MW01133586

The Hamsa

By

E.S. Kraay

"Raphael answered, 'I will go with him; so do not fear.
We shall leave in good health and return to you in good health,
because the way is safe.'"
Tobit 5:16

This book is a work of historical fiction. While certain names, businesses, organizations, places, events and incidents used in this book are or may have been real, this book and the story contained herein is purely the product of the author's imagination and entirely fictitious in nature. Any content or characterizations contained herein that resembles actual persons, living or dead, events or locales is entirely coincidental

DEDICATION

To my Dad's best friend
Louis Green
July 19, 1919 – July 19, 1994
Pittsfield, Massachusetts

And to the competitors in the 1936 Winter Olympics who died
from September 1939 to 1945 including

Karl Leban, Austria
Franz Schußler, Austria
Hans Tatzer, Austria
Martial Van Schelle, Belgium
Eduard Hiiop, Estonia
Aleksander Mitt, Estonia
Birger Wasenius, Finland
Kalle Jalkanen, Finland
Frans Heikkinen, Finland
Jean, Marquis de Suarez d'Aulan, France
Freddie Tomlins, Great Britain
Rudi Cranz, Germany
Paul Krauß, Germany
Herbert Leupold, Germany
Hans Marr, Germany
Matthias Wörndle, Germany
Roman Wörndle, Germany
Herbert Bertulsons, Latvia
Janis Rozīte, Latvia
Hildegarde Švarce, Latvia
Józef Stogowski, Poland and to
Bronisław Czech, Poland

Data is unavailable for Japanese Olympians from 1920 – 1936

Also by E.S. Kraay

The Olympian: A Tale of Ancient Hellas

The Hamsa

The Hamsa

Prologue

My mother had a dog. His name was Zegar. He was a sheepdog. Zegar was born with a single front leg, and his owner, *Pan* Kupiec, a good man was prepared to put the pup down thinking that the animal would live in misery without the benefit of its fourth leg. Mother would not allow it, and despite my father's inclination to leave the animal to whatever fate his owner decreed, my mother's passionate pleas won the day, and she brought the dog home. *Pan* Kupiec remained a good friend to mother and father. Perhaps they console one another today. He had six sons and each found his way here to this place within days after I arrived. I knew them well enough when we were children, but they never experienced the thrill of athletic competition at the level I did, not that it matters of course. Odd that we would meet again in this place that seems so distant from the real world. Of course, it has occurred to me that this place now *is* the real world and everything beyond our sight and hearing has disappeared. How sad if that is true. I saw Józef last night. His brothers? They are all gone. All that is left are the stories and the memories.

My *Babcia* knew more stories than any one I have ever known. I fondly recall those times when my brother, my two sisters and I would gather at her feet before a roaring fire. We knew she was in the mood to tell a tale, when sitting with eyes closed, humming an ancient tune, a smile would caress her face as she remembered her favorites. As I think of Zegar, I remember her story of the clock maker who only had one arm. "He made a clock for the king," she told us, "a clock the king cherished above all his possessions." There was nothing particularly special about the clock, but the king considered it priceless because a man with only one arm made it. Like the clock to the king, Zegar was special to my mother. All of us grew fond of the dog that could run as well on three legs as other dogs on four. One spring, my mother was lost in an ocean of snow that rolled down the mountains in an avalanche. For two days, my distraught father and the other highlanders, the *gorales*, searched untiringly, but could find no trace of her. Late in the afternoon of the second day, Zegar's mournful howl rose from the distant slopes. Father, and the other mountaineers, quickly descended to the dog's position. Zegar had burrowed into the snow and found my mother. When the men arrived, they saw him tugging gently on her sleeve. As her hand reached out ever softly, Zegar smiled as only dogs can...

Last night, I held my own dog as he took his last breath. I cried. Maybe the dog was really holding me, and not I, him. His name was Raphael. I think he was an angel. I am ready to follow him to the feet of God.

My fever continues to rise. Typhus is a willing accomplice of its master, death, who rules without mercy.

I am 35-years-old, and I know with certainty that tomorrow I will no longer be. My time on Earth is finished. I hope to see the sun rise one final time, but if fate or God denies me that sight, it will be okay and I will understand and hold no ill will. Although you may come to doubt it, my life has been full. I have but one regret. I wanted to be a father, to have a son who would bear my name, who would live free and happy, and enjoy the world as I did when I was a boy.

I will find no sleep on this lonely night, but I am not afraid of death, rather I welcome its finality despite the regret I bear in silence. Death has been too long coming in a place that tries so hard to destroy life's meaning for me and the others who pass through these iron portals. Time plays in death's favor. The first 30 years of my life were so short, but these last five have been so terribly long. My end comes as no accident, so my life will not flash before me in an instant like they say it does when a man meets his end in an unexpected instant. No, this is no surprise for me. I will lie dead in the morning, so I have only this night, however long or short it may seem, to reflect on those things I've done, the people I've known, the wonders I've seen, good and bad. I have watched other men twist and scream in agony as they struggle to hold onto their lives, but I will resist any temptation to cry out. I will take my final breath with the same dignity with which I took my first when God breathed life into my soul 35 years ago.

When we arrived here years ago, they called us outlaws. Few like me, whose number is inked permanently on his chest, remain. In five years, I've not looked in a mirror, but I know the digits well: three, four and nine; 349; three-hundred-forty-nine. My crime is my life, my mission to preserve my country, and for this, I am a criminal. My allegiance to my country is strong, has not and never will falter. This I swear. I will die, but Poland will live. I rub the fabric of my clothing between my finger and my thumb. This shirt and these pants are like old friends, the elbows and knees worn thin from subservience to far lesser men than I hope I have been.

I thirst but I refuse the cup my friend offers; it is for the living, not the dead. No matter. The night is colder than one would expect in June. The cold never bothered me until I came to this place, not until I had to stand in the frigid wind without shoes, without a cap on my head, without gloves. I can endure anything on this, my last night, but I am thankful that it is the cold of June and not January. Tonight's cold will be no discomfort. I will pass my final night on Earth with memories, not tears. I will smile, for it is the strongest medicine of all. I wonder what they are doing in heaven tonight, for tomorrow, I will be with them ...

Chapter One: Winter 1918

In the Beginning

Na początku Bóg stworzył niebo I ziemię.

I have always loved language.

Am Anfang schuf Gott die Himmel und die Erde.

The human voice and the words it forms fascinate me.

I begynnelsen skapte Gud himmelen og jorden.

I never attended school beyond my fifteenth year and never had the benefit of formal training in any language.

Au commencement, Dieu créa les cieux et la terre.

Nevertheless, languages have come easy to me and for a very simple reason. In our home, we had a single book that occupied a special place on the fireplace mantel. My *Babcia*, a short woman would rise to her toes each evening, reverently take the volume and, holding it before her with arms outstretched, make her way to the ancient rocking chair reserved for only her. I do not remember how old I was when she began reading to me, but I do remember that very first story. I think my older sister and brother had heard it before, but they acted as though they had not, just like I would when *Babcia* would read it to my younger sister Janina in years to come. *"Na początku Bóg stworzył niebo I ziemię,"* she would read in whispered tones, "and the Earth was without form and void and darkness was upon the face of the deep." Her eyes opened wide as she paused to see the expressions of awe on our young faces. "And the Spirit of God moved upon the face of the waters, and God said 'Let there be light,' and there was light." Most certainly, I have tried to retain within my heart, that same light amid the dark void of my recent years. No matter ...

As I grew older, my parents – with the Bible as my textbook – taught me to read. Their lessons have served me well for as an older man traveling even to America, I burned with an intense desire to learn other languages, and it occurred to me that the Bible says the same thing in Polish that it says in German, Norwegian, and French... The words are always the same.

"In the beginning, God created the heavens and the earth..."

I am 10-years old. My father tells me I was born in the year of the bright nights when the skies glowed so that a man could read a newspaper at midnight. "What happened?" I ask him. He shrugs his shoulders with arms akimbo, then twirls the right tip of his handlebar moustache and says, "God decided not to sleep those nights."

Father says I am a special boy, and today will be a special day, so I rise from my bed well before the sun and sit at the table and wait. The candles burn low and the coals in the fireplace cast a dim light into the darkness. I hear the calm, muted lowing from the nearby stable, and know that mother and father are already up and outside, he to fetch more wood for the fire, she to milk the cow. My *Babcia*

– my grandmother – stands at the stove preparing breakfast. The other children are still asleep.

Boże błogosław nasz dom. God bless our house.

I stare at the woodcut that hangs on the wall behind our table as I warm my hands on the steaming, tin cup that my *Babcia* has placed before me. "Let it cool," she tells me and returns to the stove. I nod and smile but never take my eyes from the carved image of Jesus, the faintest of smiles on his lips. Do other people see that smile, I wonder, or is it meant only for me? Probably not because my father carved that woodcut many years before I was born, of course maybe he saw me then in his mind and did put the smile on Jesus' face just for me. The tea will be weak but sweet with honey. *Babcia* knows I like it that way and she always adds a touch of cream for me. I think I am her 'special one;' at least she makes me feel that way. Would the others say the same? Probably. She prepares herself a cup and returns to sit at the table with me.

"To be a skier, one has to love the cold." That is what *Babcia* tells me. "Skiers don't tolerate the cold," she says, "They love the cold. The icy wind, and every frigid gust in the skier's face invigorates him as he flies fearlessly above the mountain slope; the wind turns his cheeks crimson and draws involuntary tears of joy that seep from the corners of his eyes. You must love the cold. Let it be your friend!" *Babcia* fusses with my hair, then returns to the stove. Two years ago, she lost the tip of her thumb. Cut it right off with the axe. She never cried out, and it has healed well. Nevertheless, father tells her to leave the firewood to my brother and me. The Tatra winds can be cruel and the avalanches that are known to accompany them, deadly. *Pani*

Murach long-widowed and her fatherless children at the
far side of town can attest to that. However, I do not fear
the mountains or their dangers. I have learned that from
Babcia. "Your fate is in the hands of God," she says and
always blesses herself when she says it. "If he deems the
mountains to take you, go with an open heart for it is God's
will. Never forget it: the mountains, the winds and the
cold must always be your friends."

I hear the children move in the bed they shared with
Babcia last night. "Is it morning yet?" one asks from beneath the covers. "Soon," I answer.

Babcia turns and winks at me. "I hope you are hungry,
children. This morning I make *pączki*."

Three heads peak over the edge of the quilt. "When?"
one asks.

"Right now," she answers and my younger sister Janka
and our neighbor Stanisław and his cousin Andrzej scramble from beneath their covers and draw chairs close to the
stove, as much for the heat as to watch *Babcia* make her donuts. "Be careful," she cautions them. "The night was very
cold, but this stove is very hot!" She dips her wooden spoon
into the thick batter and then lets the heavy dough drip
into the hot oil. As the cast iron pot sizzles and the frying
dough bobs up and down in the hot lard, the children clap
their hands and giggle.

"Please try to be quiet," my older brother Władi
mumbles from his cot. The oldest, my sister Stasia adds,
"And do not eat them all because I know you will and
father will let you if I don't say something." Both roll
in their cots toward the wall and the darkness they find
there.

Within minutes, *Babcia* takes the now golden-brown balls from the pot and places them on paper to cool. She starts another batch. "Be patient," she cautions Janka and her friends as they lean closely to steal as much of the aroma as they can. "Mother and Father will return shortly, maybe five, maybe 10 minutes." An eternity for a young child with the smell of fresh *pączki* wafting in the air!

After she makes three dozen, she brings the first 12 to the long, wooden table, and the chairs make loud scraping noises as the children pull them up to the table. The door opens, and father walks in stomping the snow from his boots and licking the ice that has gathered in his moustache. In his arms is a bundle of wood that he places near the fireplace. My mother follows him with a tin of milk. "Ha, ha," my father laughs as he turns and places his cold hands on his mother's face, "I can smell our breakfast! Your *Babcia* has done it again, children. I'm certain of it by the aroma alone, and look," he points to the platter that steams in the center of the table, "The perfect *pączki*!" *Babcia* shoos him away. "Just go sit down and don't be so crazy," she says as he hugs her and kisses her cheek.

"Whose turn is it, Mother?" He always calls my mother 'Mother' and his mother '*Babcia*.'

"I think one of our guests should say the blessing," she answers. "What about you Stanisław Marusarz? Can you say the blessing?"

Five-year-old Stanisław smiles meekly, places his index finger over his lips and says, "Shhhhh," then leans his head toward Włady and Stasia.

"Oh, don't mind them, Stashu. Your blessing is more important than their sleep."

Stashu smiles 'okay,' closes his eyes tightly and bows his head. We all follow suit and he begins, "Please bless this food, God. And please bless the Czech family who lets me and Andrzej stay with them when our parents are away to Warsaw. Amen."

My mother puts an arm around him. "That was very nice, Stanisław. God will take care of us all and your parents, too." Even in the candle's soft light, we can see his blushed cheeks.

Boże błogosław nasz dom, I say to myself.

The platter is emptied as it makes its way around the table, and *Babcia* replenishes it with the second dozen. Father is right: the perfect *pączki*! The crust is crisp and the dough inside soft and still warm. I spoon honey on mine while the other children prefer a pat of butter and the adults nothing at all.

The sun announces a new day as it crests the distant horizon and throws its bright beams into our simple home. The cloudless day will be cold, but the sun's rays will surely melt some of the snow that remains on the roof. Long, heavy icicles will drip from the eaves and form cold puddles on the ground below. The children will occupy their day battling the icicles with their wooden sticks. It can be a dangerous game. The activity is too much fun and our enjoyment diverts our attention from the danger inherent when large chunks of ice crash to the ground splintering into jewel-like pieces that scatter as if they are frozen fireflies released from a bottle. As youngsters, we become quite adept at dodging the projectiles.

Janka, Stanisław and Andrzej scurry back to the warmth of the bed and bury themselves beneath the quilt. Włady and Stasia remain motionless in their cots. My mother and *Babcia* clear the table and tend to the stove and fire. Today they will do laundry.

My father fills his pipe with tobacco, and walking to the fireplace, lights it with a slender stick. I love the smell, as it meanders through the room, overpowering the sweet fragrance that lingers from *Babcia's pączki*. He draws deeply on the stem and exhales a long stream of white, fragrant smoke that drifts through the sunlight that continues to stream uninterrupted through the windows on the east side of our home. I look out the windows to the south and see the mountains sparkle as they rise steeply from the plain into the clear blue sky. The Tatras. They are beautiful! They are mine!

For me this day is special, and it is not because I will waste it on this child's game that I have played countless times through my 10 years. Things that are more important than icicles on the roof beckon me. Today, my father and I will climb higher into the mountains than I have ever been before.

"Today," he tells me and exhales another, smooth column of smoke, "you will learn to race, to move quickly down the mountains without fear." I cannot remember when my father first bound skis to my feet, but since that time, I have learned to move easily, some say even gracefully through the white powder. Everyone in my village knows how to ski, some better than others. Włady and Stasia ski for necessity, not so much for pleasure. We must learn to ski in Zakopane in order to move from one place to another during the long winter months when our world is white. My mother goes to market on skis, we go to school on skis, and our family goes to church on skis. We carry the babies bundled on our backs, and we make flat paths for the old people who no longer can strap the wooden planks to their shoes and slide through the snow. All of it, we do on skis. The old ones like my *Babcia* who have not skied for years shuffle along, much slower now, but they shuffle with the same movement they used in by-gone days when they stood comfortably on skis. You can always tell when thoughts of those days enter their minds, for at those moments, smiles transform their faces. They remember. *Babcia* says it is good to remember. "Never forget the wonderful things in your life," she tells us. "If you never forget, they will always be a part of you and will forever bring you pleasure." I will come to learn how right she is. So, *Babcia* always smiles when she shuffles and never seems quite as old as she is.

Babcia turns from the stove, wipes her hands on her apron and asks my father, "Giewont?" He nods and she smiles with approval.

"It is a big mountain, but you are a big enough boy to reach the summit. Be watchful as you climb and look for the cavern," she says to me and returns her attention to the dishes she is cleaning. Some day it will be my mother's responsibility to tell these stories to her grand-children, stories of the White Eagle, of *Domowoj* the house spirit, of Bolesław and his knights to whom she refers to now. Bolesław and his knights. It is a grand tale, and when she tells it, she tells it with the same reverence she would if it were a story from our Holy Bible. It is one of my favorite stories. Sometimes when she tells it, my fa-ther takes his violin and plays it softly beneath her words.

Bolesław, a hero like Joshua or Samson, maybe more like David, yes, David, a king as well. *Babcia* says he still sleeps with his knights in a cavern in the very mountains my father and I will climb today, somewhere in the peaks of the Tatras. I stare at those mountains through the window. Indeed the silhouette portrays the very image of the sleeping knight who, *Babcia* claims hides himself in those white and windy slopes. Perhaps it is only her stories that make me see the mountains that way, but I do see him there, Bolesław, once a great king. *Babcia* says he and his knights only sleep, and they have been at rest in the Tatras for a thousand years! "They are patient, and they wait in peace," *Babcia* says, "but their bows and lances are always within their grasp. They are ready to return when Poland needs them, but someone has to wake them from their slumber. That is why you should stay alert and look for the cavern. Someone needs to know how to find it if the time should come when they are needed."

"Have you found them, father?" I ask. "Did you look for the cavern when you were a boy? Do you know where they are?" He ignores my question and I know better than to ask a second time.

Our small farm is at the very edge of town. To call it a farm is probably not quite accurate for we have only a single cow for milk, and we harvest only enough produce for ourselves and for the neighbors with whom we share. Father and I move quickly up the gentle slope toward the mountains knowing that our pace will slow when we reach the tree line, some 400 meters away. The only tracks are our own. As we approach the trees, we see the familiar footprints of the large rabbits that father hunts and mother turns into my favorite stew. I have had much practice moving on level ground and gentle slopes with my skis. They say I am strong for my age. The pace is quick for me, leisurely for my father whose long legs move forward in steady rhythm with his pumping arms. Running on skis in the cross-country fashion is all about rhythm. When you find it, you know it and it feels as if you are gliding effortlessly on the clouds.

We penetrate the tree line. The spruces are heavy with snow, but as we climb, so does the sun, and the trees begin to shed their white coats. Soon the slope steepens and we can no longer slide on our skis. We begin to waddle like ducks, our tips pointed outward as we grip the snow with our inside edges. It is easier for me than for my father as I follow his wide V-like track. Steeper still. Steam engulfs our sweating bodies and rises, as I would imagine as a genie from his bottle. I laugh and father glances over his shoulder and asks if I am alright. "Yes," I say and laugh aloud again. "As you breathe you remind me of the locomotives." Even steeper. We can't do it in our herringbone fashion, and we turn sideways, perpendicular to the slope and continue to work our way higher with sidesteps. So steep now that we remove our skis and carry them over our shoulders as my father's path moves upward and winds through the small spruce trees that dot the mountain meadows. I am working too hard to look back and I concentrate on the path my father creates for me. We never stop to rest. Upward, ever upward. We exchange even fewer words.

One hour passes, and my thighs burn. My father finally stops, turns and says, "Yes. This will be fine. From here you will learn to race!" He plants his skis vertically in the snow and leans back against them to rest. I do the same. He nods his head again, reaches inside his jacket and retrieves his pipe and tobacco. Side by side, we gaze back in the direction of the village. We have climbed 300 meters. From this distance, our house and small barn are mere dots; a thin wisp of smoke rises from the chimney joined by a hundred others in Zakopane, which sits in the background. I see a shadow float across the snowfield that stretches below us. I shield my eyes and raise them toward the sun. "Ah," my father breathes, "The eagle has come to watch you. This is a good sign!"

He points to the sky. "The sun tells us we've trekked for 60 minutes to climb this high, Bronisław. It won't take us 10 minutes to get back. Two years from now, five minutes." He returns his pipe to his mouth and speaks through clenched teeth that hold the stem as he leans forward and tightens the laces on his boots. "We'll rest for a few more minutes and then begin our descent. You have good balance, son. I see it when you run through the icy streets on your skis. This is all about balance. Turn with the uphill edge of your downhill ski while you shift your weight. It will happen quickly. Do you understand?" I do. "Remember: uphill edge of the downhill ski."

I watch the eagle and envy his freedom. That is what skiing means to me: freedom. As I sit here and squint at the glaring whiteness that stretches beneath me, I cherish the thought that I am free, and because I ski, freer than most although they do not know it. I think that soon, my father will teach me to jump. He is so good at jumping! For now, I can only imagine what that must feel like, to be free from earthly bonds like the great bird, if only for a

few seconds. The eagle continues his lazy circles in the sky
but stays with us. He waits and watches to see if I have the
courage to challenge the slope with speed. I do and will
not fail my father or this great spectator who has graced us
with his very presence. I mimic my father and tighten the
laces of my boots.

"Are you ready, Bronisław?"

"Yes."

He embraces my shoulders with his large hands and
holds me at arms' length. He need say no words for I see
the pride in his eyes. My siblings would be envious if they
saw it, but they do not love the cold as I do, or the freedom
that these slopes can bring. No fear and no concern in his
eyes, only pride. We bind our wooden slats to our feet and
take firm hold of the pole that each of us carries.

"I am heavier than you are so I will be faster. You may
lose sight of me as we weave through the trees. Don't worry. Try to stay in my tracks. We will take no jumps today,
but our path will be steep and you will feel the speed that
comes when you attack these mountains. Stay back on your
skis to keep your heels on the boards as best you can. That
is what will give you control of them. Don't forget: uphill
edge on the downhill ski. I will stop halfway down and
wait for you. Don't be late! Okay?"

He knows I am and wastes no time waiting for my answer. In one fluid motion, he raises himself with his pole,
rotates his body so his skis point downhill and he is gone!
I have no time to reconsider and immediately fall as I try
to mimic my father's initial gymnastics. I am not mad or
disappointed, only focused on the task at hand, and I rise
quickly on my skis. I'm onto his tracks and moving as he

disappears into the trees trailing a cloud of soft powder that rises from the end of his skis.

The path he prepares presents a challenge and I force myself not to hurry. This is my first time in the high mountains and he does not expect me to keep pace with him, only to follow him. My brain is on fire as I struggle to remember: uphill edge, downhill ski. At first his turns, though smooth lead me perpendicular to the slope. They are quick and frequent and in a short time, his advice is habit, a part of me that I do without thought. The rapid series of turns enables me to control my velocity and slows me down, but soon, his turns become less frequent and I feel the speed build. It is quiet. The snow is soft and powdery. His path veers sharply to the left. I am comfortable and feel no need to slow down, so I continue through the trees. Suddenly, I am as free as the eagle. The earth abandons me and I find myself floating some three meters above the ground. Taken off guard by my premature flight, a lump rises in my throat. I cannot control my body as it pitches forward. My arms flail like a wounded bird's and I reach forward and prepare to meet the ground with my open hands and not my head. Somehow, my skis remain bound to my feet and as I tumble forward, they regain purchase in the exploding snow. They are beneath me again, and I continue to move down the slope. Fear has fled. I laugh aloud, exhilarated by the unplanned for experience that I have negotiated and conquered.

I see no tracks before me but sense my father must be somewhere to my left. I turn in that direction hoping to intercept his path. Soon I find his tracks and fall into step. Within a minute, I am through the trees and see him some

200 meters down the open slope. His pipe is back in his mouth and he waves. I make gentle turns to the left and right of his straight path, then turn sharply to my left, slide the final 10 meters perpendicular to the mountain and come to a stop just beyond where my father stands.

He claps his hands. "Bravo," he says. "You arrived sooner than I expected. Apparently you had no problems."

"None," I answer while I catch my breath. To our right, I see the tracks we made in our ascent. So long to climb, I think, yet so fast to descend.

My father knows what I am thinking. "Is it worth the work?" he asks.

I look down the hill toward our home and then back up the steep mountain. We both smile knowing that it is.

The lower slopes provide no challenge. I have been on them many times and only regret that we did not climb higher. We return to the warmth of our house and remove our gear. Mother and the children gather round us. *Babcia* has prepared a strong cup of coffee for my father; she offers me warm milk, and I wrap my hands around the wooden cup to dispel the cold that has tried so hard to have its way with my first downhill experience.

"You fall?" my little sister Janka asks with a look of concern.

"Were you scared?" the Marusarz boys ask in unison.

Father looks over his cup and winks at me. "I never saw him fall once," he says and takes a sip.

"Were you scared?" Stanisław asks again. "You must have been scared when you were so high on the mountain. I think I would have been scared."

Stanisław's grandmothers – both of them – died before he was born. "What does my *Babcia* say, Stashu?"
He shrugs his shoulders. Before *Babcia* can tell him I say,
"'Love the cold' is what she teaches me. 'Do not be afraid
of the mountains.'"

Babcia smiles. "And with good reason," she says. "If
you are afraid of the mountains and if you do not love the
cold, you will never ski or feel the freedom it gives you."
We are silent while her words fall like a whispered prayer
on each of us. Władzy and Stasia are not so sure.

"What is beyond these mountains, father? What does
the eagle see when he crests the summit?" I ask.

"You will learn soon enough," he answers. "You are
only 10-years-old. By the time you reach your 15th birthday, I will have taken you to the very top and beyond. Our
borders lay not so far from here, Czechoslovakia is on the
other side."

I sip my warm milk. "Our name is Czech. Why are we
not from Czechoslovakia?"

"Because your grandfather came over those mountains
when he was a child. He married your *Babcia* after the
Uprising and made a life for all of us here. You and I — we
were born Poles and we live in Poland."

His answer is enough to satisfy my curiosity. "Like
your *Dziadek*, I am a mountaineer, and you will be one too.
We know the secret ways through the mountain passes.
There are not many like us. A mountaineer can take an
inexperienced man to the other side of the Tatras in a few
days. He knows the path of the eagle. Without a guide, a
man is forced to travel northeast for 500 kilometers to go
around the Karpaty. It can take weeks.

"For now, Bronisław, take pride in your small victory today. I see great things in store for you. Life will be grand."

Chapter Two, 1923

To Gaze Upon the King

It is June. Even though snow remains in patches on the mountains, the sun is bright and the temperature climbs even at the highest elevations. We stop in a clearing to feel the full force of the sun. My father removes his hat and wipes his sweaty brow with his sleeve.

"Just a few more kilometers and we will reach the high pass, the one that takes us through the peaks to the other side. From there, you will see the rest of the world. For now," he says, "we'll rest and have our lunch." He points to the north and to the east. "That is what you know." He turns and points upward, toward the pass. "That is what you don't know. A lesson for you, son, and one not to forget: you never will know as much as you think you do."

We have left the tree line and its mountain pine behind us. When we return, we will collect the magical herbs that *Babcia* has asked us to find. Someday, I will bring Janka to these heights to show her where the herbs hide. These mountains hold so many secrets, and year after year, journey after journey my father reveals them to me.

We are a full day's travel from our home in the lowlands. As with other journeys my father and I have shared in these mountains, we spend the night beneath a clear sky and gaze through the branches above us at the millions of stars that dot the black canvas of night. I do treasure this trip above all others for I know it will be the last that my father and I share. The high pass is the final piece of lore. Once he has shown me the way, it will be my responsibility to learn new secrets, unknown even to him. New secrets that will add to our accumulated knowledge that I will pass on to my children. I remember every detail of every step I have taken with my father in these mountains. I commit every turn, every rock, and every tree to memory. For his sake, I will not forget.

We travel light. Each has his pack. We are stingy with the bread that *Babcia* has made us, but we know the return trip will take less time than the arduous climb to the pass. As we approach the summit, we eat more frequently to build the energy we will need for the final assault on the pass. Water from the snowmelt is plentiful in the Tatras, and in these high grasslands, we find wild onions to add flavor to our simple meals. My aim with my slingshot yesterday was true. I killed a large hare at 30 meters, and today we feast on that. My father has his gun and plans to take down a boar or deer on our return trip. While he hunts tomorrow, I will fish for trout. We will bring home a fine feast for mother, Włady, Stasia, Janka and *Babcia*.

There is no manmade trail in the mountains; the *górale* simply remember the way. My eyes are constantly moving. I want to see everything and feel everything so that I can find my way here blindfolded. In time, I see the pass. The peaks climb to our left and right, but our path is true. We split the peaks and emerge on the other side. The vista opens and I feel as if I can see forever. The world to the west enfolds before me.

"That way, 250 kilometers," he points to the southwest, "is Bratislava. It is as nearly as far from Zakopane in that direction as Warsaw is to the northeast. And that way," he looks directly west, "Prague. North from there, Berlin."

"Have you been to these places?"

He nods his head, "A few times," but says no more.

"What are those cities like?"

"Not much different than Warsaw. I prefer the solitude of these mountains and the quiet of Zakopane."

"Can we go further?"

"There is no need, and our family is waiting."

I look to the west a final time and seal the picture in my brain: Bratislava, Prague and Berlin. I will remember. They say I have some talent to draw. While that may be, my heart compels me to race on my skis, so I make no pretense that I desire to be a professional artist. I am like my father, for he sees images in wood and brings them out with knives, hammers and chisels; I see the images on paper and bring them to life with my pencil. When I return to our house, I will record this image of the Western horizon on paper. I will remember.

He places his arm around my shoulder. At 15 years, I am nearly as tall as he is now. With an undeniable degree of sorrow, my father says, "You and I will never journey this far again together as father and son. I love you Bronisław." The pressure from his hand noticeably increases. He shades his eyes and squints at the sun. "We have plenty of daylight left," he says. "We must be on our way. I have but one secret left to share with you."

"A final secret? We have no secrets."

Father smiles. "You will see."

When we turn back to the east, we are startled and freeze in our tracks as five young men, about my age, confront us. They stand shoulder to shoulder not 10 paces from us. So stealthily did they approach that we never heard them.

The one in the middle, the tallest of the five is the first to speak and he addresses my father, "He is your son?"

"He is."

"Where are you from?"

"Zakopane, to the west."

"I am from Nitra, to the east. We will race in Zakopane this winter, my friends and I. How far from here?"

"On skis, not far, but to climb to this pass in the winter from your lowlands — it will take you a week."

"We'll see," he answers, and then asks me, "Are you a skier?"

"Yes," I say and I step forward and offer my hand.

He takes it and we shake. "Then perhaps we will meet again in a few months."

"Perhaps," I say.

"My name is Antonín, Antonín Bartoň."

"Bronisław, Bronisław Czech."

He bows. "We must be off," he says. "We are in a competition with the *Sokół*, our skiers and their gymnasts. We race to this peak from Martin in the Žilina Region and we are well in front of the gymnasts and want to stay that way. See you in a few months, Bronisław Czech, when the snow is deep." Each skier nods amiably as he files past us and they wave over their shoulders as they march down the western slope.

"Nice young men," my father says as we watch them disappear over the ridge. "I think they'll be good competition this winter if they come to Zakopane like they say."

"I like them, too. Confident, he is very confident. I will not forget his name. Antonín."

By late-morning, the melting snow is well behind us and we enter the forests again. We make our way to a small mountain lake left here millions of years ago by a great glacier. That mass of ice moved so slowly down these slopes it appeared not to move at all. During its journey, it carved the valley where we live. We have been here before, more than once, and we find the stream that flows from it. We walk another mile, and it is more than a stream but not yet a river, and home to many trout. This is where we will camp for our final night in the mountains.

My father puts his pack on the ground and takes the *Jagerstutzen* from his back. It is the same rifle he claims his father used at the Battle of Węgrów. My *Dziadek* died when I was a baby and I never met him though I very much would have liked to. Father says he was a hero and single-handedly turned the tide against the Russians in Masovia. I have no reason to doubt him.

"I will return before dark, and I will have meat with me. While I am gone, you collect the herbs you promised your *Babcia* and catch us some fish for our supper." Father surveys the area once more while he loads the muzzle, a task he can do with his eyes shut. As he reaches into his pocket for the ball, he nods toward the moving water and says, "Two hundred meters downstream, you will find a small brook that empties into this stream. Follow it to its source." He looks at the sun and measures its height in the sky then adds, "Be quick about it and you will find what you seek. If you tarry along the way, you will not." His words are cryptic, but I ask no questions. Father takes a deep breath and sniffs the air, walks no more than 10 paces and stoops to the ground brushing aside the grass. I know what he has found as he brings his cupped hand to his face and sniffs again. "Goat." He stands and wipes his hand clean on his pant leg. "*Kozice* makes a good stew. Your mother will be pleased." I now see the goat-path he stares at. He will only need one shot. When he finds the goat, his aim will be true, and he will not miss. My father is not known for his mistakes. "I'll be back," he says again and starts up the path.

My father is clear that I should waste no time. I move quickly downstream seeking the brook he told me about and have no problem finding it. I am careful with my footing as I cross the stream on slick, wet rocks worn smooth over centuries of standing obstacle to the cold water that tries in vain to sweep them from its course. Once on the other side, I drop to my knees and drink directly from the brook. I stand and straddle it with no effort. The brook flows from a steep, rocky incline, and I think its source cannot be too far from where I stand because it moves slowly in relation to the stream it joins, which has gained considerable speed over the mile it has traveled from the glacial lake.

I use my arms to help me climb the rocky face made slippery by the moss and lichen that cling to the rugged stone. My effort is rewarded as I gain the upper ledge and see the source of the brook, a cavern whose gaping mouth opens to the west. Light seems to pour from the opening, and my imagination takes me to *Babcia*'s story of Moses and the burning bush. I approach with reverence, not caution; I am not afraid.

The cavern's mouth is nearly as tall as I am. I immediately identify the cause of the intense light that seems to burst from this grotto. The cavern is not more than two meters deep and the back wall is as flat as *Babcia*'s iron skillet. A thin coat of moisture oozes from the cracks in the stone ceiling, gathers in the uppermost edge on the far side and flows slowly down the flat face. It gathers in the shallow pool of clear water that covers the floor. Gravity draw it from the cavern, down the ledge and then to the stream below. At this precise time of day, as the sun makes its way west, the light reflects off the quiet pool, strikes the back wall and returns mirror-like. It is almost blinding.

I drop to my knees to take a sip of cold water from the pool, and when I raise my face to the back wall, time stops. I become like the very stone upon which I am kneeling. Staring back at me from the smooth, glassy wall is my own reflection. I force myself to move; it moves. I smile; it smiles. I nod acknowledgment to my own being; it nods back. I cannot pull my eyes from the awestruck image reflected from the back wall, an image surrounded by the halo of light that the sun casts behind me. I am a prisoner of the reflected light until the sun moves toward the peaks at my back, the light fades, and with it, this magnificent reflection. Time is eternity and it has abandoned me. The image is gone and I see only a black, smooth wall of stone.

The report from my father's *Jagerstutzen* sounds in the distance and it calls me back to Earth. The gunshot

sharpens my senses. How long had I kneeled like a supplicant in the mouth of the cavern? A long time, for my knees
are stiff when I rise to my feet. I turn my back to the cavern
and see that as the sun falls beneath the peaks, it paints
the wave of clouds above the mountains, a fiery orange.
With certainty, the reason my father sent me alone to this
place strikes me firmly and with conviction: to find the
king.

I have found Bolesław like my father knew I would,
like he found him when he was a young man. Bolesław was
in that cavern today. He was there with my father many
years ago when his father brought him to this cave. I am
Bolesław! My father is Bolesław! My son will be, too. We
are all his knights. It is our duty as Poles to stand vigil and
to be prepared to serve our country in time of need. Now
it is clear to me. Now I understand: Bolesław and his
knights will never die because we will carry on their legacy
to protect Poland, to secure its survival. From generation
to generation, Bolesław lives. He is flesh and blood and no
specter or some imaginary character from a child's story.
He is human. He is courage. He is conviction. He and I
are one.

My encounter has kept me from my task, but I suspect my father knows there will be no fish for supper. As
dusk quickly approaches, I find my way back to our camp-
site, and as I do, the experience at the cavern evolves from
dreamlike speculation to moral conviction. I will not discuss it with my father, nor will he ask me about it. We
will both know that I know the truth about Bolesław and
his knights. If such a thing is possible, we are more than
father and son now. The shared revelation strengthens our

relationship and takes it to a new, deeper level unknown to most fathers and their sons.

I gather a supply of small sticks to start a fire with and larger pieces of wood to fuel it. Even in the summer, the nights in the mountains are cool. When all vestige of daylight has fled, my fire is warm and strong. I hear movement and see my father emerge from the shadows the flames cast into the pitch. His weapon is slung over his shoulder, and he drags the gutted carcass of a goat. Mother will be pleased. He leaves it downwind, in the shadows, and moves to the fire to take the chill from his body.

"No fish?" he comments more than asks.

"No fish."

"No matter," he says.

Our eyes lock and sparkle as the flames dance between us. That single look affirms our common knowledge. Further words are unnecessary and meaningless, but he does nod, and I smile in return.

Our supper is as special as the day. Father carefully spits the liver and heart of the goat, and roasts them over the coals. *Babcia* will be disappointed, mother and my brother and sisters will not be. *Babcia* loves the liver, and she tells us it gives us 'strong blood.' I do not know what 'strong blood' is, but if *Babcia* says it is good, I believe her and will eat the delicate liver with gusto. We cut pieces from the cooked meat, and place them on our remaining bread, soaking up the tasty juices so none are lost. This is the best day of my life, and father and I share our contentment as we spread our blankets on the ground, close enough to the stones I placed around our fire pit to draw the remaining heat from the ebbing coals.

As I lie down, father feeds more wood to the fire. A million stars fill the night sky and red sparks rise from our fire to join them. "I will beat him," I say as much to the star-studded heavens and myself as I do to my father. He responds with a snore. I turn to my side and this time whisper, "I will beat him. Antonín Bartoň."

Chapter Three, 1923

The Race

"*Babcia* says you will make a good priest." This is what Janka tells me. Właddy and Stasia roll their eyes. They have more interest in secular matters that involve their 'special friends.' There was a time when my mother and *Babcia* would frequently discuss my vocation and spiritual calling, quite often in my presence at the table. "They conspire," my father would say, and mother would answer, "You would be proud, Józef, and don't pretend you wouldn't be." *Babcia* says it more often in recent years since mother's episode with the avalanche. We are a family of skiers and mother is no different, though father and I are far more serious about it. Mother loves the mountains no less than father and I, and we cast no blame on them or the snows that buried her for a day. Mother believes it was God's will, and she claims to be stronger for it. "There is my angel," she says as she throws her arms around *Zegar*.

I have not ventured to town all week for I have no desire to see the other skiers, including those from Zakopane – though all are my friends. The visitors are there in the hostel, not far from my destination. Today is Sunday, and I will go to church and ask for God's blessing, then

I race in competition for the first time. I have prayed at St. Clement's every Sunday of my life. I will avoid Mass because I will avoid people. I wonder what kind of sin that might be. Venial? Certainly not mortal. No matter. Father Stolarczyk, an ancient priest with lines in his face as deep as a river will say Mass in three hours, at 7 a.m. I will pray now in the solitude of the quiet darkness.

I love the stillness of the cold, early morning air, and I am invigorated as I ski the three kilometers from our house to St. Clement's. It is as if I am the only man alive. No dog and no cat join me. No night birds call.

I enter the church and hesitate while my eyes adjust to the dim, blue light cast from the flickering offertory candles that glow at the feet of the Virgin. I bless myself with the holy water from the stone cistern in the vestibule. The water is clear, but it is almost ice. Father Stolarczyk will not fire the stove to take the chill from the chapel for at least two more hours. I cover my mouth to refrain from chuckling as the concept of 'holy ice' floats through my brain. I dispel the thought, walk forward, genuflect and kneel in the front pew, a position I have never occupied when other people are in the church.

The crucifix hangs from the loft above the altar. It intimidates me, more now than ever as I kneel before it alone and gaze into the unearthly shadows that rise to meet it. Try as I might, I cannot pull my eyes from it and I stare at the pale, wracked body of Christ in his moment of torment and agony captured for eternity on this piece of wood. Christ's victory frightens me in the weak light from the candles. I close my eyes and begin to pray. I believe it

selfish to pray for my own benefit, so I silently request God
to bless my family and my friends. Still, my innermost
thoughts are drawn to skiing and the race before me. God
surely knows that I have prepared myself for it, and he will
be pleased with my effort regardless of the outcome.

"Czech." My eyes spring open and my muscles tense
when I hear my name whispered from the dark shadows
somewhere behind me. Certainly, I would have heard the
old door creak open if Father Stolarczyk had entered the
church. I heard nothing but my own breathing until my
whispered name crept through the sanctuary. What's more,
Father Stolarczyk never uses my surname. 'Bronisław' he
calls me.

"Czech." I hear it again, still a whisper but louder. I
want to turn and look behind me, but fear has gripped me
in the darkness, a foolish thing in this house of God. I
slowly lift my head and dare to raise my eyes to the crucifix.
I do not move.

The rustle of clothes and the cracking sound a cold pew
makes when a body rises from it add to the mystery. "If it's
not you, Czech, I apologize and I will leave, but I'm certain
it is you, from the mountains in the summer, you and your
father. Do you remember me? Antonín, Antonín Bartoň,
from the other side of the mountains. I've come to race as I
promised you I would."

I smile to myself, embarrassed by my fear when I first
heard my name whispered from the dark corner of the
empty church. Rising from the kneeler with my cap in my
hands, I turn to face him. He nods and waves. That simple
motion moves the air ever so slightly and the candles react.
Our shadows move across the wall as we walk forward and

meet in the center of the church. Each extends his hand to the other.

"Welcome to my home," I say.

"May I call you friend?" he responds.

"Of course, but in several hours when we meet on the slopes…" I shrug my shoulders.

"We are thinking the same thing." Antonín winks at me. "What brings you here at this hour? Not even the rooster is awake."

"My mother expects me to be here every Sunday," I say.

"Then come with your mother to Mass. There is plenty of time before the race."

"This is better. And you, what brings you here at this hour? Mass is no later for you than it is for me."

He dusts his pant leg with his cap, looks beyond me and answers, "God."

"God will be here in three hours," I say, "He will wait for you."

Antonín smiles and looks back at me, "I prefer to meet him without the worshippers that crowd the pews at Mass, and as your mother does, my mother expects me to be here, too." He changes the subject, "Do you pray for victory?"

"No. Do you?"

He smiles, "Never. That would be a waste of a prayer. If God wants me to win, I will win. If not, perhaps this is your day."

"Maybe," I say and then admit, "But today is my first real race against competitors not from Zakopane. Since I was a little boy, I race with my friends from school, but never with skiers I do not know."

Antonín tries to stifle his laugh with the palm of his hand. "It is the same for me."

"You, too? But you are so confident."

He shrugs his shoulders. "I've raced, but only with my friends, and only on the Western slopes. This is my first trip over the mountains. I am the youngest skier in my group, but I am ready, ready to race and ready to win."

The echo of his voice dies without comment in the empty church.

"Well," I say, "It will take me some time to return to my home so I must be on my way. Where are you staying?"

"Two of my friends and I stay with a widow woman, *Pani* Murach. She is very nice." We walk to the door and bless ourselves with 'holy ice.' The snow crunches beneath our boots as we walk outside. *Pani* Murach's home is not too far from the church. Antonín walks to the church this morning, but now waits while I strap my skis to my boots. I'm using two poles now, and as I slip the leather loops at the ends of them around my wrists he says, "I'll see you in a few hours." He walks away.

Before I take my first stride I say, "I will beat you today." He does not turn, only raises his hand and waves.

"*Babcia* says you will make a good priest," Janka repeats as I apply an even coat of wax to the bottom of my skis.

"Perhaps I will," I tell her, "but for now, I just want to be a good skier." My skis are old, older than I am by many years, but they are still sturdy and I have learned to rely upon them. If I take care of my skis, my skis will take care of me. So, I stand with a block of white wax in hand and my skis leaned against the fence in front of the house. For what seems like the twentieth time, I draw the wax down the bottoms of my skis. The white stuff fills any imperfections that may distort the smooth surface. *Babcia* has warmed the iron and Janka retrieves it from the house. She still holds the wooden handle with two hands.

"Thanks, little sister." I take it with my thumb and index finger, by the narrow space between her small hands, careful that neither of us is burned. The iron cools quickly and when the temperature is right, I pass it slowly, in one, smooth motion over the skis. The wax melts and fills even the imperfections our eyes cannot see. When I finish, I move my fingertips purposely over the smooth surface, from the tips to the heels seeking any blemish that might remain. There are too many things that we have no control over – the temperature, the wind, and the condition of the snow – so it is imperative that we take advantage of those things we can. The surface of my skis is one of those things.

"Yes?" Janka asks. I smile and nod.

Zegar barks as he and father walk from the barn on the hard, packed snow. The dog is aging. He does not follow me into the mountains anymore. He is content to curl himself before the fireplace in the winter and to find the shade of the spruce trees when summer's days are long and hot. Father puffs on his pipe to keep the tobacco hot and glowing. "You'll be leaving soon?" he asks.

"Yes," I say and nod toward the town. We see a line of skiers leaving the village headed to Kuźnice, three kilometers south where all the contestants will assemble and receive final instructions.

"You know that mother, *Babcia*, and your sisters and brother will be there at the end of the race."

"I know you will." Janka has always been my favorite fan. Truth be told, I don't think Włady and Stasia care much at all about the outcome of this race, but they will make an appearance so they can see their other friends. The entire village will wait at the finish line. It is always a grand time. "I'll get my pack and be on my way."

I follow my father into the house. *Babcia* stands by the fireplace and pokes the smoking logs with an iron rod. "Your pack is ready," she says, but we have something special for you.

"I am already blessed with special things, *Babcia*. I need nothing more."

"Well," father says, "You have no choice in this matter. *Babcia* and your mother have decreed it. Here." He passes me a package wrapped in old paper secured with string. "Be quick about it. They won't wait for you in Kuźnice."

I carefully remove the string and paper to reveal a new pair of white woolen pants, and a jacket as well. *Babcia* has decorated them with colorful *parzenice*. They are beautiful.

"They are not only to look at," father says. "We expect you to wear them!"

"Thank you, thank you all." I take my *Babcia* and my mother in open arms and hug them closely.

When I release them, *Babcia* waves a finger and says, "Today you race against Slovaks and Russians. I think there are Germans here as well. You must look like a Pole. Be proud. Beat them. Your father tells me you fly on your skis, faster than he ever has, faster than your *Dziadek* before him. Fly like the eagle, Bronisław. Do not be afraid. Beat them." *Babcia* is so proud of me. Tears well in my mother's eyes. I will not disappoint them.

I change into my new clothes thinking I will only wear them on special occasions like this one. My family is pleased. Even Włady smiles and nods his approval without a trace of jealousy. Stasia rises to her toes and kisses my cheek. "Good luck, brother," she says. With a wave of my brimmed hat, I walk outside, strap my skis to my boots and head south to Kuźnice. Janka and Stashu Marusarz have already donned their skis and plead to come with me. I tell them it is okay. It will not take us long to get there. Father and mother will bring *Babcia* to the lodge later in the afternoon to cheer me and the other racers to the finish line.

The contestants assemble at the lodge by mid-morning. I have no watch, but the sun and the shadows it casts tell me that I am not late, even though most of the other skiers are already there. I join my friends who wave when they see me approach. All six of the Kupiec brothers are here but only the two oldest, Jan and Jóźef will race.

I see Amalia and Friedrich. They stand aside from the skiers and the crowd of spectators, who have gathered for the start of the race. Amalia and Friedrich are Jews and I feel shame that there are people here, who would prefer that my friends had stayed home, but friends they are, and I have known them since childhood. They understand the importance of this day to me personally. It is my first real race, so they have come to wish me luck. I motion them over, pleased that they have come and proud to call them friends. Friedrich walks reluctantly. His hands are deep in his trouser pockets and his eyes are downcast. Not so, Amalia. She holds her head high, looks only at me and ignores the other skiers. She is beautiful. Other families in Zakopane have not been as friendly to the Jews as has our family. "God made Jews just like he made Catholics," *Babcia* would say. Father Stolarczyk agrees, but while some parishioners nod their heads for that hour in church on Sunday mornings, they are not so apt to do so the other six days of the week. "But only Catholics will go to heaven, right *Babcia*?" "Don't believe everything you hear on the streets," she always says then adds, "When you get past who is right and who is wrong and can distinguish what is right from what is wrong, then – and only then – will you understand God."

Amalia! Her hair is as black as the raven's wings, her eyes dark and mysterious, and her smile as bright as the brilliant sun that blinds us in this field of white, and when she smiles – she brings the light from her world to mine and makes my life more complete. How can anyone deny the power of that smile, Jew or Gentile, what difference can it make?

Amalia! My heart secretly longs for her – I will not deny it – and that is why – bless you, mother, bless you, *Babcia* – I will never make a good priest! She stands before me with that disarming smile of hers. My heart beats faster when she takes one of my gloved hands and places something in it. Before I can look down to see what it is, she closes my fingers over my palm. She shakes her head quickly so no one will see. I lean forward so she can whisper in my ear, "It's the *hamsa*, the hand of God. It's for good luck. Look later. Race now." Her breath is warm. I am touched, even more so by her wish to keep this our secret. Without look-ing at the small piece and the thin letter strap that holds it,

I remove my glove and carefully put the *hamsa* in my vest pocket. "Thank you," I tell her.

Amalia steps back and says, "You look so handsome in your new outfit, Bronisław. See how all of the girls are staring at you."

"Hmmm," I respond with mock concern not bothering to look, "That may be a problem. I had hoped to strike fear in the hearts of the other skiers, not love and adoration from the girls!" Amalia tosses her head back and laughs.

"Unlikely, with or without the new outfit," Friedrich says to me. "You are the youngest, least experienced racer here. Only the Kupiec brothers know you. Not even the other skiers from Poland know you, those guys from Zywiec and Wisla. To them as well as to the Germans and Slovaks, you are a dandy, BUT," and Friedrich emphasizes the word 'but,' "although you are the youngest, I think you are the fastest!" He winks. Typical Friedrich, pragmatic on the one hand, optimistic on the other.

Janka tugs on my jacket and I lean over so she can whisper in my ear through her cupped hands. "She likes you." I hope Janka is right, but I straighten up and shake my head 'no' without looking at her. Janka turns her head sideways and looks at me from the corner of her eyes as her smile says, 'She does too!"

Suddenly the sharp peal of a bell pierces the clear air. No doubt, my parents can hear it in Zakopane as well. Spectators leave the area in front of the lodge, while the contestants gather. Each skier remains in his own group by city or country; I join the Kupiec boys and the other Poles. There are more than 60 competitors, most from both sides of the *Karpaty*: Poland, Czechoslovakia, Austria and even the Ukraine, but there are many Germans here and even a skier from Norway. Every ear turns to Doktor Świerz who presides over this event.

"Welcome to Zakopane," he says. We clap our hands and cheer, each man's breath visible in the cold air. "You have much work ahead of you so I will take little of your time," he continues. "My friend, Captain Radzim will lead you to the starting point near *Kopa Kondracka*." The Captain wears a bright strip of red ribbon around his arm so he is easy to identify, but I know him, and try to pretend that I do not. The Captain and my father have been the best of friends since '98 when father came to Zakopane from Podlasia. As I look around me, I see Antonín. "Please form a single line and take a number. Radzim will check each number against his list when you reach the summit. The race will not begin until you are all accounted for. Your starting order will be determined by your order of arrival at *Kondracka*. First to the top, first to the bottom. Don't waste your time getting to the summit." Laughter greets the Doktor's final remark. His instructions are simple and clear. There are no questions. The line moves quickly. I am number 49. We don our skis and begin the five-hour trek to *Kopa Kondracka*. I look back one time to find Amalia in the crowd that will thin, and then, in several hours swell in anticipation of the finish. She waves and I tip my hat to her. Janka and Stashu stand with her and Friedrich.

We depart in a single line, one man behind the other. The man in front sets the pace, but after 100 meters, the Captain signals that each man can advance at his own rate. As we continue to trek, the length of the line grows as the spacing between different groups becomes larger, but this is not a race to the top of the mountain – although the first man up will have the advantage coming down – and it is important to conserve as much energy as possible. The Kupiec boys and I stay together in the middle of the pack. In two hours, we have reached *Hala Kondratowa*, and the Captain blows a whistle to signal all participants to stop; it is time to rest and take our lunch of bread and cheese. The real work begins now, as the path grows steeper. It will take us a full three hours to climb to the starting point on *Kondracka*.

The preceding two hours was easy compared to what we face now. As I stare toward the summit, I realize I have yet to look at the gift – the *hamsa* she called it – that Amalia gave me. I take it from my pocket to examine it. It could be a mere lump of coal and it would please me simply because it is a gift from Amalia, but it immediately strikes me with its simple beauty. It is an amulet of sorts, and she has fashioned this charm with her own hands from clay. It is a thin, flat piece in the shape of an open hand no larger than four centimeters. She has painted it blue, like the sky, and has attached it to a thin, leather strap. Symbols are inscribed on it. I recognize them as Hebrew letters though I have no idea what they might mean. I close my hand around the small gift, think of Amalia and return it to my pocket. The Captain blows his whistle to signal it is time to continue our ascent.

Ever upward we trudge, step by step. I judge the strength of my competitors by their relative position in this line of skiers that continues to spread out as groups thin. All will achieve the summit, albeit the strongest skiers sooner, providing them a few minutes to rest their weary legs. The final man to the top will have little time to catch his breath before the Captain announces that the race will begin. The snowfields are pure and bright and they sparkle as the sun reaches its zenith. This is not my first time to *Kondracka*, and I will not deny my advantage over the other skiers who are not so familiar with the terrain. I am certain most believe their racing experience will carry the day for them. Other than my own countrymen, and Antonín Bartoň, few know who I am, and no one seems to care.

I enter eternity as I climb, and time disappears. The scope of my vision collapses, and I see no one, only my skis as I move them step by step up the steep slope. Other skiers converse with one another, but I refuse to waste my breath on chatter.

"Well done, young Bronisław." Indeed, I have lost track of time and the voice of the Captain calls me from my otherworld. He makes notes on in his pad and reports, "Only eight skiers have arrived so far. I would have expected you near the end, not the beginning." The tone in his voice is encouraging though I suspect others would not recognize it. As I stand resting on my ski poles, I look back to see the long line of men extended behind me. I have at least 15 minutes to gather my strength, maybe more. Antonín is already here. He catches my eye and nods. I smile and address the Captain, "Then I think Doktor Świerz will really be surprised when I am the first man to the finish line."

He cautions me, "Let your skis speak for you." He raises his frosty eyebrows, and I am able to silently complete the sentence, 'and not your mouth,' but I cannot refrain from answering aloud, "I will." So much like my father, the Captain fills his pipe bowl and the aroma of cherry wood lingers in the air around him.

The sun is at our backs as the final skier joins us, and I know by the time we reach the finish line, shadows will envelope the lodge in Kuźnice, and the temperature will plummet below freezing. In the distance, I see a thin column of smoke that marks our objective.

Notepad in hand, the Captain moves to the edge of the precipice. "By my count we have 67 skiers. Those who climbed the fastest will be rewarded with a forward position. We will start with three rows of five skiers, 15 in all. Four rows of six will follow. The remaining 28 skiers will be in four rows of seven." He reads from his list and each skier moves into his assigned position. Antonín is in the first row; I am in the second. "At my signal," the Captain says, "we'll start the race. On every count of 10, I will release another row. That means the brave hearts in the first row will be more than a full 90 seconds ahead of those skiers in the final row." He turns to those in the front rows and says, "Your strength honors you," and bows. He makes eye contact with Jan Kupiec who finds himself in the back row. "You men in the final row have much to prove! May luck, and God if he will, be with you." He knocks the remaining ash from his pipe with two well-placed taps with the palm of his hand and returns his pipe to his pocket. "I will follow the final row, but I will stop for no one. Skiers ready?" he asks with a strong voice. Without waiting for an answer he says, "Good. Row one, set." The skiers crouch before me. The Captain instinctively raises his arm and drops it while saying, "Go!"

The first five explode down the mountain and I shuffle into position with the others in my row. The Captain's count of 10 passes in the blink of an eye. I never hear his "Set," and find myself staring at the backs of the other four as the Captain's "Go!" echoes down the mountain. I'm over the edge with a strong push from my poles.

The once smooth and velvety surface is now choppy and ragged. The initial descent is so steep that I have to make an immediate sharp turn to my left to keep my speed in check. I squint through the flying snow and search for an untouched path. I will control my own race and not follow the course set by those in the first row. Within seconds, my hat has flown my head and flutters hanging from the leather strap that holds it secure around my neck.

I see little separation in the first group and do not sense that I am gaining on it. I glance quickly to the left and right. A tear makes its way to the corner of my eye and then flies from my face into the very maelstrom I am creating. I lead my own group. For now, that is enough.

I have been here before and I am prepared for the steep and rapid descent, but I wrestle with the slope for the first 15 minutes. I am willing to take risks to gain ground on the forward group, but I fight to maintain control. It is very easy to let the mountain take me. I refuse to let that happen knowing that if it does, my first race will end in a violent fall. On the other hand, I do not try to conquer the mountain. We must work together, the mountain and I. The victory must be shared by both of us. It is a fine balance between risk and speed. I revel in the wind and find music in the hissing sound my runners make in the open snow. I find joy in the quick turns I am forced to make to control the rate of my descent.

My thighs are strong, but they begin to burn as I push myself to catch the skiers in the front row. I ski for the love of skiing. I could walk through town like other people, but I choose to ski simply because I love it. When you love something with passion, it becomes far more than necessity, it becomes life. But as I plunge forward, I realize this is not recreation, and as much as I love it, I have an intense desire to be the best on this day. At this moment of yearning, I don't think to question my priorities, and I will myself to increase my speed. I will overtake them and fulfill the promise I made to Antonín in the early morning darkness outside of St. Clement's. In less than five minutes, steepest part of the mountain will be behind me.

The distance between the frontrunners and me shrinks. I watch them veer right as a group to slide between outcrops of stone. I cut left. Their course will lead them back to the left; mine will take me to a small cliff that I will jump with confidence, just as I have done before. When I return to Earth, I will be in front of them. Within seconds, I am through the stand of scraggly spruce at the upper edge of the tree line. I turn my skis downhill and quickly gain speed. I time the run perfectly. As I leave the ground, I float silently over the five skiers who have taken their turn to the left to avoid this precipice. There are no tracks in the snow before me. I prepare myself to meet the Earth and feel the backs of my skis slice into the snow. I've done it. Somewhere behind me – not more than a few seconds – are the other skiers. I laugh aloud, but my victory is short-lived. As I vainly raise my poles skyward to celebrate my momentary triumph, the tip of my right ski catches a stray limb. The scales are tipped and my balance fails as time slows to a crawl. I cannot prevent my body from rotating to the right and soon I am facing uphill. I fall backwards down the steep slope with the snow flying blizzard-like around me, and I tumble for many meters before I come to a stop. The other skiers fly past me as if I am nothing more than a stray rock or stump. The screech of sliding skis sends a shower of white powder that washes over me like a wave. My heart sinks. I struggled up this mountain for hours, and my labor comes to naught in a matter of a few miserable seconds.

I try to gather my wits, as well as my equipment. I am fortunate that my skis still hang to my legs by the leather straps that bind them to my boots. I raise my hands and am without one glove and one pole. I am chilled with the snow that has found its way beneath my clothes and clings to my back. As I swing my legs down slope, pain rips through my right ankle as if I have stepped into a steely-jawed bear trap. I try to rise but the pain in my ankle drives me back to the ground. I lay swathed in self-pity, which is far more debilitating than the pain in my leg or the discomfort of the snow up my back. The final skier skis by me. I am angry. He is too cautious, but here I am, the bold one whose reckless charge down the mountain will leave me in last place. The Captain glides by me shaking his head. At least he acknowledged me even though he didn't say a word.

"Stay where you are and don't move." I wipe the frost from my eyebrows and the snow from my squinting eyes. Is it a man, or some mythical shape shifter, a *Leszy* come

to protect the animals of the forest from intruders such as
me? I stifle a painful cry when I try to move, and again I
hear, "I told you not to move." I recognize the voice. It is
authoritative. My vision clears and standing above me with
my pole and glove in his hand is Antonín.

"Give me that," I shout at him, "and be on your way.
You've already lost a full minute on the pack." He does not
budge. "Leave!" This time I scream at him, and the instant
the word leaves my mouth, I wish I had not raised my voice
in anger. He pays no mind to my outburst.

"Ankle or leg?" he asks calmly as he watches the Captain
and the final skiers disappear into the tree line.

"Didn't you hear me?" My voice is now a plea. "Please
leave. You were in front. This race is yours to win."

He removes his cap and dusts the snow from it. "No,
you were winning the race there for those few seconds as
you flew over the top of me and the other leaders. At that
moment, I was certain it was your race to lose." He pauses
and adds matter-of-factly, "You did." Antonín squats low
and sits back on his skis in the snow. "I'll ask you again.
Ankle or leg?"

"Ankle. I'm sure of it."

"Well, that's better than the leg. We will leave the
boot on tight to control the swelling, but I think we had
better get moving. It will take us quite a while and we
want to get back to Kuźnice before dark. I think we can
do it."

"I don't understand. You came here to win a race.
We're not even countrymen, yet you stop to help me?"

He laughs. "I train and study with Sokół, but I have
my own thoughts. The ideas of Sokół are not exclusive to

Czechoslovakia, as many of my countrymen would believe them to be. We are brothers are we not? I'm a Slovak. You are a Pole. So what? You are still my brother. We share the same air, we enjoy this mountain together, and right now, brother, you need help. I am here to help you." He rises to his feet. "You would know better than I, but I think we are past the steepest slopes?"

I nod my head, yes to both: I do need his help, and we are beyond the steepest slopes. "The Hala Kondratowa is less than half a kilometer. There, the slope turns gentle and we can follow an easy path to the lodge at Kuźnice. Still, it will take hours with me limping along. Just go ahead. I can make it on my own."

He rises to his full height and stretches. "First things first. Let's get you up and get the skis off. We will strap them to your back. I have seen this done once before and I know we can do it. We'll strap your legs to mine just below our knees, and you will rest your weight on my back, boots on my skis. That is how we will make it down before dark. What do you think Bronisław? Can we do it?"

His confidence dispel my doubts, and I am willing to put my fate in his hands this day. "Yes we can."

The cold numbs my ankle. Antonín's steps are my steps, his path mine. He takes me down the mountain skillfully and carefully as if he has done the same thing a hundred times before. I feel his body strain to its limit to hold our collective balance in check and we never fall.

As daylight flees and dusk takes her place, we keep moving forward, ever forward. The moon rises. Antonín's head is always down as his eyes scan the ground as if he fears

we will fall into some bottomless abyss; at other times, I fear
he is sleeping. Finally, I whisper, "look." He raises his head
and sees the glow of a bonfire that fills a small, orange circle
and reveals the lodge at Kuźnice. Antonín shows no reaction and does not relax or allow any sense of relief to divert
his mind from his mission. The cold has stolen feeling from
my ankle, but I would not say the same for my friend's legs
that have remained flexed and strained for hours. I know
he is tired but he stays his path. There is no crowd, only a
handful of silhouettes, which move like phantoms in front
of the fire. As we near the lodge and the beckoning warmth
of the fire, Antonín's pace noticeably quickens.

"Hello," Antonín calls from the darkness with no weariness in his voice. "Have we won the race?"

The silhouettes become real people: my father, my
mother, the Captain, Doktor Świerz and Amalia. When
I see Amalia, I remember the *hamsa*. I consider the worth
of the charm. It did not prevent my accident – of course,
my downfall was due to my own carelessness – but it may
have contributed to my safe return, the charm and my new
friend, no, to my new brother Antonín. I strain to reach my
pocket, and when I do, I find it empty. I close my eyes and
curse my foolishness again. The *hamsa* is lost in the deep
snow on the high mountain.

My father and the Captain are the first to reach us. Each
crosses his arms and they firmly grip the other's hands, fash-
ioning a seat, which they place beneath me. I fall into it
and they carry me into the lodge. Its intoxicating warmth
pours over me in waves. Antonín and I have been outside
in the cold for nearly 12 hours, twice as long as we had
planned to be.

"It's my ankle," I say as mother embraces me.

When the Doktor carefully removes my boot and sock. Amalia stifles her cry with the palm of her hand. "It doesn't take a physician to see that your ankle is broken," the Doktor says and then grimaces. "The season is over for you, but the ankle will heal in time and you will be as good as new."

"The rewards of risk can be great," the Captain says, "but failure in the face of risk carries its consequences. This afternoon, you have tasted the punishment risk can inflict. Your chances of reward have increased. Never be afraid to dare, never shy from risk. The Doktor is right; your ankle will heal. Don't let it leave a scar on your courage, young Bronek."

I force a smile as my father pats my shoulder. "And so we owe great thanks to the Slovak, the hero who carried my son down from the mountain." We turn toward the doorway, but it is empty. In my father's urgency to get me inside, we have forgotten Antonín. "Where is he?"

"I don't remember that he came in with us," Amalia whispers. My father walks outside. The bonfire consumes itself and is now a pile of red coals. Antonín is not there.

It is mid-morning and I awake with a groan. My ankle, now bound tightly in boards my father has fashioned with the Doktor's instructions, still throbs, even more than it did before I fell asleep. I silently thank God for yesterday's numbing cold.

I open my eyes and see *Babcia* and *Pani* Murach at the table. "It still throbs?" *Babcia* asks.

I must be brave but I cannot prevent myself from answering, "Yes."

"I think some Żubrówka will help," *Pani* Murach says and sips from her steaming cup of tea.

"*Pani*..." *Babcia* waves a finger at her friend. *Pani* Murach shrugs her shoulders and says, "The throb in his head will replace the throb in his ankle." *Pani* Murach offers a toothless grin. The old women share a smile and *Babcia* goes outside and retrieves the nearly full bottle of liquor that father 'hides' in the shed. Unlike many of his friends, Father is not known for his drinking prowess.

"Just one sip," *Babcia* says. *Pani* adds with a wink and a whisper, "And don't tell your mother."

I raise myself on my elbows not certain that I want the 'medicine.' "Go ahead. *Pani* is right, it will ease the pain, or at least substitute one for another." I take a healthy mouthful and nearly gag as I force myself to swallow. Though the vodka is ice cold, it warms my stomach and I feel my head spin. *Babcia* fluffs the pillow and puts it back beneath my head.

Pani Murach approaches my bed. "Here." She extends her open hand, and in it is Amalia's *hamsa*.

My eyes open wide. "Where did you get this?"

"From the Slovak skier. He stayed at my house and told me to make sure I gave this to you."

"Where did he.... Tell him to come," I say.

She shakes her head. "He and his comrades left before the sunrise." I fall back in bed disappointed but happily drugged. I stare at the blue charm. What was lost is found. I will see my friend again. I know it.

Chapter Four, 1927

Giewont

The Captain is my father's dearest friend. Janka teases them that they look alike, though that is no bad thing. Both are handsome men with thick, black hair and heavy moustaches. Each is tall and one can only see the initial stage of a bald spot when they are sitting down. Neither is vain and takes no issue with this first sign of age. No one ever talks about the Captain's family, and no one asks. As far as I know, he has never had a wife or children. I cannot remember a time when he was not with our family, and so, I have few memories that do not include the Captain. I have never seen him ski, yet everyone in Zakopane says he is the best. His experience with the sport and his knowledge of the mountains is so vast anyone who wants to be a competitive skier comes to the Captain. He lives alone in a small cottage at the edge of the meadow. I believe the skiers from our village are the best in Poland, and it is because of the Captain's influence and example. His mere presence is an inspiration to these would-be champions.

There are days when I believe he has deeper feelings for my older brother and my sisters than he does for me. I find that odd since I am the one who loves to ski and who shares his passion for the mountains. Still, my respect for him never wavers and I follow his advice as if it comes from the mouth of God.

Many years ago, I asked my father, "How does he know so much?"

"Years before you were born," he told me, "The Captain and I lived in these mountains, and we knew every tree, every stream, and every square centimeter from north to south, the east slopes and the west ones. The Captain and I skied these mountains and others you've never seen and dare not even imagine."

"But why have I never seen him ski, father?"

"It's not a question you should ask, nor one that I will answer." He turns from my inquisitive look and stares into the distance. "Give it no more thought, but believe me when I tell you, he is the greatest skier who has ever lived, and you are fortunate that he is your teacher." I never asked again.

"Don't let me down, Czech. I have been taking chances on you all your life. Make it worth my while." The Captain never fails to challenge and inspire me with the simplest of words.

So, with the Captain's exhortation ringing in my ears, I begin this training session running like a fool while my teammates follow at a brisk walk. No doubt, they are chuckling amongst themselves. This morning, we climb Giewont, but our thoughts are on St. Moritz where we will travel in seven short months. The hike will take us near to the king's secret place. I'm certain other teammates have visited the grotto, but its existence remains unspoken to preserve the mystical power it possesses for us and for those who will follow in our paths. I make pilgrimage to the cavern every year to remind myself who I am, and of the obligation I have to my country. The mountain will test my endurance and my legs will burn today, but I will take pleasure in the pain knowing that my thighs will be strong like the steel of Bolesław's sword when I climb the slopes in Switzerland in the winter.

I will ski for Poland in the Olympic Games. I do not know much about these games, but father tells me the Olympic Games follow an ancient tradition that began in Greece thousands of years ago and were later abandoned to lay dormant for another millennium and more. Father explains that only 30 years ago, a Frenchman started the games again, and just three years ago, his countrymen staged winter games for the first time, in Chamonix. Next year, the Swiss will stage winter games – the second Winter Olympic Games – in the Alps. I've not seen those mountains, but father tells me they are spectacular, high praise from a man who has spent his adult life in the Tatras! The popularity of our sport is growing and I am overjoyed to be a part of it. I will be the youngest Polish skier at St. Moritz; I am determined to be the fastest.

Our goal today at nearly 2,000 meters: the steel cross on Great Giewont. I marvel every time I glimpse the cross. Nearly 30 years ago – while athletes raced at those new Olympic Games in Athens – my father, the Captain and their highlander friends erected the cross. What devotion each man had as he experienced his own Christ-like passion, dragging the steel beams to the top of this mountain. My climb today is an easy stroll compared to the arduous trek my father and the Captain completed when they carried the heavy beams to the mountaintop. I can hardly imagine their effort, and then at the summit, the *górales* built the cross, which has survived the wind, ice, and rain and lightening for three decades.

With poles in hand, I work my arms in the same motion that will help propel me on the snow. Within minutes, I am well ahead of my teammates and no longer hear their casual chatter, but only my steady breathing as I continue to surge forward and upward. My hair falls over my brow and into my eyes as I vigorously shake the beads of sweat that continually flow down my forehead on this warm day. I think to run my fingers through my hair, but it is of no use for my locks are determined to rest on my forehead. The kerchief tied loosely around my neck is soon drenched with perspiration and I feel cool drops sliding down my chest. I take both ski poles in my left hand and place my right palm over my sternum. I maintain my pace and am reinvigorated when I feel the *hamsa* beneath the thin fabric of my wet shirt. I will not lose it again, ever. It hangs from my neck on a thin leather strap with a small cross that I carved from a single piece of wood, a replica of the cross I travel to this day.

Time passes unnoticed. Finally, as I move up the North face of the mountain, the steel cross emerges on the summit. I climb now with my hands as well as my feet. My body is tired but I have learned not to associate fatigue with pain. I will not concede to the ache that invades my thighs with every step I take. To yield to the pain would demonstrate weakness and *górales* show no weakness. The scrub grasses that grow on this steep slope offer me some purchase, but I am on my own for the final 100 meters. I drop to my knees like a supplicant animal and crawl the final distance to the base of the cross. Is that not what I am, merely an animal who has purged his brain of pain during this assault of the mountain just to kneel on the hard, stone slabs that surround the base of this monument? Not an animal, rather a man who understands that this place, in the shadow of this cross, is a place of reverence.

Pulling myself to my feet, I catch my breath, and I read the weathered sign that my father and his comrades placed on this site, "To Jesus Christ, from the Highlanders of Zakopane. 1900." Such is the mind and will of my father and men like him, unbending like the steel beams they carried up this mountain, and for a single purpose: to praise their God. I want to be like my father and his friends.

I kneel on the rocky surface, face the cross and gaze upward to its apex. It is midday. The sun is directly above me and the crossbeams filter the sun's warm rays over me in a river of brilliant light. It soaks me with its warmth. I open my mind and I pray, for what I do not remember, but I pray and it makes me feel good. I think of my mother and know that she may have stood on this very spot when my father and his comrades raised this cross. I look to the north and my country enfolds before me. It is green beyond green. Can any land be as beautiful as Poland? I have never been beyond its border, only gazed to the west where Czechoslovakia follows the Tatras as its peaks climb to the north and veer to the sunset. Soon enough, I will venture beyond the *Karpaty*, and I will bear the colors of Poland; its White Eagle will soar.

I dream of glory on that day, glory for Poland, glory for my family, and glory for me. Everyone will know Bronisław

Czech. My country, my family and my name will be known well beyond Zakopane and the Tatras. In my mind's eye, I see myself flying from the jump in Switzerland. I rise to my toes on Mt. Giewont as I feel the Earth fall beneath me. I am suspended in air and close my eyes to the wind in my face. The crowd holds its breath and watches admiringly as I lean forward over the tips of my skis and soar effortlessly and in perfect form. As the ground rushes towards me, my daydream is interrupted.

"Hey, pretty boy, open your eyes and welcome me." It is Andrzej Krzeptowski. He was in France, at Chamonix at the first winter games, and that makes him a veteran. My father respects him and advises me it is good to be his friend. "What's the idea?" he asks. "You are putting us all to shame!"

The wind whistles through the steel beams of the cross. I want to be proud and defiant, but I remember what my father says about Andrzej, so I humbly lower my eyes and search for an answer that might satisfy this experienced competitor.

"Whew," he gasps. While he scans the horizon, I can tell he is watching me from the corner of his eyes, just as I watch him thinking he does not notice. Without warning, Andrzej delivers a hardy slap to my back. "Hey, my young friend. It is okay. I mean no offense. Frankly, I am glad we have some-one like you to push us. We were not so strong in Chamonix. *'Nie chwal dnia przed zachodem słońca,'* I told my teammates, and I'll say it again now, 'Don't praise the day before sunset.'"

Andrzej puts me at ease and I am comfortable looking into his eyes. "Yes, Bronek, I agreed with the Captain when he said we need you on this team. Make us all work harder! Show the world what a Pole is made of."

My confidence swells and I am ready to return to Zakopane. I correctly suspect that Andrzej will take a few more minutes rest. I bid him goodbye, take a final look at the cross and bless myself as I begin my descent. "Keep the dinner warm for us," Andrzej calls after me.

The summer night is clear and warm, the stars arranged in a brilliant mosaic across the black sky from horizon to horizon. Even with just a sliver of a moon, there are shadows that sway almost imperceptibly in the faint breeze that dares disturb the foliage. Distant owls call to one another across fields that sparkle with lightning bugs, and the constant chirp of crickets gives the night music a special rhythm. The song is always the same. It is a song that comforts children and old men and lulls them to sleep while it draws lovers to each other's arms.

It is very late. Hours ago, tired, stocking-capped men and their wives blew out any candles that had not burned down. Zakopane sleeps, but I cannot. The restlessness that I endure crept to me like a specter months, no, years ago. It is Amalia who haunts me. Every time I close my eyes, her image appears beneath my lids. She makes no overtures to me, now or ever, but I cannot escape her. She is proud like a lioness and seems to flaunt her jewishness, yet she has always been cautious around me, more for my sake, I think than hers. She has no desire to see me labeled a 'Jew lover,' as is so often done by ignorant men who have neither compassion in their hearts nor the silent voice of God in their souls. Still we are friends. She does not rebuff me but does not seek me out as she used to when I was a young boy.

As children, our friendship was open and unhindered; as we become adults, it is closed and restricted, even forbidden in some circles.

The world changes, people change, but my fondness for Amalia does not. It is as constant as that very star that shines so brightly in the northern sky. It pained me when she went to University. Warsaw is not so far away, but when Amalia left for school, it seemed as distant as heaven is from earth. She comes home for several weeks each summer. She returned yesterday. Amalia no longer looks like a peasant. Her new clothes accentuate her femininity and make my body stir. My entire demeanor is animated, but she would not know it, for I hide in the shadows when she disembarks from the train. Amalia used to come home mid-winter at Christmastime, when the Jews celebrate their festival of lights. Last year she stayed in Warsaw. I did not ask her why.

So I enter the village and walk through the empty streets and I wonder if Amalia thinks of me as often as I think of her. I expect nothing, only to gaze upon her quiet house in the starlight. I pretend it will be enough.

My home in the foothills is large like most farmhouses. Amalia's house is small and plain. She has no siblings, but relatives from Warsaw have moved in and taken refuge from the violence that occurs frequently in Warsaw and in other cities since Poland declared its independence just 10 years ago. The older I get, the more I understand. I learn that *Babcia* is right when she tells *Pani* Murach, "The Jews will never be safe." There is more room in the house for her mother and father and their guests when Amalia is at the university. The Statters live among the other Zakopane Jews – some 200 families – in a compact neighborhood on the far side of town away from the mountains. How Amalia escapes discrimination at the university I do not know. Of course maybe she doesn't. Maybe she just refuses to discuss it and pretends it does not happen.

When he spies me coming up the narrow street, a dog barks and trots towards me. I stop and pat him on the head. He is a sheepdog and reminds me of *Zegar*, but this friendly dog has all four of his legs. He sniffs my pant leg with no mal intent. I run my fingers through the thick hair at the nape of his neck. He moves on. I think each of us has made a new friend.

I reach a crossroads. The neighborhood before me and to my right is the Jewish neighborhood. Amalia's house is the corner house; it is plain and simple like the other houses in the Jewish sector. I take a seat on a bench beneath a large tree on the opposite side of the street. I disappear in the leafy shadows as I stare at the dark house. My wooden bench backs to a well-groomed hedge that runs the length of the street. As the tired breeze moves through the limbs above me, I imagine that the sound it makes is the collective breath of those men, women and children who rest in their warm beds preparing for the coming day. The sound is comforting and masks the tension that seems to be an integral part every Jew's life. Something not quite right lurks in the background like a dream once seen but never remembered. Perhaps it is a nightmare.

I am mildly startled when muffled voices and the scruffy sound of shuffling feet approach from the street behind me. I freeze and become a part of the bench, my stillness my only camouflage. I hear whispers and then restrained laughter.

"Be quiet!" someone says in a hushed but urgent tone.

"Don't be so scared," another replies. "We'll be heroes. Do you really think anybody cares?"

Five boys pass me and take no notice. I know them, but not by choice. Two sets of brothers and a friend, the oldest is five years younger than I am. Like their fathers who work in the sawmill, they are ruffians and take an unhealthy pride in their crudeness. I have heard it said that Oblinski and Gabryszak participated in the pogrom at Zawoja many years ago. Neither denies it, and neither hides his dislike of Jews. While their sentiments are uncomfortably popular, I do not share them, nor do most of the highlanders.

The boys stand defiantly in the middle of the cross-roads with no concern of discovery. Wisław, a teenager is the oldest. They gather round him and watch in a near worshipful way as he takes a single cigarette and a single match from his shirt pocket. He carefully strikes the match on the edge of the small knife he carries. The flare briefly blinds them as Wisław puts the flame to his cigarette. He inhales deeply and expels a thin column of white smoke that quickly dissipates in the faint breeze. He does not cough; he has done this before. One of his friends extends his hand for the cigarette. Wisław slaps it away. "Get your own," he admonishes his friend and then blows smoke into his face. The others laugh, louder than what they should. Their brazenness will serve them no good, now or ever.

"Who has the bucket?" Wisław asks.

The smallest boy raises it carefully with two hands. It is Mirek. Too bad. He could be a good boy.

Singing insects cease their chatter and go still when the loud creak of old hinges on an even older door cuts the air. The sound is not quick and sharp, but slow and piercing, like fingernails on a chalkboard. Wisław takes a final drag on his cigarette and throws it to the ground. He waits unafraid.

"Who is it?" Amalia ask. When no one responds, she steps from the shelter of the porch and into the starlight. Her wool nightshirt hangs straight from her shoulders. The image is not angelic, rather fearless and threatening. "Who is it?" she asks again in a hushed tone so as not to wake those inside the house.

"We're the painters," Wisław finally says, "See how chipped the paint is on your miserable house? We have come to help you." Wisław's cronies softly chuckle. "You'd best go back inside and we'll be about our business."

"You have no business here you little goat. Take your kids and go back to the barn."

"Or what, *Żydówki*? What will you do?" Wisław takes a menacing step forward. When Amalia moves forward to meet him, his gang is not so quick to follow.

"Maybe we should go," Wisław's younger brother Krzysztof mumbles.

"And maybe I should tell our father how brave you are?" he lashes out. "Be quiet!" Wisław turns back toward Amalia. "Little goat, you say? You go back inside, *Żydówki* or I'll have more fun with you than you can possibly imagine." He hitches up his trousers in a poor effort to act like a man. Seconds pass. They are at impasse. "I think it's time to give you a lesson, *Żydówki*."

Amalia is 21-years-old, thin but fit. I think she could handle this puffed up clown herself, but I am concerned with numbers, and I do believe Wisław would use his knife willingly. Before he can take a single step forward, I rise from the bench and stride boldly to the broken down gate to stand between Amalia and Wisław and his gang. "I think the lesson will be yours, Wisław Oblinski." My unexpected entrance paralyzes the boys. A sigh of relief follows Amalia's initial gasp. "I have no time for your tricks or your games," I tell the boys, "We have nothing to discuss, so be on your way."

He finds himself in a corner and must decide if his bravado will serve him. It will not, because he has already crossed the line with his disrespectful threats. I will tolerate no more and begin to count silently to myself. When I reach 10, he must be gone or I will act.

"Jew-lover," he hisses at me with a smirk on his pock-mocked face. Although in essence he may be correct, his mean-spiritedness intends the term as a slur, not a compliment. I love dogs. I do not like cats, and Wisław's outburst reminds me of an angry cat confronted by a dog.

As I move forward, he steps back and raises his arms like a boxer might do. Before Amalia can say 'stop,' I snatch the open bucket of paint from Mirek and place it swiftly, firmly and sloppily over Wisław's head. He struggles to remove it, then tosses it to the ground. White paint drips slowly down his face and back. He bends forward to wipe the paint from his eyes and catlike, spits it from his mouth. His whiteness glows like a beacon in the faint starlight.

"You fucker!" he shouts.

I grab his shirt collar in one hand and the seat of his baggy pants in the other. I throw him to the ground and kick dust at him. His gang runs down the street not waiting to see what will happen. Wisław cowers as I move toward him dusting my hands. "You may leave," I say in a calm voice, "But before you do, you may apologize to Miss Statter."

"To a *Żyd*? Never!" he screams.

My anger rises and is about to fall like an avalanche upon this young boy who tries so hard to be a gangster thinking it will make his father proud. I have my temper under control, but still I pick up the empty bucket and throw it at him. It bangs off his head and he falls back, arms raised defensively once more. As I move forward, he scrambles to his feet and stumbles up the street. He just has to yell back a final, stupid statement, "Fuck you, Jewlover and your fucking *Żydówki*!" I'll waste no more time on him.

The glow of a candle moves past the window in Amalia's house and comes to rest in the open doorway behind her. The light filters through her flimsy nightgown, and I see the curves of a body I am not meant to see.

"What is it, Amalia?"

"It's nothing, Papa. Go back to bed," she answers.

"But I heard voices."

"Papa, please go back to bed. It is nothing." She says it as more of an order and less of a plea. University has made her stronger of mind and body. The floorboards creak as her father shuffles back to his bed.

"What was it?" his wife asks from the her bed.

"Nothing," he answers, "Amalia says it is nothing. Go back to sleep."

A bullfrog from a nearby pond loudly croaks twice as if he is a conductor tapping his baton on his music stand, and the night denizens resume their symphony. The lightening bugs return after the dust settles. I remember running through these nearby fields when the grass was taller than I was catching the tiny creatures and holding them in my hand as if their meager light would keep me safe from dangerous, unseen things in the dark.

"Are you okay?" I begin to say, but Amalia puts her fingers to my lips.

"Shhhhh, Bronek! You'll wake them again." She takes me by the elbow and leads me back toward the bench. "What are you doing here anyway? It is the middle of the night."

She is annoyed, and I assume it is because of the incident in front of her house. "Don't worry," I say, "They are gone and they won't come back. Their fight is with me now, not you."

She shakes her head. "Why are you here in front of my house at whatever time of the night this is? You have no business here. Leave."

Her words have no affect on me. Impulsively, I take her in my arms and clumsily kiss her lips. Is my awkward inexperience as obvious to her as it is to me? Though she allows me to kiss her, she stiffens, and I know I have made a mistake, so I release her and step away, embarrassed. As the distance between us grows so too does the ache in my heart. What have I done?

She reaches for my hand and draws me back to the bench and we sit. There is love in her touch, but not the passion that burns in mine. "Oh, I do love you, Bronek," she says and puts her arms around me. I hold mine painfully in my lap like a whipped schoolboy, not the man who just beat off a gang of trespassers. "But don't you see? You and I? It's impossible." She drops her arms and takes my hand.

I am too humiliated to look into her eyes so I stare straight ahead and say, "Nothing is impossible."

She does not answer, and the night music fills the void that flows from our silence. She does not see what I see. She does not feel what I feel. I am lost and without direction. I have nowhere to go, and I struggle to think of the right words to say.

I dare to speak. "I have loved you since I was a little boy, from the first time you waved at me when my father and I delivered wood to your neighborhood. I was five-years-old, you were seven. I looked up to you then, you were taller than I was."

"I remember," she says and I feel her smile.

"You were unafraid then, and you are unafraid now." I lean forward, my elbows on my knees and my chin cupped in my hands. The *hamsa* and the cross fall from my open shirt and swing from the strap around my neck.

She takes them fondly and rubs them gently with her fingertips. "These two, they are powerful together, Bronek. I do remember, and I will never forget."

I stand and the weathered strap breaks but Amalia is quick to catch the charms in her hand. I curb the desire to take her in my arms again. "There doesn't need to be anything to forget." Now I am pleading. "When I return from the games in Switzerland, I will return for you. We will leave together and find a new home, free of the prejudice that makes you think we cannot be together."

"I am so sorry, Bronek, but that can never happen." She takes a deep breath, then says the words that strike me like a thousand daggers, "You see, Bronek, when I leave for Warsaw at the end of the summer, I leave to be married." The words cut so deeply, I nearly collapse in a heap on the dusty road.

"Bronek." She rises. I pull my hand from her grasp, raise my arm and motion her to stop. I can bear no more. I don't care whom, how, where or why. I cannot overcome the urge to cry, and a sob escapes me like a child leaving his mother on the first day of school.

Amalia tries to comfort me, but how can you comfort those who cannot be comforted? That is truly impossible! Another sob forces its way through my pursed lips, and I feel tears streaming down my cheeks. She reaches to brush them away, but I turn my back to her.

"I am okay," I burble for lack of anything else of substance to say.

"I'm so sorry, Bronek." She hasn't the strength to turn me around so, moving in front of me, she takes me in her arms, her head on my chest. The scent of her hair chokes me, but I refuse to respond and stand stoically like stone.

"I must leave," I lie. I pull back and wipe the tears from my eyes. I look at her and force a smile. "I will be okay."

As I turn to leave, she holds my sleeve and says, "Wait." She slips the hamsa from the strap and puts it in my hand as she did once before. "May I keep this one?" she asks and cups the cross, still on the strap, to her chest.

I repair the broken leather strap with a knot, and I slip the loop over her head so that the cross rests between her breasts. I am beyond thinking. I nod, "May God be with you and your husband." She kisses the cross, then her fingertips and places them softly on my mouth. "And may His hand keep you from harm at the games and protect you always."

I bow my head and disappear into the darkness.

Chapter Five, 1928

Highlander

On the one hand, I am sure that I am moving faster than I have ever moved in my life, but am I really? My passenger car is rolling rapidly down the rails, yet I sit, seemingly motionless, gazing upon the landscape as it floats past the window. I look down at the cinders that line the tracks below, and watch as they race by in a blur, and then raise my eyes to the trees in the distance that appear to stand still. It is an interesting illusion, one that I have plenty of time to contemplate as the locomotive steams its way to the heart of Europe. We travel past landscapes I have not seen before; landscapes that seem vaguely familiar, as if each consists of a basic design, common to all.

I have never been on a vehicle powered by anything other than an animal. I have seen a horse lug a thousand kilograms of lumber through heavy snow in the Tatra foothills, but they say the engine that pulls this train has the power of a team of a thousand stallions pulling in unison. I have never seen a thousand horses in one place at one time, but I imagine they could move a mountain.

The old men say that January is the coldest month, but on this day in February, I would disagree. The clouds hang low and threaten snow. This train journey, my first, distorts my sense of time, and I judge the hours only by the rising and setting of the sun. I have no idea when we will reach our destination, so I patiently continue to stare out the window. Twenty-five teammates accompany me in this open car. The coaches and other representatives from our sporting committee – all of them that is except the Captain who refuses the luxury afforded to him by the Polish Olympic Committee – ride in sleeping compartments. "How can I judge the condition of my athletes," he says, "if I eat caviar and sleep in a warm bed while my skiers snatch naps between games of cards on hard wooden benches." He is my Captain.

The glass is cold on my forehead. I breathe on the window creating a canvas of condensation for my finger drawings, and realize that I have subconsciously scribbled a small and inexact outline of my *hamsa*. The amulet hangs from my neck on a new, metal chain that I hope will outlast its leather predecessor.

"So you are an artist now, pretty boy?" It is Andrzej Krzeptowski. He means no harm and only pokes fun at me, but I truly wish he would not call me 'pretty boy.' As I erase the picture from the window with my sleeve, he whispers, "If that is what I think it is, you need to be careful." I choose not to react to his word of caution.

I have been sitting with a hockey player, Karol Szenajch. Karol smokes cigarettes; I do not. Unlike the Captain's pipe tobacco that soothes me, cigarette smoke is quite acrid and it annoys me; Karol knows this so he excuses himself to go outside into the frigid air to 'enjoy' his cigarette. I wonder how it is possible to do that, to enjoy a cigarette. They smell like burned cow dung to me, and I have no reason to think they taste differently.

"May I?" Andrzej points to the empty seat beside me. He sits before I can answer. "First time away from home?" he asks.

"Yes."

"You are the youngest member of our team, and there will not be many athletes with your youth at the games. We all know that, and we will watch out for you. The Captain likes you. You are a good skier and you soar like an eagle when you jump. You will be fine, but be careful … with the *hamsa*. Do not give anyone an excuse not to be your friend."

The moment is awkward, and I do not know how to react, so I say the first thing that comes to mind, "Please don't call me 'pretty boy.'"

Andrzej is satisfied that he has made his point and will not belabor the issue. He slaps my thigh and laughs, "I'll try to remember that, young friend, but I am certain that the ladies in St. Moritz will find you so. Don't let them distract you."

The train rolls on and the monotonous sound of the iron wheels on the iron tracks creates a thumping, metallic cadence of its own. I close my eyes and doze off only to awaken at night, physically rested but mentally restless.

Several benches behind me, one of my mates, Jerzy Bardziński, the oldest member of our team plays his *konzertina*. Jerzy will ride the skeleton, much faster I am sure than the easy rhythm he has set with his instrument. He has taken the steady beat of the speeding locomotive and slowed it to his own comfortable pace. A handful of my teammates hum to the familiar melody, and with no forethought, I stand and raise a foot to the bench. In the dim light of the cabin, I lend my voice to the song, "Góralu, czy ci nie żal ...

> "Highlander, don't you feel sad
> To leave your native lands,
> From the green forests and meadows
> And the silvery streams?"

My teammates join in the chorus. Even the Captain lends his deep, strong voice to our makeshift ensemble. Not a man among us claims to be a professional singer, but together our combined voices do justice to the song!

> "Highlander, don't you feel sad?
> Highlander, return to the meadows!
> Highlander, don't you feel sad?
> Highlander, return to the meadows!"

I continue, and Jerzy, with obvious musical talent on the konzertina joins me with bass harmony.

> "And the highlander gazes at the mountains
> And wipes away a tear with his sleeve.
> Because he must leave the mountains
> For bread, Sir, for bread.
> Highlander don't you feel sad?
> Highlander, return to the meadows ..."

And so we continue into the night using song to remind us of our roots, our homeland and the mountains that bred us. Jerzy plays *Boże Coś Polskę* and follows with *Z Dymem Pożarów*. All of us know the words and have discarded any fear we might have that our voices are not good enough to carry a song. We are loud, we are proud. Our spirits rise with each note. As our songs drift away, so too does the night as the horizon behind us begins to brighten. Jerzy returns his *konzertina* to its case. I have never been beyond the Tatras and I return to my seat and lay my head against the window, straining for my first glimpse of Switzerland.

Slowly, the sun creeps over the landscape and paints the Alps on the Western canvas. I stare in wonder. They are much higher and much more rugged than I expected them to be. Our Tatras look small in comparison. They rise defiantly and dare me to challenge their steepest slopes and their most rugged terrain. I am not afraid.

The train slows and my teammates and I move to the seats on the left where we can see the lake, completely frozen now and ready for the games three days hence. The sky is cloudless, and they say this is typical in the city that some refer to as "the top of the world."

With a final, labored groan, our locomotive comes to a heavy halt at the station and we file out the right side of the car. Our contingent is 37 strong: 26 athletes, six coaches and five committee members including Alexander Bobkowski, the president of our ski association. Of the athletes, our hockey team accounts for 11, five are bob-sledders and 10 of us are skiers. We retrieve our gear and wait patiently as *Pan* Bobkowski smiles and meets with the members of the host organization. Cheery heads nod as the contingents shake hands. Good will rules the day.

Dignitaries pass through our ranks, tip their hats and say, "Willkommen und viel Glück!" Their rosy cheeks and smiling faces do make us feel welcome, and I am happy to be here with my teammates. After several minutes of well wishing, *Pan* Bobkowski gives a final bow, then gets our attention with a clap of his hands. He waves his arm forward and we follow him up the street toward the village. The mountains dwarf the town and are much closer to it than the Tatras are to Zakopane. A magnificent castle rules the shore of the lake. I envy the inhabitants who live in this large, beautiful and grand building. I have seen nothing like it. It rises at least 10 stories into the blue sky. On the western end of the building, the Swiss flag, red with its white cross, waves proudly from the pointed roof of the castle's highest parapet. Another flag flies beneath it in the center of the structure. The street we are walking will take us directly in front of the palace; I am eager to get a closer look.

"It's much nicer than the hotel we stayed at four years ago in France. Of course, just seven of us were there and the uncertainty of what to expect suggested to Bobkowski that humble accommodations would suit our needs. This event will be much grander than Chamonix."

"I'm sorry, I was daydreaming and didn't hear you. What did you say?"

"This hotel," Andrzej points at the castle, "It's much nicer than the one we stayed at in France."

I am confused. "That is a hotel?"

"It is. The very one where we will be staying at these 10 days."

"We are staying there?" I cannot believe it.

"Yes, pretty boy, we are staying there. By the way, you will room with me. Captain's request, not mine, though I do find you a pleasant and entertaining lad. Your singing last night was an inspiration, and I suspect you'll draw the ladies like bees to honey. I'm okay with that. Just stay close so I can keep you out of trouble."

Andrzej enjoys teasing me, but it is no matter for the prospects of spending my time in this castle overwhelms me. The small awning above the entrance bears the name 'Badrutt's Palace Hotel.' I was right, it is a palace, and we enter a world of royalty when we walk through the small door. The ceilings soar and the foyer expands beyond us in all directions. There is energy everywhere as quests meet and chat while staff scurries across the polished, stone floors. The youngest of us are górale and have rarely, if ever been beyond the borders of our small towns and villages. This is all too new and difficult for our imaginations to comprehend. To live in a palace.

"Andrzej!" I hear a loud voice call, and the name echoes from the vaulted ceilings. Some banter ceases while people search for the source of the shout, but the quiet lasts for only seconds and then the cacophony resumes in its mingled tones and multilingual conversations.

"Andrzej," this time not so loud and much closer. A well-dressed man approaches Andrzej and takes him in his arms. The man is not athletic nor does he appear very strong for that matter, but he raises Andrzej in a bear hug, and I fear they will topple. I catch my breath and only release it after this man unsteadily settles my teammate back to the ground.

"Adam," Andrzej beams, "So you did come!"

"Of course, of course, and why not? Very important to my career," the man says. He pats Andrzej firmly on his shoulders and continues, "You look terrific. Are you up to the task?" With a sarcastic sneer on his face, Andrzej extends his arms with open palms. "Of course you are," Adam answers his own question. "What a silly question. And the rest of our team? What about them?"

"Judge by the youngest," Andrzej says and pulls me forward as if he is an auctioneer and I am the product on the block. "This one is Bronisław. Fast and brave. Flies like an eagle." I stand mute. The Captain is nearby and catches my eye. He looks over his shoulder and winks at me.

"Meet my big brother," Andrzej says. "Bronek, this is Adam." I remove my glove and we shake hands, his is small and his grasp, not firm. I wonder again how he could have lifted his brother from the floor in a bear hug.

Adam retreats a step, closes one eye and stares through the frame he has created with his hands. "Another good face. Are we Poles the handsomest men on the Continent?" They laugh, but the joke is lost on me.

"He claims he will make films, the moving ones," Andrzej explains to me, "and he's always looking for talent."

"I have brought my cameras here, but these Swiss are not convinced I can add value to the games by recording them on film." Adam waves enthusiastically to someone behind us. "Okay, brother. I have to run. Meet me this evening in the bar and we'll talk." Without looking at either of us, he says, "Nice to meet you," and leaves in pursuit of his next 'talent.'

Our rooms are spacious, but our committee has only reserved four, thus our 26 athletes and our six coaches will sleep eight to a room. As the youngest man on the team, I watch my roommates draw lots for the two beds. I will be content to sleep on the floor, not far from the radiator that hisses quietly in the corner.

The veterans and older athletes do allow me to use a dresser drawer, and in it, I find a book, "Die Bibel." A cross graces the leather cover above the title, and as I leaf through the pages, I find pictures of biblical events: Moses with his tablets; the young David holding the head of Goliath; and Jesus on his cross and a dozen other pictures. I deduce that this is a bible in the native tongue of the Swiss, which I will come to recognize as German though the Swiss do speak other languages. If I am correct, then 'Die Bibel' must mean 'The Bible.' My discovery and inference brings a smile to my face.

Andrzej is our leader and has the honor to carry our flag in the opening ceremony. "The train ride was a long one," he says. "We'll meet for dinner this evening. Until then, you should rest and relax." He means that our time is free and we can do with it as we please. He trusts that we will not waste it or be foolish with it. He flops on a bed and covers his eyes with his cap. Józef Bujak takes the other bed.

The train ride has confined me too long and I must move and exercise my legs. As I open the door, Andrzej says with eyes closed, "Don't get lost, pretty boy, and don't be late for dinner." I hesitate and think to take the book. "I will return in a few hours," I tell him.

We arrived from the east, so I turn west when I depart the hotel. St. Moritz is small, maybe smaller than Zakopane, but the population has increased many fold with athletes and spectators who have come together to celebrate life through sport. Men tip their hats and women smile as we pass each other in the busy street. I bow in a casual way holding the book with both hands behind my back as I look at each passerby and attempt to discern nationality. I doubt that I can, nor does it matter. We are all clearly pleased to be here on this glorious day. The village stands on the north side of the small lake, and pedestrian traffic is sparse when I reach the far end. I see a path and follow it to the frozen shoreline where a weathered wooden bench beckons me to sit. I accept the invitation and the peace and quiet it affords me. I close my eyes, sit and lean forward with my elbows on my knees and drink the stillness that surrounds me. There is not enough to satisfy me, but I take what I can and sit up to rest my back against the bench as I open the book I carried with me. I stare at the page that reads *"Buch I, Genesis,"* and I have no doubts that my translation – Book One, Genesis – is correct. The light breeze turns the thin page for me. *"Am Anfang schuf Gott die Himmel und die Erde."* I smile to myself, certain that this means, "In the beginning God created the Heavens and the Earth ..." *Babcia* has told me the stories – all of them – many times, and just as many times, I have read the stories myself. If I know the stories in Polish, how difficult can it be for me to learn them in another language, and so I begin my instruction. With this book, I teach myself German.

I have never had such a meal, and I finish it with some difficulty, refusing to waste a morsel. I decline the rich *sachertorte* and ice cream that my teammates attack with enthusiasm. The cake hardly looks real with its two chocolate layers perfectly aligned next to a delicate spoonful of whipped cream. It looks so delicious, but I have had my fill and then some. The waiter clears our table. Apparently, the bill is paid but I never see money exchange hands. I am beginning to understand that to be an Olympic athlete is special, and the dinner will overcome any discomfort my sleeping quarters might impose. A clock chimes nine times and the Captain scoots his chair back from the table and tells the skiers to meet at sunrise for an early morning run. While most of our team returns to the rooms for the evening, Andrzej invites me to join him and his brother in the bar. I know no better and go with him.

We seem to have the dimly lit room to ourselves. Andrzej explains that it is still very early in society circles and that the room will be full by midnight. I hope to be fast asleep by then. We take seats at the bar and as I stare at my reflection in the long mirror on the wall, I see Adam walk in and dust the snow from the thick, fur collar of his overcoat. He unbuttons the coat as he walks towards us.

"Good evening, gentlemen," he says, "Glad you could spare some time with your brother, Andrzej."

"An hour at most," Andrzej replies. "I have to tuck young Bronek into his blankets before the Captain checks our room at midnight."

Adam removes his coat and folds it over a chair at a table behind us. "One hour is enough for tonight." The bartender wipes the bar by habit and asks what we would like. Andrzej defers to Adam. "Wine for my brother and me. Perhaps the *Chateau Filhot Sauternes*, 1908. You have it?"

"But of course," the barman answers, "If it is your pleasure."

"And you, Bronek?"

I smile and comment, "That is the year I was born. I'm sorry, but I don't drink," and add too late not to be obvious, "… much."

The brothers exchange a grin. "Fair enough, young man. Perhaps you are not ready for wine. How about a beer? I think that is better. Do you agree, Andrzej?"

"I think so."

The barman nods. "Two glasses of the Sauternes and a Müller Brau for the other gentleman."

The brothers Krzeptowski engage in a lively conversation. Their home is not far from my own — Kościelisko — but I did not know Adam at all. I learn that Adam loves the Tatras but has no athletic talent; he is more inclined to exercise his mind than his body. While the mountains schooled Andrzej, his older brother attended university and the nightlife of the city lured him to its secret and forbidden places. I sit quietly and listen while I sip the strong beer. It has a curious flavor, much different from the vodka I tasted, but only on those rare occasions when I am sick, or for special celebrations with my Father.

Adam studies photography. The art form and recent innovations in moving pictures enamor him. "I'm going to make films," he tells us enthusiastically. "Have you seen moving pictures?" he asks me. I shake my head 'no.' I do not even know what a moving picture is, but I keep that confession to myself.

"No? Then I will take you. There is a small theater here in St. Moritz. One night we will go. You will find it amazing." He lights a cigarette and I make no fuss about it. "The Americans are producing some fabulous pictures," he explains, "But right here, talented film-makers are beginning to gain notice and attention. Even in Poland, we have Eduard Puchalski. I have met him. Wonderful man with great vision. I will make films even better than Puchalski."

Andrzej sips his wine and asks, "And what will your films be about?"

"Love, I think, and adventure, also. I will stage them all in the Tatras! You can be a part of this, Andrzej, and you, too Bronek!"

I have no idea what he is talking about, but I smile as if I do. Suddenly, Adam's attention is drawn to the foyer. He snubs out his half-smoked cigarette. "Just a minute. Wait here." He walks quickly from the bar into the lobby and greets a woman. They are laughing. Adam points to us. She nods, and he leads her back to the bar. Andrzej immediately stands up and I follow his lead.

"My friends," Adam says to Andrzej and me in a grand way, "I present my accomplice and the future star of my moving pictures: the beautiful Miss Janina Fischer." Miss Fischer is quite beautiful with a figure that her overcoat cannot conceal. Her blonde curls cling to her head like leaves of gold.

Andrzej acts with assurance, takes her extended hand, and places his lips briefly and softly upon the ring that adorns her finger. She bows appreciatively yet ever so slightly, the smile of an angel sculpted on her countenance. I am neither so bold nor confident. I cannot hide my smile as I return hers, and gesture with a touch of my finger to my brow. Andrzej offers her his seat at the bar, and I force myself not to stare like a schoolboy at her exposed knee as she climbs into the chair.

"Skiers?"

"We are," Andrzej replies.

"Me, too, but not competitively. I ski only for pleasure, and I love the mountains." Her voice is high-pitched and squeaky, not what I expected from such a beautiful woman.

"There are not many women who ski," Andrzej adds.

"I think more will," Janina responds. "It is a healthy, invigorating pursuit that is becoming more popular in these Alps."

"An actress who skis," I add with as much composure as I can muster. "A rare combination!" The dryness in my throat disappears with another draft of my beer. The barman brings another glass of wine for Adam's future star.

"Here's to our film," Adam says and raises his glass in a toast.

"And to your success at these games," Janina adds.

Adam offers her a cigarette. As she reaches for it, one of her gloves falls to the carpeted floor. I am quick to retrieve it. Adam strikes a match, and her eyes sparkle. As I return the glove, her smile fades and she says, "Are you a Jew?"

The barman noticeably hesitates and the few other drinkers who sit at the table to our right turn towards us. Even Adam's expression turns cold.

I check my first reaction to respond as if I am offended then calmly answer, "I am not, but what if I am. Does it make a difference?"

She ignores the question and touches my chest with the hand holding the cigarette so that the smoke rises to my eyes forcing me to squint. "You wear the Jewish good luck charm." She taps it twice with her finger. I look down and see the *hamsa*. As I retrieved Janina's glove, the *hamsa* made its way between the buttons on my shirt and now hangs exposed from its chain. I cover it with my hand and slide it back beneath my shirt.

"It is nothing," I say. "I found it on the street and find it pretty." The lie immediately humiliates me and I fight to conceal my shame.

She raises her eyebrows and exhales smoke. "Nothing to you maybe, but revealing to others."

Andrzej rescues me. "A pretty charm for a pretty boy. He is no Jew," he says and firmly slaps my back. "You will see. No Jew flies like this one." He turns to the bartender. "A final glass of wine for me, my friend."

Half of my first and only beer remains when Andrzej finishes his drink. He excuses us to return to our room for rest. As we leave, I can hear Janina's squeaky voice comment, "The young one is a pretty boy, isn't he." Andrzej grabs the nape of my neck and keeps us moving.

Loud snores greet us as we enter our dark room; there is no need for us to be quiet. Andrzej stumbles to the bathroom and turns on the bright light. When he is finished, I take my turn. I will sleep in my under-shorts and I remove my clothing and stare at the mirror above the washbasin. I remember the same image in the cavern of Bolesław. I remind myself, with conviction, that I am a part of the king just as he is a part of me. I am here for a purpose. The *hamsa* draws my attention like a full moon on a clear night. As I lean forward, it swings from its chain above my naked chest. How simple to remove it and to discard it in some obscure ditch, here in the Alps. Who would know? I imagine it falling from my hand to balance dangerously on a gutter grate. I am afraid it will not fall and that someone has seen my crime. It teeters, and then slides between the iron bars and into the sewer, lost forever below the city streets. It can be over that fast, I think, and as it falls to the abyss, it takes with it the association with Jews that seems to concern so many people. I will do it. I will throw this from my life. I clutch the amulet, but I stay my hand before I can rip it from my neck. Why do I hesitate? I answer my own question: because if I tear this from my neck, I tear it from my heart, and I will know. I am not a Jew, and I know only one thing about them that matters: we worship the same God, perhaps in different ways, but he is the same. If I remove the *hamsa*, I deny my belief that God created all of us in his image and equal in his sight. If I rip the charm from my neck, I tear Amalia from my heart. Is that what I want? If she marries another man, does that mean I can no longer love her? Does it mean I cannot love ever again? I am confused and the thoughts torment me as I find my way to the corner of the room that is mine.

Janina Fischer enters my dreams, and as she does – despite Amalia's stated intentions – I feel strangely unfaithful to my Jewish friend, to this beautiful woman I have known all of my life. I dispel the image of Janina from my dreams, but I know it will return.

Chapter Six, 1928

The Föhn

The weather has been perfect since the day of our arrival, however, I awake on Saturday to confront a storm that blows in from the mountains and slams our hotel with no regard that today the games begin in the stadium, just a short walk from our hotel. While the wind wails outside, the air in the room is sour with the smell of the rich food to which we highlanders are not accustomed. A teammate farts, not quietly, and not a man among us restrains his laughter.

"Sorry, gents, but we're not going to open the window," Andrzej tell us as he rises and pulls back the curtains. Gray light enters the room.

Józef Bujak bolts for the bathroom and slams the door, muffling the eruption of sorts that quickly follows. We are thankful for the toilet and the running water. "Hey," he calls from behind the door, "Who used up all the toilet paper?"

We take our turns in the reeking bathroom, appreciative that we do have running water. That convenience outweighs the annoying smell that invades our room each time the door opens or closes. We are Poles and thankful for what we have, not ungrateful for that which we do not.

I am glad that Andrzej is our flag bearer. He is a friendly and likeable sort, and we respect him as a person and revere him as an athlete. His work ethics set an example for the team, and I strive to be as serious about my sport as he is about his. Andrzej hurries us along so that we are in the lobby and ready when the Captain and the other coaches arrive. We wear red flannel coats, gray pants and black boots. A white scarf and a black newsboy cap complete this outfit. I consider these the best clothes I have ever had. I am proud to wear them.

As the strong wind weakens, the visibility improves, but conditions remain quite blustery. "Button up, boys," the Captain instructs us, "In just a few minutes, we'll be taking our place in the line of contestants. We'll march into the stadium and wait for the arrival of the dignitaries."

"Who are the dignitaries?" someone asks.

"Who cares," another answers and we share another bonding moment of laughter.

"There will be plenty of festivities and speeches," the Captain says, "Bear with them; it is your duty as an athlete and your obligation to Poland. Bobkowski tells me the show is finished when they release one hundred white birds. Enjoy the ceremony, but when it is over, return to your rooms and rest before this evening's banquet with the other athletes. Questions?" There are none and we follow Andrzej and our flag into the cold air.

Men with brooms and shovels continue their never-ending task to keep the streets and sidewalks clear. The blizzard has passed mercifully and left mountains and lakes buried deep in fresh snow. I think it is an omen that favors us. For me, the quality of the snow matters most, not necessarily its depth. I snatch a handful and toss it into the air. It is very light and the breeze, like a magician, carries it away in an instant.

Twenty-five nations compete in these games. Most are European, but four teams travel from the Americas, and a small contingent of skiers is here from Japan. I know very little about the Americas except for the United States. Everyone knows about the United States. *Pani* Murach, ancient now, tells us of her young niece from Wilna who left Poland for the United States many years ago. She writes to say that America is beautiful. Everyone has a job, everyone works and makes money. "You can buy things in America," she writes. "Things you cannot even imagine."

We see a sign in front of us that says, "Pologne." I walk next to Jerzy Bardziński, the *konzertina* player. "That's us," he says, "Pologne. It is French and means Poland."

"And Norvège," I ask, "what is that?"

"Norway, the best skiers. They want us to believe they invented the sport."

"Did they?"

"Who knows. I think the Russians."

The Norwegians have not arrived yet. Their space is empty, but standing in the area beyond the "Norvège" sign are five small and dark-skinned men huddled together, shivering, and wrapped in a blanket. Their placarded sign reads "Mexique." Like Italy's, three wide vertical stripes – green, white and red – adorn their flag, but in the center is a curious image of a strange bird with a snake in its talons. "What is that?" I ask Jerzy.

"Mexico," he says.

A vague recollection rises in my mind but the details remain hidden. "Where is Mexico?"

"In the Americas. It shares its northern border with the United States."

Aha, I have it! I remember three things I learned about the United States as a boy: George Washington, General Custer and the Alamo, where a large army of Mexicans slaughtered a handful of Americans — as we so often refer to those people who live in the United States — but the defeat inspired the Americans to fight harder, something like the Spartans at Thermopylae. Drawn up under the blanket, the Mexicans look timid, not at all formidable. "Do they ski?" I ask Jerzy.

He shrugs his shoulders, "Don't know."

"Probably not," I conclude thinking that they appear afraid and lack the courage to tackle the slopes. They would do well to follow my *Babcia*'s advice: love the cold. I do not think these little Mexicans do.

There is movement behind us and I turn to watch the Norwegians approach in formation — like military men — behind their flag bearer who carries his banner with solemnity as if it was a sacred relic. They exude a confidence — not arrogance — that suggests the foregone conclusion that they are here to win, that they will win. I see it in the flag bearer's countenance. He neither smiles nor frowns, but only intimidates. The Mexicans cower before them, afraid to look in the Norwegians' eyes. I will not tremble before these Northmen, but their visage and reputation command my respect. Each looks neither left nor right but keeps his eyes ever forward. Jerzy elbows me and says, "Now these men are skiers! They are the ones to beat."

As they march past us, I notice three women among them, all young like me. One is very pretty with wide, bright eyes. She breaks protocol and catches me staring at her. She winks at me and infects me with her smile. I overcome the urge to avert my eyes, and touching the small brim of my cap, bow gallantly to her. She approves with a slight turn of her head.

Immersed in the excitement of the moment, we ignore the blowing snow, and soon the line begins to move taking nearly 500 athletes to the stadium, which will host the hockey games and skating events over the next nine days. A band plays inspiring music that lifts spirits even higher. A large crowd awaits us and raises its collective voice to welcome the Germans who lead this illustrious parade into the stadium. The contingent from Germany is very large, with perhaps twice as many athletes as our team. Every athlete — even the solemn Norwegians — is enrapt in the celebration and waves as he passes through the portal. Arms become heavy, but remain in the air to express joy and appreciation. Spectators line both sides of the wide path that we follow.

"*Powodzenia Polska*, good luck to Poland," Someone yells from the crowd and elicits good-natured laughter from both spectators and competitors. The squeaky voice is unmistakable; it is Janina Fischer in her tight, blonde curls. She waves at the team, then points at me and blows a kiss. I am too excited and happy to be embarrassed, but I take pleasant note of her gesture. Adam escorts her, and bouncing like a jumping jack, raises his clasped hands in a sign of victory. If it were only that easy, I think.

Within an hour the final team, a small group of Yugoslavians, is in its proper place. The cheering subsides momentarily as a large sleigh pulled by a team of powerful horses with a second sleigh in its wake enters the stadium. Accompanied by the clean, crisp sound of jingling bells, the transports stop before a podium positioned centrally in front of the grandstand that dominates the north side of the arena. There on the podium, stand the dignitaries, and with them, His Royal Highness Prince Consort of the Netherlands, Honorary President of the Dutch Olympic Federation. The Dutch will host summer games in Amsterdam in just a few months. Right now, however, none of us cares about those games. Our moment is here now with the eyes of the world turned toward us, the skiers, the winter athletes, as passionate about our sport as the 100-meter man is about his. These dignitaries move nobly as they climb to the platform and seat themselves according to protocol.

The spectators in the grandstand take their seats while thousands more stand and wait. The wind still blows but no longer howls so it is possible for us to hear the opening remarks of Mr. Schulthess, President of the Swiss Confederation. He addresses us in French, a language I do not understand, but I see the approving nods of the few teammates who do. Andrzej knows the language and tells me afterwards that it was a good speech.

After another speech, the orchestra performs a solemn hymn. A chorus blends in and lifts its voice to heaven on our behalf. As it does, a large, white flag with five intersecting, colored circles in two rows, three on top, two on the bottom ascends the pole behind the grandstand. The

moment is quite emotional. As the singers and the orchestra hold their final, triumphant note and the flag reaches its
zenith, the sun breaks through the clouds and 100 white
birds, doves fly free from their hidden cage behind the
podium. Like the music, they soar into the clearing skies,
circle us, and then follow the wind westward. Athletes and
spectators gasp in unison. It is for this moment in time
that I was born. I close my eyes and wish my family could
be here, in this stadium, to share this occasion with me, and
with my fellow athletes.

A trumpet blares three times and a bass drum joined by
the "rat-a-tat-tat" of snare drums pounds out a marching
rhythm. The 25 flag bearers raise their sacred banners, and
move forward and assemble in a semi-circle in front of the
podium. As I stare at the national flags and the Olympic
flag waving high above them, it occurs to me that the colors
of each nation's flag are represented by the circles that adorn
the Olympic flag. A solitary athlete ascends the platform,
stands behind the podium and raises his right hand. The
crowd is still. In a clear, loud voice he says, *"Nous le jure.
Nous allons participer à des Jeux Olympiques dans un esprit de
chevalerie ..."*

In a single voice, all participants repeat the words, in
French.

Jerzy whispers to me, "I will translate for you. 'We
swear. We will take part in the Olympic Games in a spirit
of chivalry, for the honor of our country and for the glory
of sport.'" I think hard on those words and make them a
part of me.

I challenge anyone to tell me there is a greater honor
than this.

We remove our caps as the choir sings the Swiss anthem. The Swiss team and its thousands of countrymen are not shy at all, and add their loud voices to the choristers'. Jerzy knows the tune and sings it to me in Polish. I learn the melody quickly and hum along as the volume grows throughout the stadium.

"When the morning skies grow red

And o'er us their radiance shed,

Thou, O Lord, appearest in their light.

When the Alps glow bright with splendor,

Pray to God, to Him surrender,

For you feel and understand,

That He dwelleth in this land ..."

We applaud each other when the final note leaves our lips. Officials direct us to clear the stadium for the artistic program scheduled to begin in a few minutes.

As I walk from the ice, someone taps me lightly. It is the young Norwegian girl. *"Mitt navn er Sonja,"* she says. I smile but must raise my hands in such a way that she knows I do not understand. *"Parlez-vous Français?"* she offers. I look bewildered and have no idea what she is saying. She sighs and returns to her teammates who are waving at her. It is at that very moment that I promise myself to be even more attentive to language. I have missed much during the ceremony, and who knows what wonderful things this girl would like to tell me.

As we clear the stadium, the clouds return and the snow resumes — perhaps with less intensity than it had through the night — but while it may hamper visibility, it cannot dampen the enthusiasm and excitement that runs unbridled through spectators and participants alike. I want to stay for the show and to watch the hockey match that will follow. The host team from Switzerland will battle the team from nearby Austrians. The Captain turns to face the windblown snow, gauges the weather then shakes his head. He spreads the word that we skiers are to return to the hotel; the hockey team can stay to watch one of the four afternoon games to gauge its competition. I am disappointed that I cannot stay, but pleased nonetheless to be part of such a grand event.

The warmth of the hotel envelops us as we return to gather in front of the fireplace that blazes night and day. The floors become treacherous as we walk through the lobby, snow melting from our boots. Near the entrance stands a small army of young boys, mops at the ready. Their task is to keep the entrance clean and dry as visitors come and go.

The senior members of the team take seats on the plush sofas and chairs that invite guests to relax in lavish comfort. "Gentleman," the Captain begins, "the games are now officially open. While I want you to enjoy yourselves, you are here for a single purpose: to compete for your country. Our history is long and storied, but the world has only recognized us as a nation for a single decade. To the people who have traveled to Switzerland for these games, we are Poland. They will judge our country based on how we perform in competition. That is no surprise, but more importantly, they will form their opinions of Poland based on how we act when we are not competing. To win is our ultimate goal, but winning is only of value if we do it with dignity. I will emphasize that throughout these games. Perform hard as if your life depends upon it, and do it fairly. Above all, compete with dignity.

"We do not ski for several days," he says while he passes schedules among us. "We ski and we play hockey. Our skaters take the ice tomorrow against the Swedes. We must all be there to give them our support. Trust me, gentlemen, there will be few Poles attending these games. Most of the attendees will be Swiss, but I expect large contingents of spectators from Germany, France and Italy, possibly even the Nordic states. We must rely on each other for the support that other teams will draw from their visiting countrymen.

"We wait for three more days, until Tuesday, when our distance runners will race for 50 kilometers. I expect you to exercise several hours each day to condition yourselves and to accustom your bodies to the environment. This storm may dump a meter of new snow, maybe more. That much new snow may level the playing field a bit.

"A final note. Be in bed — your bed — by midnight. Breakfast together at 0600. If your regimen requires eight hours of sleep, be in bed by 2200. Banquet tonight at the Hotel Kulm, just up the street. Meet here at 1900. We walk up as a team. Look sharp."

I will compete in two events: the Nordic combined – ski jumping and an 18-kilometer race – and in the individual ski-jumping event. I do not race or jump until Friday. The wait and the uncertain weather conditions make me irritable. It continues to snow on Sunday and is still snowing lightly Tuesday morning when we assemble at the starting point for the 50-kilometer race. Andrzej is the best of the four skiers who will compete for Poland. He limits his conversation at the breakfast table to 'yes' or 'no' responses, and soon it is clear that we should leave him to his own thoughts as he prepares for his race.

I follow at a distance as Andrzej and his fellow skiers make their way to the starting area. The Captain chats with them during the walk, but Andrzej does not react. His lack of response is not disrespectful but demonstrates his nearly demonic concentration. The officials start the race promptly at 0800.

We estimate four, maybe four-and-a-half hours to complete the 50-kilometer course, but we do not anticipate the disaster that will develop. Like the other spectators, my teammates return to the hotel after the skiers depart, but I have taken a liking to Andrzej and he to me, so I decide to wait with the Captain. He pulls his pipe from the pack he always carries on his back and asks, "You will wait with me?" he asks. I smile and he nods approvingly.

We clear 30 cm of new snow from two chairs and take a seat at an outside table. "It is important for me to know what my skiers feel," he explains and waves his hand in the air. "The wind, the temperature. All very important." He looks at the large window where he sees the crowd gathered inside. "They will never fully appreciate what these racers endure unless they remain outside through the entire race. Even then, they can only guess at what a man's legs feel like after racing for four hours through deep snow.

"They are all good men," the Captain says as he lights his pipe, "but that Andrzej is special. I would never tell him this, but I do not think he will ever win a race at this level. Though not our best skier, no one will out-work him. That is why he will be a member of this team as long as it is in his heart. He inspires us all to work harder than we think we can, to try to work as hard as he does. Do you understand Bronek? We need men like him on our team. I think you are like him." He pats my shoulder in a fatherly way, and I feel special.

An hour passes and the Captain sniffs the air. His brow furrows. He stares into the wind toward the peaks. Following his gaze, I note that the snow has stopped falling. While random conversations continue around us, I feel the same uncomfortable quiet descend from the nearby mountains that he does.

The Germans call it the "*föhn*." My father and his highlander friends call it "the snow-eater." The *föhn* flies over the mountains quickly and brings with it warm temperatures, very warm temperatures. As we wait for spring on the leeward side of the Tatras in Zakopane, we welcome the snow-eater. The warm wind gives us reason to be thankful for the joy and pleasure we have experienced in the winter cold and snow, and it reminds us that spring, with its gift of new life will soon be with us. We have much experience with this phenomenon at home, but here, now, in February? No one could have anticipated this.

As he faces the mountains to the northwest, the Captain exhales a large cloud of tobacco smoke. The *föhn* blows it back in his face. "Not good," he says and breathes deeply of the warm air.

"What can we do?" I ask.

The Captain pulls a map from his knapsack and spreads it on the table. It is a diagram of the race. The skiers race southwest along the foothills and circumvent three lakes before turning northeast, not quite halfway through the course. At the 30km mark, they turn sharply to the south and climb to the highest point. There, they retrace their path north, back to the *Silser See*, where they face the final 10 kilometers to the finish. Using the stem of his pipe he points to the portion of the outbound leg, which passes north of the *Silser See*.

"There is nothing we can do but wait," the Captain says. "The wax on their skis will be worthless as the temperature rises. I have more suitable wax in my knapsack, but it will be of no use now." He pounds the table with his fist.

"I can run up this part of the course," I tell him, almost pleading. "I will wait for our men at the south side of the lake. When I find them, I will apply the new wax for their final 10 kilometers. It can make a difference."

"Indeed it would, Bronek, but the rules will not allow it. We can only wait." He blesses himself quietly and raises his eyes. "If Andrzej has different wax with him, he will use it. If not, I know he and his teammates will do the best they can."

Two hours later, a man appears in the distance. He is walking toward us with his skis over his shoulder and his poles in his hand. It is Stanisław Wilczyński. We jog 200 meters through the deep snow to meet him. He is smiling and says with no remorse, "My ski broke."

The temperature was a comfortable 0° C when the racers left the starting gate. The blizzard passed and scattered flurries followed. Four hours later, I remove my parka and my sweater. The Captain and I stand in puddles. The thermometer reads 25° C, warm even on a late spring or early summer day. Still no sign of skiers. I begin to wonder what effect this will have on my events in three days. I can see the jump in the distance, and although it remains white, workers desperately shovel snow from the sides of the jump to its surface.

The wind carries the clang of a distant bell, signaling that the first skier is approaching. He is still some 1600 meters from the finish line. The ringing proclamation calls hundreds of spectators – some in sleeveless shirts – from the nearby restaurants and taverns to join us to greet the medalists as they complete the race. The Captain pulls his watch from his pocket and performs a quick calculation. It has been nearly five hours since the racers departed. "Unbelievable," he comments, "At Chamonix in '24, less than four hours."

The results are unexpected. The crowd rushes to line both sides of the final 400 meters. The red Norwegian flag with its blue cross, outlined in white dominates the welcoming spectators as they wave their flags and rattle their cowbells to create a festive atmosphere in the warm weather. But as the lone figure continues his methodical arm and leg movements and closes the distance to the finish line, we can see that his colors are not the Norwegian red, white and blue, but the blue and yellow of the neighboring Swedes. When he crosses the finish line, he collapses into the arms of his waiting teammates. He has discarded his jacket, and his drenched sweater hangs heavy from his aching shoulders. His flushed face drips perspiration. The Swedes are elated and for good reason. I learn that the top Swede racer was ill and did not even compete, which makes this man's victory even sweeter. His happy countrymen will celebrate well into the night.

More than 10 minutes pass before the final two medal-ists arrive, both Swedes. Only a Swede might have guessed at the medal sweep, but I doubt he would have placed money on such an outlandish bet. As we wait for our Polish skiers, we feel the Norwegians' disappointment as their top two skiers come in three minutes apart, but more than 20 minutes behind the gold medal-winning Swede.

When the first six places have been claimed, the crowd disperses. Even my other teammates have left. I wait and stand vigil with the Captain. I will not abandon my friend who is still on the course, for I am certain his labor in the race – like that of every man who crosses that finish line – is no less than the efforts of the medals winners. Watching one man's disappointment as his race ends, I realize that not a man entered this race with the thought of failure. No, each athlete takes his first step with the clear intention to win the race, not lose it. Regardless of the outcome, a man that starts and finishes the race bears no shame. He has done the task and overcome the fear of losing, and for that, he is no longer a common man. I respect each man — teammate and opponent — and so I wait thinking that my mere presence will be worth something to every exhausted athlete who crosses the finish line. Maybe someone will honor me in the same way.

"What do you think?" I ask the Captain.

"I think no Pole will give up." He holds his gaze on the course. A Finn, yet another Swede and another Norwegian, a pair of Germans and a Slovak. As the snow continues to melt and fall from the trees, it becomes more difficult to spot the racers, but I can see the next one, barely. I stand on the table, and I shield my eyes.

I hop down, relieved. "It is one of us," I report to the Captain, "I'm certain his cap is red." The Captain squints hard and smiles.

"It is Andrzej. I knew it," he exclaims, "He may not win the race, but he will set the pace for our team."

The few people who remain at the finish line applaud politely. The Captain and I catch Andrzej before he can fall to the soaking wet ground. He is breathing hard and strains for each breath. "I'll be okay," he manages to say. We help him to a bench and I kneel to remove his skis.

"The others?" the Captain asks.

"Don't know. I passed them long ago." Andrzej shakes his head. "It's the wax. When the temperature rises, the wet snow clings to our skis. It is the same for everyone, so I make no excuse." He leans over heavily and takes his throbbing head in his hands. "At 30 kilometers, I was still in contention. I even took the lead as the Swedes and Norwegians stopped to service their skis. They carried other wax. I didn't, so I skied past them, but within 5 kilometers, I could hear them breathing hard behind me, and when they finally passed me, it was as if I was standing still, my skis mired in wet snow as they quickly glided past."

The two other Poles complete the race almost a full hour after the first Swede claimed the gold medal. The Captain, Andrzej and I greet them with broad smiles on our faces. "Well done Józef and Franciszek. Poland is proud of you," the Captain congratulates them. "We are proud of you," I add, then turn to Andrzej and say, "And you, too. Even you, Wilczyński. You walked across the finish line with your broken skis on your shoulder, but you finished the race you started. Bravo for all of you!"

My four teammates are exhausted and disappointed, but they will not let the lack of a medal diminish their accomplishment. Their spirits remain high. "Give me your skis," I say. They look at me with some doubt. "Here," I repeat, "Give me your skis. You have done enough work for the day. Let me honor you."

"And I will carry your poles," the Captain says.

"Give them to me," Andrzej says, "You are the Captain. You do not carry our gear."

The Captain refuses. "For men such as you who give their all for the glory of Poland, I'll carry your equipment to the ends of the earth."

"But we brought no glory to Poland in this race," Franciszek says and lowers his head.

"More than you know," the Captain is quick to respond. "Never doubt yourself."

The four join arms and begin their walk back to the hotel with the Captain and me in trail carrying their skis and poles. As the snow-eater wreaks havoc on the facilities, the warm air inspires a festive mood in the village. Spectators occupy every available sidewalk chair and raise frothy glasses of beer in good cheer. They laugh and smile oblivious of the impending disaster that can result from the warm weather. The *föhn* is no friend to the athletes here. Nevertheless, the spirit of camaraderie, the happy crowd exudes inspires and comforts us. Often considered a stern man, the Captain surprises us when he begins to hum, and then to sing as we walk through the cobbled streets to the hotel. He sings our favorite, the same song we sang on the locomotive as it steamed its way through the mountains. "Góralu, czy ci nie żal…" The four skiers and I join him, and we are singing so loudly and shamelessly that we attract the attention of the street revelers. They begin to follow us and soon we are a parade. Our new friends may not know the words, but they are quick to pick up the tune.

"Well done, men of Poland," a deep voice cries. I look to my left where the very Swede who won the race raises his glass to salute us. The Captain is right. The glory comes from the game itself, not the result. Poland can be proud of us.

Wednesday morning and it is raining. Slush covers the streets and sidewalks. The precipitation ends on Thursday, but the temperature remains warm. I am nervous and my anxiety drives me from my room. I walk aimlessly through the village and conquer the temptation to stare at the jump. I will face it tomorrow regardless of the weather and the temperature. The delegations have been meeting with the authorities and there has been some talk of delaying or even canceling the remainder of the events.

The street leads me to the stadium. I enter and sit in the grandstand not far from where the skaters assemble. My mind continues to wander. I consciously pull it back from some frivolous daydream to the here and now. Tomorrow at this time, I remind myself, I will be on the 18-kilometer course, the first part of the Nordic Combined. My strength is the jump, and it can pull me to the top of the competition if I do race well enough to stay close to the experienced competitors who I challenge.

"How are you, friend?" A young man about my age sits next to me. "Hans," he says and we shake hands. "You see that girl, the one in the striped jacket?" He points to where the skaters are, and I see the young pixie.

"The one with the white beret?"

"Yes, that's the one. She wants to know your name." He speaks perfect Polish, but his accent betrays him. He is Scandinavian.

"Why?"

He studies me from head to toe then says, "I would not know. You must ask her."

I try to disguise my interest and say matter-of-factly, "Bronisław. My name is Bronisław."

"A strong Polish name. And where is the strength of your athletic prowess, Bronisław?"

"The combination. I race and I jump. Better in the jump."

"Then I will see you tomorrow. I too race and jump, but I race better than I jump. If you keep pace with me in the race, and your strength is in the jump, you may have a chance to win the combination. Anyway, she wants to learn your name. I will tell her."

He stands and bows formally, but before he can leave, I ask him, "What is her name?"

He laughs. "Seriously, you don't know who that is?" I shake my head. "That is Sonja."

"Who is Sonja?"

"You are serious, aren't you?" He shakes his head. "You'll know soon enough. The Americans think they will win this competition, the figures. They are wrong. Sonja will win. See you tomorrow, and good luck."

"Good luck," I say and look past him at the pretty girl from Norway whose name is Sonja.

Friday finally arrives. This is my day, the day I will don the colors of Poland in the Nordic Combined. The *föhn* has moved on and cold weather well below freezing returns. Heavy wool scarves mute the laughter outdoors; they help to fend off the chill that attacks the face like a thousand icy pinpricks. Conditions are not ideal. Puddles have turned to ice, and the walk from the hotel to the starting point is no longer a simple task, but a perilous journey. The frigid temperature holds the crowds indoors and the streets are empty compared to what we've seen in recent days. Few spectators are with us for the start of the race.

Bujak, Rozmus, the Motyka cousins who I know from Zakopane and Andrzej will race with me, or more accurately, I will race with them. Bujak is our best cross-country man in this short distance. Rozmus and Stanisław Motyka race with me as part of the combined event. As we cautiously make our way through the town, Zdzisław Motyka slips and falls hard to the cobblestoned street.

"Are you alright?" his cousin asks.

"Yes," Zdz answers, probably more embarrassed than he is hurt.

We arrive at 8 o'clock, one hour before the race is set to begin. The Captain spends several minutes walking amongst the different teams, nodding his head in friendly greeting. But when he returns, we know he has been studying our opponents.

"Most skiers are applying hard white wax," he tells us. "The Americans are using *Old Black Dope*."

"Something to do with their Negroes?" Józef asks.

"No," the Captain responds, "It's a wax they developed from whale sperm. Can you believe it? Pine pitch makes it black." Our laughter breaks the tension.

"So what do we use?" Aleksander asks.

The Captain answers, "I don't think we can generate enough sperm for all of our skis." We laugh again.

"The course will be dangerous today and it will demand all of your skill, particularly in areas of descent. Zdz already demonstrated that to us on the way over. He slipped and fell and he was only walking in his boots. Imagine what will happen when you are faced with a sheet of ice in a 10-meter descent. While speed is the obvious choice, it may not be our best option. I wager that half the skiers who start the race will not finish. The ice will break bones and strain muscles. Today, we trade speed for stability. We stay on our feet to avoid the splits that will surely elimi-nate your ability to make sperm when you need it most, and I remind you again, that is not here in St. Moritz!" The Captain takes an envelope from his knapsack. In the envelope are six sheets of paper; he hands one to each of us.

I am the first to remove my gloves to learn that the paper is smooth on one side and very coarse and hard on the other.

"It's called 'sandpaper.'" The Captain watches as each of us studies his sheet, examining it closely on one side, then the other.

"What's it for?" I ask.

"Turn one ski over, Bronek. Step back and hold it near the tip. That's it." I do as I'm told with the tip of the ski resting on my shoulder. It is angled maybe sixty-degrees from the ground. "Everyone watch." The Captain places the coarse side of the paper flat against the ski and draws it slowly from the tip to the tail. The sandpaper etches shallow marks on the surface. He works both skis, running his bare fingertips over the ski after every swipe. When he is satisfied, he tells each of us to feel the surface of my skis. It is no longer smooth with the clear wax, but rough, ever so slightly rough. "You feel the difference?" he asks.

We do.

"The whale sperm or any other wax will do more harm than good in these conditions," he explains. "This sandpaper?" He holds it up. "This will enable your skis to grip the ice that you will confront and that you cannot avoid. It will give you more control. While others slip and slide, your steps will be sure."

I do not know if it will work, but we are thankful the Captain is our coach and prepared to face any challenge. He is not afraid to try new ideas, and his fearlessness gives us confidence. We set to the task of readying our skis, following his example.

We draw numbers from a box to determine our starting positions. The first racer will depart at 9 o'clock sharp, and the rest will follow at 30-second intervals. Where a racer starts is another of those things beyond his control, it is solely the luck of the draw, but I believe most skiers prefer to be further back at the beginning of the race, allowing them to see and gauge the temper of the skiers who lead at any given time. I draw number seven; I would prefer Stanisław's 18, but I accept my lot without complaint. The Captain offers each of us a bit of individual advice. "Your strength is in the jump," he tells me. "I think if you can finish in the top 10 of this race, you can win a medal with a strong jump this afternoon. If you maintain good pace, catch all six racers in front of you and let no one pass you, you will probably have one of the 10 best times, and that is your objective. Understand?"

I am not sure that I do. I am an artist, not a mathematician. I gaze into the white expanse before me and think only of skiing. The brotherhood of my own teammates and the camaraderie of the men from other nations dominate my emotions. If I win, I win. If I do not, life will go on, and I, because of my presence here, am changed forever. I stare at the backs of the men who will precede me. Even if I pass them, and even if I win, I know I am no better than any other man who skis this course with me today. For the next few hours, I will fight them all for the medal, but at day's end, my respect for them will have grown and I will be grateful to have been a player on this grand stage.

"I don't think you do." The Captain disrupts my thoughts, and we stare at each other while he waits for a response. I cannot disagree, but I will not admit it with words. I am silent. He's not dismayed and says, "Go, Bronek. Take your place in line, and above all, enjoy yourself." He takes two steps backwards, offers me a salute and moves down the line to advise Stanisław and the others.

Several spectators wield cowbells to announce the departure of each skier with a persistent din from their simple instruments. As the seconds count down, I offer a prayer and bless myself with my right hand, then tap the hidden *hamsa* with my left.

"*Aller*! Go!" the judge exclaims and taps my shoulder. I step forward into the track of the man who preceded me, and I feel my sandpapered skis grip the slick surface. The cowbells jangle wildly and the Captain's deep voice cries *"Powodzenia"* a final time as I explode from the gate with a powerful step. It is a good way to start the race.

Within two minutes, I am comfortably into the course and the distant sounds from spectators fade. The beating of my heart keeps the cadence I feel in my chest while my skis scrape the icy surface. The mountains watch silently, but they do not threaten, at least not yet. These mountains are written by God's own hand, and while they may pass judgment, they will not intercede. We climb some 400 meters on the outbound leg and then descend on the return. This is nothing, I think compared to the countless assaults I've made on Giewont. The vision of King Bolesław flashes like lightning through my mind's eye and strengthens my resolve to work hard in Poland's name.

Like a thousand tiny fingers, the grip of my roughened skis holds firm to the slick surface, allowing me to glide swiftly toward the mountains. This is no illusion – the grasp of the skis on the ice – nor is my thought that the skiers ahead of me are growing larger. I am gaining ground and time on them. The Captain's gambit has given us an advantage. As I begin a gradual ascent, I am tempted to look back at the field behind me, but I resist. My pace is comfortable, and I will not let the other skiers intimidate me. I can only work as hard as I can, and I revel in the hard flex of my muscles with every step I take. As I continue to gain on the leaders, I note they can no longer move directly up the slope and now traverse it, much as a schooner would tack into the wind. My skis, however, and the grip they afford, enable me to hold my direct path much farther than those who preceded me. The distance between us narrows.

As they approach the top flag, the slope becomes too steep for them to traverse, and the men before me begin to side step. The gap between us closes as I hold my traverse higher and longer than they could, and because I am able to '*herring-bone*' my way up the section they were forced to sidestep. Only a few short meters separate me from the man who left the gate 30 seconds ahead of me. I pass him. Neither of us speaks. Thank you, my Captain.

My breath comes hard and fast when I reach the summit, but I am satisfied with my effort, and am confident I will pass each of the six skiers who left before me. The Captain was right: I did not understand all of his instructions, but I did listen closely. I will pass those six skiers, and will do it with no fewer than eight kilometers remaining in the race. I pause to take a drink of cold water and I chance a look back down the slope I just ascended. I am shocked. Even at this distance, I see a large group moving at a very fast pace and they are gaining ground while I rest. Unacceptable. I must move on.

I begin my descent and see that two of the remaining five racers in front of me have tumbled and slid well off the course. I will be aggressive but will not abandon caution.

Within 200 meters, I am moving too quickly. I need this reckless velocity for the jump, but not on this slope, if I intend to make it down riding my skis, not flailing them in the air above me. If I fall and veer off the course in an uncontrolled slide, it will take me an hour to get back on course, much like the two I see far below me in the ravine. The slope is a pure sheet of ice and offers no security to the bravest of skiers that challenge it. I turn hard to my left and try to dig into the surface with my uphill edges but continue to slide perpendicular to the slope, and the tips of my long skis vibrate and chatter like a wooden tuning fork. I remember Wilczyński's lot in the grand race three days ago, and I pray that my skis will not break and snap off as his did. I grit my teeth and bite down hard as I force the uphill edge of my downhill ski into the unforgiving ice that holds the course hostage. My right thigh begins to burn and shake. I fight to maintain a semblance of control. My poles provide balance but are of no other use in this crazy maneuver. I fight to keep myself perpendicular to the slope even as I feel my skis trying to turn me backwards. I will not let that happen and continue to battle the ice. After 30 seconds, that feels more like 30 long minutes, I slow and stop. Despite the frigid air, sweat pours down my brow and stings my eyes. I take count of where I am, pleased that somehow, some way, I remain on the course though I stand dangerously close to the edge of the ravine that has claimed three of the skiers ahead of me. They are within shouting distance and I call out, "Are you alright?"

One waves and points to the other. He cups his hands and yells back, "Broken leg, but he'll be okay. I'll get him out."

Confidently I yell back, "I'll be the first one to cross the finish line and I will send help." They clap their hands in gratitude, and one shouts, "Good luck and stay safe, brave heart!"

I survey the course before me and am thankful for the slight wisp of overcast. The thin layer of cloud minimizes the glare that would otherwise hamper my vision on a sunny day. My poles cannot penetrate the thick crust unless I deliver a forceful blow like some ancient hunter, thrusting his spear deep into his prey. There is no time to waste. I will catch the remaining skiers, who I can barely see in the distance, and I must forge ahead with urgency so the band of racers climbing the slope behind me does not overtake me.

The downhill run is far more difficult and dangerous than the climb. The inertia created by even a small amount of speed on this frictionless surface can be disastrous. An hour after the start of the race, I have successfully negotiated the highest part of the course and now return to relatively level ground. I do not recall a more difficult task. My thighs ache with the effort, but the final six kilometers lay before me. I begin my rhythmic strides concerned that determination alone will not enable me to catch the two racers still in front of me. I disassociate myself from the pain in my legs and envision the locomotive that brought me to St. Moritz a week ago. I see its powerful, iron arm turning the heavy wheels with unemotional regularity. The arm never tires. The train never stops. I survive unconscious minutes lost in this mechanical vision of strength and power, and when I return to the real world, I see two skiers less than 50 meters in front of me. My pulse quickens, but before I take any satisfaction that I will overtake these two, I hear the steady "swish … swish … swish" of skier behind me eating up the meters that separate us. No need to look over my shoulder to know that he is there. I increase my pace, and close rapidly on the leaders, but ever still, the ghost-like sound behind me gains volume, "Swish … swish … swish."

I fight past the two, but within a minute, my peripheral vision picks up the pumping arms of another. He nods respectfully and literally runs by me. I simply haven't the strength to match his pace and can only stare at the 10 cm Norwegian flag embroidered on the back of his jacket. I have no knowledge of the Norseman's starting position, but given his rate of speed, I suspect the gold medal is his whether or not he catches the lone runner before him.

Exhaustion looms like a mountain ogre and threatens to overcome my resolve. I banish the condition from my tired limbs. Distant cowbells ring once more. The mournful, proud call of the alpenhorn joins them to tell me that the first man has run his race. I round the forest at the edge of the lake, and the cowbells and alpenhorn raise their voices again: the second man is home.

A large and colorful crowd awaits me. With no other competitors in sight, the well-wishers cheer for me alone. My nationality makes no difference to them, nor do their nationalities make any difference to me. I am elated to finish the race, and they are excited to acknowledge the feat. Amid the frantic bells and the long, deep sound of the horn, I am the third runner to cross the finish line. The first two – the Norwegian and a Slovak – have shed their skis and now approach my spent body. Supporting me between them, they lead me to a wooden bench that welcomes this aching athlete. I will honor these two and help the skier who follows me though he is still's not entered the final straightaway. I say to the Slovak who can understand me, "There is a man with a broken leg ..." He interrupts me, "We have already reported it and help is on the way."

I remove my skis, then stand and raise my arms in victory, victory not realized from accolades and medals, but from completing the challenging task in honorable fashion.

I value my weariness knowing that too many people might say, "Why would he do this? Why does he push himself to the edge of consciousness?" Unless he has done it himself, no one can know the satisfaction a man earns from total fatigue that results from a noble effort.

The Captain and I embrace. "You've run a good race under very difficult conditions, Bronek. By my watch, you are well under two hours. We will see when the others arrive, but I think we'll find that you did what you needed to do to stay in contention. You have but three short hours to rest and then we take to the hill. That is where you can win this competition. Understand?" This time I do.

The Captain's prediction holds true: only five racers record faster times. My teammates are not among them, so Poland's hope of a medal in the Nordic combined rests with me.

It remains cold, but the afternoon sun dissolves the clouds and a clear blue sky frames the jump hill and its steep ramp that rises 100 meters before us. The flags at the bottom of the hill wave across the face of the mountain. The air is perfect, but the ice presents controversy as the officials discuss where on the ramp we should start our runs.

The Captain and the three of us who jump in the combination wait patiently at the bottom of the hill. Andrzej and the others who will only compete in tomorrow's jumping event are with us to study the conditions and the factors at play on this hill. The officials conclude their meeting and *Pan* Bobkowski meets us to explain what will happen. "Physical science is at play here, Captain. Many representatives say their jumpers fear that excessive speed on the ramp will propel them from the jump in such an uncontrolled way that they might face serious injury." 'Physical science' means nothing to my highlander teammates and me. Our skis are an extension of our bodies and we feel the surface with them, just as we feel the wind on our faces. We sense speed as we accelerate down the ramp, and we adapt our bodies for it. We don't need pencils and papers to analyze the mountain, only our God-given senses.

"It is a question of speed and safety," Bobkowski concludes, "so the committee has agreed to move the starting point farther down the ramp. The decision has been made." He turns to us, tips his stovepipe hat and wishes us good luck. "You have a chance here, Czech. Take advantage of it." He shakes the Captain's hand and returns towards the group of dignitaries who disperse into the large crowd gathered behind us. As Bobkowski walks away, the Captain raises his thick eyebrows and says, "I think he expects you to win, Bronek." The others laugh.

"Okay," the Captain says, "I know you have no questions, and I have nothing to tell you. If you haven't learned it from the countless jumps you've taken in Zakopane, I can't tell you how to do it here." He shields his eyes from the sun, brilliant now in the cloudless sky. "This hill is a bit bigger than ours, but a hill is a hill. You'll see as you climb it. Will it be fast? Of course it will be. It's a sheet of ice. If you are afraid, don't do it. Off with you now."

At least a hundred horse drawn carriages have arrived and an occasional 'whinny' breaks the constant murmur of the endless parade of pedestrians. As we climb the wooded path to the left of the ramp, we see several thousand spectators below us, most waving the small flags of many nations.

The jump attracts more spectators than any other event simply because the human mind thirsts for danger, especially when it cannot touch them. Watch how people taunt the caged lion in the zoo. Many adjectives – most of them extreme – describe jumpers: 'brave' and 'courageous,' sometimes even 'crazy.' I think there is a bit of each in all of us.

We climb the hill and will jump in the order of our finish in the 18 kilometers. I am sixth in line and follow a German. A Norwegian is behind me. Two of his teammates are in front of me including Hans, the one I met yesterday at the rink. My legs are just a bit heavy from the morning race, and I don't complain when I see that the officials have moved the starting point of the in-run a full 30 meters down the hill. I think 30 meters on this ramp – a ramp that I estimate at 100 meters high – is a bit extreme, but if that is the decision, I willingly abide by it.

I stare into the forest, away from the action while the first jumpers make their runs. The vocal reaction of the crowd suggests the quality and distance of each jump. I can't help but watch the German in front of me. There is an awkwardness about him as he climbs the hill, and it becomes more noticeable the higher we climb. When his turn arrives, he struggles to maintain a position perpendicular to the slick ramp. Time at the top is his enemy for it allows him to think too much. Time allows fear to reach its thin, spider web-like fingers into the athlete's mind. The German nearly falls as he makes the 90-degree hop to begin his run but catches himself on his outside edge. The entire maneuver slows him down, and when he gets to the lift-off point, he does not leap, rather he drops from the end of the ramp. Momentum can take a jumper only so far, and it is not very far when compared to the distances his fellow competitors reach who leap with power from the end of the ramp. The German does not soar, but drops like a wounded bird well short of the flag that marks the par distance that each skier aims to surpass. The crowd's polite applause lacks the enthusiasm with which they awarded the Norwegians. At just 36 meters, his jump is well short of the 50 meters announced through the scratchy public address system in several languages for the previous jumpers.

"Next competitor: Bronisław Czech, Poland." When they call my name, the official at the starting point invites me to take my position and jump. I can use 60 seconds to prepare, but I am not one to wait; waiting only promotes anxiety and uneasiness, and I've no time for either. Besides, what would I wait for anyway?

I accelerate down the ramp and hear nothing but the wind – no cheers, no voices – only the wind. I crouch low to present the smallest silhouette to the air that I can. They say control is everything, but without speed, it is nothing. The runway is fast, very fast and I flex my legs to keep my balance as the end of the platform approaches faster than the locomotive that brought me here a week ago. I time the maneuver as well as anyone and I leap with all my might into the open expanse of air as if to grasp the lonely cloud that floats lazily over the village. I close my eyes and feel the joy, but only for an instant, and that instant feels like an eternity of freedom and pleasure. The air lifts me even higher. I begin my return to earth as the hill rushes toward me. I extend as far as I can but the laws of gravity inevitably rule and the back edge of my skis finally make contact. I smoothly kneel in a Telemark position and hold it well while paying homage to the God who gives me such pleasure as to inspire me to dare what other men fear. In this way at this moment, I genuflect as I do at church. I stand and calmly turn my body perpendicular to the slope and apply pressure to my edges. I come to a stop as my rattling skis break the ice and it scatters like shards in a kaleidoscope. The roar of the crowd replaces the rush of the wind. I look back as the officials take their measurement. One walks to the podium and offers the announcer a piece of paper. The crowd quiets. The announcer nods, clears his voice and says, "Fifty-one meters." Cheers from the crowd and thousands of hands clap. "Next jumper: Ole Kolterud, Norway."

I remove my skis and return to my teammates. Most are there. The Captain does not exhibit the unbridled enthusiasm that has taken hold of my fellows. He pulls me aside. "Fifty-one meters is okay, Bronek, but you must do better. Everyone can do fifty-one meters," he scoffs. "You must do sixty."

The Captain is right. After the first round, few jump-ers have not at least approached 50 meters, but I will not let disappointment impede my thoughts of victory. I enjoy this too much. If the 50-meter jump brought such joy to me as I soared above the 8,000 or so who watched and soared with me, imagine the delight they will experience when I exceed my physical limits and reach for 60 meters. "I can do that," I tell my Captain.

There is a commotion and the contestants gather at the podium. The interruption will give the surface of the ramp time to gather itself in the cold, and freeze more solidly than it was on the first run down. The Swiss jumpers are speaking passionately to the judges, but the Swedes and the Americans are equally emotional, defiantly waving their hands and shaking their heads. "What are they saying?" I ask the Captain.

"It seems that the Swiss want to start at the very top of the ramp, but the Scandinavians and the Americans say it is too dangerous." He looks at me and asks, "What do you think, Bronek? Is it too dangerous from the top?"

"There is danger in every jump," I answer. "It makes no difference from where it begins or what the conditions might be. If a man fears danger, he should not jump. Is it too dangerous? What is 'too dangerous?'"

He is satisfied with my answer, and has no cause to respond. We wait. Another exercise in patience lost on the Scandinavians and the Americans. Nearly an hour passes before a decision is made. When it is, the Swiss smile and raise their hands in victory. Ever pragmatic, the Swedes defer to the Swiss and matter-of-factly accept the outcome; the Yanks, as they're called, sullenly walk away like spoilt children. We begin our procession back up the hill to the highest point on the ramp. A maintenance crew breaks up the frozen surface to make the path to the top easier to negotiate. I nod appreciatively to one worker who has stopped to rest on his way back down, and I think it is likely I will make it to the base of the mountain sooner than he will.

A favorable roar from the crowd greets each contestant as he departs the ramp, but I pay no particular heed to the jumpers before me except for the German. The beads of sweat that have gathered on his forehead in the freezing temperature are born of more than the physical work of the arduous climb. They betray his nervousness. Indeed, as I survey the vista and gaze at the bottom of the mountain, I conclude the extra 30 meters I've climbed may as well have been 30 kilometers; the people below look like insects at this distance. The German has 60 seconds to take the ramp. His hesitation is obvious to the judges who wait with little patience as the afternoon minutes pass quickly to usher in the dusk. "Schnell," one of the judges says. I step up and put my hand on his shoulder and see the fear in his eyes when he looks into mine. He would not understand any words I might say, so I offer him a simple smile and a nod of confidence. His eyes soften when he acknowledges my effort. He turns back to the task and is on his way without vacillation. His jump is straight and true and farther than his first. I wait until his run-out is complete. He looks back up the mountain and waves — I know — to me. I return the gesture as the address system announces his distance — 48 meters this time, a full dozen more than his first jump — followed by my name.

I move onto the runway, make my 90-degree hop to the right, tuck and plunge down the precipitous ramp. It is a sheet of ice and there is no friction to hold me back. Once again, I celebrate the speed and acceleration that embodies the descent. I have never moved so fast in my life. Thought is beyond me, and I merely react with an Olympian effort as I leap into the sky, into the heavens that welcome me with its unrestricted vastness. No creature has ever felt what I feel in this moment of pure exhilaration. Time has stopped and life has ceased on Earth. I remain the sole creation who can enjoy this moment of beauty. If the *hamsa* is the hand of God, he raises me higher. The seconds above the Earth are timeless, and I rue my return from this glimpse of eternity.

But as I will learn can happen so often in life, exhilaration can plummet to the deepest and darkest holes in our hearts in the wake of disaster. The very instant my skis contact the ground and return me to reality, I know I am leaning too far forward. The pleasure of the act has distracted me from the task at hand. I struggle and fail to capture the Telemark. I know the effort is useless, but I move my arms rapidly like a wounded bird hoping I can learn to fly. With no control over my flailing body, I concede to failure when my weight shifts to the right and my shoulder scrapes the ground. Disembodied, I watch myself tumble like a discarded rag doll with no rhyme or reason to how my limbs are connected to my torso. My muscles are strained and pulled to their limits, and I am fortunate to escape serious injury as my body comes to its painful rest at the bottom of the hill.

The Captain precedes the crowd that converges upon my limp body. "Are you okay?" he asks. I laugh inwardly. For the first time in my life, I consider the Captain's question rather silly. The breath has been knocked from my lungs and I struggle and gasp to regain it. Over the Captain's shoulder, I see the face of the Norwegian skater, concern etched on her pretty face. I sense she is going to reach for me, and then another body brazenly pushes the Captain aside and reaches toward me. It is Janina. The Captain stays her arms before she can take me. "Please, madam," the Captain says, we mustn't move him until we know the condition of his bones. She raises her hands to her red lips. I continue to gasp for air like a flopping fish out of water.

I hear the speaker announce my distance — 60.5 meters — followed quickly by a word that I hear repeated in Polish, "Disqualified." I squeeze my eyes tightly. The pain that racks my body is nothing compared to the agony that racks my soul. The word echoes distastefully in my mind: disqualified.

The crowd that surrounds me watches as a physician opens my coat and shirt to place his stethoscope on my bare chest. He sees the *hamsa* and moves it to the side with his fingers. His disapproving glance does not go unnoticed by those near enough to see. I hear another word, "Jude!" It is as cold and heartless as the metal disk of the doctor's instrument. The world turns black and I lose consciousness.

Chapter Seven, 1932

Biały Ślad

I avoid the attention that comes with notoriety. I have noticed that those who enjoy it find themselves obligated to act in a certain way, and most do, simply to maintain their celebrity status regardless of their true feelings. I've never met a highlander who has succumbed to the temptation, though we can act the role when necessary. I last visited the Villa Marilor in the summer of 1929 to celebrate my father's 50th birthday, a grand and festive event organized by his good friend, the Captain. No one on that special night could have imagined greed would bring the world's economy to its knees by the end of the year. It means nothing to a simple highlander like me, but to the wealthy, it means everything. As the economy worsened, my family grew stronger. We have our cow that gives us her milk and we have our chickens that share their eggs with us. We are blessed with our faith and don't need much more. *Babcia* is gone and rests in the cemetery behind the church. Włady and Stasia have moved away, he to Kraków and she with her husband to the Ukraine. I remain close in spirit with Janka, and we continue to share the house with mother and father. Our parents are not fond of the cities, so Janka alone accompanies me this evening.

"What will it be like?" Janka asks. Her exuberance leaps from her pretty smile, and I think of *Babcia* and wish that she could have seen me at the games in St. Moritz and those soon to come in the United States. *Babcia* was so full of life and that is what the games are about, and that is what this evening is about and I am so pleased that my sister is with me.

"Warsaw? It's just a big city, Janka, bigger buildings, more buildings, more people, and automobiles."

"I know that," she says. "I mean the moving picture. What will it be like?"

"I've not seen one either, little sister. I can't tell you. We'll just have to wait and see."

"I think it will be magical. I can't wait."

The Villa is an elegant place and reminds me somewhat of the Badrutt in St. Moritz, though on a smaller scale. Fewer vacationers have attended our ski school in recent years, which is fine with me. I am jealous and would keep the Tatras to myself if I could. Not so, Andrzej's brother Adam. He so much loves the mountains and wants to share them with the world. "My film will bring people to these mountains," he says with passion. "Damn the depression! We'll have none of it here." Even before Janka and I enter the Villa, Adam's voice rings loudly and clearly from the lobby's open door. Like my mother, Janka loves the spring when things come verdantly to life. I, like my father, prefer the bold, bright colors that adorn the trees in autumn. They foreshadow the snows of winter that will lure us to the mountains for six long, dark and cold months. Janka sees the beginning's explosive activity; I see rest and reflection at the end.

Adam names his film *Biały Ślad*, and he has used us Zakopane skiers in it. And why not? His story is a love story, not just between a man and a woman, but also between a people and its environment. Skiing is at its heart. Who better to play the roles than the real skiers, the men of the Tatras? Andrzej and his friend Stanisław Sieczka, a jumper like me, play major roles as they vie for the attention of the ever-beautiful Janina Fischer, cast as Hanka, a wealthy girl returned to the mountains from school. Adam includes the Marusarz boys and me in the film, I think only because he likes us, certainly not because of our acting skills. Of course, neither Andrzej nor Stanisław are professional actors, but I believe they perform well in Janina's shadow.

A butler greets us and escorts Janka and me to a large sitting room where the production staff and guests are gathered. Adam sees me and snubs his cigarette. He exchanges a knowing glance with the valet who closes the large paneled doors behind me.

"This is it, gentlemen," Adam proudly proclaims as he passes out the rail tickets. "Janina, Lina and Józef are in Warsaw and will meet us at the Polonia where we will dine after the premiere. I thank each of you for your contribution." The valet returns with a tray of bubbling, stemmed glasses. Champagne. I allow Janka to take a glass, albeit with the stipulation that she only wet her lips and that she not tell mother. She is radiant in the tailored dress from *Pani* Gromelski, mother's friend. Though not orphaned, my sister is like the character Zośka in Adam's film, pure and innocent, she lives in a foothills cabin with her brother. I want the night to be perfect for Janka. She has never been treated with the admiration afforded an Olympic skier or an actress, but she is no less deserving of such veneration. I put my arm about her shoulder and say, "Good things happen to good people, Janka, and you are a good person."

"To the success of *Biały Ślad*." We raise our glasses with Andrzej to toast his brother and the film. "*Na zdrowie*, to life!" I touch my glass to Janka's and the sharp 'ring' complements the sparkle in her eyes.

With a single exception, we are in formal attire. The Captain has no interest in moving pictures and will not come with us to Warsaw. He stands on the periphery in his hunter's trousers and a knitted brown sweater. The sweet fragrance of his pipe balances the stringent smell of cigarettes, the smoke of choice among those people who feel the necessity to climb the social ladder. He taps the stem of his pipe on his glass to get our attention and says, "And to our Olympians who will travel to America for the winter games."

"*Na zdrowie*," we say again. The stewards refill our glasses and Adam adds a final toast, "And to Poland, may she forever stand proud and free!"

Approaching Warsaw, evening creeps upon us, and the lights of the city grow. So many lights, I think. In Zakopane, I gaze into the night sky and see millions of stars spread across God's black palette. In Warsaw, I look into the glare of the electric street lamp that gobbles up the twinkle of starlight and hides it from view. Flexing my legs to rid them of stiffness, I realize how short this four-hour train ride is compared to the journey to America. In a few months time, we will traverse an ocean, a vast expanse I have never seen, but only imagined.

We board a tramcar that carries us to the Polonia where we will meet Janina Fischer and the other members of her entourage.

There are so many lights in front of the hotel that it could be daylight. Extending into the infinite darkness, spotlight beams fence one another in the sky. Passing motorists blow their loud horns. This must be 'glamour,' I think. So many people in such snobbish finery for no apparent reason other than to be noticed as someone with social status.

Janka tugs at my coat sleeve. "I look like a maid," she says. I put my arm around my sister, pull her close and whisper in her ear, "If maids look like you, Janka, every woman here will be envious and looking for house work tomorrow morning."

Adam is proud of his film, and we are his chosen ones, those who will accompany him to the first showing at the Atlantic. I know little of such things, but it is rumored that Eugeniusz Bodo, the king of Polish actors will be in the audience. They say that if Bodo is pleased with the film, all of Poland will agree.

Conversation is lively and gay when I hear the unmistakable voice of Janina Fischer, "Janka, Janka," she shouts above the crowd. Janina is very kind to my sister. "I am so glad you could come with your brother." She holds Janka at arms' length. "My, but you are so beautiful. You put all of us glamorous socialites to shame. I'm afraid all eyes will be on you and not the film. Therefore, little sister, you must sit with me. It is settled." I offer no resistance, and with Janina on my left arm and Janka on my right, we enjoy the short walk from the hotel to the new Atlantic Theater on Chmielna Street.

I smell the newness of the theater the second I walk through the door. A giant oriental carpet flows like a sea of red and gold before us. A dark, mahogany wall separates the lobby from the auditorium. A smiling usher escorts us up the elegantly enclosed staircase that leads to the balcony. From our seats, we look down on the audience of wealthy patrons whose curiosity continues to draw it to moving picture premieres. A large chandelier hangs well above us and casts its dim light onto the audience waiting patiently below. A small orchestra plays music that was written specifically for our 'film,' the word Adam uses when he refers to our moving picture. I like this music. It is grand and majestic like our mountains, yet interspersed with playful transitions that describe what the amateur skier might feel on a recreational run down a shallow slope.

As I am about to ask Janka what she thinks of this, the music stops with a tap of the conductor's baton, and the casual conversation that fills the hall fades to a whisper, then silence. Adam enters the stage from the left and the crowd applauds. He walks to the front edge of center stage and quiets the audience with his outstretched arms and open palms. Graciously, he thanks them for attending, then introduces a handful of celebrities and guests. Bodo stands at his front row seat and faces the crowd when Adam thanks him for his appearance at this premiere. Bodo's faint smile is as much a sneer, tainted with a glint of arrogance. Janina waves when Adam calls her name. It is all quite formal, but I pay more attention to Janka's reaction than to anything else. My parents would have enjoyed this, and I say a silent prayer for *Babcia*. I do believe she is here.

After Adam concludes his planned statement of welcome and gratitude, he walks backward, stage left and his out-stretched left arm seems to draw open the tall, red curtain with him. The lights dim, and with the theater completely dark, the ratcheting sound of gears accompanies a strong beam of light that cuts through the auditorium smoke. Suddenly and astonishingly, the wall before us fills with the bright image of our own Tatras! The audience applauds. I am amazed how Adam's camera captures the mountains from so many angles and directions. An ancient *Dziadek* in a wheelchair who has spent his entire life in the city can now see the beauty of the mountains as I've seen them all my life. What a great invention these moving pictures are. Janka's eyes open wide, her fingers cover her lips to stifle the thrill of watching Adam's tapestry come to life on the flat wall in front of us.

The hour passes too quickly. There is skiing and adventure! Romance! Adam's film has it all, and the reaction from the audience says it approves, with or without the great Bodo's endorsement. Janka takes Janina's hand when the actress first appears in the picture. Frankly, I can hardly identify myself when I enter the screen because I am covered in shadows, but I do find it strange to watch my image move on the wall. Janka elbows me and looks bewildered as she glances from the wall to me and back again. The smile never leaves her face, not even as Janina and Andrzej are swept away in an avalanche. Andrzej and my fellow jumper Stanisław are the two heroes in the story. I think in real life, Stanisław would get the girl — he is a very handsome man — but in Adam's picture, it is Andrzej who wins the prize, possibly, because they are brothers in real life. No one seems to mind.

The final image of a heart-broken Stanisław — Jasiek in the story — standing atop a lonely, Tatra peak fades into darkness on the wall, the electric light from the chandelier rises, and so too does the audience. The long, loud and continuous applause leaves no doubt that the moving picture is well received. With cries of "Bravo, Bravo," the audience turns collectively and raises its arms towards us in the balcony.

We descend the grand staircase and gather in the lobby to greet the audience as it exits. "Don't wander off," I tell Janka. "I want to know where you are all the time." I am protective of my sister and as she evolves into a beautiful woman, admiring eyes will follow her every move.

The audience floods the lobby and gathers around Adam and his main players.

"And where is your Captain?" It is *Pan* Bobkowski. I bow respectfully and introduce my sister. "Charmed," he says, "More beautiful than your brother is handsome."

"Agreed," adds the tiara'd woman at his side extending her hands to Janka and me.

"My wife," Bobkowski notes.

"*Pan i Pani* Bobkowski, I am pleased to see you here," I say. Janka blushes when she curtsies.

"Splendid picture, don't you think, young Janka?" he asks. "With so many of my skiers in this film, I simply had to come, but no Captain?"

"He prefers the solitude of the mountains over the crowds and the bustle of the city," I offer.

"He may be wiser than all of us," *Pani* Bobkowski says.

I have never met *Pani* Bobkowski, and I find her very pleasant. I learn that she is well traveled and for that reason, found no need to be with us in St. Moritz. "But America!" she says, "I've never been to America, and I will travel with you this winter. I so look forward to it."

Bobkowski twists his white gloves in his hands. "Quite perplexing. This depression that started in America with their lame financial organization is sweeping Europe as well."

"We can't blame it all on the Americans, Alexander," his wife playfully admonishes him with a wave of her hand. "It's the Brits and their gold standard."

"Regardless," he says, "you highlanders may not feel it like we do in Warsaw, but you will see that our team will be much smaller in America than it was in St. Moritz. We've not the funds to support it. And yet, I have the personal resources to take my wife? I must be crazy!"

She doesn't apologize. "I suspect this will be my final opportunity to travel to America. I will not let it pass."

"We will welcome your company, Madam," I say. Bobkowski and his wife excuse themselves and stroll toward Andrzej and Stanisław.

I enjoy this event, but certainly as much for my sister as for myself. I am glad she is with me. Like the Captain, I prefer the mountains, their majesty and their solitude. I smile when I recall the final scene of the picture that shows brave Stanisław on the snow-covered peak. I find more beauty in the sparkle of ice and snow than I do in the sequined dresses that fill this room. I am ready to return to the hotel for dinner, but protocol demands otherwise.

Janka pulls my sleeve and draws me close so she can whisper in my ear. "I think you are in for a big surprise," she says. Before I can ask her to explain, two arms reach from behind me, and perfumed hands cover my eyes. They are a woman's small hands. I place mine on top of them. I draw a deep breath as I remove the hands from my eyes and gather them at my waist. Janka's face glows as she shifts her gaze to the person behind me. I turn and face the woman. It is Amalia.

I haven't seen her since that night in front of her home when I learned she would marry. Oh, how long those four, short years seem to me. Amalia is radiant and her apparel suggests that life has been good to her. I am happy for her. Her raven hair is much shorter than I remember but still stunning as it frames her beautiful face. The small wooden cross I handcrafted as a boy contrasts her elegant dress and hangs from a gold chain where the neckline dips. As my eyes linger on the cross, she touches it with the fingers of her left hand and, with the fingers of her right, reaches to my chest and feels the *hamsa* beneath my shirt. A look of knowingness passes silently between us as she holds my gaze with a bittersweet smile.

"So this is Bronisław, the man of whom I've heard so much," her escort says.

"It is, darling," she answers without taking her eyes from mine, "and this is his sister, Janka. May I present my husband Max."

We shake hands. He is much older than Amalia. "We enjoyed the picture very much," he says with enthusiasm and sincerity. "Since the picture house opened two years ago, we come often. I congratulate you and your fellow filmmakers. I must say this is one of the best I've seen."

"You are too gracious, Max. A filmmaker I am not. In the hour, I appear, what, maybe five minutes?"

"But it was the best five minutes, wasn't it, Amalia?" Janka says.

"It was," Amalia answers smiling broadly at Janka. "I remember last seeing you four or five years ago. You were still a child. Look at you now, Janka, you have become a woman! And so beautiful! Your mother and father must be so proud of you both."

Janka's blush makes her even more attractive.

"And Wisław and Stasia? They are well?"

"They are. Life for us is simple but sweet. I ski, Janka finishes school."

"And do you have a sweetheart?" Amalia boldly asks me.

I put both arms around Janka and say, "This is my sweetheart, my favorite sister whom I cherish above all other women."

"Except mother," Janka adds.

"Except mother," I agree.

Janka wriggles free. "I think he may be too shy," she says and they laugh. "You see this one here?" Janka nods toward Janina Fischer. "The only reason she is with Stanisław and not Bronek is because my brother is too shy."

"But far more handsome," Amalia adds.

"Enough of this," I say. "And you and Max live in Warsaw? Children?"

"No children," she says, "We live here in Warsaw, and both work at the university. Max teaches fourth year history. I teach philosophy. It is a good combination. We live nearby, maybe one kilometer." I don't have to ask, for there is little doubt in my mind that Amalia met her Max years ago while a student in his class. When I returned from Switzerland, she was gone, her entire family, too. My broken heart suppressed my compulsion to ask questions. Time has healed my wounds, but my memory remains clearer than a moving picture. How many nights I've awoken with the image of this woman in my mind, I can barely count. But it is the small amulet that hangs on my chest that keeps her memory alive regardless of where she might be or whom she is with. I have no intention of forgetting her or casting her from my thoughts. I want her to remember me as someone she will always love – even if only as a friend – and to whom she can turn for anything. I cannot deny the fact that Amalia is one of the reasons I strive to excel in my sport. If I achieve any notoriety, my name will appear in the newspapers, and she will see it whether she is in Warsaw or London. Olympic athletes' names travel the globe. So too, I am learning, will the names of people associated with moving pictures.

The lobby doors open and the crowd begins its exit.

"Can you join us at the Polonia for dinner, Max?"

"Unfortunately, no," he says. "We're not so welcome at the Polonia. I lectured there several months ago, and a group attended that did not quite share my views on Polish sovereignty."

"We don't need to discuss it," Amalia interrupts.

"I'm sorry," I say. "I have little inclination for political things."

Max turns his head and casually remarks, "Someday you may."

Janka furrows her brow.

"This topic is not appropriate for such a wonderful night," Amalia firmly suggests. "No, regretfully we cannot join you for dinner, but I want you to come visit us if you have reason to return to Warsaw, though you love Zakopane like a woman, Bronek." We laugh. She opens her purse and gives me a small card that reads 'Haas' on one side, their address printed on the other. "Really, it is not far from this theater."

"Can we come back soon, Bronek? I would so love to visit Amalia and Max and to see the university here. It is so much different than home, so much more alive."

I don't agree with my sister. "Alive? That, Janka is purely a matter of one's perspective. I'll take Zakopane, and I mean no offense to you, my friends." As I see Adam wave, signaling that it is time for us to leave, a thought occurs to me that I am certain will please Janka. "I have an idea. In January, I leave for the games in America. I will be gone for two months. Would it be possible for Janka to come for an extended visit? If it would not be an inconvenience to you, I know it would be of great value to Janka to experience the academic lifestyle you find so comfortable and stimulating. I'm sorry, I am being to forward and presumptive."

"Not at all," Max replies with a grin. "We would love to have her stay with us."

"Can I, Bronek? Will it be okay with you? What will father and mother say? If, of course Max and Amalia permit it."

"I think mother and father will be agreeable to it. We will work this out and put a plan together," I say to everyone's approval. "Our team gathers in Warsaw in January. I will write to you before Christmas to make sure you remain comfortable with the idea."

"Consider it settled," Max says. Amalia's smile is her sign of approval.

We leave the theater and walk the single block to Marszałkowska Street where Janka and I exchange farewells with Amalia and her husband. They wave and stroll north, arm in arm, toward the university. I watch them walk away and place my hand on my chest to feel my heart pound through the small, clay *hamsa*.

"You are still fond of her?" Janka asks. My eyes tell her I am, while my heart tells me I can't be. "Let's go." Taking her arm in mine, we quietly return to the Polonia and the celebratory dinner.

Chapter Eight, 1932

West to America

I have become somewhat accustomed to these rides on the locomotive. I discover they are easier to endure, if only I can find it within myself to enjoy them. With mother and father's approval, I left Janka with Amalia and Max in Warsaw – my sister was so pleased — and, with my teammates, boarded this train to Hamburg where we will depart for our sea voyage to America. Not a one of us has been on a steamship. The concept of floating in an iron hull on the vastness of the ocean, dominates our thoughts to a point just shy of intimidation. Heavy iron on water? It does not seem possible to me. Józef Stogowski, who has the honor to carry our flag at these games, has an interest in 'technical things.' He is quick to tell us that our ship is not a steamship, rather a motor ship. The difference is too complicated for me to understand and I really don't care as long as we arrive safely on the other side of the ocean.

Not even the immensity of the sea could prevent the financial difficulties of American banks from invading Europe. Whatever those American bankers did, we see their disruptive and destructive effects everywhere. A subdued air lingers in the railway stations and far fewer passengers travel by rail than what I have seen in the past. In

1928, our Polish contingent in St. Moritz numbered nearly
40. We travel to America with only half of that. Our
team numbers but 15, five skiers and the 10 skaters on our
hockey team. True to her desire, *Pani* Bobkowski travels
with her husband. Good for her, I think. She is a nice lady.
I like her.

We spend one night in a cheap, Hamburg hotel where
heavily rouged women, who pretend to enjoy our Polish
accents, crowd the small lobby. The youngest members
of our team, the cousins Marusarz, Andrzej and Stanisław,
enjoy the attention afforded them by these ladies whose
demeanor does not conceal their profession.

I am compelled to confess my crime. I departed St.
Moritz with the German Bible I found in the dresser at
the Badrutt. Knowing my interest in language, Max and
Amalia gave me an English Bible at Christmas. I have
gained some proficiency in German and I look forward to
practicing my English in America. My ability to commu-
nicate, however primitive, gives me confidence, and I will
not feel so lost when I arrive. A final admission: I acquired
a Norwegian Bible and have given some attention to that
difficult tongue should I ever cross paths with the figure
skater I met in Switzerland. As a ski instructor and mountain guide in Zakopane, I have had some opportunity to
advance my newly acquired language skills. Although the
depression has reduced the number of international visitors
to our mountains, my services have been required enough
to allow me to practice my speaking skills. When I first set
my mind to studying other dialects, an Englishman told me
the only way to learn a language is to practice. His guidance is sound: a student can learn much more from practical

application than he can from a book. I take his advice to heart and use foreign parlance whenever the opportunity presents itself, though I'm not sure what linguistic value there is in a discussion on politics or finance with a prostitute. I'll leave the Marusarz boys to find out and tell me.

We rise early, have a simple breakfast and assemble in the street. The sky is overcast and dark, and a feathery mist carries the scent of salt even though we are some 70 kilometers from the North Sea. It is there that our ship will enter open water. The Captain tells us the short walk to the dock will be good for us, since it will be more than a week before we touch dry land again. This is not a comforting thought for men of the hills.

We are a young, inexperienced team. Only five of us competed in St. Moritz. At nineteen, I was the youngest member. The Marusarz cousins are only eighteen and three of our hockey players are only nineteen. I feel responsible for them in the same way that Andrzej Krzeptowski took care of me in Switzerland. Andrzej is not with us, lured instead to visions of fame and fortune that his brother claims will be theirs in the picture industry. I wish them both luck.

A steamship's hoarse call cuts through the fog and directs our way to the bank of the Elbe River. Our party follows the sorrowful sound through the narrow streets that lead to the dock. The horn bellows again, this time close and very loud, a frightening sound for us, who are unaccustomed to life in a port. The fog thins and before us is the monstrosity of the ship that will take us to America. Its name is the *St. Louis*. At 175 meters long, it dwarfs the small vessels, the tugboats and schooners that are busy on the river. The forward mast must be at least 25 meters tall and nearly disappears into the low clouds that hang above the river. Two giant smokestacks sit behind the mast midway down the boat. There are larger ships in port with three stacks, and I even see one with four. Black smoke curls from them and stains the sky. A wide footpath rises from the pier with steps to the deck of the ship. I'm not quite comfortable with this, but the Captain shows no fear as he climbs the gangway and steps aboard the boat. Hoping to waylay the fears of my younger teammates, I follow his lead, and with staged confidence, imitate his ascent.

Pan Bobkowski offers a half-hearted apology that limited funding from our federation requires that we athletes make the voyage in steerage accommodations. "You will find it not too uncomfortable," he says as he and his wife leave us and follow a steward who guides them to the first cabin salon.

"Okay, boys," the Captain says, "Lucjan and I are assigned to the second cabin where we will share a room." Lucjan manages our hockey team. "We will spend seven nights on this boat before we reach port in America. Lucjan and I have decided we will exchange beds with you throughout the journey. We will spend our nights in steerage with you, and each night two of you will sleep in our second cabin room. Fair enough, Lucjan?"

"Fair enough," Lucjan answers. "Tonight, the honors go to Józef our flag bearer, and Zdzisław, our senior skier." We applaud Lucjan and the Captain for their generosity and their choice of sleeping arrangements for the initial night of the voyage.

We share our steerage compartments with hundreds of passengers. Bunks are stacked one atop the other. Two men are supposed to sleep in each bed. Even the smallest man in our party will find his space cramped.

Three hours pass before the horn loudly announces our departure. We sense the deep rumble and feel the vibration of the giant motor as it begins to turn. We climb to the deck as the driver of this iron whale – assisted by smaller boats called tugboats – moves us carefully and slowly away from the pier. When we are safely away, he turns upriver to the North Sea. Sunshine breaks the afternoon clouds and spills through them as we enter open water. The continent drifts behind us. After several hours, I feel more secure, but several of my teammates find traveling on the ocean not as agreeable. Kazimierz Sokołowski may be a furious wolf in the hockey rink, but on this boat, he is more a lamb as he slumps forward on the railing and empties his stomach into the churning water. Me? If I look down at the water, my head spins with my stomach and I feel the urge to lean so far over that I might fall! So I stay a full step back from the rail, keep my eyes focused on the distance, and watch the sun sink toward the western horizon. My teammates return to their quarters and alone, I remain on deck, captivated by the wonders spread before me, an unending tapestry of rolling waves and churning water. The sea is so expansive, no boundaries. I have seen nothing like it. A steady sense of motion caresses my face as the cold wind blows my hair back. I close my eyes and feel as if I am jumping, but I never land, I just keep soaring with the wind in my face. Time is silent.

The sky is afire as the sun falls beneath the waves. Light lingers longer on the open sea than it does in the foothills of the Tatras. When the sun disappears behind the mountains, darkness follows quickly. The light fights to keep its hold, but the struggle is futile. I sigh and breathe a silent prayer for no special purpose other than to thank God for giving me this day.

I find my teammates in steerage where most of them have either been resting all afternoon, or hiding from the elements on deck. The Captain insists that we will dine together as a team. He looks at me, and then his watch. He clicks it shut. "Don't make us wait next time, Czech." I understand and he need say no more.

Led by the strong aroma of a stew, fresh bread and tobacco smoke, we have no difficulty finding the area set up as our dining room. It is a large area and necessarily so, for it seems that most fellow travelers are in steerage, separated in so many ways – beyond the level our respective decks – from the passengers in the first and second cabins. A pair of burly men, one squinting from the cigarette smoke that rises from the butt in his mouth, spoons out the evening meal. We take our places in line. With each spoonful that 'plops' into our wooden bowls, the one with the cigarette mutters through his clenched teeth, "Breakfast at 6:00 a.m."

"How will we know when it is 6:00 a.m.?" Andrzej asks.

The other chef places a slice of bread on Andrzej's stew and answers, "You won't." The two laugh cheerfully. "We've got plenty of beer, so take what you want," he says, then cautions us with a wave of his serving ladle, "But no one gets drunk!"

"Only happy!" his partner adds with a wink, and their bellies jovially roll once more.

We sit on benches at long, plank tables. Smiling, I recall the dinner I enjoyed with my sister at the Polonia after the moving picture premier in Warsaw. Dressed in formal attire and finery, we would make quite a scene at this table! With an open collar and my shirtsleeves rolled up, I prefer this environment. The stew abounds with large chunks of meat surrounded by carrots, potatoes and beets, all swimming in thick gravy. It is good and exceeds my expectations. Gaunt faced mothers and fathers shepherd their raggedy yet happy children. This may be the best meal they have shared in quite some time. Their belief that this meal proclaims what they can expect when they reach the shores of America fuels their smiles. Can America answer their prayers? I hope so.

With the meal finished, a fiddle calls from the corner. The rhythm soars as men stomp their feet and women and children clap their hands. A second fiddle joins the first. Jerzy retrieves his *konzertina* and effortlessly accompanies the talented players. The gay music tantalizes the crowd, and men push the tables and benches to the side, making space for those who are driven to dance the *tarantella*. A handsome young man with dark, curly hair moves to the center of the room and spins and whirls on his toes. "*Olimpico*," an old woman says proudly to her friend nodding at the dancer. Both grandmothers smile toothless grins. Each wears a colorful babushka tied beneath her chin to cover her thinning gray hair. I surmise correctly that the Italian team shares this ship with us. The dancer is very good and very athletic. Perhaps he is a jumper like me. As he spins, he stoops low and then leaps into the air, ducking his head to avoid the low ceiling.

Our crazy Stanisław vaults onto the floor to create his own *tarantella*. The Italian accepts Stashu's friendly, unspoken challenge and the two mimic and mirror each other. From the far side of the room the Italian contingent chants, "Severino, Severino." They sing to the music that flows happily from the fiddles and Jerzy's *konzertina*. For our part, we counter, "Stashu, Stashu." Even the Captain lowers his guard and allows himself to enjoy this moment. Suddenly Andrzej Marusarz rises from his bench and strides across the room, dodging the two dancers. He bows grace-fully to another Italian athlete who rises willingly to greet him. They hold hands and extend their free hands to their teammates. I must be a part of this special moment, so I join the athletes that encircle, and then move around Stashu and Severino. In that moment, the fellowship of athletes is unrivaled and consummate in its purity and simplicity. Who is more tired? The musicians, the two dancers, the lively audience or me? The familiar odor of sweat rises in the room, but no one seems to mind.

Someone takes hold of the 'X' formed by my suspend-ers, at first, I think to slow me down, but then I feel the 'snap' when he releases the straps. I look over my shoulder and see a face I have not seen in eight years. It is Antonín Bartoň, the Czechoslovakian skier.

"I thought so," he says, "It is you, Czech. Are the Poles taking you to America to wax their skis or are you actually on the team?"

We hug like bears for as I have learned when two men embrace in friendship, the ground shakes, or in this case, the boat rocks. "Let me tell you what happened," I say. "I went to Warsaw to become a cook and got in the wrong line. They handed me a pair of skis and said, 'Take these to America.' So here I am."

We embrace again. "It's good to see you," he says. "And the leg? No problems?"

"After eight years I hope not."

"Let's sit and have a beer. You have time?"

"Only about a week."

The music and dancing will be a welcomed part of every evening for the entire journey. Three teams travel together aboard this boat: the Italians, the Czechoslovakians and us Poles. As I renew my friendship with Antonín, I see new friendships blossoming without regard to geographical borders, political sovereignty or religious preferences. The Marusarz boys and Severino and his Italian mates are as natural together as bread and butter. Stashu and his cousin do not speak Italian, and the Roman athletes are probably not proficient in Polish. The languages are too different; our roots are Slavic, theirs are Latin – you see I've learned much since my time in Switzerland! But language raises no barrier in this celebration.

Antonín and I take seats near the narrow doorway with a man and his happy family.

"You have been well?" I ask. He nods and I comment, "You weren't at the last games."

"I wasn't good enough to make our team," he replies, "But you were there! My friend Rudolf brought us a medal, bronze in the ski jump. He recounted a Polish jumper who soared like an eagle but landed like a brick. Said his name was Czech. I laughed when he told me."

I raise my glass to his. "That was me, alright."

"Hey Bronek," someone calls loudly above the din. "Where did you get the beer?" It is Józef with Zdzisław.

I point with my glass to the barrel that sits tapped on a table at the far end. "What are you doing down here?" I ask. "You have but this single night in the second cabin."

"Fuck the second cabin," Józef says in his crude way. "We know why Lucjan and the Captain were ready to give it up. Too stuffy up there."

"Not the air, the people," Zdzisław adds. "I can't even imagine what it is like in the first cabin. No fun. Not like down here. Hot air does rise!"

"Here's something you want to know," Józef says over the music. "There is no liquor in America." He notes the surprise in our faces. "It's true. The Americans haven't had legal alcohol for over 10 years. Can you imagine that? Get your fill on this boat because you won't get any after we make land." They pat my back, acknowledge Antonín with a nod and make their way through the crowded room to the keg.

"So you were the Polish jumper who fell in St. Moritz like the eagle of Aeschylus."

"Whose eagle?" I ask.

"Aeschylus, the Greek playwright. Come now, Czech," he leans closer, "I have seen your moving picture. You're an actor now. You should know these things."

I lean back while he offers me a toast. "I'm no actor, Antonín. The others in the film are my friends. Two were with me in Switzerland. One, a mentor of sorts. His brother made the picture and needed some skiers. It was fun."

"I'll bet it was, particularly that blonde girl. I imagine she is fun."

"She is a nice person," I say to quench his curiosity.

"In any event, the moving picture was a good one, better than those dark and dreary pictures that come from the Germans. My girlfriend loves the moving pictures and we go often. When I told her you were my friend, she wanted me to bring her to Poland to meet you. She thinks you are famous." We laugh.

Antonín and I talk for nearly an hour as if no time has passed to distance us through the years. I remember to thank him for returning my *hamsa*.

"Our rendezvous in the church in Zakopane tells me you are not a Jew," he comments, "but I have wondered why a good Catholic boy like you would wear such a trinket. Quite unusual."

I offer little explanation, "From a friend."

"Strange bedfellows."

"Not a bedfellow, just a girl, a special girl whose friendship I will never betray."

"Odd that you should use that strong word, 'betray.'" I let his remark pass without further comment and guide our conversation to safer ground. We have no need to talk of politics or religion or other things that threaten world harmony.

We part late. The children who travel with us in steerage have long since retired. Only a few graybeards remain, smoking their pipes and reminiscing of days long past, the memories of the homelands that they left forever when the shoreline sank beneath the waves behind us.

Antonín and I meet often during the crossing. It never occurs to us that our kinship is stronger than the friendship we share with any of our teammates. We are both jumpers and will both compete in the combined event, just as I did in St. Moritz. Such is the way of the athlete. We love our sport with such passion that we are drawn to others who share similar dreams and visions. Ideology is meaningless. Each Yank who competes wants to win as much as each Brit, as each Pole, Czech and Swede. We respect each other for our sacrifice and for our obsession, for each man's desire to be the best.

As the sun rises behind us on our ninth day at sea, the pilot of the ship announces, "Land Ho!" The day is clear and presents a deep purple sky to the west in contrast to the fiery orange behind us. I strain my eyes and am finally rewarded with the sight of land climbing on the horizon. Passengers crowd the deck for their first glimpse of America. For my teammates and me, this is just another stop on our endless road to compete. For other travelers on this ship, America is their new home. I overheard someone comment that the migration to America is slowing. If that is true, it must have been something 10 or 20 years ago when they say that twice as many people were coming to America.

The boat slows and creeps toward the land and into a bay not unlike the area from which we departed Europe. There is no sting in the wind as there is on open water. In the distance, a statue rises from the water. It is a robed woman crowned with seven sharp spikes like beams of sunlight. She holds a tablet in one hand, close to her breast; in the other, she raises a torch high above her head. We crowd the deck and watch in awe, transfixed by this majestic woman. The nearer we approach, the more I realize how large and beautiful she is. I've seen nothing like her. I recollect my history lessons and the Colossus of Rhodes. It's said that the ancient statue rose 30 meters above the island it guarded. As we pass this crowned woman, I think she reaches 50 meters. If the Colossus was a wonder of the world, imagine this! The excited steerage crowd cannot withhold its pleasure. It whoops and hollers, while young people dance, old husbands and wives hug each other with tears streaming down their faces.

The bay narrows just beyond the woman with her torch, and a tugboat greets us with a hearty blast of its horn to escort us up the river. Unlike the 75 kilometers or so we sailed upriver from Hamburg to reach the open sea, it is just a short distance upriver to where we make port, in a town called Hoboken. I am ever so grateful when my feet finally touch dry land!

Yellow taxicabs take us across the river to New York City to the train terminal. Two things are obvious to me: everything in America is new; and everything in America is big. As our boat approached the crowned lady, we glimpsed a building that strained to reach heaven. As we enter its shadow, I stick my head out the cab window and strain my neck to see the very top. I fail. The building is so tall that it is cloaked in clouds. This city is built on an island and surrounded by water, but so many people desire to live here that they build higher and higher. This would never happen in Poland.

By noon, we board a train. As I take my seat, I find a book that has slipped to the side of the bench, *The Light of*

Western Stars by Zane Grey. The cover depicts men with
big, wide-brimmed hats on horses. Reading it will be good
for my language skills and an interesting departure from
my biblical studies in English. Zane Grey will help me
pass the time on our journey north. The conductor tells
us we'll arrive at our final destination, Lake Placid, in 18
hours, which means very early tomorrow morning. The
railroad tracks follow a river north from New York City,
then several hours later, we turn west to follow another
river. Light fades as the day ends.

My book is about cowboys and Mexicans. It holds my
interest, and I race the fading light to finish it. The conductor passes through our car and points out the window. "The
Mohawk River," he says. I love the names the Americans
assign to their cities and landmarks. Sometimes, they refer
to their European roots: New York, English; Syracuse,
Greek; Rome, Italy. Other times, they plagiarize the name
of some indigenous tribe of natives who once roamed this
vast, open land, or sometimes they steal a native word:
Mohawk, Oneonta, Adirondacks. American history is so
recent but ours, so ancient. I finish the book not a minute
too soon. The first stars paint the sky, and despite the week
of rest at sea, the steady rhythm of the heavy wheels upon
the iron tracks lulls me to sleep. The undulating motion
of a boat brings sleep easily to those inclined to escape
boredom from the endless water stretching from horizon
to horizon. The train rocks, almost imperceptibly, and it is
noisy, but the very sound, its repetitiveness as grating as it
might be, evolves into a mechanical lullaby that makes eyes
heavy. I am eager to escape the coffin-like spaces I've been
confined to since I left home. I decide to sleep through

these final hours to Lake Placid.   As darkness covers us, there is nothing left to see.   The subdued sounds of sleep that escape the parted lips of my teammates and the other travelers, replace the music and revelry from the boat.   I turn toward the dark window, away from my seatmate and quickly fall asleep

Chapter Nine, 1932

Praise the Nations

As the sun peeks above the mountains to the east, the train decelerates and the squeal of iron on iron awakens me as the engineer applies his brakes. Lifting my head from my elbow, I stretch to relieve my body of the lassitude that sleeping upright can produce. The whistle blows as we make a final turn and the train delivers us to our final destination. Typical of my brief American experience, the station is large and brand new. Colorful flags and banners proclaim this as home to these third Winter Olympic Games and invite officials, spectators and participants to enjoy their sojourn in Lake Placid. 'Red, White and Blue' are the dominant colors, and the abundance of 'stars and stripes' leaves no doubt that this is America. Three other trains are in the yard and there is room for more.

The sun clears the mountaintops as we step from the train. I breathe deeply. The air is clean and fresh but not too cold, even at this early hour of the morning.

Not far from the train, a man holds a sign that says, "Polska, Poland." A small boy, maybe seven or eight, presumably his son, stands next to him and timidly waves a Polish flag attached to a stick. The Captain and *Pan*

Bobkowski approach the small welcoming committee, and the Captain doffs his hat.

"*Czy polska drużyna?*" the man asks. His pronunciation is poor, but at least he tries.

"Yes, we are the team from Poland," the Captain answers.

The young boy's eyes open wide as he gazes up at the Captain, then at the 15 of us standing behind our bags on the platform. He grins sheepishly and waves his flag in our direction. A handful of us wave back, the rest smile.

"I have a bus," the father says and points to a nearby vehicle idling white exhaust into the fresh air. Large letters scripted in red, white and blue identify the bus as 'The Adirondack Stagecoach.' The Captain waves us over. "The car is for your officials," the man adds. "They will be staying at the club?"

"We are," Bobkowski confirms. The man signals to the car, and the driver loads Bobkowski's luggage into the trunk.

"How far to our hotel?" the Captain asks.

"Not a hotel," the man responds. "It's a house, Mrs. Jordan's house. You will like her, and she is a good cook. Not far, a mile or two."

"I will walk," says the Captain.

"My son will guide you."

"May I come with you and the boy?" I ask. "My legs need the exercise."

"Of course." The Captain lights his pipe and looks down at the boy. "What is your name, young man?"

"Johnny."

"And I am Martin," Johnny's father says. "I will be with you throughout the games. If you need anything, ask me and I will do my best to tend to your needs. Okay?"

The Captain nods. "Boys," he says to the team, "Martin will take you to the house. Bronek and I will walk with young Johnny."

We wait for the bus to depart, then the Captain says to the boy, "Lead on."

We don't walk far when we approach a 'T' in the road. Johnny points right. "To the bob run and the ski jumps." Then he points at the street sign. "Main Street. It will take you just about anywhere in Lake Placid." We go left on Main Street and cross a bridge that spans a brook connecting two small ponds. Despite the warm temperature, they are still frozen. Main Street continues left at the next crossroads where Johnny stops, for just a moment, to point straight ahead. "The Club. Rich people." In the distance, the land slopes gently down to the lakeshore. "Mirror Lake," Johnny says in his terse monotone. He's not quite sure of us yet. Large hotels and homes not unlike those I remember from St. Moritz stand like royalty high on the hill. Yet even from this distance, I can see that these buildings are wood, not stone and concrete like the Badrutt in St. Moritz or the other grand hotels in Europe. We continue left on Main Street, which apparently means we are not 'rich people.' For the Captain and me that is fine, for a highlander's riches have little to do with money.

The village is very small, like Zakopane, and it wraps itself around a lake, Mirror Lake, not Lake Placid. The town's namesake lake is a considerably larger body of water that lays one or two kilometers to our north. Autos and pedestrians crowd the streets, and the people smile and wave. The boy's plaid flannel jacket is clearly a hand-me-down. The elbows are patched and the hem is frayed.

"Do you have brothers?" the Captain asks Johnny.

Johnny raises his hand, and reveals the patched elbows of his jacket. "All older," he says. It does not occur to him that his mitten prevents us from counting his fingers, but 'all' leads us to assume that he has at least three older brothers.

"Do you have skaters on your team?" Johnny asks.

"Hockey," I answer.

"No," Johnny corrects me, "I mean skaters, speed skaters."

"No speed skaters."

"That's good. You see this boy running towards us?"

A jogger in a red sweater with "U.S.A." in large blue letters waves and cheerily says, "Hi, Johnny." He greets us with a smile as he passes by. His icy white breath disappears quickly.

"Hi, Jack," Johnny replies then says to us, "He will win the gold medals in the speed skating. He is the fastest and the strongest. My father says no one can beat Jack Shea."

The Captain and I exchange a glance above the boy's head. While some men can't be beat, anyone can lose, but we'll not sully Johnny's image of 'Jack' or his belief in his father's prediction.

As we walk north up Main Street we pass the Olympic Stadium and the Olympic Arena on our left. The Mirror Lake sits behind the houses and buildings on the narrow shoreline on our right. American flags fly everywhere and the Arena is dressed impressively with large red, white and blue banners draped from every ledge deep enough to hold one. Near the top of the street, we approach a large brick building – the neon lights on the façade identify it as "The Palace Theater" – and the marquee announces "Rainbow Trail" as the current show. It is a moving picture theater. As we walk by, I glance at the colorful poster. It is a picture of a cowboy and a lady, and right there it says "Zane Grey's Rainbow Trail."

"I know who that man is," I proudly say as I point at the poster.

The Captain and Johnny shrug their shoulders. "What man?"

"The cowboy?" Johnny asks.

"No, the writer, Zane Grey. I read his book on the train from New York."

"Then you should come back tonight to see the picture," Johnny says.

"Maybe we will, but for now, let's get to our house." The Captain takes Johnny by his shoulders and points him up the street. A large inn sits on a hill just beyond the theater. Once we pass it, we turn left on Saranac Avenue where a large, three-storied building commands the corner. A large group of USA-clad athletes emerges from beneath the portico and strolls up the path towards us. I wave amiably. No one waves back. Jack Shea appeared to be a friendly, happy chap. These gents are rather stern.

"The Americans stay there," Johnny comments, "That was our hockey team. Here in Lake Placid, hockey is war. Don't be offended. Those men rarely smile. Too many missing teeth.

"The Jordan house is just up the road."

Martin's bus is parked on the side of the busy street ahead of us. The matron of the house, Mrs. Jordan, stands on her porch grinning broadly. She wears an apron over her flowered dress and does not seem to mind the cold. "Do they speak English, Martin?" she asks. The bus driver mounts the steps leading to the porch that runs the width of her home. "Not many of them," he answers as he places a large duffel bag to the right of the front door. As our team carries bags up the stairs, Martin and Mrs. Jordan attempt to simplify and expand their verbal instructions with hand signals. "Over here," Mrs. Jordan says very loudly to Czesław Marchewczyk, a young hockey player who does not speak English. Why do people speak loudly to those who do not understand their language, as if adding decibels to their voices will magically make the words understandable. Czesław smiles broadly revealing his missing front tooth.

"*Witaj w moim domu.* Welcome to my home," Mrs. Jordan tries valiantly to greet us in Polish. We appreciate her effort, but her inflections and pronunciations are so bad that the lads don't know what she is trying to say. Each smiles politely.

Kaz smiles at her while he tells Jożef, "She thinks we are from another planet, maybe the moon."

With a smiling Mrs. Jordan before them, Jożef nods politely and says aloud to Kaz, "The moon is not a planet, stupid."

"Madam," I intercede, "I can help." I suspect my English may be better than her Polish.

"Oh my goodness," she raises her hands to her mouth and says through her fingers, "you speak English," as if it is not possible for a Pole to learn this difficult language.

"He does too," I nod toward the Captain. She glances once, then twice at him. She is smitten. He is quite the dashing chap, after all, and she finds our English, seasoned with our Slavic accent, amusing if not beguiling. At a loss for something to say, she takes the corners of her apron in her hands and curtsies. The Captain returns her gesture with a bow.

A long table adorns Mrs. Jordan's dining room, allowing us to eat together and not in shifts. Her parlor is inviting. Over-stuffed chairs and a sofa command the fireplace, and well-stocked bookshelves surround the room. I tell my teammates, "A good way to learn language is to read books. It will also help us to relax in the evenings. Read books." Stashu tells me that is a good idea and he would like to learn English. Those of us who went to school have read at least some writing from Henryk Sienkiewicz. "Aha," I exclaim as I take a book from the shelf. "Here, Stashu. You have read this book in Polish so you know what it says. Try reading it in English. You will learn." He takes the copy of *Quo Vadis*, hefts it in his hand and says, "Thanks, Bronek. I will give it a try."

"Another way to improve our language skills is to attend the theater," I tell my mates. "The movie house is just around the corner."

"I like that idea better," Kazimierz offers with enthusiasm. "I can't even read Polish, and you think I can read English?" We laugh. "I remember the book and could not finish it. Maybe there is a moving picture." I will not get his hopes up by telling him that there is, but it is an Italian picture, and I know it will not find its way to The Palace

Theater in Lake Placid, America, at least not while we are here.

In contrast to the great New York City, Lake Placid is small and easy to navigate. Martin is always ready with the bus, but the only venues that are of any considerable distance from our lodging are the ski jump and the bob run. The ski jump is a short walk, maybe 30 minutes from Mrs. Jordan's, and the bob run, another four kilometers beyond the jump. Those events are scheduled late in the games, and the Captain insists we take the bus to those sites. "Other than that," he tells Martin, "rest your bus and walk with us."

Our first week in Lake Placid passes quickly and the officials are pleased as heavy snow falls to relieve their concerns events may have to be cancelled or delayed.

On the eve of the opening ceremony, we assemble for supper. Mrs. Jordan has prepared a hearty stew with large chunks of tender venison and goodly portions of vegetables – carrots, potatoes, corn, peas and celery. After four nights in her home, we know she serves promptly at 6:00 p.m. No need for a clock for we are drawn to her dining room by the splendid aroma of the stew and the sweet bread she bakes for us every day. Her home, she insists, is our home. A picture of Jesus, standing before a small and simple home in the twilight, hangs on the wall behind the head of the table. This place of honor beneath the portrait is reserved for the Captain. The picture is imprinted with the same blessing as the woodcut in my home, but in English. Stashu takes my advice and reads from Sienkiewicz every night. This night, like every other, we stand behind our assigned seats and await Mrs. Jordan. When she finishes preparing the table and is ready to sit, Stashu points at the picture and proudly says in English, "God bless our home."

The Captain looks over his shoulder at the picture. "Well done, Stashu," he says.   "I think knowledge of English will benefit you more 50 years from now than your ability to ski will!"

We have reached an agreement with Mrs. Jordan. She will try to learn Polish during our visit, and we will speak only in English. Easy for the Captain and me, not so for Mrs. Jordan and most of the other members of our team. Still, we hold true to our pact and help each other improve our language skills. In just four days, her Polish has improved and even Kazimierz Materski who can't even speak Polish correctly is learning English words and phrases, qualifying him as more than a mere tourist.

With the table set and everyone seated, we join hands and bow our heads. Mrs. Jordan blesses our meal – in Polish – and the Captain prays – in English – that our collective strength, courage and wisdom will carry us through the games.

Our bedrooms are small but adequate. With me are Zdzisław Motyka, Stanisław Skupień and the Marusarz boys. We share our room with an alarm clock that sits atop the bureau. Throughout the night, its "tick-tock" attempts to lure us to sleep. However, few hours pass this night when I do not hear the hourly call of the cuckoo from the clock in Mrs. Jordan's parlor. Józef's loud snoring, does not steal sleep from the younger skaters. No. Their nerves are yet to be forged in the fire of Olympic competition, and their inexperience denies them the rest they need. Tomorrow afternoon, following the opening ceremony and the first match between the Yanks and the Canucks, our hockey team will face off against the Germans. Only four teams have entered the hockey competition and Germany will be our easiest opponent. Ice hockey is an American game. The Canadians call it 'their' game, but the Americans are very good as well. We will play each team twice, and if we can't beat the Germans, it is unlikely we will fare well against either team from North America. As athletes, we enter every competition to win, but we are also keenly aware of our opponents, their strengths and their weaknesses. Our boys will know where they stand after tomorrow's games.

When the cuckoo sings six times, I climb from my bed and pull back the window curtain. Auto headlamps brighten the dark street, a far-off locomotive whistle announces the arrival of another train and I'm certain I hear the distant drone of an airplane as well. The lamps are no longer lit, but even this early hour, many people walk the streets. This is an important and eventful day. I wash the sleep from my eyes and dress in five minutes. The strong odor of frying bacon drifts up the stairs and greets me as I open the bedroom door.

"Leave the door open," a drowsy Stashu says. "I love that smell."

"Me too," his cousin adds as he rolls over. "What time is it?"

"You have another half hour," I tell him. He pulls the blanket over his head.

I quietly leave the house, the cold air slapping my face as I walk down the steps. God creates another day, and his dim, dawn light reveals thin columns of smoke that rise from snow-covered roofs, only to dissipate in the cloudless sky. The day will be perfect for these opening ceremonies. I am glad to be alive and extraordinarily fortunate to be an actor on this grand, international stage. I walk to the corner and look down Main Street. The rising sun reveals a cascade of colors from the national flags of the 17 nations who will compete here. The flags decorate every lamppost. Their colors are joined in the five circles of the Olympic banners that hang lifeless in the still morning air. Another whistle, as another train arrives. I look down the road at the long parade of autos, making their way up Main Street. The Games will begin in just a few short hours and spectators are willing to brave the dawn cold to get one of the 5,000 seats in the bleachers. I will not compete for another week, so I relish this early morning walk.

The recent snow allows us to practice on the jump, and though none of us knows the exact course of the 18km race, we skiers have taken to the woods that surround the village to maintain our fitness as we wait for our personal judgment days. Idleness irritates me, and I spend my time doing things that can improve my chance of success.

As I near the stadium at the south end of town, the sidewalks become more and more crowded. Drivers' toot their horns, but only in celebration, not in anger. Many pedestrians support their teams with flags and banners that prominently display national colors. When colors are the same, a mark or symbol distinguishes one nation from another, stars for the United States, and a cross for Norway.

As I pass beneath a sign for the Lake Placid Marcy Hotel, a woman's voice calls, "Hey you. Do you speak English yet?" I am reluctant to turn, or acknowledge the question is directed at me, but when she cries out, "Yes you. Polish skier. You know I am talking to you," I must learn who beckons me.

I stop, as indifferently as I can, and turn toward the stairs leading to the porch in front of the hotel. Standing at the railing is the Norwegian pixie from St. Moritz. Her heavy fur coat cannot hide the fact that she has matured. I remember the pretty, teenage girl I saw in Switzerland; I see a beautiful young woman and can't help but smile.

"Aha," she exclaims, "I've caught you now. You do speak English."

"Og jeg har lært akkurat nok norsk til å snakke til deg."

"Oh my God," she says, "that is terrible! Do you know what you said?"

"I think I said 'I know enough Norwegian to speak with you,'" I answer, thinking now that I may have offended her with something inane and ridiculous.

"Close enough," she answers as she floats down the steps, "but I think we will do better in English. Let's start again." She takes my arm and says, "I'm Sonja and I am pleased to finally and formally meet you."

"And I am Bronisław, and I will tell you I hoped that we might meet again at these games although I doubted very much that you would remember me. You are very famous, I am not." Her smile is infectious. With her arm in mine, we begin to stroll toward the stadium.

"Famous or not," she says, "You are a handsome man. I wanted to tell you that four years ago in Switzerland."

I blush. "Handsome is nothing," I say. "Particularly when standing next to you." She removes her arm from mine, stands on her toes and pulls me close to kiss my cheek. I smell her perfume and I am dizzy.

One kiss. "You are a handsome man," she repeats, turns and walks back to her hotel without another word.

I am breathless and can only mouth the word, "Wait." It is too late. She is lost in the crowd and I can see her nowhere. I retrace my steps and search the porch of the Marcy hotel. She has disappeared. I return to Mrs. Jordan's house to share breakfast with my teammates, all the while telling myself that this girl Sonja is a distraction I do not need.

Sitting next to me at the table, Czesław Marchewczyk says, "Is that your perfume I smell, Mother Jordan?"

"No it is not!" she says quite definitely. Czesław looks at me, then sniffs, mouse-like. "Hmmm," is his final comment before he devours his breakfast.

This time, as we pass the American residence on our way to the opening ceremony, the Yanks wave and greet us affably. We meet the Norwegian men as we turn onto Main Street. They reside not far from us. We allow them to pass; Sonja is not with them. I berate myself as I search for a glimpse of her. When we reach the hotel, she skips gracefully down the stairs to join her teammates. She assumes a prominent position near the front of her delegation. The crowds on the sidewalks become deeper as we approach the stadium. Fewer spectators and athletes have journeyed here than what I remember in St. Moritz, but these Americans are a loud and happy bunch and make much more noise. They wave flags and blow horns, some even throw confetti. This is crazy, I think, but I love it nonetheless. Automobiles divert to side streets leaving the snow-packed Main Street to the pedestrians. We return the enthusiastic greetings of the spectators, but I find myself always looking from the corner of my eye toward the Norwegians to see if Sonja will even look at me. At last, she spins 360-degrees in a single, fluid motion, never losing step with her teammates. She catches my eye and I turn directly towards her. She smiles broadly, points to me and blows a kiss. I wave, but she doesn't see it. "Okay," I tell myself. "That is it. No more. Her kiss is good enough and I will dispel further thoughts of this angel until the games are complete. My mind speaks with finality, but my heart tells me it will be no easy task blocking this vision of heaven from my thoughts. The Captain walks behind, and I feel his eyes before he taps my shoulder.

"Did you see that?" he shouts in my ear to make himself heard. "That girl just blew me a kiss."

"She's pretty," I say in such a cavalier way, as to demonstrate my disinterest.

He takes my shoulders, leans close and says, "Of course she's pretty, Bronek, but forget about her. You are here to ski." He shakes me firmly.

We arrive outside the stadium. The sky is clear and the sun brilliant. The flags of the 17 nations wave above the perimeter of the stadium, their colors sharp and distinct against the deep blue of the Adirondack winter sky.

The loud and continuous roll of a snare drum slices the air. Conversation wanes, and then ceases as the band opens these games with the national anthem of the United States of America. The Americans are the last team in the parade and well behind us, but as the band plays the anthem, the athletes and their countrymen raise their voices to honor their nation. The American athletes behind us are singing more loudly than the crowd in the stadium does or those that jam the streets do. Though ours is a friendly but serious competition, like soldiers, we feel pride when we represent our countries. The crowd noise swells as the band holds the final note, which finally escapes the stadium and flees to the surrounding mountains. After a brief pause, the band begins to play a lively march and the Austrians lead the parade into the stadium.

We shuffle our feet as the line moves forward, but as soon as we stride onto the ice in the stadium, our steps become precise and we move as a single unit driven by the rhythm of the band. Many of the older athletes have served their countries in uniforms far more sacred than these colorful slacks and jackets we don today. Marching is natural for them and so we follow their lead.

Józef — our senior member — carries our flag and leads us into the stadium. A young man precedes Józef, carrying a sign that says "Poland" just in case there is any doubt as to who we are and where we are from. I am certain that few people in the stands do not have any knowledge of my country, nor do they know how similar Zakopane is to their hamlet. As we pass before the reviewing stand, Józef dips the flag to salute the dignitaries assembled there. I do recognize Count Baillet-Latour, the president of the International Olympic Committee, from the games in Switzerland, but I cannot identify the central figure on the reviewing stand, a tall, proud man who holds a cane. While others on the stand chat with each other, this man makes eye contact with every athlete who passes before him. He takes our gesture of honor seriously and holds his hat over his heart as each national flag dips in salute. He looks into each man's eyes, even if briefly, but I swear that after he looks at each Pole, he looks back at me with a wisp of a smile on his lips. I suppose the Captain will tell me later that the man was looking at him!

After all 17 teams have entered the stadium, our flag bearers assemble in front of the reviewing stand. The crowd quiets and the man with the cane is introduced as "His Excellency, Franklin D. Roosevelt, Governor of the State of New York." The title takes me by surprise. I am unaware that in these United States they refer to any of their elected officials as 'His Excellency.' This is the great democracy. Why do they call this man 'His Excellency?'

Roosevelt takes his place at the microphone, the greatest athletes in the world assembled on the stadium floor before him. Thousands of people, unable to secure a seat in the stadium for this event, gather outside. Roosevelt's words are few but they are well chosen. They echo from the speakers arranged around the perimeter wall, so that even the huge crowd outside can hear his speech. "Athletes participate in these games," he says, "for no recognition other than a simple medal." His sincerity is profound when he adds words that will forever remain with me, "I wish that in these later days, the Olympic ideals of 2800 years ago could be carried out in one further part. In those days, it was the custom every four years to cease all obligations of armies during the period of the games. Can those early Olympic ideals," he asks, almost pleads, "be revived throughout all the world so that we can contribute in a larger measure?" He pauses briefly. The crowd is still and its silence rises like a voiceless prayer, but before his words can suppress the high spirits of the participants or the spectators, Roosevelt smiles and raises his voice to conclude, "And so we are glad to welcome our sister nations as guests of the American people and the State of New York, and I proclaim open the third Olympic Winter Games, celebrating the tenth Olympiad of the modern era."

Bugles blare and cannons roar, directing our attention to the end of the stadium where the white Olympic flag is finally raised. One of the Americans — I can see now that it is Johnny's friend Jack in white hat and white jacket over blue flannel pants — climbs to a wooden platform that workers have quickly set up on the ice in front of the flag bearers. He faces the spectators.

Jack raises his right hand. Every athlete follows suit. Jack swears the oath on behalf of all athletes participating in these games: "We swear that we will take part in the Olympic Games in loyal competition respecting the regulations which govern them and desirous of participating in them in the true spirit of sportsmanship for the honor of our country and for the glory of sport." I close my eyes and remember my *Babcia* and think of my parents, my brother and sisters and all of my friends who will never experience the pride that comes when a person speaks those words: "for the honor of my country." The Games are officially open, and by the end of the day, young Jack will have his first gold medal. I imagine what it might have been like for that very first athlete who ran that very first race on the stadium floor at Olympia nearly 3,000 years ago. No words can describe it. I merely accept that I am a part of his heritage and, as I represent my country, I represent that first runner no less.

The day is too splendid to leave the stadium and the activities that will occur here. My teammates are of the same mind. We have not brought any speed skaters to these games, and the 500-meter heats will begin in just a few minutes. I look in vain for Sonja and conclude that the Captain is right: I do not need the distraction.

I think I have become Johnny's favorite and he waits for me as I walk off the ice with my mates. I signal to him and he follows us to the small bleachers left of the main grandstand; it is reserved for the athletes. Not a single spectator leaves the stands so it is a good thing that special seating is available for the athletes. Even the surrounding hills offer vantage to hundreds of people who were not able to purchase seats inside the stadium. The organizers hope the weather holds true so that the outdoor stadium can accommodate as many events as possible. If the weather turns, the indoor arena to our north is ready.

A Canadian bests Jack Shea in the first heat of the 500-meter race. Jack's second-place finish is still good enough for him to advance, with the top two finishers in the other preliminary heats, to the finals.

"I don't know, Johnny," I say skeptically. "The Canadian looked very strong."

My young friend is not concerned. "Just watch," he replies confidently. "I told you no one can beat Jack Shea. He did what he had to do. Now he will win the final. Those other racers will only see the bottoms of Jack's skates as they toss ice chips into their faces. You'll see."

The boy is right. The speed skating track is 400 meters, so the 500-meter race is just over one lap. Jack explodes from his starting position like a bullet from my father's old *Jagerstutzen*. Each long and fluid step reveals the outlines of powerful thigh muscles through the tight fabric of his skating suit. He increases his lead with every stroke, and in just over 40 seconds, he crosses the finish line two full steps ahead of the second-place Norwegian. The three Canadians and the other American are well behind Jack and the Norwegian. He did make it look easy. While the other skaters lean forward, their hands on their knees, Jack stands straight up and raises his arms above his head. He holds his pose while his momentum carries him another 100 meters. We sit 50 meters beyond the finish line. As he glides past our position, Jack glimpses Johnny and waves to him. Cowbells clang and horns blow random notes, creating a wild cacophony that accompanies Jack for his complete victory lap. I am happy for him and for my friend Johnny whose dreams rode with Jack for those 44 brief but explosive and exciting seconds. The Americans will celebrate their hometown hero's victory for the rest of the day.

The two hockey powerhouses take the ice before a standing room only crowd. Our team will watch. Perhaps the Americans and Canadians will inspire us to play well against the Germans this afternoon.

I have seen our team play many times and I admit that the North Americans play the game with more technical skill than we do. If it is possible, our boys will neutralize the skill and artistry of our opponents with our spirit and desire to win. From the opening whistle, the evenly paired teams stage an entertaining match. The game is scoreless after the first period, but the Americans strike early in the second and manage to hold the goal advantage as the final period gets underway. I credit the American goalkeeper for protecting his net under a constant assault from his northern neighbors. It is inevitable that the Canucks will score and they finally do, but with less than 10 minutes to play. The 1 − 1 score after three periods sends the match into overtime. The Americans catch their second wind and balance the play, but seven minutes into the overtime period, the Canadians break out on a counter-attack and beat the American keeper. The Yanks are understandably disappointed, but the fans in the stadium and those watching from the hillside applaud heartily and show their appreciation for a well-contested match that either team could have won.

"Good game," the Captain says. "I hope we can be as competitive." Our team leaves the stadium for the building that sits behind the main grandstand. There, they will don their uniforms and prepare for their match with the Germans, two hours hence. The other skiers and I wait with the Captain to watch the 5,000-meter races.

Delicious aromas drift our way from the stoves and wood fires set to prepare food and drink for the hungry spectators. The smell of strong coffee cannot completely overpower the sweet smell of hot chocolate.

"I'm hungry," Stashu says to his cousin.

The Captain stands to stretch and lights his pipe. "From the looks of it, there are plenty of good things to tempt your appetites."

"Can we go back to the house?" Stanisław Skupień asks.

"I suppose so, but I think you should return to support our hockey players."

"We will."

"What about you, Bronek?" the Captain asks. "Are you hungry?"

"I am."

"Then let's you and I see what type of food these Americans offer their European brethren."

The area around the stadium is as maze of heavy, pedestrian traffic. The band never stops playing, and automobiles, passing along the main street east of the stadium, raise their celebratory horns to complement the lively march.

Above the music, the cheering, and the crowd chatter we hear the Polish words, "Dzień dobry ci moi bracia! Good day to you my brothers." I turn and see a colorful vending cart with the name "Nathan" printed in large, green letters on a sign attached to the roof. The vendor waves us over, even as he serves two customers, standing with their backs to us. He wipes his hands on his apron and says to his clients, "Excuse me, please. I must say hello to my countrymen."

"Of course, of course," a gentleman says, and when he turns towards us, I recognize him as 'his Excellency.' "Ah, men from Poland," he continues as he acknowledges our uniforms. "Poles like my good friend Nathan here. Best hot dogs in the world. Show them, Eleanor." The woman with him raises her hands to show us two buns, each with a steaming sausage peeking through a mound of bright yellow mustard. "They are quite good," she says and endeavors to hold them away from her body, thus avoiding the mustard that threatens to drip from the sides of the buns. "Franklin and I are quite fond of this particular fare, and often enjoy them in New York City."

"Well, good luck to you, gentleman," Franklin says. "If you can perform as well as Nathan and Ida prepare their hot dogs, you'll have a successful trip. Your names?" he asks and leans forward to listen.

"This is the Captain. He is our leader, and I am Bronisław Czech, a skier and jumper."

"*The* Captain," Roosevelt repeats. With the assistance of his cane, he stands very erect and says, "Quite imposing, sir. You've got the look of my wife's uncle, a bit of a rough-rider, are you?"

"A highlander," the Captain answers.

"Well then, Captain, best of luck to you and your wards."

The Captain bows while I say, "Thank you, your Excellency."

Roosevelt laughs with gusto and dismisses the title with a wave of his hand. "Not hardly. Whoever made that one up needs to rethink his American history. Come now Eleanor, the races will begin shortly." He winks. "I think we'll take another gold medal. Good day to you, highlanders."

As the Roosevelts meld with the crowd, the vendor says, "He's a nice man, the Governor is." The governor and his wife are not the only ones who like Nathan's hot dogs. A line begins to form in front of his cart. "Murray, can you handle this for just a few minutes." A young boy with curly brown hair climbs a box behind the counter and begins to fill orders. His clientele waits without complaint.

"You are Nathan and you are from Poland?" I ask as I point at the sign on top of the cart.

"I am Nathan Handwerker, Schlomo when I came to America as a baby with my mother. She did not speak English, so I grew up learning many languages, Polish, English, German, Hebrew, too. I am a Jew. I am an American citizen now, but I cherish my European roots. While I may not be the first to welcome you to America, I may be among the happiest. I am glad you are here, and I will be cheering for you." Nathan steps outside his cart and hugs us, then firmly shakes hands. "I have a gift for you. Ida and Murray," he shouts back to the cart, "for the duration of these games, free frankfurters and Coca Cola for all Poles. If they are athletes dressed like this or spectators waving the Polish flag, free hot dogs."

"Okay, Papa," Murray answers from his perch on the cart.

"Here," Ida says as she reaches out and hands each of us a frankfurter, then two curved bottles filled with a dark liquid. The Captain eyes the bottle suspiciously and holds it up to the sunlight. Murray laughs from behind the counter.

"It's okay," Nathan says. "It's Coca-Cola and it goes well with the hot dogs." I cautiously dare a sip. The drink is very sweet and it tickles my tongue. I take a larger draught and immediately hiccup.

"More powerful than beer," I comment.

"But no alcohol," Nathan responds.

"Thank you for your kindness and generosity," the Captain says, "but we must return to our seats. The race is about to begin."

"Remember, free frankfurters and Coca-Colas for all Poles. Let your friends know."

I raise my bottle to him. "We will."

The Yanks are strong in the 5000-meter race and take the gold and silver medals. Only a final lunge prevents a sweep as one of the Canadians beats the third American by less than a second.

Our hockey match with the Germans is the day's final event. There is little general interest in the contest and the crowd thins, as spectators leave the stadium for their hotels. Someone calls my name from the small group in the grandstand. Stashu waves from the near empty stands. He and the other skiers sit with *Pan* and *Pani* Bobkowski. There is no reason not to join them, so the Captain, Johnny and I move to the grandstand where we have a better view of the game. The German Olympic team, like ours is few in numbers. In addition to its hockey team, one figure skater and nine bobsledders represent Germany. They too take seats in the grandstand, as do a handful of committee officials who refuse to abandon us. I think the officials are embarrassed that so few people remain to watch the match.

"We could have played this game in Berlin," I whisper to the Captain.

"Come now, Bronek. The opening ceremony alone was worth the trip was it not?" The Captain is right. Few Europeans have made the trip to these games, fewer still from Asia, represented only by Japanese skiers, speed skaters and figure skaters. I should not be surprised and promise myself that I will not allow the world economy to dampen my spirit, or the spirit of these games.

As the teams warm-up on the ice, Nathan comes around the corner with two boxes tied to the sled he drags. He waves and shouts, "Free colas for you and for your German friends." He uses a special key to remove the cap from the bottles and Murray carries them two by two into the stands. He hands one to each German, most donned in their knickers and heavy wool sweaters. Johnny skips down and asks Nathan if he can help Murray. "Of course you can!" the jovial Pole responds. War may soon erupt on the ice, but those of us in the grandstand remain brothers-in-arms as we share our Coca-Cola.

After the players are announced, the band plays each team's national anthem. We Poles are not bashful, and stand and sing quite loudly so that the people on Main Street will know who we are. We are engaged in friendly competition with the Germans to see who can sing louder, though not necessarily better. We applaud their efforts and they, ours in return. The musicians place their instruments in their black cases and leave, all save a lone accordion player who decides to stay. His nimble fingers make lively tunes, enticing the sun to remain for the duration of our match. The accordionist is a master and keeps us happy with polkas and German drinking songs, until the opening whistle sounds and the referee drops the puck. The game is on.

For the opening 20 minutes, our goaltender, Józef Stogowski is under siege. We take some comfort when the first period ends scoreless. The truth is, however, if it wasn't for the tremendous play of Józef, we could easily be trailing by several goals. We know it, the team knows it and undoubtedly, the Germans know it. Their confidence grows with each shot. If we had three chances on goal, the Germans had 15. Józef removes his cap between periods and when he shakes his head, beads of sweat fly from his disheveled hair. He is tired and working very hard, but his poise matches the Germans' confidence. I catch his eye and raise my thumb. He actually winks at me as if to say he has the game under control.

The accordion player must favor us – not because he is Polish, which he may be – but because people love to cheer those fellows who continue to fight with their backs against the wall. He plays only polkas during the break, I suppose to help keep our spirits high and our wits about us.

"What is your name?" I shout to him.

"Ernie," he shouts back.

"Keep playing, Ernie," I yell.

For whatever reason Ernie plays his polkas, the result is favorable. We remain very much in this game.

However, disaster strikes faster than a snake. If a spectator had diverted his attention for just an instant, he would have missed it. At the second period face off, the puck flies backward to the German defender. The forwards race up the wings, and the center player and off defender join them. Our forwards rush the defender with the puck. In a single, deft move, he slides the puck between them and the Germans quickly have a numerical advantage in their attacking third. One touch right to the forward behind the net, and a quick pass to the charging center who deftly raises the puck quickly and accurately above Józef's wide goal tending stick. Bang, bang, bang, bang, bang. Five touches, and just 12 seconds into the second period, we trail by a goal. Józef rises from his split and slams his blade to the ice. He blames no one but himself, however he received little support from his teammates, who seemed as frozen as ice sculptures while the Germans easily maneuvered the puck around them. Józef's outburst is instantaneous and short-lived. I focus on him because he is the oldest member of our team and he will set the mental attitude of his teammates. He takes the responsibility very seriously. While the few spectators who remain watch the German celebration, I see Józef wipe his brow with the back of his over-sized glove, adjust his pads and re-set himself firmly in front of his net. Our team gathers around him.

Whatever it is he says, the message is not lost on his mates for when the game resumes, our team attacks the ice with the ferocity the North Americans displayed in the previous match. Our pace quickens with new commitment, and we put the Germans back on their heels as we skate purposefully and powerfully, moving the puck into the attacking third.

"Credit to Józef," the Captain says to me. "He is one of those rare athletes who refuses to lose."

As the clock moves into the 11th minute, Aleksander Kowalski slams into the German skater carrying the puck, and sends him over the meter-high wall. The Germans scream for a penalty, but the Canadian referee denies their plea and waves the play on. With no hesitation, Aleksander kicks the puck forward with his skate and charges the German net with no defenders before him, save the brawny goalkeeper. Alek fakes once to his left, then to his right. With a pair of defenders in pursuit, he spins a full 360-degrees and emerges from the maneuver with a forceful shot that rises over the keeper's right shoulder and slams into the corner of the netting.

The street traffic hears our raucous celebration and chimes in with cowbells and whistles. The game is tied at a goal apiece. The war is on. As the Germans mill about the ice, the skater who was checked over the wall, climbs back onto the rink and moves toward Alek with fire in his eyes. As the celebration wanes, and our team gathers behind our goal scorer, the Germans circle us like a swarm of angry wasps. The American referee blows his whistle, decisively summoning the skaters back to center ice.

The final ten minutes of the second period are brutal and the referees frequently blow their whistles to stop play. Three Germans find themselves in the penalty box during the closing minutes of the period, but we cannot break through. With a handful of seconds remaining and both teams at full strength, Kaz Sokołowski is whistled for high-sticking and directed to the empty penalty box. With blood flowing freely from his nose, he questions the referee's decision. I think Kaz is right; he raised his stick in self-defense. The ref ignores him, and we'll start the third, and final period a man down, Józef and our four skaters will battle their six.

As a young man, I loved my history lessons above all other studies, but I was not very good with numbers. I have a fondness for Greek mythology and remember that even the great Zeus, king of the gods, was subject to the power of the three fates. I've learned that fate can be cruel, and so it is on this late afternoon in February. With Kaz in the penalty box, Włod Krygier stands at center ice to take the face off. The numerical advantage is with the Germans, and all five take forward positions, confident that their net minder will not be threatened, for at least the opening two minutes of this final period. And so, they are taken by surprise when Włod grabs the puck and drives through his opponent, as if he weren't there at all. We cheer and collectively hold our breath. There is no way any German player can catch him. He has a clear path to goal. With a full head of steam, and not more than 10 meters from the net, Włod loses his balance and falls forward. He watches as the puck slides harmlessly to the German goalkeeper who slaps it quickly to his teammate well up the ice on his left.

The five German skaters assault our net like a wolf pack drunk on the scent of blood, and our three standing skaters chase them with little hope they can stay the attack. Józef parries a pair of lightning quick shots. He extends his right leg as far as possible to block the third, but we watch as the puck caroms off his ankle, turning end over end and continues its flight toward the net. Józef waves his glove at it but misses. The German skaters and their followers raise their arms as the black puck falls painfully across the line and tumbles slowly to the back of the net. I check the clock: less than a minute has transpired and we are down a goal. Our spirits fall with the sun as it dips below the mountains and dusk creeps silently over the stadium ice. Józef continues to battle valiantly and will not allow another goal, but our skaters are tired. Two more earn costly rest time in the penalty box, while the Germans remain at full strength for the remainder of the contest. When the final whistle blows, we are on the short end of the score line of a game we all believe we had to win. There is little doubt, the Americans and Canadians bring more speed, strength and technical ability to the ice than either us or the Germans.

The game was physical and brutal, but the contestants shake hands and exchange only words of praise. There is no lack of respect on either side. Several of our players leave the ice with heads bowed, but not Józef. He keeps his head held high and exhorts his teammates to follow his example.

Józef is disappointed – no doubt – but he also understands he faces five more games in the coming 10 days.

"Take a lesson from our flag bearer," the Captain tells me as we leave the grandstand. "Józef refuses to lose, but no man can avoid defeat. When victory escapes you, think of Józef. He understands it is okay to lose as long as he does so with dignity. Look at him now. Józef looks and acts like a winner. Because he does, he is a winner." I promise myself I will remember the Captain's words and carry the image of Józef with me.

Chapter Ten, 1932

Moonshine

I suspect God cares little for ice hockey, and I think he gives little notice to other athletic endeavors as well. He enjoys them and is pleased that sport brings value to our lives, but his concerns are grander than these Olympic Games. He takes as much pleasure in two children who play catch as he does in Jack Shea, or any other man who competes at these games. We lost, by a respectable three-goal margin, 1 – 4, to the Americans on Friday. Józef was tough as nails, and Adam scored our lone goal, a blistering crack from a dozen meters that I don't think the American goalkeeper so much as glimpsed, but, alas, his tally was far too little and way too late. On this early Sunday morning, we walk to St. Agnes Church and attend Mass as a team.

As we leave the warm confines of the church following the service, the Marusarz boys share their prayers. "I prayed that we will beat the Canadians," Andrzej tells his cousin.

Stashu is more realistic and more specific. Quietly so no one can hear, Stashu responds, "I don't think we can win. I prayed that we stay within three goals and can make it a match."

"I think you are more reasonable," Andrzej agrees. "Maybe I wasted my prayer."

I am now certain God cares little for ice hockey. My revelation comes in the wake of our afternoon match; the Canadians blank us nine goals to zero.

At the Switzerland games, the athletes attended several dinners and events hosted by the Olympic Committee. The financial mayhem the planet faces in 1932, demands moderation. In Lake Placid, the committee invites us to a single, social affair, a tea at the main club across the lake where – according to Johnny – the 'rich people live.' After the shellacking we take at the hands of the Canadians, we tell the Captain we have no desire to attend the gathering. The Captain bobs his head in contemplation, as the familiar thin wisp of white smoke rises from his pipe bowl to fill Mrs. Jordan's sitting room. I am fond of the new aroma created by the blend of the smoke with the scent of book leather and musty pages. "So," he finally says, "Are we all agreed, then that Poland has been so humbled in a game played on skates that we cannot keep our heads raised proudly and say, 'Yes, we are Poland?'"

The 'tick-tock' of the cuckoo clock is the only sound and the rising smoke from the Captain's pipe, the only movement in the room.

"Nonsense." It is Józef. "I will go with you, Captain," he says, "and I am the goat who allowed nine goals!" We laugh. "Could I have played better?" he asks. "Maybe, but when I took the ice, I wanted to win no less than those Canucks. They are a great team and I credit them for their win, but I played as hard as I can, and I believe they respect me for that as well. I find no shame in the loss. Our history as Poles is long, but we are a new nation and it is important we participate in a friendly way with the other nations of the world. Poland made that decision when it attended the first games in '24. We are here to celebrate our membership in the international community. Losing a game will not deter me from showing my colors at this event. The rest of you can stay here and sulk if you want, but I prefer some friendly conversation to the monotony of the cuckoo's call." With that, Józef dons his cap and walks out the door followed closely by the Captain and me. The rest are quick to follow.

"I will have cocoa for you when you return," Mrs. Jordan calls after us, as she closes the door.

The hosts try to create a semblance of European elegance, but it is difficult for the Americans to shed their cowboy image, and, to me, not necessary. There is history in the great northern forests of America, but it is brief and there are few people to share it with. It seems to me that the entire European continent is a series of towns and villages, one after the other, some large, most small, but all connected by roads, paths, rail lines and waterways. Here in this northern tier of America, one can travel for miles and miles without encountering a town or village. I cannot help be reminded of the wide-open spaces that Zane Grey writes about and that we saw in the picture show we attended when we arrived. As far as I can tell, the only difference between the 'Wild West' as they call it and the northern tier is the trees. As I read about it in books and see it in pictures, the American West is an open, vast desert with high, rugged mountains, a landscape I have not experienced; as I see it in Lake Placid, the American North is a forest. Regardless of where in this vast country you may reside, the carefree, cowboy attitude permeates American society beyond the confines of the big cities like New York. Hence, we meet at the Lake Placid Club not in formal attire, like we did in St. Moritz, but in our sweaters, our knickers and our boots.

The Club is a series of buildings, some large, none small. Roads, paths, stairways and hallways connect this confusing labyrinth. The Zakopane style hides transparently behind the façade as exposed cedar beams hover above us and wood planks cover the floors and walls. Even though I know this club exists for 'the rich,' I am comfortable here. It is not unique to me. Even a poor Pole in Zakopane has a home in this style, only smaller.

The center of activity is in a very large room that manages to accommodate all the athletes and dignitaries. Stairways rise to balconies that surround this great room, and at least two libraries, furnished with large, plush leather chairs afford some privacy for intimate conversation. 'Adams's Albany Empire State Band' plays from a stage at the far end of the room and its music wafts about us. Adam announces his next song as "Buffalo Gals." I like it. I see only smiling, happy faces, and I am glad I came. My Captain is right: there are no losers here. In no time, Józef and a Canadian player embrace. Alek and the Hun he sent flying over the boards, soon join them. They will compete again later this week, but at this moment, they are friends. They make light of the aggressive and violent nature of their sport and the seriousness with which each plays it.

I meander through the crowd to the large bar staffed by no fewer than six tenders. As we learned on the ship, no liquor in America, no legal liquor, that is. One of our hockey players has learned that the locals manufacture a strong drink. They call it moonshine because they brew it secretly, in the light of the moon. The Captain advises against it, but gazing at the 30-foot mirror behind the bar, I see an occasional flask passed covertly through the crowd. I think it is moonshine. A stuffed moose head stares stoically from the wall above the mirror, probably alert for any authority that might be about in search of the bootlegged drink. Frankly, since Nathan introduced me to it, I have become partial to Coca-Cola, so the absence of alcohol is of no consequence to me.

I think the moose, fish and the other stuffed animals hanging on the walls are the only emotionless objects in this boisterous room. I scan the mirror again and this time, spot the reflection of my Czechoslovakian friend Antonín Bartoň. He sees me and points to one of the wide stairways where we meet to shake hands and embrace.

"How are you, brother," I ask, "and what do you make of all this?"

"I think this is wonderful," he says with obvious pleasure. "I was so afraid the immensity of America would overshadow these Games, but in this small town, that is not the case. Not that different from your own Zakopane, no?"

"Even the architecture," I add, then change the subject. "So where do you and your teammates stay?"

"Not far from here. A small but comfortable cottage just to the north of the pond by the railroad station. We are only six, plus our coaches, so it is fine."

A server walks by with a full tray of Coca-Cola. We each take one and tap our bottles together. "May luck be with you, my friend when our paths cross later this week, in competition," he says.

A heavy hand takes my shoulder, but gently. "It's the friend of the Polish Roughrider, or more accurately, the highlander. Bronisław, if I remember correctly. Enjoying yourself, son?"

"I am, sir," I answer the individual introduced at the ceremonies as 'Excellency,' the Governor of New York. I like this man. I find nothing 'regal' about him. He moves through the crowd without an air of importance, only a simple and humble sophistication, happy to greet everyone he meets, and quick to remember little facts about each.

"And who is your friend, Bronisław?" He leans forward for a better look at the small flag embroidered on the left breast of Antonín's sweater. "Hmmm," he ponders, "Not a Pole. Ah, yes, the red, white and the blue triangle of Czechoslovakia, a nation rich in history, yet new in international recognition. Welcome to America, my friend." He extends his hand to Antonín who grasps it firmly.

"Antonín Bartoň, may I present our host, the Governor of the State of New York."

"And you boys know one another? One from Poland, the other from Czechoslovakia." the Governor asks.

"For many years, now," I say. "We chanced to meet on a mountaintop in the Carpathians that serve as a border for our countries. I skied my first race against this man."

"And who won?" the Governor asks in a playful way.

"He did," we both say. The Governor appreciates our camaraderie and laughs heartily.

I put my arm around Antonín's shoulders and say with great respect and sincerity, "Honestly, sir, my friend was the greatest racer that day. Early in the race and very high on the mountain, I fell and broke my leg. This man stopped, put me on his back and carried me to the bottom of the mountain."

"He's as much your hero as he is your friend, then?"

"He is, sir, he and my Captain." As I answer, I feel the miniscule weight of the *hamsa* that hangs beneath my shirt and recall most vividly that day when it was lost, then found.

"This man needs no heroes," a beguiling, feminine voice interrupts us, and Sonja, dressed to the nines, boldly but effortlessly enters our private circle.

"Oh my goodness," the Governor exclaims, taking a small step backwards. "This woman is genuine royalty and needs no introduction. It is my honor to meet you at last, Miss Henie. With all due respect to my friends from Poland and Czechoslovakia, I believe you to be the star of these games and certainly the belle of this ball."

Sonja reaches up, and taking hold of his lapel, pulls the Governor closer. "Please, Franklin," she says and then adds quite coyly, "I can call you Franklin, can't I?" Her eyes sparkle. "Of course I can," she answers her question before he can say a word. "Please stay close. I'm hiding." The three of us glance up cautiously, as if holding some great state secret amongst us. "Yes, I'm hiding, hiding from those awful Italians who seem to think they are so very special. Where does that attitude come from? Caesar? On the other hand, maybe the Pope? They follow me like lapdogs." We are quite taken aback, but humored nonetheless at this young girl's brashness. "No, no," she corrects herself, "It is neither Caesar nor the Pope. It is that dreadful Mussolini." Sonja certainly is maturing into a woman of great confidence, and it shows as much in her out-spoken demeanor as it does in her vibrant personality. While the Governor appears humored, the stunned look remains etched on Antonín's face.

The Governor smiles, and in a fatherly way, takes her hand and says, "I regret to tell you, my dear, but I am obliged to maintain neutrality in these matters. I find no fault with the Italians, neither with Caesar nor with the Pope. Regardless, while I will gladly give you safe harbor from their worshipful adoration, I think it better if our mutual friend, Bronisław, from the great nation of Poland, take you for a whirl upon the dance floor."

Sonja raises her expectant eyes to mine, removes the cola bottle from my hand and gives it to Antonín. "Wonderful advice, Franklin," she says. "Shall we, Bronek?" I am as handcuffed as a Zane Grey bandit but am glad to be the prisoner of such a beautiful captor. I am no dancer and fortunately, the 'Empire State Band' slows the beat to an easy, rhythmical tune that will not challenge my limited dancing skills. Sonja, on the other hand, is known for her deftness and agility on the ice, and I pray that my clumsiness will not offend her. She pulls me close as we move comfortably to the lilting voice of the singer,

> *"Embrace me, my sweet embraceable you.*
> *Embrace me, my irreplaceable you.*
> *Just to look at you my heart grows tipsy in me.*
> *You and you alone bring out the gypsy in me."*

The lyrics embarrass me, particularly when I become uncomfortably aware of the fact the other dancers have left the floor to Sonja and me. All eyes are on us, admiration in some, jealousy in others. My emotions run amok and I want to play ostrich again, but my honor will not allow it. As the song ends, the guests in the room applaud and the singer extends her arms toward us and says, "Ladies and gentlemen, Miss Sonja Henie." Even as I think 'what about me,' the Governor takes the microphone and says, "And her capable partner Mr. Bronisław Czech from Poland." In front of 400 people, Sonja stands on her toes and kisses my cheek. My temperature rises 10 degrees and my face is as red as a beet.

Nearly lost in the shadows cast from the dim light in the library, the Captain watches me. He shows no emotion. I recall his advice at the stadium three days prior. "You are here to ski," he told me. He is right. I must break the spell the Norwegian girl has cast upon me. I am no different than the others, I think. She is the three sirens in a single, beautiful body with the power to lure me to Charybdis.

Her perfume intoxicates me as I kiss her cheeks. "Thank you, Sonja," I say and then add, with some finality, "But I must go."

"You can't," she says, "Not now." Sonja places her palm on my chest, and, through the fabric of my clothes, she fondles the *hamsa*. Then, I remember. Four years ago as I lay on my back gasping for breath at the base of the jump in St. Moritz, Sonja's face drifted behind the Captain's. She remembers, too, and the vision flees when she cocks her head and quizzically whispers, "Jew?" I shake my head 'no.' "It doesn't matter," she says. I shake my head again, step backward, turn and leave.

The week of my competition finally arrives. I will race on Wednesday and jump Thursday and Friday. Physically, I am ready, but psychologically, I have never been as distracted as I am now, and the perpetrator is the Norwegian. I have stayed active on the many trails that surround the lakes, and also on the 30-meter hill next to the Stadium, where we practice our jumping while crews work feverishly to prepare the Intervales Hill for the Thursday's competition. Intervales is about three kilometers south of the village, a healthy walk from Mrs. Jordan's house, but I decide to visit the jump to help keep my mind focused. Johnny often accompanies me and insists that he carry my skis "just for practice" he says. The first trek was awkward and comical, as I slowed my pace so this small boy could feel that he was making a valuable contribution to my efforts. Now, after several trips, Johnny wields my gear with ease.

Automobiles and pedestrian traffic continue to crowd the streets. The men's figure skating began yesterday and concludes today, Tuesday. As the men complete their competition, the women begin theirs.

Johnny nods toward the Arena as we walk by and asks, "Have you been inside?"

"Once," I answer, "to watch a practice session. It is huge."

"No empty seats today," Johnny comments. "A mouse couldn't get in without a ticket. People love the figure skating, and they love that girl from Norway."

"Have you seen her?" I ask. He nods, 'yes' without looking at me. "Do you think she's pretty?" He nods again and tries unsuccessfully to hide his broad smile. I continue to torture myself with thoughts of this girl. Am I that undisciplined that I cannot focus on the reason I am here? I snatch a handful of snow from the top of a railing and spread it across my face. Johnny thinks I'm crazy.

Antonín and I first met high in the Tatras in the summer of 1923, and our paths crossed again the following winter in Zakopane. Sport has brought us together again a full continent and an entire ocean away from the comfort of our homelands. I suspect we have not spent more than several hours together since that first time we met. Much of that time, I was incoherent as he lugged me with my broken leg down the drift-covered mountain. Still, I feel as if we have been friends through our entire lives, and that is why it is so easy for me to refer to him as 'brother.' Today we ski with the hope that the countless hours, we have expended in preparation for this race, will be rewarded by a worthy effort.

It is Ash Wednesday. It surprises me how few people are willing to interrupt their activities to take ashes. The church echoes its emptiness when the Marusarz boys and I enter for early morning Mass. Antonín kneels in the last pew. We exchange no words, but each knows the other is there.

I learned on that mountainside in '23 that Antonín is a man of strength: physical strength, mental strength, and spiritual strength. Other than his teammates, few know him at these games. With their long and storied history in the skiing competitions, the Swedes, the Finns and the Norwegians are the heavy favorites. They are such strong skiers that even an event is named for them, the Nordic Combined. No one gives much notice to the rest of us. Because I skied and jumped in St. Moritz, the competition knows me – and also, no doubt, due to my time on the dance floor with Miss Henie – but no one knows Antonín, nor do they know the great strength and endurance that he brings to the hills.

New snow blankets Lake Placid, but the sky is clear and blue when we assemble in the stadium. Today is my first event, the 18-kilometer cross-country race, the short race. Over 60 skiers from 11 nations will participate. An odd thought hits me as I scan the competition and see several Japanese skiers. Where are the Mexicans? This is America. If they came to Switzerland, why would they not come to the United States? The question does not beg an answer. Temperatures remain unseasonably high, so I expect the course to be slow and sluggish, and void of the icy dangers that plagued the course in St. Moritz. We drew our numbers on Sunday and I will be starting the race just two positions ahead of Antonín. Racers set out at one-minute intervals.

When the Captain, my teammates and I enter the stadium with Johnny in tow, Antonín sits on the bottom row of the bleachers. His posture is very erect; he is alone and breathes deeply and thoughtfully, his eyes fixed on some virgin point in the mountains, while his mind envisions the race he will ski. I leave him to his mental preparation.

A somewhat listless crowd gathers in the stadium, disappointed, no doubt that they were unable to acquire tickets to watch the women figure skaters in the arena next to the stadium. This event is their alternative. The real excitement of a cross-country event often takes place on the trail, deep in the forest. The spectator will only glimpse the initial and final rushes of the contest, deprived of the drama that occurs between the start and the finish. While our pace is steady and graceful, it lacks the creativity the women will display in the arena, with their daring jumps, twists, turns and spins. I will admit figure skating can be quite exciting and beautiful.

No man here has the advantage of practice on the course we ski today, not even the Americans. Last night after dinner, we gathered in Mrs. Jordan's sitting room and waited patiently for our Captain who attended the pre-race meeting. He returned late with maps of the course we will run this morning. They call it the Mt. Whitney course for the obvious reason that we will race in the shadow of that mountain. Northeast of the village, it rises some 800 meters. "The race will be won on this mountain," the Captain explained as the fire danced and crackled behind him. "This race belongs to the skier who has the strength to attack the mountain without regard to the pain his legs may feel, as he begins the ascent for, he knows that the descent will lead him back to the finish line." I did not sleep much last night, but it will be enough. I have memorized the map, every turn, every rise and every fall I will face through all 18 kilometers. I am ready.

The race begins, and the starter releases a skier from the gate every 60 seconds. As my position approaches, I stand and stretch, then step onto my skis. I twist, turn and bend to stretch the bindings in all directions with as much stress as I am able to exert. I know the course will push my equipment to its limit, well beyond what I can do here on this flat surface, but this stationary test will suffice. I punch my gloved fists together, satisfied we are one, my equipment and I. My skis will serve me well.

"Attack the mountain, Bronek, but don't be lazy on the downhill runs," the Captain passes his final words of advice and pats my back as I step up to the starting line.

"Ready, son?" the official asks while he stares at his watch. Whether or not he sees me nod, he smiles in return. When he looks up, I see the ashes on his forehead. "Get set," he says and begins his reverse count, "ten, nine, eight..." I work to control my heart rate. "Three, two, one, GO!"

My first stride is long and powerful. My poles bite the snow-covered ground and my arms pull me forward for added speed and momentum. The crowd roars its approval and I realize, while I was lost in my preparation and concentration, more and more spectators have arrived, filling the stadium to its 6,000 seat capacity. Excitement and anticipation replace the earlier apathy. *"Powodzenia, bracie!* Good luck, brother!"* I recognize Nathan's voice as he shouts above the crowd noise.

The first three kilometers take us east of Mirror Lake to a small pond identified on the map as Cherry Patch. As we leave the stadium, we climb an easy slope for a kilometer, then descend the next two toward the pond. With the sounds of Lake Placid behind me, I set my pace and rhythm when I reach Cherry Patch, and then move into the solitude of the woods behind the club. The brooks and streams that babble softly in the summer months are mute now and lie buried beneath this deep blanket of snow. No one changes positions in this early part of the race. We are content to maintain pace knowing we face a moderate climb when our route turns to the west and to another small pond, they call Mud Pond. The early stage of each race brings me great peace. My heart has yet to begin its pounding beat, and my muscles are still loose and comfortable. A raven calls like a chanting monk and jays cackle wildly as they congregate in the trees near the pond. The American Jays are larger than those that populate Poland, and their plumage lacks the brown in our species. A skier notes these things during his many hours in the forest. They dispel the monotony of the journey, comfort him and divert the skier's attention from the ache that grows into pain in the latter stages of the race.

This frozen pond, now blanketed by deep snow, is merely an open space in the woods. As I approach it, a wooden sign marked with a bold, black arrow directs me to turn left. Of course, I don't need the placard: the trail blazed by the men who precede me is clear enough to follow. No sounds before me; no sounds behind.

I ski west for two kilometers and climb 100 meters, then turn back northeast, into the snow-clad pines that present a white, inviting tunnel. Before I enter the forest, I glimpse Mt. Whitney, the highest point of the course. I easily negotiated the initial climb, and this next short leg slopes downhill. I slow my breathing in the descent where each stride carries me five to 10 meters. Other skiers are apt to glide on these down sloped and let gravity move them forward. The Captain teaches us to attack these downhill runs with the same intensity that we attack the mountains. Still no sounds behind me, but I can hear the faint 'schuss' of another pair of skis before me. I am gaining ground. The land rises before me and I heed the Captain's advice. With seven kilometers behind me, I know if I am to win this race, I will do it on this mountain over the next six kilometers that climb more than 250 meters. The path is steeper than the course in Switzerland, but there is no ice. I will herringbone if I must, but I will not resort to sidestepping. Either will kill my pace and momentum, and destroy any advantage I may be attaining. I feel very strong, and I continue to pump my legs like a locomotive and use my arms to pull and push me forward and upward. I will not allow this mountain to steal my strength.

I charge up the slope – not the steepest I will encounter – that takes me to the East Bay of Lake Placid itself. As I do, I glimpse the back of the first man I will overtake. No wait; there are two of them. I will catch them both over the next kilometer before turning south toward Mt. Whitney.

They are halfway up this slope, and already struggle with the herringbone. Both resort to sidestepping. Their day is finished, I think. One hundred meters short of the top, I move into deep drifts to pass them. The snow is heavy and tries to impede my progress, but my objective is clear. I increase my pace and clear them in five strides. One is an Italian, the other a Frenchman. *"Bonne chance!"* I say. Neither responds. I leave them and charge down the short slope that heralds the climb up Mt. Whitney. I reach to my soul and gather my wits and the strength to face this mountain that craves to defeat each skier who dares climb it.

Stashu started the race at least five places in front of me, but as I move up the hill, I recognize his voice as he hums an old and familiar Polish melody. My strides are longer than his are and I soon pass him. "I'm thinking of Poland," he says cheerfully. "That is a good thing to think of," I respond. "For Poland," I say. "For Poland," he answers and I move through the clearing and back into the woods.

One kilometer short of the highest point of the race, the slope steepens sharply and my momentum dies. I disregard the pain in my calves and thighs and concede that I will not conquer the incline unless I switch to the herringbone. Someone calls out, "I'm coming, Bronek. Don't let me catch you." I don't have to turn around. It is Antonín. "You are slowing down," he says, louder as he closes the distance between us. I do not want to waste my waning energy on words. I will my legs to move faster, but to no avail, I can work no harder. Antonín is the stronger man this day. He slips by me and when he does, I see that, for every step I take, he takes two. I try to match his movements and it does help me some. When we reach the top of the slope, I am but a few paces behind. He disappears and I follow him over the edge. I leave my pain behind me. The steep slope on the trail down reminds me of my first race in Zakopane. I caution myself: no flying in this race. I use my poles to propel me forward even faster, and the distance between us closes. We pass two Americans, a Nipponese and a Canadian. They ski in a tight group and proceed cautiously down the treacherous backside of the mountain. Less than four kilometers to the Stadium, we pass a large water tank and the angle of the slope decreases.

My continuous poling returns its dividends as I creep closer to Antonín, then unexpectedly, his binding breaks! He topples, and one ski flies from his boot, skidding like a flat rock on water, toward the trees in front of us. The wayward ski comes to rest in a bramble of fallen trees 30 meters down the trail.

"I'm fine," he calls out. "I'll see you at the Stadium." As I pass him, my mind evokes the day of my first race in Zakopane when I lay in the deep snow, high on a mountain with a broken leg. Can I possibly continue this race and leave him? What if his leg is broken? I work quickly to retrieve his ski and I return it to him as he pulls a spare leather strap from his small backpack. "Don't be stupid, Bronek," he says. "You are losing time."

"I'd rather be stupid than to leave a man in trouble. I'd rather lose time and a race, than a friend. For me to leave now would be to betray you. Are you hurt?"

"No," he answers. "I just need to rebind." The tone of his voice carries many colors: disgust for the mishap; disappointment that I stopped; but pride and pleasure that our friendship means so much to me that I would lose this race to help him. I throw my gloves to the ground and we rebind the ski. The Americans are closing on us. Antonín is ready in less than 60 seconds. I salute him and am off before the Americans reach the clearing.

The final kilometers cross level ground. Antonín and I trade places one time, but ski side by side, as we approach the finish line at the Stadium. I move as fast as my tired body allows me. I watch Antonín from the corner of my eye and wonder if he is trying as hard as he can, or does he defer the finish line to me because I stopped to help him? I slow to see what he will do. He slows when I slow, and increases his speed when I increase mine. His objective is no longer a secret to me. Strange, yet wonderful, the power of friendship and the way it moves men to react in such noble ways. After all, what will matter most in an old man's life? The medals he's won or the friends he's made and preserved through the best and worst of times? Can a man who has friends be called a failure?

Cowbells clang and horns blow when the large crowd that returned to the Stadium sees us approach. Onlookers cheer for both of us. We hold pace and position and I cross the line a step ahead of my friend. That is how it is meant to be.

The Canadians embarrass our hockey team in the re-match. We don't score a single goal, and we play Swiss cheese defense and watch as the Canucks strike for 10 goals. Even our opponents are sadly surprised at the ease of their victory. Because only four teams compete in the event, we play Germany again on Saturday with the bronze medal at stake. Can you believe it? We lose a game by 10 goals and we are still in medal contention. Lucjan says we cannot play worse. He is probably right, so he takes the boys out to a secret club in the woods where he's been told he can get each of his players a stiff drink of moonshine. Maybe this is what they need.

I am tempted to return to the Arena to watch the con-clusion of the women's figure skating. After yesterday's mandatory figures, Sonja firmly controls the competition. This evening's free figures attracts a capacity crowd while other well-wishers wait outside the Arena for the results. I jump tomorrow and decide it is best for me to concen-trate on my own tasks rather than Sonja's. In three short days, Motyka and Skupień face the grueling 50-kilometer course. My jumping partners and the racers retire soon after Mrs. Jordan feeds us another satisfying dinner. I linger a bit longer.

The fire burns slowly in the sitting room, and a single lamp barely disturbs the warm and comfortable darkness that fills the corners. The Captain sits angled toward the fireplace in a heavily cushioned chair. Like ghostly fingers, smoke rises from his pipe bowl. A book sits on his lap but he certainly can't read it by firelight alone, and the shaded lamp is too far away to offer much help. Too exhausted to sleep, I relax in a wooden rocking chair at the opposite end of the hearth; worn from years of steady use, it groans softly as I lower myself to the seat.

"You will never win, you know," the Captain says with casual finality. I turn my eyes towards him. He draws on his pipe and fills the room with the sweet aroma of black cherry. "I know what happened on the course today." When I don't respond, he asks, "Is winning important to you, Bronek?"

I place my elbow on the rocker's arm, put my chin in my hand and stare into the glowing embers. For the first time in my life, I struggle to answer. He rises to place another log on the fire and then returns to his chair.

"But there are things of greater importance?" he suggests. I nod my head. "But not the girl?" he adds.

"No, my Captain," I answer, "But not the girl." I move the logs with the iron poker and watch the sparks fly up the chimney, like a swarm of frightened fireflies.

"No," he concludes, "You will never win," then clarifies, "You will never win a race, that is, and neither will your friend."

Mrs. Jordan turns out the kitchen light, and comes in to say, "I'm turning in for the night. You raced well today. Leave that light on for your teammates. I think they'll have difficulties enough when they return, and a dark house won't help them."

"Good night, Madam," the Captain says. "You have been too kind to us." She flaps her apron at us and retires to the bed she's made for herself in the pantry, allowing us the use of her personal bedroom.

"You and that boy from Czechoslovakia. Not so different from your Father and me. By God, he could ski, your Father." His eyes glisten with the reflection from the dancing flames that now rise to consume the new logs the Captain has offered them.

"When did you conclude that I will never win?" I ask as my rocking chair creaks with age.

"Many years ago."

"Then why am I on this team?"

"The simple answer? Because you are the best skier in Poland. You earned your spot on the team in '28, and you earned your spot on this team. I believe you'll be here in '36 as well. Beyond that? I think it unlikely."

"Fair enough," I say. I take no offense. "And the not so simple answer?"

He leans forward, taps his pipe on the large, iron ball atop the andiron, then sits back, and refills it. "You are on this team because you are the type of man that all Poles should strive to be. You live with a lust for life. That is obvious every time you strap skis to your boots and take to the mountains. You don't need to be in a race. You do it for the simple reason that you love the Tatras and you love the sport. If all men could take your example and not only appreciate creation, but also take an active part in it ... I think life would be grand. Most importantly, you recognize there are things more meaningful to a man, than a medal or a prize won in a race or on a jumping hill.

"Would you be here and on this team if you were not the best? Possibly not, but because you are and because of the manner in which you represent Poland, I am honored as a compatriot that you wear our colors at the Olympic Games.

"To win, you must cherish winning above all other things and you must be willing to sacrifice more than your time and body to the sport. You do not, Bronek, and you cannot. Nor can your friend. If you did, you would not trade victory to help your fallen comrade with his broken binding. Think about this, Bronek." He points the stem of his pipe at me. "When all is said and done, you and your friend will be in the top 10 Nordic competitors at these games. Consider what your position might have been had you not stopped to help him today."

"Are you telling me I have the wrong attitude?" I ask.

"No, you have the right attitude. Take no offense, Bronek. I find no fault with your choice. Your action today on the course is a greater victory than the gold medal. Few know what you did, fewer recognize why. Trust that I do, just as your friend does, and I am pleased to sit here in this room on this night and share your triumph proudly and quietly with you. Victory in life is defined by more than medals and championships. You may have first learned that, the day you fell and broke your leg. In that first race, when you were just a boy, and another boy, one you hardly knew, exchanged his chance to win for an opportunity to help a fallen comrade. You both have my enduring respect. No, Bronek. I'll never question your attitude. It is sound and it is inspiring."

The cuckoo announces 9:00 p.m.

"Do you know why I walk with this limp?" he asks.

I have known the Captain all my life and it has never occurred to me why he limps. I take my father's advice and ask this man no questions. We all know he was once a great skier. In Zakopane, every conversation about skiing includes the Captain. He has always been on the mountains, and he has always walked with his limp. We take his limp for granted and give it no notice. He is the Captain, and that is the way the Captain walks.

"When I was a young man," he reminisces, "I loved to ski and jump no less than you do, no less than your Father did. We were proud highlanders and when we did not work our farms, we spent our time in the mountains, throwing ourselves at the steepest slopes and the highest jumps. We loved the snow and had no fear of the cold. We had no games like these Olympic Games, but during the winter months, we often roamed the mountains in search of others like us who shared our love of the sport. We challenged them in friendly competition. Those were wonderful times for us. We did not ski for notoriety or prizes. We skied because we loved it and it was as natural for us as walking.

"But that changed when I was not much older than you are now." He draws thoughtfully on his pipe.

"Before Father Józef came to our church, an old Russian priest served us well and faithfully. His name was Kazimierza. He was humble of heart and lived his life in poverty, not in spirit, mind you, but only in body. Father Kazimierza was plagued with a cough that never failed to erupt, sometimes violently during his sermons. His church, like his small room was never properly heated in the winter and his cassock too thin to ward off the cold. Pneumonia mercifully took him the year before you were born. Father Kazimierza first voiced the improbable thought of raising a cross to Christ on the summit of Giewont."

During the race as I passed by Mt. Whitney, I thought of Giewont today. This New York 'mountain' is but a hill, dwarfed by Giewont and the Tatras. Of course, that failed to make the challenge any less difficult.

"You see that giant cross today, and accept the fact that it is there – has always been there – just like we accept that the great pyramids rise from the sands of Egypt. We give little thought to how they got there, only that they exist, as if they have been there forever. Now imagine how they got there." He draws again and his smoke settles on my silence. "You can't. However, your father and I were among the highlanders who brought those 2,000 kilograms of iron beams to the summit. It was difficult, and it was dangerous. We loaded the beams on wagons and moved them as high on the mountain as the horses could take us. Then Górecki, the man who designed the cross in Kraków created a series of pulleys and ropes we used to drag the metal beams the final steep meters to the summit. No one has ever seen anything like this. It seemed utterly impossible, if not witnessed with your own eyes. Instinctively, the horses pulled their cargo upward. We walked alongside the wagons, and it was my horrible fortune to be near the wheel spokes when, like dry sticks in summer, they exploded outward. It happened so quickly there was no time to react. In that instant, the wagon tumbled to its side. I was trapped beneath, my legs pinned to the ground. The horse was screaming wildly with the wagon atop its rear legs as well. I heard a gunshot. The screaming stopped. Your father and the other highlanders emptied the wagon and then lifted it while Górecki dragged me from beneath it. Like the spokes of the wheel, my leg had snapped and broke clean through just below my hip." I wince as the Captain recalls the painful memory.

"With no hesitation or protest from me or the others, your father raises me to his back and begins the long trek down the mountain through the Hala Kondratowa to Zakopane. That's my story, Bronek. That is why I acknowledge victory in your action today."

The fire cracks and cackles amidst the hiss of boiling sap that steams from the end of the log.

"And you never raced again?" I ask.

"Never. I was back on my skis that winter, but I never raced again, nor did your father. We were content to enjoy each other's company in the solitude and peace that only the mountains can provide."

The Captain stands and stretches his arms. "The hour is late and tired or not, Bronek, you must get some sleep, or at least rest your muscles. We'll leave for the jump at noon."

I rise from the rocker and cannot restrain myself from taking the Captain in my arms. "Thank you," I whisper. Indeed, the earth moves.

Batter drips from Mrs. Jordan's ladle as she waves it at the Captain. He joins the jumpers for a breakfast of flapjacks, eggs and bacon. "No more moonshine," she says.

"Do we have a problem, Mrs. Jordan?" the Captain asks as he scoots his chair to the table. Breakfast is always less formal than dinner.

"Not so much anymore," she says. "I did not hear your skaters come in, but when I got up? You would not believe the mess in my sink." She threateningly brandishes the ladle again, and says slowly and deliberately, "Remember: no more moonshine. You tell Lucjan, and tell him twice. Once in Polish and once in English." She turns back to her stove.

The Captain secures his napkin to the top button on his shirt and 'mouths' to the Marusarz boys, "No more moonshine!" We smile and raise our index fingers to our lips.

My time at Mrs. Jordan's cottage is so much more enjoyable than my previous experience at the Badrutt in St. Moritz. Mrs. Jordan's unassuming, motherly manner and her home-style meals replace the Badrutt's stuffy elegance. Her home is our home. As we join hands and ask God's blessing on our meal, I am drawn to the picture of Jesus above the Captain's chair. After a pointed and direct caution to avoid the moonshine, or risk her wrath, she happily serves up plenty of maple syrup with her flapjacks. I love that English word, 'flapjack.' They call these 'pancakes' as well. At home, we serve our *placki* with fruits, berries and jam, but here in America they use syrup, sap from the maple tree, a process the early Americans learned from the natives that inhabited these forests long before Europeans invaded their shores. The syrup is so deliciously sweet and with the butter, flows slowly down the sides of my flapjacks, merging in a thick yellow river.

The Captain wipes amber syrup from his moustache, and dares a sip from his steaming cup of black coffee. He pulls a sheet of paper from his shirt pocket, adjusts his glasses and studies it for a full minute. We continue to eat and patiently wait for the Captain to explain the situation to us. He clears his throat and peers over the rims of his spectacles. "Here's where we stand, boys," he finally says. "Bronek is our strongest finisher in the 18-K." My teammates applaud. The Captain raises his hand. "But, of the 64 contestants, he finished in the 18th position, 13 minutes behind the Swedes." Our cheers turn to groans. "Stashu was in 27th position, and Stanisław and Zdzisław both finished in the top half.

"But there is good news," he continues. "Bronek is sixth in the combined event after the race. His friend from Czechoslovakia is fifth and Stashu, you are in 10th." When we don't react, the Captain claps his hands and says, "Now you can congratulate yourselves. Be proud, highlanders. Lift your spirits as you will lift your wings today. We are in contention. With good jumps, who knows? We might win a medal."

To our disappointment, at the end of the day, our efforts fall short. Those skiers with faster times than mine in the 18-K race match my 50-meter jumps. One Swede and a Norwegian jump over 60 meters. I finish in seventh position, Antonín in sixth.

Darkness descends with the temperature as Johnny and I hike back to the village. I feel as if I have disappointed the Captain, and I am despondent. A long line of vehicles passes us on the crusty road. One bus stops, momentarily, and Antonín disembarks and joins us. We shake hands. Johnny walks between us.

"Will you jump tomorrow in the individual event?" I ask him.

"Of course."

"Can you do better?" Johnny asks me.

"Yes."

"Will you do better?"

"I have to."

"And if you don't?"

I ruffle his hunter's cap and look over the top of his head at my friend who smiles.

"It is of no consequence," I answer.

"Then what's the point?" Johnny retorts.

"What's the point? Stop right where you are." Antonín and I freeze in our tracks. Johnny takes another short step.

"Why are we stopping?" Johnny says. "We have a long ways to go and it is getting dark."

"That's the point, Johnny. Look back along the road to where you began to ask your question." Antonín and Johnny remain where they are as I pace off 10 meters and turn to face them. "You are right, Johnny. We still have a long walk back to the village, but the distance from here, where I stand, to you," I point at the two of them, "That short distance, Johnny, is the difference between the man who will win tomorrow and the man who will finish last. Forty jumpers will compete. The winner will make it to where you are, and the man who finishes last will only trail him by the distance between you and me.

"Thousands of spectators will watch from the stands tomorrow, just like today. People love to watch the jump, to pretend it is they, not I who sails above the mountain, but they fear it because it is steeped in speed and danger. Secretly, they hope to see one of us crash and fall, to see a man slide on his back, uncontrolled, and smash into the hay bales stacked in front of the bleachers. That's the point, Johnny. I love jumping and do not fear it like these people, who ride back to the village in the comfort of their cars and buses. I no longer need to win. To compete is enough for me.

"You watch," I add. "Someday your own Jack Shea will feel the same way. When he does, don't be disappointed in him. Just understand that he loves doing what he does and that is enough. Life is filled with pleasure and pain. I've learned not to make the pleasures painful."

We walk into the deepening darkness guided by the lights of the village. "Are we too young to understand this?" Antonín asks.

"Maybe we're not supposed to," I answer.

Chapter Eleven, 1932

Aeschylus

The jump at the Intervales Hill rises over 70 meters into the steel blue sky. From its summit, a jumper gazes northeast to the high mountains of the Adirondacks. Lake Placid and its village sit to the jumper's left. Nearly 5,000 spectators have gathered for the event. In years past, the jumpers were the daredevils of the mountains. Today, we share the danger with the bobsledders. The screech of the blades on the icy track and the raw speed and power of the plummeting sleds, lure men to gawk as the bobsledder confronts disaster at every turn. Still, people love to watch jumpers fly of their own accord without the support of wings or powered by motors. Ski jumping evokes fantastic images of mythical gods with no attachment to the ground save the gravitational pull that no man can overcome. For six seconds, the jumper is free from the bonds of earth, a child of space, and a member of no tribe with temporal or spiritual designs on his fellows.

The morning temperature is well above the freezing mark and the run out area at the bottom of the hill is slush. As the sun continues its daily course, the jump hides in the afternoon shade and the temperature drops. Conditions are perfect as we climb the broad stairs on the side of the ramp to reach today's starting point. The judges have set it several meters below the very top of the jump.

Thirty-four jumpers begin the day, but two fall with injuries and are unable to make their second jump. One is an American whose 68 meters would easily have been the longest jump in the first round, but the slushy conditions at the bottom of the hill toppled him into a wave of wet snow and water. He looks like a sea monster as his spinning body throws slush in all directions. He plays his gambit and pays the price with a broken collarbone. He is out of the competition. While he physically dampens the crowd with his watery ride and spray, he does not dampen its spirits. The audience cries for more, urging the next jumper to best the American's failed effort to earn gold.

The 56 meters I post on my first jump well exceeds my best effort yesterday in the combined event. I take some satisfaction from that fact, but several jumpers fly beyond 60 meters. I know I can get that far too, and convince myself of it as I climb to the top for my second jump. I want to remember it as my best effort.

The Marusarz boys precede me up the stairway. Stashu's head is bowed, but Andrzej wears the dumb smile you might expect from a youngster. The results of our second efforts will be predetermined by our attitudes: Stashu's resignation, Andrzej's enthusiasm, and my confidence.

"Lift your head up," I shout to Stashu in Polish so no one else will understand. "It is a wonderful day and we are here. Look around you. Listen to that crowd below us." He ignores me.

About 130 meters from the launch point, 500 spectators stand on either side of the run-out. The volume and enthusiasm in their voices give us the best indication of the distance jumpers attain. The crescendo begins as the jumper leaves the ramp and concludes as he lands and slides to a stop. Stashu's jump is greeted with polite applause and nothing more. Likewise for Andrzej. I learn afterwards that they jumped approximately the same distance, but Stashu's 53 meters were short of his first jump, and Andrzej's 54 meters bested his first effort by nearly three meters. Attitude.

The temperature continues to drop. The ramp is faster, and the slush in the run-out turns to rutted ice. The landing will be dangerous, but I am certain I can reach 60 meters on this jump. The announcer calls my name and the official at the top of the ramp waves me forward and says, "Good luck, son."

Saying "Thank you," I hop onto the ramp, legs bent and flexed like coils, skis pointed down. In seconds, the wind is screaming in my ears and my hair is blown back from my temples. I smile in the freedom that comes with flight. I bend low keeping my profile as small as possible. I think I can reach a speed of 100 km/hr. The iced ramp is much faster than yesterday or the earlier run this afternoon. I know I am close to my target speed when I reach the bottom of the ramp and explode into the air, tips up and arms out-stretched. As I fly through the cold air, I hear the rising voice of the crowd above the rush in my ears. I stretch, extend and stretch even further before I finally permit my skis to touch ground. The crowd cheers appreciatively. My jump is a good one, my best of the day. I stem my skis and turn perpendicular to the run-out. More ice than slush precedes my approach to the boards that separate the bleachers from the end of the landing area. I fight for balance, digging my edges into the ice, and come perilously close to the boards before I finally stop. Those in the front row raise their arms delightfully, albeit in defense, warding off the ice and slush that I cannot help but spray in their direction.

A tall man dressed in the white coat and knickers of the American Olympic Committee, removes his glasses to clear them. He laughs and says to me, "Was that as much fun for you as it appeared to be?"

"It was," I say.

The hatless man next to him wears the winter gear of an American military man. He reaches out and pats my shoulder. "I've been to the North Pole, boy, and I can assure you I'd be more scared to fly down that ramp of yours than you would be to challenge the tundra on a sled. Well done, son. Safe journey to you and your team." I glance at his nametag before I schuss away. "Byrd."

I remove my skis and weave my way around the crowd, and find the Captain and my mates standing with Johnny and his father, in front of the Adirondack Stage bus. The hockey team has not recovered from its determined battle with the moonshine. They collectively shield red eyes from the sunlight receding behind the mountains. Bless their hearts, I think. Not even the moonshine could keep them from supporting us at the jump today. The Captain offers me a gratifying smile and says, "You did it, Bronek. You reached 60 meters, but with not a centimeter to spare." I bow respectfully, but am disappointed when I learn that the three Norwegians who claimed the top positions exceeded my best effort on each of their jumps. One even surpassed 70 meters, and that on his first jump when the ramp was still slow! The Captain indicates Stashu and Andrzej and says, "These two boys ... they will do better in the future. They can be good jumpers and good skiers." He points to his head and says, "If there is one thing you learn from this experience, and keep with you for the rest of your life, make it this. You don't measure the size of a man from the ground up. You measure the size of a man from the neck up." Our teammates congratulate us.

Adam Kowalski nudges Józef and whispers, "I don't get it. The neck up?" Józef cuffs the back of Adam's head sending his flat cap to the ground.

"That's a good lesson for you, too Johnny," Martin tells his young son.

"We're done here," the Captain says. "Good effort from Bronek and the Marusarz cousins. Enjoy the evening. You others have more work tomorrow."

Andrzej raises his hand like a schoolboy. "Can we enjoy the evening with moonshine?"

"No more moonshine!" we shout back at him as the Captain points his index finger in Andrzej's face. Witalis holds his head with one hand and clenches his stomach with the other as he surrenders to a final bout of dry heaves. The hockey team gathers around its ailing comrade, and Lucjan waves his arms above them like a symphony conductor. They repeat Mrs. Jordan's new edict, "No more moonshine!"

I am satisfied that I gave my best effort to Poland on the slopes and on the jump. I find no shame in my undertaking and I dispel my disappointment in short order, so I am content to spend my final day of these games at the Stadium – from the start of the 50-kilometer race to the conclusion of the closing ceremonies. There is nothing more gratifying than to join my teammates and brothers-in-arms at the hub of activity on this final day of competition and celebration. Walking through the parlor, I notice our hockey team and skiers have already left. It appears that I will be the last one out the door. As I reach for the doorknob, a soft sniffle distracts me. I step back and peer through the kitchen door. Mrs. Jordan sits alone at her table. She weeps softly and holds a black rosary in her hands.

"Mrs. Jordan?" I whisper. She raises her head, puts the rosary in her pocket and wipes her eyes with her checkered apron. She tries to speak but a sob muffles her unintelligible words.

"Is there something wrong, Mrs. Jordan? Can I help you?" She waves me away. Instead, I approach her quietly and place my hands on her shoulders. She lays her hands on mine and I feel compelled to lean forward and kiss the top of her graying head.

"I'm just a foolish old woman," she manages to say. "There is nothing wrong. I'm just sitting in this house thinking how quiet it will be when you and your friends leave tomorrow." She pulls the rosary out and spreads it on the table before her. "I always use these when I feel sorry for myself," she says. "I'm just being selfish. Pay me no mind, Bronek and be on your way."

I sit at the table and take her hands. This woman is not so different from my mother and my *Babcia*. Why must she be lonely?

"It's okay to cry, *Pani*," I say. "I can assure you, all of us will fight back our tears when we are forced to say farewell.

You have been much more than a hostess. You have become as dear to us as our mothers."

"Nonsense," she says dabbing her eyes with her apron. We sit quietly for a moment and let the stillness ease her solitude.

"Have you left this house at all during these games?" I ask her.

"Not often," she answers with a shake of her head. "Only to keep the pantry filled with good things for my boys from Poland."

"Well then, it is time for you to enjoy some of the festivities, *Pani.*" I gently pull her to her feet. "Grab your coat! Today, you will be my date at the games."

"That's not necessary. You are such a handsome man, and I am certain the young ladies are waiting for you in the village."

"Now *that* is nonsense." I retrieve her worn coat, a hat and a scarf from the closet.

As I do she pleads, "Are you sure?" However, her eyes sparkle as her spirits rise. I am sure.

"Shall we?" I say. She takes my arm and we step outdoors into the dazzling sunshine.

The energy in the village is as vibrant on this final day as it was 10 days ago when the good Governor opened the games. The melting ice on the stadium rink has forced our bronze medal match against the Germans into the arena. As we walk through the doors, a young girl asks for Mrs. Jordan's ticket. Before I can make my plea to gain her entry without a ticket, a man behind us says, "That's okay, young lady. They are with me." It is Byrd and his entourage. "Please," he says to me and directs us into the

arena. "No one should be excluded from these games, particularly not a high-flyer and his escort. Madam," he says
graciously, and hands Mrs. Jordan a pair of tickets that simply say 'Grandstand Season Ticket.' "Win or lose, enjoy
the match." With that, Byrd departs with his men in tow.
Whoever he is, Byrd is a nice man and I am grateful to him.

Mrs. Jordan is so happy to be in the arena with me that
she refuses to remain in her seat. The energy of the athletes and the enthusiasm of the audience sweep her from her
everyday existence into a world of excitement and daring
where men vie for victory and the honor of their nations.
She cheers wildly whenever our Poles snatch the puck and
move toward the German net, or when Józef throws himself daringly in front of a vicious shot. Her 'boo' wisely
evolves into a groan when the Germans take a one-goal lead
five minutes into the second period, but she rises to her
feet with hands above her head when Aleksander levels the
score. Our team swarms around him as he puts us back into
the medal race, but our joy is short-lived when the Huns
take the lead for good less than two minutes later.

Despite the 4-1 score line, the match was enjoyable and
exciting. The teams show respect for each other as the skaters – who just minutes before were slamming each other
against the boards with dire intent – join hands and skate
around the perimeter of the rink waving to the fans that
cheered nonstop for both teams through the entire battle.

"That is what sport is about," I tell Mrs. Jordan. "You
compete like hell, and then leave the field as friends, each
respecting the other. If you don't, you are playing for the
wrong reason."

Leaving the Arena, we return to the crowded street. "That was wonderful," she says. "I will see you and your teammates at the dinner table at 8:00 p.m."

"You don't have to go," I say, hoping that she will spend the afternoon with me. "In just a few short hours, your Americans and the Canadians will play for the gold medal. The closing ceremonies will begin immediately following the match. You will enjoy it."

"Thank you for your offer, Bronek, but I must be on my way. I have a special dinner planned for you and your teammates." She stands firm in her decision. I take her hands and lean forward to kiss both her cheeks.

"*Dziękuję*," I say.

"*Nie, to ja dziękuję*," she replies. "No, it is I who thank you." She waves and walks up the street.

"I knew it," a girl shouts and a snowball knocks my cap from my head. I raise my shoulders and brush the snow from my collar before any more finds its way down my back. I turn to see Sonja brushing the snow from her hands. The three Norwegian jumpers, who bested me in the individual jump, accompany her. "Yes, I knew it," she cheerfully repeats, goodwill in her voice. "There is always another woman. Don't think I didn't see her."

"You've found me out," I play into her game. "As your teammates have conquered me on the mountain, Miss Henie, you will conquer my heart." She steps backward and curtsies while her teammates applaud my admission and my bravado. The melting snow contorts my body and drips to the small of my back and beyond.

"Sorry about the snowball," she says, "but after you left me on the dance floor at the club, I imagined this might be the best way to get your attention."

I bow to her teammates and rise to an onslaught of Sonja's adoring crowd. Her fans passionately approach to request an autograph – hers, not mine – on whatever scrap of paper they might have handy. "I don't believe you lack for attention."

"This is not the attention I want," she is quick to respond.

"Miss Henie," someone calls out. "Miss Henie." A hand waves to catch her attention. She waves back.

"That's George," she tells me without looking up. "Domestic radio station. NBC or something like that." She waves again, "In a minute, George. Just give me a minute." George smiles broadly beneath his cocked beret and seats himself on a nearby bench to wait patiently for his chance to interview the lovely star of these games. I am quite sure Lake Placid would argue that its own Jack Shea – though I would not refer to him as 'lovely' – is most deserving of the plaudits and equal star status.

"I'm sorry, Bronek. I have to go. I do want to see you, though. At the ceremony?"

"Okay."

The Americans and Canadians fight hard in the final hockey game, but after three overtime periods, the match ends in a 2-2 draw. Unfortunately, for the Yanks, the Canadians take the gold medal by virtue of their 2-1 win over the U.S. on the opening day of the games. The energy from the match does not dissipate when the arena empties for the final time at these Olympic Games. The crowds move toward the stadium, where the participants assemble for the grand finale.

The stadium is once again filled to capacity. Even the bleachers are full. Every area outside the stadium that affords a glimpse of the closing ceremony is occupied. Dark clouds threaten from the west, but no one seems to care as the orchestra's uplifting music refuses to allow the approaching darkness to encroach upon the spirit and success of these games. From the south, many people wave and cheer from open windows in the nearby high school. Banners and flags flutter in the breeze that sails down the western slopes and follows the road and railroad tracks up the valley. Flurries dance on the wind and as the sun sets, the lights surrounding the stadium illuminate. The storm intensifies. The flurries evolve into giant snowflakes and glisten like a million diamonds from heaven in the bright light that tries to cut them.

The teams assemble in front of the grandstand. One by one, the medalists climb a three-tiered platform where the winner of the event takes the highest position while the band honors him with his national anthem. I do envy them, but I remain thankful that I have had the opportunity to compete against them and with them on this great stage that promotes fellowship of nations through athletic contests. Over 250 men and women from 17 nations gathered here two weeks ago, and 87 from 10 countries will leave with at least one medal to his credit. A medal to be cherished, no doubt, but many will tarnish or be lost over time. The memories will always remain.

Sonja takes her place on the highest platform and receives her gold medal. She is beautiful, and the crowd loves her as much for her skill as for her flamboyant but pleasing character. The blizzard strengthens and the surging wind swirls the snow creating a magical ballet of white ghosts in the strong lights.

After the final recipient accepts his award, the handsome, white-haired President of the International Olympic Committee, Count de Baillet-Latour mounts the top platform and officially declares that the games closed. He directs our attention to the south end of the stadium where an honor guard lowers and reverently folds the large Olympic flag. It will not wave again for another four years. We are covered with white amidst this raging storm, but no one is ready to leave. The teams disperse and athletes seek out their friends and peers from other nations to bid them continued good luck, farewell and Godspeed.

Impervious to the cheers and laughter, I stand mute and search the colorful crowd for Sonja. She is running toward me across the snow-covered ice with no fear of falling, her gold medal sways from her neck. I brace myself as this beautiful, young woman leaps into my arms. I hold her tightly and feel her warm breath on my neck as she buries her face in my shoulder. She raises her eyes. She is weeping through the magnetic smile she shares with me. We are too close and I cannot refrain from a single kiss that she willingly returns. My head spins wildly as I look into the glittering snowflakes that continue to spread their spell on this celebration of life, a celebration that refuses to end. For this one second, only the two of us are here. If only I could take her in my arms and escape into this blizzard, just she and I. She is not a Norwegian; I am not a Pole. She is not a skater; I am not a skier. We are just two people embracing a single, sweet moment in time … I lower her gently to the ground.

"Will I see you again?" she asks through her tears.

"In four years," I say. "Remember me."

She wipes the tears from her eyes and softly touches my cheek with the palm of her hand. Someone calls her name. "I must go," she says. "Safe journey to you." She takes a small step back. Her hand runs down my chest and her fingers brush the outline of the *hamsa* beneath my sweater. She kisses her fingertips and raises them to my lips then turns and disappears into the milling crowd.

As still as an ice sculpture covered with snow, I stare after her. A friendly hand dusts the flakes from my shoulders. It is Antonín. "Don't worry, Bronek," he says. "You will see her again." Whether or not I do, life is grand. I return to earth with a smile, and with exaggerated gallantry, I offer Antonín my arm. He accepts it, and soon we find the Marusarz cousins, who join us. In turn, they capture a Nipponese and a Swede. We become over 30 strong, arms intertwined and we dance joyfully around the stadium floor.

A white whirlwind of snow rises into the dark. At first, I imagine it a lost spirit, and then realize, no, it is an angel.

Chapter Twelve, 1936

Bavaria

The Captain's cottage, in the way of the highlanders, is small. It sits in the cool shadow of the trees at the edge of the forest where the mountains desert the lowlands and rise steeply, searching for heaven. He rests on his porch rocking in an ancient chair that I suspect served his father and his grandfather too. "Too many people die too young," he says. "For that reason, I have no need for birthday celebrations. They mean nothing to me and only make me sad."

My father and the Captain were born on the same day, the third day of June in 1880. The partitioners from Austria and Russia still ruled the country. It was a hot summer day, and the midwife was particularly busy.

"I've come by myself, Captain. I am alone," I say. "No celebration, just a gift." I hand him an unframed canvas, loosely rolled and tied with a piece of string.

He takes it and says, "So you feel the pressure from the younger skiers and you seek my favor. Is that it, Bronek?" He jests and I answer in kind, "That must be it."

He carefully works the string loop off the end, unrolls the canvas and stares at it appreciatively. He smiles, "I think you'll be on the team one more time." I have drawn a charcoal picture of the Captain and my father as I remember them in the winter of 1930. Grinning broadly beneath their wide-brimmed *górale* hats, they stand in front of the heavy sleigh that has belonged to my family for nearly a century.

"You do fine work, my friend."

"Portraits are not my strength," I admit. "But this is special for you and another for my father. May you both live long." I bless myself with the sign of the cross, and sit on the top step that leads to his porch. The Captain continues to rock behind me. "I will cherish this," he says. He hides his emotion well, always has, but the tear that appears in the corner of his eye speaks louder than any words he might say.

"If Janka was here, she would have framed it for you. I'll have it done when she visits," I tell him. As much as he may like the picture, it will gather dust on top of his cupboard unless someone frames it for him.

"How long has it been?" he asks. "Four years now in Warsaw for your sister? She must like it."

"She does," I tell him. "Very much. She has become accustomed to life in the city, and life at the University suits her. She is much smarter than I am now, or ever was for that matter." I laugh. He smiles and points the stem of his pipe at me. "Intelligence does not come from books, Bronek. Your father attended school no more than six years, and he is the smartest man I know." My silence tells him I agree.

The Captain rocks, grateful for the peace he enjoys here, and for his opportunity to appreciate life without the technology that suspiciously steals toward us like a thief. It threatens the highlanders' old ways and concerns us both.

For now, we enjoy the twitter of happy songbirds. My father will make his way here later today. He will probably bring his Żubrówka.

"It's not so far this time," he says as he looks at the picture a final time. Satisfied, he neatly rolls it up and holds it in his lap.

"What's not so far?"

"The games this winter. They are not so far away, not like America."

"No, not so far away," I comment lazily, "not like America. I enjoyed it there. I like the Americans and their cowboy ways. Bavaria will be like Zakopane, more like home." Remembering Jack Shea I add, "Probably more formal, though, like the Swiss." The bees hum in the wildflowers that surround the cabin. "If I lived in America, I would want to be a cowboy. If an American lived here, he would want to be a Górale. No question about it."

The Captain taps the bowl of his pipe on the arm of his chair. "You think so?"

"I do. Some people would dread the isolation of these mountains, just as someone might dread life in the open range in America. American cowboys would cherish our seclusion." I breathe deeply and smell the sweat air. "I can see the sky. Buildings do not confine my mind like they do in Warsaw, and like they surely would in New York City. Maybe I am comfortable not understanding what is happening in our own country. One day everyone likes Piłsudski, the next day no one will support him. Me? I pay no attention to *Sanacja* and things political. I can't do anything about it anyway."

"Probably, not." The shadow of passing cloud announces its farewell to the east.

"But you know what, Captain? I've been reading a book."

"You always have your head buried in a book," he laughs.

"I do," I continue. "Now, when I travel to a new country, I find book written in that country's language. I start with the *Bible* because I know exactly what it says. Then I add a book or two that I know nothing about. This year, I am reading a book called *Mein Kampf*. The man the Germans call *Führer* wrote this book many years ago. I read a book to learn the language, but this one makes me very uncomfortable. The concepts this man writes about are dangerous. He does not like the Jews."

"He is no different than Poles and Russians, Americans too," the Captain comments offhandedly, albeit with little conviction or interest. He is content to leave the fate of the world in the hands of those he perceives more capable to manage it. As long as his home at the edge of this forest is not disturbed, he is content. The shadow of the house creeps slowly along the valley, toward the village.

In one sense, the Captain is right. Too many pogroms have occurred within our borders, and violence against the Jews in Russia is well documented. No pogroms in America, but stuffiness at the club in Lake Placid hinted at anti-Semitism. Nothing obvious, but it was there. In 1932, the large crowds at the stadium in 1932 offered unmatched support for Jack Shea when he took his gold medals in the 500 and 1500-meter races. The same crowds greeted fellow American Irving Jaffe with polite applause when he captured gold in the 5,000 and 10,000-meter races. I fondly recall when Jaffe – who I learned later was a Jewish immigrant from Russia – fell as he approached the finish line. Despite 20 grueling minutes of hard skating, he still managed to slide across the line ahead of the Norwegian and Canadian who were not more than a breath away. The cheers from the international contingent rang out more loudly and enthusiastically than from the American spectators. "What a race," I said to young Johnny who stood by me in the stands. "He's a *kike*," Johnny answered. "A what?" I asked. "A *kike*. A Jew. That's what they call them at the club." We discussed it no more.

It is not my business to educate the Captain, but I have read Hitler's words. He is a dangerous man, and when dangerous men ascend the power ladder of any government … even a simple highlander like me can see the difficulties ahead. It does not portend well for that country or for the countries that surround it. This winter, we will be in Hitler's country and these games will be his showcase. He hates the Jews; that is very clear from the words he writes in his book.

"Leave the politics to the politicians," he says. "We command the slopes; they command the chancelleries. You've already said it, Bronek. We can't do anything about it anyway."

"I suppose that's what bothers me," I tell my Captain. "Maybe the problem is us. We live peacefully in our mountains and ignore the talk in the cities. When conflict strikes, we are the first to answer the call."

"And the first to die," he adds. "But Poland exists because of men like us. Our faith in God and our resistance to change our language, or to adopt the ways of the par-titioners has preserved Poland through the most difficult times. While the men in the cities often bow to the invad-ers, the farmers and highlanders refuse to change. We always stand prepared to undo those things we never sup-ported to begin with. Our steadfastness will continue to make us strong regardless of what happens in the halls of government."

I stand and stretch while the breeze caresses my face and rustles leaves in the quiet trees. The sounds of nature are the most profound and they penetrate my being. No man can reproduce them, and they are mine at no cost.

"I must be on my way," I tell him.

"Where to?"

"To meet with the King."

"Like me," he says, "Your Father smiles upon you on this day. I thank you, Bronek." He waves the rolled canvas at me. I nod and continue my journey up the mountain.

We travel by train to Bavaria. The tracks run so close to the road that Fedor's cigarette butt almost reaches the gravel that peeks through the snow-covered surface when he flicks it from the open window. Traffic is sparse but in a few days, the highways will be jammed with automobiles on their way to these fourth Winter Olympic Games. The train travels east through Prague, then south to Munich and on to Garmisch-Partenkirchen. Hitler's power exceeds reason. One year ago, two small towns occupied a pristine valley in Bavaria, not 10 kilometers from the Austrian bor-der. Today, it is one town, Garmisch-Partenkirchen ... con-solidated by Hitler's decree, with no regard to the desires of the respective mayors and their citizenry. Nothing matters to this man. He acts with impunity.

"Shut that window," Józef yells from the back of the car. "It's cold enough in here without you letting in more freezing air." He's right; we see our breath with each word we speak. Józef has successfully defended his goalkeeping position despite fierce competition from a handful of players 15 years his junior. While most hockey players reach their best level of performance in their late twenties, they say that goalkeepers become better with age and can compete well into their thirties. At 36, Józef is the oldest member of our team. I am 27, and only three other teammates are older than I am. These games will be my third. I think I can go a fourth, maybe a fifth. Nonetheless, I recognize the future of sport rests with the young.

My language skills continue to improve. My expanding fluencies include German, Norwegian, French and English. My studies teach me that our Slavic language has roots much different from the romance languages like English and French, which are based in Latin, and the Indo-European tongues that include German and Norwegian. Consequently, while a German and a Norwegian find similarities in their words and language structure, they would not and could not recognize words in Polish, nor could a Pole understand words in German. That is a good thing. My young colleague Fedor Weinschenk is a Jew.

As we race through the primeval forests of central Europe and cross the German-Czechoslovakian border headed for Munich, a large sign greets us. It stands prominently between the tracks and roadside, visible to motorists and trains as well. A traveler could not enter the country without seeing it. The sign is large and reads,

"Hunde und Juden nicht erlaubt"

'Dogs and Jews not allowed.'

I exchange a furtive glance with the Captain while Adam Kowalski shouts to me, "Big sign, Bronek. What does it say? Welcome Polish Highlanders?" The others laugh, including Fedor who knows no better.

"Yes, Adam," I say over my shoulder. "That is what it says, 'Welcome Polish Highlanders and their star Kowalski.'" More laughter with no understanding of the heinous motive behind the insulting words on the sign. Am I wrong to protect Fedor from this racist stone cast directly at him and his Jewish brethren? I leave them thinking it is a joke because I do not believe the German people share a common purpose with their Führer in this regard. I shudder and revulsion rips through my body when I recall the all-revealing statement this wicked man writes in his book, "The personification of the devil as the symbol of all evil assumes the living shape of the Jew." I lean forward and wrap my arms tightly around my waste to dispel the depressing thoughts that will not leave me alone. They've haunted me like demons, ever since I opened that man's vulgar book.

The gentleman who occupies the seat across the aisle asks me in German "Are you alright?". He sits with his wife who stares blankly out the window.

"I am, sir." I say it with more conviction than I feel.

"Your German is flawed. 'Highlander' does not appear on that sign. Regardless, you did the right thing, friend," he says. "Your teammates will learn soon enough how hateful the leader of this country is. I can assure you: for every German that shares Hitler's view of the world, there are five who do not."

"I hope you are right," I answer.

He extends his hand. "Eckstein, Hersz Eckstein" he introduces himself. "My wife Natalie. We are Jews, and she is afraid." I do not know how to respond. "I make hats in Dresden." He taps his head. "To hide my baldness," he laughs, "but Natalie encourages me to move, to leave Germany. We spent last week in Warsaw, and now we visit friends in Munich before we return to Dresden."

"Bronisław." I shake his hand and nod toward his wife who offers me the slightest of smiles.

"An athlete?"

"Yes, a skier."

He studies the other passengers within earshot, including my teammates. He rightly concludes that, save for the Captain who sits next to me, no one is eavesdropping on our conversation and that few, if any of my teammates speak German.

I introduce the Captain. "My mentor." They shake hands. Eckstein and the Captain are about the same age.

"Jews?" Eckstein asks.

"Poles."

"Your reaction to that sign bespeaks your disapproval of the Führer's opinion of Jews. If you thought otherwise, the sign would have elicited laughter, not the revulsion I see."

"As a trainer of athletes," the Captain says in flawless German, "I leave politics to the politicians, but it is difficult to ignore the brash ignorance the sign displays. On behalf of humanity, I apologize."

"Not required from you," Eckstein says.

I reach beneath my sweater to show Eckstein my amulet. He smiles. "The *hamsa*. Why does a Gentile wear the *hamsa* and why – of all places – into the lair of the beast?"

"I ask him the same question," the Captain says with a shake of his head. "You will never learn, will you, Bronek?"

"I have nothing to learn about this, Captain. Someday you will understand why I refuse to give this up. I am not a Jew, but even if I was, there is no law against it."

"Not yet," Eckstein grimaces. "May I look more closely?" I take the *hamsa* from my neck and he places it on his open palm. "Do you know what it is?"

"I know it is for luck," I say. "I am from Zakopane. I was fifteen and preparing to enter my first real race. A beautiful Jewish girl, three years my senior gave it to me minutes before I headed up the mountain with the other skiers. She told me it is the Hand of God. 'It's for good luck,' she said. I have worn it ever since. Whether other men judge my life as good or bad, I believe it is better than it might have been because God blesses me for I wear his *hamsa*."

"Interesting that a Gentile would feel this way about a Hebrew amulet. I believe she made this herself?" Eckstein asks.

"I believe she did."

"It is simple, but beautiful. Some call it the Hand of Miriam, the sister of Moses and Aaron. You see the five digits of the hand?" He raises his left hand, and wiggles his thumb and fingers. "The Torah. The five books of Moses." He hands the charm back to me and I return it to my neck. "May the hand of God protect you, Bronisław and bring you luck at these games."

"It will. If I finish in 22nd place, I know I would have finished in 23rd without it."

Eckstein pats my knee and smiles. "So tell, me. Where is this beautiful woman now who gave you this *hamsa* so many years ago?"

I sigh, not intentionally. "She and her husband live in Warsaw."

"Ah," he says. "Unrequited love. The most painful of emotions." His wife glances at him and rolls her eyes. "Never mind her. She will never understand how a hat maker can be a romantic as well."

"We remain very close friends. My younger sister Janina lived with my friend and her husband – both professors – when she attended university. City life suits Janka and she shares an apartment with several girlfriends there today."

"You know Warsaw?"

"I prefer my mountains, but I visit occasionally, not too often. Janka always has a 'special friend' she wants me to meet, a new boyfriend."

"You be thankful for that," the Captain intercedes. "At least she seeks your advice with important decisions. Too many young people don't do that."

"He's right," Eckstein says. "Natalie and I have no children, but our friends who are parents? It is frightening the things that young people do with no regard to their parents' wishes."

"Janka is a good girl, and Amalia and Max have had a positive influence on her life. Our parents are pleased with Janka's situation in Warsaw."

"So how do you perceive Warsaw? Is it safe ... for a Jewish hat maker and his wife?"

The Captain will not hide his displeasure. "This is the best answer I can give you: Nowhere in Poland, including Warsaw have I ever seen a sign like the one we passed minutes ago. Safe? I don't know what is safe anymore, but if I were a Jew, I would not want to live in a country where the leader permits the display of such signs."

"Permits?" I say. "Encourages would be more accurate. What motivates the Germans to think it is acceptable to promote such garbage?"

"Not the Germans," Eckstein counters. "More accurately the Nazis and their *sturmabteilung*, their brownshirts."

"When you ask, Eckstein, we'll tell you what we think," the Captain gravely adds, "No one wants to mislead you. There are problems to be sure in Poland. We have not been our own country for 20 years yet, but our traditions span centuries. The Russians hold no love for Jews, nor do the Ukrainians in the south. There has been violence and there is hate, but maybe not so much as here in Germany."

"He's right," I add. "My Jewish friends in Warsaw feel secure at the university. Perhaps their elevated status as professors protects them from the cruelties that they might otherwise experience in another profession."

"And a hat maker?" Eckstein asks. "How will a simple hat maker fare?"

Neither the Captain nor I answer. Our silence reveals our uncertainty. I ponder the thought that in my own country, a simple man like this may not be safe from the physical animosity fashioned by the bias and prejudice of fellow human beings.

Eckstein takes an ornate watch from his pocket and tells us we will arrive in Munich within the hour. "You are good men," he says with a grateful smile. "Thank you for sharing your thoughts. I wish you and your teammates the best of luck in your games."

The train leaves the Munich terminal with no empty seats, and some passengers must stand and grasp the rail above their heads to maintain their balance. We speed south for the remaining 80 kilometers to our final destination in Garmisch-Partenkirchen. The tracks lead us through wooded valleys framed by steep, white mountains that hide the late afternoon sun as we arrive. Conversation in our car is loud and animated despite a pair of stern-faced men dressed in sharply pressed, black uniforms, each wearing a red armband displaying a swastika. I make eye contact with the younger one, a man about my age. His cold glare is meant to intimidate me. When I continue staring, he stands and walks towards me.

"*Was ist los?*" he challenges me.

"*Nichts.* Nothing," I answer and smile.

"*Haben sie ein problem?*"

I shake my head 'no.' He shifts his hard gaze to the Captain who meets it with an icy, defiant glare of his own. The Nazi tugs firmly on the hem of his black coat and bows almost imperceptibly to the Captain and returns to his seat without further incident.

"Welcome to Deutschland," the Captain says.

I never take for granted my chance to represent my country. We are a good people, probably no better and certainly no worse than other men that call this planet 'home.' I am proud to take my place in the spotlight on behalf of my countrymen. As the train glides through the valley on its approach to Garmisch, I glimpse the village, blurred in the fog on the window where the Captain's breath melts the frost to create a postcard-like image, sharp in the center, less clear on the edges. Garmisch is yet another small town likened to St. Moritz, Lake Placid and Zakopane where wispy columns of white smoke rise from the homes that grace the narrow streets. However, those others, particularly Lake Placid seem more remote. In America, one journeys through countless kilometers of valleys and mountains populated by nothing but tall, snow-covered conifers. Few towns or villages line the iron tracks that lead us to their doorsteps. In Garmisch, we are less than 100 kilometers from Munich, and both Prague and Vienna – Bern, too – are close enough that these fourth winter Olympic games are likely to attract larger crowds than the other three did.

The festive mood threatens to evaporate when our train arrives at the Garmisch-Partenkirchen terminal. The Nazi officials who I learn are members of what they call the *Schutzstaffel* are first to rise from their seats and move to the exits. They walk by us with an obvious swagger that annoys me. When they roughly push an old man back in his seat so that they can pass, I stand and reach out for the assailant. The Captain quickly stays my hand. "Leave it alone, Bronek. You are here to ski. Hold your tongue and your hand. Your dignity, in the face of their impudence, does them more harm than anything you could say or do with your fists." I am not known for my temper, but I grip the top of the seat in front of me in order to check the feeling of rage that tries to take hold of me. Better to grab the seat than the jacket of the *SS* man. "Don't be a tough guy," the Captain cautions me, "Not here, not now. Do you understand?"

"Do I have a choice?" I answer under my breath.

"All of life is a series of choices," he says. "Don't make a bad one here."

I stare after the *SS* official as he greets another group dressed in the same black coats with swastika armbands. As they spot each other, they extend their arms upward at 45-degree angles with fingers pointed skyward. 'Heil Hitler,' they call to each other, hail Hitler.

"Bronek!" The Captain snatches my attention, "Leave it alone."

We allow the other passengers to disembark, and then we leave the train as a team. Clouds hide the mountain peaks in the late afternoon and street lamps prepare to ward off the early winter darkness. The smell of snow hangs in the air, invisible but unmistakable. Ten minutes pass and we are alone with our gear in front of the empty train station. No one greets us with the royalty afforded us in Switzerland, and there is no Martin or Johnny with friendly, smiling faces to welcome us and escort us through the village. We wait patiently and the warm glow of the street lamps rise as darkness falls. A solitary man approaches. "Poland?" he asks as he removes his fedora. "Yes, we're from Poland," several of us respond.

"Good, good," he says. "I'm not too late, am I?" I stand close enough to this elfish man to taste the smell of alcohol that hangs heavy on his breath. "Had to run an errand, you know, and the crowds are so big. Too large for our small town. But," he concludes, "We are glad you have come to the games in Garmisch-Partenkirchen. *Bitte.*" With no introductions, this strange, little man turns on his heels and proceeds up a narrow street, not seeming to care if we follow him or not.

He is right about one thing. The lighted storefronts and restaurants do not lack clientele. Even at this hour, the streets are crowded, but when the games start, spectators will be required to leave this little village to the athletes. For now, it is their town, too.

As much as I enjoyed our accommodations at Mrs. Jordan's home in America, I dislike our lodging in Germany. We stay in an old hotel, which is fine with me, but the people here seem so impersonal. Mrs. Jordan was special, but even the staff at the Badrutt in St. Moritz accorded us a courtesy and respect that was sincere and noticeable. Not so at the Ludwig Hotel where the guests are simply occupants.

Our party of 20 athletes and 10 trainers, officials and guests crowds the small lobby where other groups are waiting to check in as well. I step outside, preferring the cold to the stuffy, busy lobby. I am only 27-years-old, but I am a veteran, and that is one reason why I have the honor to carry our flag at the opening ceremonies. These are my third games. No other Pole – save the Captain of course – can make that claim.

"It's cold out here, Bronek." Adam Kowalski, our goal scorer joins me and slaps the sides of his coat after lighting a cigarette. I ignore the smoke. Adam and his older brother

Aleksander are my friends. They are from Warsaw and I always visit them when I travel to see my sister. I think Adam is quite fond of Janka, but Warsaw has made her an independent woman. To Janka, Adam is just a funny, frivolous man with no future as an athlete. She may think the same of me, but she would never say it.

"I was thinking," I tell him, "If Aleksander was here, this would have been his third competition. As it is, I am the old one."

"Neither of you are old," he says, and then exhales the smoke through his nostrils, examining it as if it might be part of his brain that evaporates into the air. Hockey players are unusual, but nonetheless entertaining people both on and off the ice.

"He is still a good player, your brother is."

"He's lost his taste for the game. Maybe not so much that," he corrects himself, "but he has found the soldier's life more favorable."

"Some men like it."

The Captain and the others return to the street. "It will take some time to check us in," he says. "Here is enough money for each of you to have a good supper. There are plenty of restaurants nearby to satisfy even Józef." We share the joke as the Captain distributes our stipend for the night. He points to a large street clock on a nearby corner. "It is just past six o'clock. I will be back here by eight o'clock. Please return no later than ten o'clock and I will have your room assignments. Questions?"

I plan to dine with the Marusarz boys, but before I can make that arrangement, the Captain motions me to him, and hands me a small envelope. "This was waiting for you at the desk." My name is written plainly on it in a delicate hand. "Be careful," he says, and I give him a questioning look. "Just be careful," he repeats and leaves me under the street lamp in the lightly falling snow.

I turn the envelope over in my hands several times and notice that the seal has been broken. Within it, a folded note with a simple message: "Meet me in the *rathskeller* on Von-Brug Strasse at 7:00 p.m." I return the note to its envelope, the Captain's caution still in my ear, "Be careful." My heart races, for I suspect whose hand crafted the note and left it at the hotel. Maybe the Captain does too, and if he does, he could have kept the note from me, but he does not. Uncertainly, I remove the note for a second look and stare at the black ink on the pale, pink paper. Looking up from the street, I see the last of my teammates disappear around the corner. I am drawn to them, but the siren's song is stronger. My feet are frozen on the cobblestone street. My will weakens. The wind picks up and the snow swirls in the light from the lamp that illumes the clock, which urges me to act as its hands advanced to six-thirty. I return to the crowded lobby, hoping that it might keep me captive and distract my desire to race to the rendezvous. A single empty chair beckons me. As soon as I sink into its deep cushions, I realize that it faces the large window, which frames the street clock.

I bury my head in a magazine, but the clock at the front desk chimes a quarter-'til-seven. The sound forces me to look at the street clock for confirmation. There is no mistake. A bellhop walks by. "Excuse, me. Can you give me directions to Von-Burg Strasse?" I walk out the door, convinced I will go to the *rathskeller* only to learn the identity of the note sender. I become lost and ask for more directions. After 30 minutes, I find the dimly lit stairway leading down to the bar. I hesitate at the top of the stairs and stare at the sign that is posted above the door, *Die Krone von Bayern*, the Crown of Bavaria. I brush the snow from my shoulders and descend the stairway. Reaching for the doorknob, I command myself to leave, but I stay. I will talk to no one. The note draws my hand to my pocket. It has not disappeared; it is still there, and I must discover who authored it. A couple laughs intimately and walks down the steps. I smile at them and stand aside. They enter and the door closes in my face. I turn to walk back up the steps and leave, but another couple comes down to seal my fate. I follow them into smoky laughter hanging in the stuffy air, warmed by a cast iron stove hiding in the corner of the large room.

I run my fingers through my wet hair as the snow melts and puddles at my feet just inside the doorway. The *rathskeller* is crowded and amber beer glistens in clear glass mugs as a large, busty waitress carries it from the bar. She catches my eye and grins broadly.

I feel foolish and turn to leave when a young man taps my shoulder and motions me to follow him. As we make our way through the crowded room, I hear her voice call out, "Bronek. Over here, Bronek." We push through the crowd until I glimpse Sonja, trapped behind a table at the far end of the room. She struggles to her feet, slides around the table, and physically – if not intentionally – falls into my arms. I hold her close, as much to protect her from the crowd as to experience the bittersweet wave of emotion I remember from New York.

"I didn't think you would come," she says. I consider it odd that everyone in the establishment, including Sonja uses only German. Surely, like Sonja and me there are guests from other countries.

"I didn't think I would, either," I answer in Norwegian.

"You don't speak German?" she asks then adds quickly, "But I think you do by your very response. We are in Germany, darling. Use the language." She laughs and waves at her friends sitting at the table, but I cannot take my eyes from her. Her scent overpowers the heavy odor of smoke. She takes my hand and leads me back to the table. I sit and she takes her place squarely on my lap. The delicate touch of her fingers excites me as she peels the coat from my shoulders and folds it over the back of the wooden chair.

"Look at you," she says like a schoolgirl. "You never change. Is he the handsomest man in the *rathskeller?*" The tedious looks from the men at the table suggest they really don't care, but her female friends smile with disarming interest.

"Your vision haunts me every time I close my eyes," I whisper in her ear. She smiles and kisses me indifferently on the forehead. I expected more.

"This is my friend Christl and her brother Rolf, both alpine skiers."

I nod courteously and say to Rolf, "These are my third Olympic games and I have great respect for you Norwegians."

Christl shares a boisterous laugh with her friends at the table. "But we are not Norwegians," Rolf says as he lights a cigarette. "We are Germans." He blows the smoke in my face. "What about you Mr. Handsomest Man? From where do you hail?"

"My apologies," I reply politely and wave my hand in front of my face to disperse the smoke. "Poland. I'm from Poland." It means nothing to him. I may as well be from Mars. He turns his attention to his other friends at the table.

"A beer?" Sonja asks. "Would you like a beer?"

"No, thank you. I can't stay long," I respond. My moment with Sonja is spoiled.

"Just one? Please?" She pouts and her lips brush mine. I casually wipe the small beads of sweat from my forehead. Is the room that warm?

"Just one. Then I must be on my way." She snaps her fingers at the barmaid who acknowledges her request with a toothy smile. "How did you find me?" I ask.

"Have you ever smoked a cigarette? I tried one once. Horrible stuff. My father smokes a pipe. The aromas are strong but sweet. Cigarettes? I don't like them, but there is nothing I can do. Rolf and his friends think they are special and try to impress me with their cigarettes." The barmaid returns with the drinks. How she can hold four glasses in each of her hands is beyond physical law. "It is easy to learn things here in Germany if you know the right people to ask," she says. "Do you see that man sitting at the end of the bar?"

"The one in the black coat with the armband?"

"Yes. He is the one."

"I saw another like him on the train today. Very rude."

"That man is my escort. The Führer himself assigned Karl to me. He is a member of the *Schutzstaffel*, the Führer's personal guards. He is very nice and not rude at all and he knows everything. 'Can you tell me where the Polish team will stay?' I ask him. Within an hour he knows and carries my message to you."

"Not before reading it," I say.

"Pardon me?"

"Nothing." Thinking I would much rather drink from her lips, I raise my stein and take a draught, then cool my forehead with the cold glass. She traces the moisture slowly with her fingertip and looks – just for a moment – deeply into my eyes, and I glimpse the same emotions in her that are pounding through my veins.

Her spell breaks as quickly as she cast it when one of the boys at the table calls out, "Who wants to play a game?" Certainly not me, I think, but Sonja claps her hands like a child and the others at the table begin to chant, "Game, game, game…"

"What about you, Pole?" Rolf asks. "What was your name again?"

"Bronisław."

"Do you want to play a game?"

His boyish looks suggest he is the youngest person at the table. I think he is still a teenager yet his teammates concede to him as if he is the one most deserving of their respect. I don't like his arrogance. "That is why we are here, to play games," I respond. "What game do you want to play?"

He takes hold of a passing barmaid and whispers in her ear. She smiles and returns with a black, cardboard box. Rolf and his friends clear the table of glasses and ashtrays, and the maid wipes it clean, then Rolf opens the box and produces a board, which he places in the center of the table. The board depicts a walled city map, and the name of the game appears on the board in large, bold letters, "**Juden Raus**," "Jews Out!" The people gathered at the table and those nearby laugh hysterically and begin to chant, "Out with the Jews! Out with the Jews!" Within moments, everyone in the *rathskeller* takes up the cry.

I do not share their amusement, nor do I hide my disapproval. Sonja smiles politely and says to me, "It is just a joke, Bronek. Don't be so grim." I stare across the wooden table at another German team member who picks up a playing piece, a distorted Jewish caricature with a pointed hat. The German holds it near his grinning mouth and in a high, squeaky voice mimics, "Send me to Palestine, please." As the laughter intensifies, my annoyance grows into anger. Some people find this so funny they have tears in their eyes. The Captain's voice echoes in my head, "Be careful." Could he have possibly anticipated this? The world is upside down when people treat fellow human beings like dogs and play games of chance that test their skills at driving men from their borders. They show no more concern than they would driving a herd of cattle to the butcher's block.

A chorus of drunks at the bar begins to sing,

>"Schlomo is a friend of mine.
>He will fleece you anytime
>For an orange or a lime.
>Just one shekel suits him fine."

Others raise their glasses and chime in.

When the clamor subsides, the blonde man with pock-marked cheeks opposite me says, "The game is so simple, even a Pole can play. Roll the dice and get your Jews out of the city and on their way to Palestine." He begins to position pieces on the board and says, "Who's playing?"

I notice that Sonja's 'friend' from the *Schutzstaffel* watches us closely from the end of the bar, a smirk spread overtly across his face. Sonja glances at him. I cannot believe it when she says, "I'll play, and Christl, too. Bronek, will you play?"

How can this be, I ask myself? How have I found my way into this den of thieves who take pleasure in stealing a man's dignity with hateful words and more? How can this girl who I find so beautiful be not so innocent? I can stay here no longer. I fled from her once in America, and I flee again in *Bayern*.

"I'm sorry," I tell her, and I truly am, "but I must go."

"We don't have to play," she says. "Maybe we can find another table?" It is far too late for that.

I want to pull her to me, to take her hand and leave, but in less than 30 minutes, she has made a powerful statement to me about her personal values. My kiss would be wasted on a person who is willing to play this wicked game with these evil people. "That's not necessary," I say flatly.

"What's the matter, Polish man? Have you lost your competitive edge on a simple board game?" Rolf sneers at me.

I imagine turning the table over onto his lap, scattering the pieces of his board game and smashing his ashtray and beer glass on the hardwood floor, or better yet in his face. The Captain's words continue to resound in my brain. I hold my composure and force a smile to my face and only answer, "I must leave." I drain my beer glass and place it on the table with more power than I should have. Sonja follows me to the door and forces me to turn around. Her SS escort skulks several paces behind her.

"You don't have to leave, Bronek," she pleads.

"You don't have to stay," I answer. I wait for her to reply thinking that maybe, just maybe she will leave this hateful place with me. She looks back and sees her escort, then her friends at the table beyond him. They stare at her and grin. I think she does not fear her escort, but I also believe she will not leave her friends — if that is what they are — nor will I force her to make that choice. When she turns back to me, I do not permit her to speak, and I take her in my arms and kiss her for what I know will be the final time. I am certain it is wasted, but I will remember that I did it. She cannot fail to taste the salt that runs down my cheek. This is not meant to be, and this kiss cannot last forever. I break free from her embrace, walk out the door and quickly climb the steps to face the heavily falling snow that utters the single word I cannot say, "Farewell." I abandon romance in these slushy streets and return to my teammates and my Captain.

We acclimate ourselves to Garmisch-Partenkirchen throughout the week of practice. I withdraw from the crowded streets, spending more time on contemplative thought in my small hotel room. The lampposts and street signs wear alternating pennants, one bears the white Olympic flag with its five colored rings and the other displays the red Nazi flag with its prominent swastika. This is what Hitler chooses to replace the old Weimar Republic's familiar black, red and gold flag with. My teammates find me irritable but attribute it to nerves, something one would not expect from a three-time Olympian.

I believe that the spirit of the games should never fade or fail to excite every man's heart to beat faster. Every four years brings yet another exciting adventure, but these games are different. In one short week, I have encountered too many situations, seen too many things and overheard too many conversations – not all whispered – that suggest these Olympic Games are designed to benefit one man and his Nazi thugs. The Swiss and the Americans welcomed us warmly. Perhaps it is not fair to say the Germans as a people place themselves above us, but the Nazis are very clear about their perception of the rest of the world. The Nazi demeanor says, "Look at us. We are better than you are." I fail to convince myself that it is 'just me,' or that I am more sensitive to the things around me that I do not agree with than other men are. The sign on the road, the game in the *rathskeller* and the laughter it drew from the drunken crowd… Whether or not I take more offense than other people in the village makes no difference. These things are not right. Can a man ever tire of performing in these Winter Olympics? I think not, but strange thoughts swirl in my mind and disturb me. There is more at stake here than a victor's medal, and I cannot ignore the distractions that plague this Bavarian village. Perhaps the Nazis intentionally play with our psyches in order to distract athletes from the task each faces. Not all athletes give so little attention to world events as to ignore it when one man calls another a dog. I am amused when I conclude that I would rather be a dog than a Nazi.

My solitary walks lead me to a small church on the hillside high above the village. St. Anton's, it is called and home to Franciscans. The games open today. I wander to St. Anton's through the early morning darkness. Light snow falls like God's tears from the black sky. He rues what happens here but denies free will to no one. The old hinges squeak tiredly as I open the door and stomp snow from my feet on the stone floor. Unknown supplicants who whisper prayers at odd hours of these cold winter nights leave a handful of lit, votive candles that offer dim light in the empty sanctuary. I enjoy these visits most when only God and I are present. I kneel in the front pew and feel his hand upon me and the warmth and comfort it brings. I am quite certain that there is a real *hamsa*, a real hand of God and it is here to comfort all of us. In younger days, I would pray for victory, then to do my best. Today, my prayers have nothing to do with sport or games. Thousands of people have traveled to this small village where they will be touched by Hitler and his Nazis. I pray today that all men who attend these games come with strong hearts, immune to Nazi propaganda. I pray today that everyone here, all spectators and all athletes, experience true fellowship and leave with a willingness and commitment to treat all men with dignity.

Like a vigilant nighthawk, the door squeaks behind me. The air ripples and its motion crawls through the vaulted church and finds its way to the candles whose flickering shadows feign physical life to the statue of Jesus that watches me from an alcove to the right of the altar. Steps tread softly up the aisle and a body slides into the pew behind me. "Welcome friend," I say softly with no knowledge of who it might be.

"Welcome," the visitor replies. I smile. I will gladly share this time with the Captain.

"Can you do this?" An odd and curious question, but I know what he means. I will lead our parade and carry our flag into the stadium.

"With pride and with pleasure," I answer.

"I know you are bothered by this Nazi rhetoric, their crude signs and pompous attitudes. Even their coaches look down at us. Their athletes may be worse, but honestly, I think the SS watches them very closely for signs of weakness and commiseration. They are instructed to act like they do for the benefit of their leader, and no one is ready to pay the consequences of disobedience. That man is crazy. I believe most of their athletes are good men, but they follow orders so as not to forfeit their chance at personal glory. Only a handful truly support this rabble-rouser who places himself on his own pedestal, but mark my word, Bronek, sooner or later his pedestal will erode and crumble. The Germans are not a stupid people. They just have to wake up and recognize their leaders are making bad choices for them.

"Carry our flag with confidence, Bronek. Set the example for your teammates. They will follow you."

A heavy, white blanket greets us when we leave the church. Snowy conditions persist as dawn creeps up on the awakening village.

Poland is forever destined to follow Norway into the stadium unless Norway hosts the games in the future, in which case they, as host country, like Germany today, would be the last to enter the stadium. We followed Norway directly in America, but at these games, *Österreich* – Austria in America and *Autriche* at St. Moritz – separates us. The snow will not subside, but it does not deter a huge crowd from gathering in the streets leading to the stadium. More countries participate in 1936 than at any of the previous games, and far more athletes assemble to march, nearly threefold the number in America. It follows, then that the crowd that swarms this small Bavarian town is equally as large and impressive.

I stand with our flag to lead Poland's 20 men into the stadium. I look past the Austrians and search the Norwegian team for Sonja. It is not difficult to find her, for a group of young, adoring men surrounds her. She is my curse. Five other women represent Norway, two other figure skaters, and three alpine skiers. I regret that our team includes no women. Poland boasts several aggressive women skiers that I know can compete with anyone in the world. Unfortunately, our Olympic committee has not seen fit to bring them with us. The five Norwegian women stand quietly by themselves, content to concede the spotlight to Sonja. I am sure Sonja would have it no other way. She knows I am here, but even if she thinks she can see me through the Austrian team, she refuses to look in my direction. That is her choice and I will not argue with a woman whose thoughts are as firm as they might be unpredictable.

As we wait outside the stadium, a motorcade approaches, and a large, well-organized contingent of uniformed men rudely pushes people aside to clear a path for the vehicles. The men are very business-like and methodical and they simply tell us to move, not, "Please move," but just, "Move."

"Who is coming?" someone asks.

"It is the Führer." The news spreads quickly, and it means the waiting is over and the ceremony will start very soon.

Apparently, my teammates and I are too slow to the curb because a soldier reaches for me – innocently enough at first – to move me along faster.

"Do not touch the flag," I tell him.

He looks at me and sharply says, "What did you say to me?" In a heartbeat, the Captain and an SS man converge on the soldier and me. I remember the man from the train. His nametag says "Feldman."

"It's you again," Feldman says, "the man from the train who has no problems. I think you soon will." As he reaches for me, the Captain stays his hand and says, "Don't touch my athletes ... or the flag this man carries." Before Feldman can react, the lead vehicle rounds the corner. Every German in sight and even visitors from other countries raise their hands to salute the Führer who stands in the passenger seat of the black vehicle and returns their adoration with his own gesture. Feldman cannot deny his leader and shouts twice, "*Heil* Hitler. *Heil* Hitler." The Captain shepherds me to the curb with the rest of our team. Feldman jogs backwards to follow the cavalcade and points his index finger at me without saying a word. I stand my ground. Finally, he turns and follows the Nazi parade.

"Tell me, Bronek, are you really looking for trouble, or am I just imagining this?" the Captain asks. Before I can answer, a clear, loud and distinct blast of brass instruments explodes from the stadium accompanied by the elation from the large crowd gathered inside. Without exception, the athletes gathered outside applaud. It is our time. The fanfare announces Hitler's arrival and with it, the commencement of the opening ceremonies amid the blizzard that continues to assault southern Germany. The stadium is massive compared to what I remember at Lake Placid, and all the more impressive from a country decimated by war less than two decades ago.

Protocol specifics for these games are vague. They must be simple enough though for an official waits at the stadium entrance to explain how we will proceed. As each team marches into the stadium, the crowd greets it with a roar of approval followed shortly by a second wave of applause as each team passes the reviewing stand. Twice though, the crowd offers suppressed hisses, if not whispered 'boo's.' What can that mean, I wonder?

As the Austrians leave the staging area and enter the stadium to the delight of their many supporters, an official waves his hands to get my attention. "You speak German," he asks me?

"*Ja.*"

"Then you will translate so your teammates understand."

"*Ja,*" I repeat.

He tells us that I will be required to dip my flag and my teammates will be required to raise their arms in salute to the Führer as we pass the reviewing stand. He chooses his words poorly. Had he told us to salute the essence of the games, the crowd or anything else about the games – anything other than this madman – I would have complied, but to salute the German Führer, Hitler, the man who forbids "dogs and Jews" to enter his country, who promotes games to rid his country of Jews... I have seconds to respond, to determine what I will tell my teammates. My conscience commands me do what is right, but I must consider the effects of my choice on my teammates and on my country as well. "Do you understand?"

"*Ja*," I tell him, "I understand." I have 60 seconds to instruct my teammates.

In Polish, I explain, "Let me make it simple, brothers. I make the choice for all of us. I refuse to honor their leader, and I am prepared to violate their protocol. When we march into the stadium, we march in, eyes forward, and take our place on the stadium floor. No salutes to Hitler." I offer a final challenge, "If anyone wishes differently, you have 10 seconds to take this flag from my hands, and I will give it to you with regrets but without resistance."

With no hesitation, Stashu yells, "We are with you," and he offers a smile and a mock salute to the official that just briefed me. The other 18 raise closed fists in the air to show their solidarity.

"Do they understand?"

"*Ja*," I answer a fourth and final time. He nods and ushers us to the stadium entrance. The name "*Polen*, Poland" booms from the loudspeakers and the crowd raises its unified voice to welcome us to these games.

All week uniformed men – some dressed in brown, others in black but all wearing the swastika – pass each other and extend their arms in the *Hiltergruß*, the Nazi salute. It is uncomfortably similar to the Olympic salute. As we parade into the stadium, I watch the Norwegians with great interest. I know the Austrians will gladly abide by the instructions. What about the Northmen? The Norwegian flag bearer disappoints me when he dips his flag towards the reviewing stand Hitler shares with the International Olympic Committee President Henri Baillet-Latour and other dignitaries. As he lowers the flag, the athletes who follow him raise their arms in salute, which delights Hitler and the majority of spectators, mostly Germans. Hitler acknowledges the Norwegians with an insolent salute of his own.

To even louder applause, the Austrians lower their flag and raise their arms. Some even cry "Heil Hitler" as they do.

My stomach tightens as we approach the stand. I hold my breath while I hold our red and white flag erect. It blows freely and proudly in the blizzard that rages about us. Now I learn the cause of the 'hisses' and 'boos' we heard earlier when we stood outside the stadium. I look neither left nor right but raise my eyes to my flag hoping that my teammates behind me honor our pact. I cannot say how Hitler reacts, but above the audience's general disapproval, I hear scattered applause and I dare look forward at a handful of small, American flags that wave fiercely with even fewer Polish flags. I strain with my peripheral vision, and swear I see Henri Baillet-Latour – standing beside Hitler – defiantly and enthusiastically clapping his raised hands.

I am never free from the Captain. As I march through the stadium, his words swim above the receding hisses from the pro-Nazi crowd, 'Are you looking for trouble, Bronek?' "What were you thinking," he will ask me, and I will answer that I did what everyone else should have done. The Captain will agree.

The disapproving sounds fade faster than they emerged. The Romanians who follow us do not deviate from the instructions. I want to call them cowards, but at the same time, I must acknowledge their commitment to their beliefs as I hope they acknowledge mine. By the time we shuffle through the many inches of accumulated snow on center ice and take our position on the field, the Americans enter the stadium. I have the greatest respect for the Americans, and I am anxious to know if they will enforce the protocol. Their actions will validate or subvert mine.

As soon as the last Yank enters the stadium, the swirling, heroic notes from Richard Wagner's rousing "Ride of the Valkyries" charge from the loudspeakers and echo throughout the village announcing the entrance of the mighty Germans. As the home team, the Germans have the privilege to be the final team into the stadium. The rousing music turns all heads toward the tunnel entrance where the Germans walk into the field amid the din of fanatic cheers, applause and the blasting notes from the loudspeakers. The noise is so loud that it dispels thought and suffocates the other senses. With his eyes on his athletes, Hitler and his countrymen take little if any notice that the Americans, like us Polish highlanders, do not lower their flag nor do they raise their arms in a meaningless salute.

Hitler turns to the Americans as if to return the salute he expects to see. For their part, the Americans tilt their heads toward the reviewing stand and stare blankly at Hitler. Hitler frowns when he lowers his hand and says something over his shoulder to one of his cronies, then points at the Americans. He dismisses the Yanks with a loathsome gesture, then returns his attention to his team as it approaches the reviewing stand with arms outstretched. The incident lasts just seconds and appears to be generally overlooked, but I notice and share immense pride with, and respect for the Americans. I laugh at Hitler's rebuff.

When the Germans are in place with the other nations, the music stops abruptly and the cheering ebbs as Deutschland's Olympic president, Dr. Ritter von Halt moves to the podium to deliver his welcoming speech. His words of 'celebration, peace, fellowship, honor, honesty, solidarity and devotion' ring empty in my ears. Hitler follows von Halt. The rabid applause lasts forever, but this man who they say is such a gifted speaker says few words and simply declares the games open. As a member of the world community gathered here to celebrate world peace through athletic competition, I find neither man's remarks inspiring and, in fact, I question their sincerity. Neither man matches the integrity that Roosevelt brought to the American games.

With Hitler's final word, the orchestra plays a slow and rhythmical melody, and church bells ring throughout the village announcing the games are officially opened. From the nearby mountains to the west, a battery fires a series of salvos that meld favorably with the tolling bells. The Germans are intent to create an unforgettable spectacle here in their southern mountains, but I'm inclined to think that they have over-stepped their bounds, and in doing so have sacrificed the spirit of the games for the glory of Germany. The drama is impressive but pompous. The music swells as we face the mountains where our hosts have erected a tall tower at the top of the hill behind the ski jumps. I must admit that the tower reminds me of Giewont's cross, but to erect it here is nothing compared to the feat my father, the Captain and their highlander friends accomplished nearly four decades ago without the might of a nation behind them. This is no cross made of steel beams, however. High atop the tower that reaches well above the treetops is a large, metal bowl adorned with the five Olympic rings. We squint through the heavy snowfall that makes the pine trees so heavy that they appear to bow down to this Olympic tower. A lone man climbs the hill bearing a torch whose flames cut through the premature darkness the heavy, snow laden clouds give us this day. When he reaches the base of the tower, he faces us, raises his torch and holds it high above his head for everyone to see. "Behold the Olympic flame," a deep voice booms from the loudspeakers. As the words echo above the music, the torchbearer turns back towards the tower and transfers the flame from his firebrand to the metal bowl atop the tower. The flame races up one of the sturdy, steel legs, and blooms when it reaches the oil that fills the bowl. Dark smoke rises from the bright flame whipping haphazardly in the gusty wind. The flame will burn without interruption for the full 10 days of competition, and it is visible from just about anywhere in the valley. The beacon is quite stunning. With the flame lit, the huge, white Olympic flag is slowly raised and emerges, windblown above the tallest ski jump. The flame is lit, the flag is posted and the final notes of the Olympic hymn fade and race away with the wind.

The 27 other flag bearers and I move forward and form a semicircle in front of the podium. Willy Bogner, a German skier stands before the lectern. He grasps his country's flag in his left hand, raises his right and leads us in our oath.

This is the third time I have been honored to say it, "We swear at these Olympic Games to conduct ourselves with honor and to abide by the rules of the games. We will compete respectfully in the spirit of sportsmanship for the glory of our countries and the glory of sports." I say each word like I mean it, and I say each word as if it were the very first time I ever spoke them, and as I do I wonder if there is a conflict between two of those words, 'honor' and 'glory.' I think not, for there can be honor without glory and glory without honor, but here at these games, the two must co-exist, and there is no room for one without the other. The moment is always a solemn one for me, but this time my mind wanders back to the *rathskeller*, and to the German lads gathered there around that stupid board game. Do they just repeat these words like a nursery rhyme, or do they seriously contemplate what they say? What about Sonja? Does she dwell only on glory at the expense of honor?

Lost in these thoughts, the Austrian flag bearer who stands to my left says "Polen, Polen" to get my attention. Had he not, I would have remained there in my deep thoughts, naked and alone. I return with the other bearers to our teams.

The Führer leaves and we are dismissed and march from the *skistadion*.

Chapter Thirteen, 1936

Shield of Abraham

"Przybylski is very upset," Stashu announces as he joins the Captain and me for a small lunch in an even smaller café. In two hours, we will stroll to the *Kunsteis-Stadion* to watch our hockey players open their quest with a match against the defending champions from Canada. Przybylski is our attaché. "He met the hockey players before they could leave for the Rießersee. Andrzej and I were with them." I lean back in my chair as our waitress places a small plate of meat and cheese on the table.

"What's done is done," the Captain concedes. "I do not want it discussed for the remainder of our stay in Bavaria. We have games to play and races to run. We've no more time for Hitler or his politics despite what Przybylski might think." His comments bring a curious but satisfied smile to his face and he adds, "I can only tell you so many times, Bronek. You must be careful, but I cannot control your actions – on or off the slopes. I will tell you this, though," he leans forward in a conspiratorial way and concludes, "Your father would be cheering much like Baillet-Latour."

I am pleased that the Captain thinks so. Stashu adds, "Your teammates have no issues with you, Bronek, and we would do it again. Before the team could escape him,

Przybylski ranted red-faced, 'And you others.' – seriously, Bronek, the man was weeping – 'Not a one of you could say no to Czech?' Then it happened, one of those rare moments when all sound ceases except for Józef's deep voice as he said, 'Go piss up a rope.' The players left Przybylski with his jaw hanging open while me and Andrzej escaped in the opposite direction." The Captain raises his hand to his forehead and shakes his head approvingly, but in disbelief.

"There are no cowards on this team," he says, "That much is certain." Despite how our fainted-hearted attaché is reacting, I am pleased that my Captain and my team-mates support our brief but bold act of defiance in the face of this heartless man, Hitler.

"I will tell you a final story, then we will speak of this no more," the Captain says and taps the table with his butter knife. "Today, Bronek, you and your teammates fly with eagles. You remember the sign you saw from the train?"

"How can one forget it?"

"You can't," he continues. "Those signs are gone." I raise my eyebrows. "Days after our arrival, I strolled the streets and chanced to meet an old friend. We stopped in a café for tea. According to my friend, Baillet-Latour was very upset when he saw the signs. He went directly to Hitler and told him the signs must come down. Hitler scoffed at the request, said, 'This is my country, and I make the rules.'"

"The prick," Andrzej spits out.

"Precisely, but then Baillet-Latour tells Hitler that when the Olympic flag flies above the stadium, the Führer becomes the guest and the IOC makes the rules. He orders

– that's right, he's beyond requesting – he orders Hitler to take the signs down."

"Gutsy man, this Belgian count," I say. "And what happens?"

The Captain raises his hands, palms up. "The signs are gone, at least for the duration of the games."

We finish our meal and walk into the crowded street. Three boisterous and happy Brits with a large Union Jack draped around their shoulders accost us.

"You're Polish boys, aren't you?" one asks stumbling over his tongue, and Stashu retreats a step, ready to raise his fists thinking there is trouble in the air.

"We are," I answer while feigning a swat at my teammate.

"Well done, this morning, lads. At the ceremony."

"We weren't so pleased with our boys," another adds.

"Now, now," the oldest of the three chimes in. "I'm thinking we lacked the courage but not the heart. You chaps from Poland – like the Finns, the Yanks and the three boys and two girls from Estonia – have both. Balls of iron, I'd say, with apologies, of course to the women on those teams. Very well done lads, and good luck in the competitions." They bow together like an actors' troupe and continue their merry way toward the stadium. Their encouragement further strengthens my resolve.

Despite the fact that our hockey players are facing the defending champions from 1932, few spectators attend the game. While we skate on the *Rießersee*, a small lake on the southwest edge of Garmisch-Partenkirchen, the other three games on the day are scheduled at the *Kunsteis-Stadion* in the center of town, and while we face the Canadians, the Germans play the Americans, which is certain to be the marquee match of the day. As our game progresses, the sparseness of the crowd becomes a blessing. We are targets for the Canadian sharpshooters and Józef's goal little more than a sieve. We trail by five goals to none after a single period. Adam posts a lucky goal in the second period, but when the final buzzer sounds, we skate from the ice whipped soundly at 8-1. Better than 8 – 0, I rationalize with little satisfaction.

Our return to the hotel provides me an opportunity to focus on my purpose. Walking along these crowded streets, I realize that new events will make my task more challenging at these Games. I am delighted that the International Olympic Committee has added a downhill race and a slalom race to complement the cross-country races. They've even added a cross-country relay race. We refer to the cross-country events as 'Nordic,' and we call these fast races down the steep slopes, 'Alpine.' Cross-country skiing has been a means of transportation for us highlanders from the time we could walk, but our true love is the rush of wind in our faces and the speed we experience as we fly fearlessly down the steep slopes of Giewont and brother mountains in the Tatras. Transportation is one thing, to race and move as fast as you can is quite another. The added events mean that through 11 days, I will compete in six of them. The daily pace will test my endurance. As my Bibles tell me in every language, there is no rest for the wicked, if indeed I fall among that lot.

As young boys in the Tatras, we would climb to the top of the mountain and once assembled, race down in groups, each boy carving his own path. First one to the bottom wins. If he has courage to fly from a cliff, all the better assuming he negotiates the jump successfully. The event has evolved, however, and, at these games – the first to include downhill competition – all skiers will race the same course that is defined by a series of gates or obstacles, and we will be timed. The man with the fastest time wins. Simple enough, but I prefer the excitement of the old way where you can see your competition and know your position as you speed down the mountain.

The day of the downhill, clouds hide the sun helping to keep the temperature cold and the snow fast. The Captain reports 70 skiers will participate. "The Germans know this hill well," he says, "so I think they have an advantage, but I believe the Italians and the Americans will be tough competitors as well. The early racers will have the best chance because this slope will become dangerous as more and more skiers pack down and smooth the surface." He looks at the official sheet. "The best Germans have early slots. Bronek, you are number 11. Take advantage of it. Karol and Teodor, 34 and 53. Do your best."

The Olympic Committee has invited women to participate in the Alpine events, and the German Alpine specialist, Christl Cramer, the girl with Sonja in the *rathskeller* is a heavy favorite to win the gold medal. The men wait at the base of the course and watch the women fly across the finish line, Christl's time may be the slowest time of the German woman. A Norwegian girl recorded the fastest time. This might be a surprise. The Norwegians are favored in the

Nordic events, but not in these downhill races. I am happy for the Norwegian. The beauty of the Alpine competition, however, is that Christl – if she is as good as they say – can still win gold. The winner will be determined by the combined results of today's downhill and tomorrow's slalom. About half as many women as men compete in the Alpine events.

A newly constructed cable car slowly climbs the four kilometers up the mountainside. I believe the Germans built this as much to demonstrate their technical engineering proficiency as they did to accommodate the skiers. Regardless, it is quite impressive. My teammates and I take our places in the long line. Germany's highest mountain, the *Zugspitze* rises behind us and reaches for the low ceiling of clouds. From start to finish, we will descend 1,000 meters. Each car carries seven competitors and one official to the starting gate at 1,700 meters.

I am satisfied with the luck of the draw and take my place in the second group of seven, which includes a Norwegian, a Yugoslavian, a Belgian, a Canadian and a pair of Germans. One is Christl's brother Rolf, the gamer from the *rathskeller*. He tries to intimidate me with an overconfident sneer. I put him at 10 years my junior, a teenager, and teenagers who attempt to play like adults more often than not look foolish. His sneer detracts from his otherwise handsome appearance. I return his sneer with a smile. The world could do better without the weak souls who try to act tough. The cable pulls a large car before us. Its door is open, and Rolf nudges me brusquely as if to board the car in front of me.

"Hey, Jew-lover, I believe I am before you."

Smiling all the while, I answer, "I believe you are wrong," and step into the car. His teammate escorts him to the opposite end and offers me a look of apology. I do not recognize this man from the *rathskeller*, and I nod my acceptance to him. Rolf starts to open his mouth but before he can say another stupid or insulting word, his teammate puts his face very close to Rolf's and silences him with a single, commanding word, *"Schweigen,"* be silent. Unlike the revelers at the *rathskeller*, this man is serious about what he does and how his teammates represent his country.

An attendant closes the door, and the car begins its slow ascent up the face of the mountain. I study the race-course. It weaves through hundreds of spectators climbing the mountain. They crowd dangerously close to the edge of the course, particularly near the lower gates where racers will achieve their highest velocity as they surge to the finish line. The crowd is not so deep on the upper half of the mountain. Few spectators have the stamina to march through the deep snow to those higher levels. It requires tremendous effort and only the stout of heart can reach those heights. For those fit enough to face the challenge, the reward will be well worth the effort. I think of how many times, skis on my back, I have marched for hours up a mountain, only to turn and race back down the slope in minutes. I do enjoy this ride as we glide above the people and the forest. I am pleased we are building a cable like this one in Zakopane. The car sways slightly in the wind, and occasionally a small, white whirlwind rises from the field below us and tries to touch the car. Each fails and spins laterally across the mountain, then disappears into the pines. The gentle movement of the car and the subtle vibrations that accompany it lull the Belgian to sleep and he snores softly. The others smile, but not Rolf who refuses to take his cold eyes off me. He mouths 'Jew lover' again. I refuse to play his nasty game and look out the window at the harsh serenity of these cold, white mountains. As brutal as the environment can be, it cannot match the brutality of men like Rolf who call this land their home.

The 15-minute cable car ride concludes at a large platform that surrounds a wooden A-frame. The car sways uncomfortably as it comes to a jerky stop at the station. I flex my legs to keep my balance. When the car comes to rest, we file out and the official immediately puts us in proper order, which separates me from Rolf who is last in line. We trek another 400 meters to the starting point, and our legs are warm and limber when we get there. Within 15 minutes, the other German and the Norwegian are on their way down the mountain. As the Yugoslavian in front of me steps to the starting line, I wish him good luck. "Are you ready?" an official asks. He nods and in 10 seconds, he's told, "Go!"

The icy wind chills my face, forcing me to pull my red stocking cap over my ears. As my turn approaches, my heart beats faster. I will stay calm. I step to the starting line, stare down the steep precipice and breathe deeply and slowly. When I answer that I am ready, the official begins a backward count, "Five, four, three, two, one, GO!"

Like an ancient hunter, I stab the snow as if it is a threatening monster. Pushing hard with my poles, I explode onto the course. The first 300 meters are the steepest and I attack them fearlessly, perhaps recklessly. I command myself to hold nothing back. If I lose, it will not be because I was afraid and exercised too much caution. No, I will assault this course like it is a wild beast I must bring to heel. I am flying faster than I ever have on these narrow boards strapped to my boots. I make no adjusting turns or stems to check my speed, and I continue to accelerate. Then, as I enter the first, wide turn to my right, I lose my edges, both of them. No man would be strong enough to hold his balance at this speed. My skis slide from beneath me and I fight to give up as little ground as possible. I hold my skis downhill and they chatter noisily as I strain to dig into the snow and ice with my edges. I am slowing down, but I watch helplessly as I pass beneath the gate through which I am supposed to ski. Is it over so soon, I ask myself? For a brief instant, I am willing to concede the race, but then I think of my country, my teammates and yes, my Captain. I see Rolf's laughing face in the clouds. I cannot give up. Like a desperate animal trying to protect its life, I claw with my gloves and slow myself enough to find purchase with my skis and stop my downhill slide. I have no options and immediately begin sidestepping back up the hill so that I can pass through the missed gate and complete the race. Blood pounds through my ears and counts the painful seconds my recklessness has cost me.

My legs are on fire when I reach the gate and join the race for the second time. Through it all, I hear a frantic voice call above the crowd, "You've lost a full minute, Bronek. You must fly like the wind!" I negotiate four quick turns and enter another straightaway, this one not nearly as steep as the opening run, but I have no choice but to accelerate. I must go faster than I've ever raced and I must ignore the pain in my thighs that worsens as I strive to maintain my edges. This is the price of speed.

I clip several flags as I negotiate the course, and nearly fall again when the basket at the end of my pole snags a gate. I rip it free before it can pull the strap from my wrist. I've skied too many mountains not to know that as I reach the gentle curves of the final kilometer at the bottom of the course, I am moving like a bullet. The spectators hold their breaths and anticipate imminent disaster when I speed by them and fly over the small bumps and through the final curve that takes me to the finish line. I cross it and stem hard on my edges to stop. I am moving so fast that I spin and complete two frantic revolutions, then fall to the ground and slide on my back, finally coming to rest against the hay bales at the end of the run out area. My legs are spent for this day. I have nothing left to give.

The Captain jogs to me, unfastens my bindings and pulls the skis from my feet. "Well done, Bronek! No points for style, but your speed was incredible!" For once he cannot hide his personal pleasure and excitement at my performance. "You came across that line with wings on your feet. So much faster than anyone else! Listen to the crowd!" As my pulse slows and the throbbing in my ears diminishes, I hear the ovation from the thousands gathered at the finish line. With my arm draped around the Captain's shoulder, I stumble to the side with him, and clear the finish area for the next skier. I wave over my shoulder. As far up the course as I can see, men, women and children are looking at me, Bronisław Czech and applauding my effort. I remove my hat and wave it in the air, and the gesture evokes another loud roar.

Stashu joins us. "You are crazy," he says gleefully. "I've never seen anything like that." I finally catch my breath and raise my hand to the Captain and Stashu to refrain their enthusiasm.

"But you don't understand," I begin to pant through labored breath. Before I can explain, the officials announce my time at five minutes and 46 seconds.

"There must be a mistake," the Captain says, confused. "There have already been four times less than five minutes, and those skiers looked as if they walked across the finish line compared to you, Bronek." The crowd is stunned to silence.

I collapse in the snow and lay on my back to stare into the faces of the Captain and Stashu and several other people I do not even know. "I fell," I gasp as I rub the sweat from my eyes. "I fell in the first 200 meters," I explain. "I lost a lot of time." The Captain and Stashu lift me to my feet while the other spectators walk away. Fame flies quickly. It is empty. I am no longer their hero, but it felt so good for those few minutes.

"But you got up and finished," Stashu says.

"And did you miss an obstacle?" the Captain asks me.

"I slid by a gate, and when I stopped I was prepared to concede and walk off the course. In seconds, I reconsidered. To give up despite my mistake is not an option. I climbed back up the hill to rejoin the race. No, Captain. I did not miss an obstacle."

"All the better for you," he answers. "The easy path, the easy choice tempted you, but you chose to do the right thing. Few would make the same decision."

Another skier finishes his race and the biased crowd greets him with joyfully and enthusiastically. It is Rolf Cramer and his time is a good one, just over five minutes. He will certainly be in contention when we race the slalom course in two days. He and his sister stroll past me. The other German skier who rode to the top in our cable car is with them. Rolf gives me another look and says, "Tough luck, Czech, but would we expect any different from a Jew-lover? I think not." His sister finds humor in his prejudice; his teammate doesn't.

Before anyone can stop me, I reach out, grab his jacket and spin him around to face me.

"Please," the other German skier pleads.

"Stay out of this, Roman," Rolf responds and steps forward to put his face in mine. "A wager for you, friend," he challenges me. "On Sunday, you won't be within 30 seconds of me, that is, if you can even finish the race without planting your ass on the snow."

"First of all, I'm not your friend, and secondly, Olympic athletes don't wager," I answer.

"German athletes do," he says and struts off with his sister.

The other skier lingers. "He is a bad one. Like his sister, a good skier, but he is a bad one. I am Roman Wörndle, and on behalf of my teammates and me, I apologize to you and yours." He cautiously surveys the area and adds, "We are not all Nazis." He clicks the heels of his boots, bows and follows Rolf and Christl.

Józef is a wall in front of his net for two full periods before allowing a pair of goals in the third. Adam accounts for our goal, but it is one too few as our hockey team falls to the Austrians this afternoon. We played with courage and never gave up. Tomorrow, we play our third and final game against Latvia, another new nation in the grand scheme of international politics, but with an ancient history of Baltic tribes that is legendary. This evening we dine as a team. We are tired. Tomorrow is an off day for me, so I will enjoy my teammates and try to relax this evening.

Our table is by a large window and I look through it as if it is a moving picture screen. Nazi banners hang limp from the lampposts in the calm air. Passersby ignore us until a man, a woman, and their young son stroll by. The man casually glances at me, then turns back quickly with a look of recognition. He smiles at me, waves and then leans forward and says something to his son, who beams broadly and claps. The man takes an official program from his pocket and extends it toward me, making a writing motion with his hand. Andrzej watches also and says, "He wants you to sign his program, Bronek." Before I can avert my eyes from the man and his son and pretend I do not see them, Andrzej motions them in. The bell jingles at the top of the door as they enter the restaurant, stomp the snow from their boots and approach us.

The husband looks over his fogged spectacles, bows respectfully and says, "You, sir are my son's new hero. Would you be so kind as to sign his program?"

I am no hero, I think, but the boy smiles at me with such anticipation that I cannot refuse. Adam jokes with the man, "But I am the one who scored our goal this afternoon against the Austrians. I think mine is the signature the youngster wants!"

My teammates laugh, and the husband and wife smile politely. Then the father explains to Adam, "But this is the man whose time was the fastest on the mountain this morning in the downhill race. I've never seen a body move so fast on a pair of skis! He humbled all the skiers today though few know it."

"Unfortunately, you must be thinking of someone else," I say before the boy can pass me his program and pen.

"No," the father says, "I am certain you are the man, the man with wings on his feet. Did you not fall high on the hill this morning?"

"I did."

They are pleased they have found me. "We were a bit further down the slope but could see your undoing. The minute you started to slide, I looked at my watch thinking this would be the soonest anyone would be disqualified. You checked your slide not far from us, and then you got back up and climbed to the obstacle to resume the race. As you passed through the gate, I looked at my watch again. A full minute and some seconds more had expired. We cheered when you continued the race when so many others would have quit. As you sped past us, we waved and screamed, 'Fly! Fly!'"

"But my time was not nearly the fastest," I correct him and smile apologetically at his wife and son.

"Indeed it was," he explains. "We waited patiently to hear your time, and when it was announced, I simply deducted the 85 seconds that it took for you to recover from your spill and..." he seems lost for the right words, "You would have led the day by no fewer than five full seconds. Not a hero? Any athlete who does what you did is a hero." Adam pats my back and my teammates applaud rowdily, which draws the attention of the other diners who gladly join in even though they have no idea what we are discussing.

"My son has something for you." The boy reaches into his pocket, retrieves my red stocking cap and hands it to me. "You lost this on the hill."

I smile. "I don't even remember." I turn it in my hands.

"Please, sir," the boy extends his program and his mother offers me a pen.

I pretend to take them with reluctance because I am embarrassed to admit that I do enjoy the notoriety that this family extends to me. No one has ever acknowledged my efforts like this young boy and his parents. "What is your name?" I ask the happy lad.

"Yeheil."

I check myself and look deeply into his eyes, then into the eyes of his mother and father. I put my hand on his fragile shoulder and pull him near, then I reach into my blouse and produce my *hamsa*. In turn, he carefully unbuttons his top button and extracts his own. Mine is but a piece of worn clay; his is forged in silver with clear, dark Hebrew letters clearly etched into the metal. Each examines the other's. I say to him, "I'm told it says 'good luck.'" and he returns a quizzical look, surprised that I do not know what it says and that I seek confirmation from him. "I am fluent in several languages, but I am not a Jew and cannot read your letters," I explain. He and his family take no offense.

"Hamesh for the fifth letter of the alphabet, '*Heh*,' one of the holiest names of God. The hand of Miriam, Moses' sister, five fingers for the books of Torah. On one side, many, like yours, say 'good luck, *B'hatzlacha*,'" the boy tries to explain it in a way he thinks I can understand. "You see." He raises his to my face. "Mine is very clear. Yours is worn, but you can still see the letters if you look closely: □□□□□, B'hatzlacha, good luck." He turns his *hamsa* over, "But this is what you must really understand. Not all have a second inscription." I stare at different symbols on the reverse side.

"Mine reads '*Resh Aleph Hey*,'" he says softly while staring at his *hamsa*, "Finding the Way."

"And mine?"

His father leans close, studies the worn and faded letters and says to his son, "You know what it says. You can tell him."

"*Magen Avraham*, Shield of Abraham." The boy speaks the words with such reverence that even my jovial mates are captured by the silence that follows and lingers like ripples on a pool of clear mountain water.

"Thank you," I tell him. On his program I write, 'Yeheil will find the way. From your new friend, Bronek, the Shield of Abraham.' I pass it back to the boy and we briefly hold hands.

"We must be on our way," Yeheil's father says. "Thank you for your kindness, and may God be with you throughout these games."

"Please. A final gift from me to you." I give my red cap back to the boy. Yeheil smiles broadly and puts it on his head. He is only as tall as I am as I sit in the chair. We embrace in mutual gratitude.

His father touches the brim of his hat, then turns and escorts his family to the street.

I spend my off day at the *Kunsteis-Stadion* where our hockey team opens the day with its match against the Lettlanders. What a special day it is! For the first time in my three Olympic games, I see Poland's red and white triumph as Adam and his mates have their way with the luckless Letts, nine goals to two. We have been on the short end of the score line too many times not to know how they feel, so when our opponents manage a pair of goals in the final period, Józef graciously acknowledges the efforts and I even stand and cheer for them. With neither team advancing to the medal games, in the evening they meet in a *rathskeller* and share too many rounds of thick, dark beer, but they celebrate without me as I retire early in anticipation of my slalom race on the 'morrow.

The downhill race tests a man's courage, but the slalom tests his skill. I know I am a good skier, not a great one, but I will admit that I have more courage than skill. A man can train hard to improve his skill at any task, from baking bread to skating the figures, but he is born with courage and each man's portion allows him to dare only so much. Courage has its limit. There are skiers here that can cut a corner with the precision that a master window maker cuts his glass: they make no errors, the line is clean and sharp. That is my goal, to be a master, to make no errors, to clear each gate cleanly. I care little if I look clumsy, but I am intent to make each of the two runs, error-free, and I will negotiate each run with the speed and daring that my highlander teammates expect from me.

The landscape shimmers in the naked sunshine, and dark shadows at the edge of the forest frame the whiteness of the open course. The warm day invites me to remove my heavy clothing. As I climb the hill behind a Norwegian with my skis resting on my shoulder, I study the 33 obstacles, and when I reach the starting point, I know that speed will not win this race. Speed may prevail on the upper half of the course, but on the bottom, it will prove a reckless man's undoing. I force myself to accept the fact that caution will rule the day. I've learned that lesson, and it is time to apply it. I feel Rolf Cramer's hostile gaze on my back. As expected, his sister earned the gold medal in the women's Alpine event yesterday. I congratulate her, but a man with Rolf's attitude will not be up for the task. He is destined to walk in his sister's shadow as long as he competes, now and forever.

I maintain control and ski comfortably on the first run. There are many racers with slower times than my time, but alas, there are too many with faster times. I think Rolf is too concerned with his challenge to me, a wager I would never accept, and good thing for him. On his first run, he misses a gate and is penalized, and the penalty leaves his time slower than mine. On the one hand, I feel sorry for him because he was in medal contention, but if the leaders can maintain their consistency on the second and final run, Rolf will leave without a prize. So close, I think, yet his own arrogance and selfishness defeat him, and simply to prove a meaningless point to an obscure Pole like me. When I reach the top of the hill for my final chance on the course, I look back and see Rolf climbing slowly up the slope. He will not look at me, so typical of a beaten man, and here am I with no chance for a prize. I will enjoy my second run.

I smile at the official starter when he asks me if I am ready. "Of course," I say. "I'm having the time of my life. What can be better than to ski this great mountain with these great skiers in front of so many wonderful people."

"We should all share your sentiments, young man," he says. He returns my smile, counts down and sends me on my way. I charge the upper slope like a Cossack and fare well, but my aggressive approach fails me through the tight gates at the bottom. I come to a near standstill at the 20th gate; otherwise, I would have missed it, or worse, fallen. The incident at the 20th gate relegates me to the 20th position at the end of the day. I am more disappointed that I finish behind Rolf, but feel no dishonor and maintain my dignity with a simple smile.

Monday introduces another first at the Winter Olympic Games as 16 nations participate in a team sport for skiers. In the first three games, skiers skied and jumpers jumped to win individual medals. In these games, the International Committee has introduced a cross-country relay race where four men will each ski 10 kilometers. The 16 participating teams will begin the race from the same line at the same time, unlike the interval starts used in the individual events. The 16 separate starting tracks will blend into no more than three or four as the strongest racers advance to the front and the weaker ones follow in their channels. Racing against the clock as we did in the Alpine events is one thing, but racing against another human being is quite another – much like the marathon at the summer games – and the act creates excitement and anticipation amongst the competitors and the spectators. Even in the individual

E.S. Kraay

cross-country events where our starts are staggered, there are critical moments when faster skiers close in and pass slower skiers. That drama heightens in the relay race as the first 16 men await the starting gun.

A surprisingly large crowd fills the stands to capacity and this for a mere cross-country race where one sees but a small slice of the action that will unfold over several hours. Only two other events are scheduled today, *eiss-chießen*, curling at the *Rießersee* and men's figure skating at the *Kunsteis-Stadion*.

Each 10-kilometer leg begins and ends at the *Skistadion* at Gudiberg. Michał Górski is our first racer, and I will ski the final leg. Marian Orlewicz and Stanisław Karpiel complete our team. Even though I am the oldest skier of the four, I remain the fastest. The Captain hopes we are close enough when I take the course that my experience can serve us to medal. When I was a young boy, the Captain told me that I have to learn to lose before I can win. These are my third Olympic games and I have many losses behind me; I know how to lose. Perhaps my time to win has arrived. I must consider however that few people ever complete their athletic careers at this level with a victory, and that is why the love of the game pushes us harder than the need to win.

The 64 skiers and their trainers assemble before thousands of spectators who fill the same horseshoe stadium at Gudiberg that hosted the opening ceremonies. Three meters abreast separate each of the 16 teams who wait at the starting line. The Finns stand to our left and the Italians to our right. Both are formidable opponents and if we can keep pace with them, we remain in contention. As the clock moves slowly toward 9 a.m., Michał and the other

15 men representing their countries on this first leg of the race strap their skis to their boots.

I find the personalities of the teams to be as different as the languages that they speak. The Finns, ever the professionals in an amateur world exchange few words among themselves and none with us or anyone else including the official who will monitor each of their exchanges during the race. The Italians on the other hand are loud and boisterous. They enjoy the moment and they enjoy each other no less. One Italian looks at me, points at the man who will ski their first leg and says, "My teammate wishes you the silver medal."

"And the gold?" I ask knowing what his answer will be. He wastes no words and simply opens his arms wider than his broad smile. His gesture is more convincing than anything he could have said. "Good luck, friend," I cheerfully say. Sixty seconds. Michał leans forward, shifts his weight to his poles and slides his skis smoothly back and forth, back and forth. He is a good skier, but the weakest on our team. He understands his role and abides by it. We huddle as the seconds evaporate.

"If you can finish in the top eight skiers, Michał, you have done your job," the Captain tells him with confidence. "We believe in you. We know you can do it."

"I can," he responds.

The starter's gun resounds with a loud 'bang' that cuts through the crowd noise like a sharp crack of summer thunder. The racers respond with a charge into the white plain before them. The skiers from Finland, Norway and Sweden surge forward with long, powerful strides that demonstrate the strength of the Nordic countries. The Slavic skiers fade to the back of the pack but ahead of the Turk, who looks as if this is his first time ever aboard a pair of runners. His short steps elicit some laughter, but I respect him and urge him onward knowing what courage it takes for him to compete with the giants of the sport. Michał starts well and holds his position in the middle of the group as they crest a small hill, and disappear into the trees.

The Captain checks his timepiece. "Forty-five minutes. That will be a good time for Michał. Forty-five minutes." As we wait, we keep our legs warm and limber with frequent stretches and knee bends, but we spend more time resting on the bench than standing. After 30 minutes, the Captain sniffs the air like a bloodhound and tells Marian to ready himself. When the distant crowd noise grows, we know that the first racer approaches. In minutes, we see him. The Norwegian will complete the initial circuit in the first position, and his lead is formidable. A full minute passes after he gives the race to his second that the Finn and Swede, matching each other stride for stride hand the race over to their teammates.

The Captain counts the minutes and grimaces with each second that ticks when 45 minutes expire and Michał is not in sight. He shakes his head involuntarily while we search the horizon, and then we spot him. Regardless of Michał's time, the Captain concedes that his effort is a good one, as he is the sixth racer to complete the first leg. He tags Marian and collapses. We are quick to pull him to his feet so that his muscles do not cramp.

"*Powodzenia!*" I call to Marian but he probably can't hear me over the blood coursing through his ears with the sound of kettledrums. Stanisław will run the same track that Michał did, so Michał briefs him thoroughly. Michał's strength is on level ground, and he explains to Marian that the steep ascents they are required to negotiate tested his limits of pain and endurance. "It's easy coming down," he says, "but my legs burned like the fires of Hell going up!"

Midway through the race, the outcome becomes less certain as the second Norwegian tags his teammate just seconds ahead of the hotly pursuing Swede. Next, comes the Finn, who will not concede the race and follows the two by only 20 heartbeats. We maintain our sixth position when Marian tags Stanisław, but we trail the Norwegians by nearly nine minutes as they continue to build their lead. The Northmen are very strong, and halfway through the race it becomes clearer that the medals will fall into their hands.

My mouth is parched and my pulse quickens when the crowd announces the approach of the leader of the third leg. It is not the Norwegian this time but the Finn, who has passed his competitors and – though his team still trails – gains valuable seconds on the field. I bind my skis to my boots and wait patiently for Stanisław. We've lost more ground as I take the race from my friend. I know it is impossible to erase the 12-minute lead the Nordic speed-sters have amassed, but I will not verbalize it. Stanisław knows the race is lost when he tags off, but as he does he gasps, "For Poland."

The man in front of me is the German, and he leads me by more than a minute. He is the man I must catch; it may be impossible to win, but if I take them one man at a time... I see myself magically catching each one and

passing him while the crowd cheers my name! "Czech,"
they cry as I glide past Germany's favorite, then "Czech,"
again as I advance past the other racers in front of me until
I finally leave the Swede and the Norwegian in my tracks.
It is then that I glimpse the Finn, tall, blond and powerfully built. He pulses like a machine. My stride becomes
awkward and pained, but it does not matter because I
feel myself catching him as we race through the streets of
Garmisch-Partenkirchen. The spectators, young and old
are lost in their frenzied cry for "Czech! Czech!" I've never
heard such cheering for me. It spurns me onward, well
beyond the threshold of pain that I have banished from
my memory. I continue to close on the Finn. The sense
of competition is keen and the thought of victory is won-
drous. My emotions drive me forward like a taskmaster's
whip. "Czech!" they continue to scream, and now I see
the swastika'd banners laying in a heap at the base of each
lamp post, replaced by the simple red and white stripes of
Poland's flag. I am soaring like my mountain friend the
eagle, but as I emerge from the village into the final, open
stretch that leads me to the *Skistadion*, silence envelops me.
The only voice belongs to the wind; it may be soothing, but
it is not inspiring. The large crowd returns to the village
and no one pays me any mind. Stride after stride I close on
the finish line. There are no cheers; there is no orchestra to
welcome me back as the victor. My 45 minutes are gone,
and I realize that I have skied a lonely, uneventful race. I
caught no one, and no one caught me. As there is no glory,
I feel no shame. If the seventh position is respectable, then
we are a respectable team for that is where we have finished.
No shame, no glory.

Like a somber procession in a potter's field, we trudge through town to our hotel. We finished 17 minutes behind the Finns who captured the gold medal in storybook fashion. Their final racer, a superman named Kalle Jalkanen moved like an invincible machine, eliminating the 60-second lead the Norwegian held going into the final leg. Jalkanen crossed the finish line just six seconds ahead of the exhausted Norwegian.

I am not as exhausted as I think I should be and that tells me I did not give my best effort in the race. Marian and I skied the same track, and his time was nearly two minutes faster than mine was. My teammates avoid me at the hotel. No one need remind me that Marian is our youngest, most inexperienced cross-country skier. As I review the times, I understand that even if my time were five minutes faster – another impossibility – our team would have only climbed from the seventh position to the sixth. What would have, and could have been is of no count. We are who we are.

After a hot bath, I tell the Captain and my teammates that I need some time alone to gather my thoughts and regain my focus. I go for a walk. My statement is true, but my wandering is not random. I cannot explain it, but the *rathskeller* where I met Sonja draws me to it.

Pedestrian traffic on these narrow streets is heavy, but the rules are clear: after each day's final event, access to the village is restricted to the athletes, and spectators and visitors must return to their lodging in Munich or other nearby towns. The procedure benefits athletes as well as businesses across Bavaria who profit from the increased tourism. In a short time, the village will be clear of spectators, but for now, the streets are busy with people making their ways to the train terminal, or to parking areas where they have left their vehicles. The crowd is happy, satisfied and grateful. The German showcase is impressive, and these winter games at Garmisch-Partenkirchen serve as a valuable rehearsal for the summer games in Berlin in just a few short months.

As I round a busy corner on an otherwise quiet street, I come face to face with Sonja's black garbed SS escort. He reaches out – not in a threatening way – to usher the crowd to one side. Not far behind him is Sonja, her laughter unmistakable. She walks arm in arm with a man she calls "Jack," easily recognizable as an Englishman by virtue of his heavy accent. A long entourage of adoring patrons follows the couple, but scattered amidst their personal train are other SS officials.

I step to one side to prevent her seeing me. Jealousy chokes me when Jack puts his arm around her and she rests her head on his shoulder. Sonja laughs again, and some bystanders even applaud when Jack leans and kisses her tight, blonde curls. Ah, the prince and the princess. Maybe they are. While I am no peasant, I pride myself in my highlander roots. I am at peace in the outdoors, and would rather eat beets and potatoes from a wooden bowl, and drink water from the cup of my hand, than I would eat roast duckling from a china plate and drink fine wine from a stemmed glass. I reflect on my parting moments with Amalia some 10 years ago on a starlit night in Zakopane. There were tears then, but I shed my tears for Sonja at the *rathskeller*. I will not do it again. Love is not so grand that losing it ends a man's life.

As the entourage moves on, I step backward and trip. I struggle to regain my balance, but only slip on the ice. I extend my arms behind me and prepare for the embarrassing fall, when two strong arms catch me and return me to a steady, upright position. My savior is the German Alpine skier who rode the *Kreuzjoch* tramcar with me for the downhill race.

"It seems you've saved me for a second time, my friend," I say to him, "and I can't say which situation threatened the worse consequences."

He bows to me. "After the way my teammate treated you, I will remain at your service." He extends a hand and re-introduces himself. "Wörndle, Roman Wörndle."

"I remember. Bronisław Czech."

"I know," he says as we shake hands, "The speed merchant from Poland. Word spread quickly through the village. My teammates Franz and Gustav have the highest respect for you after your performance on *Kreuzjoch*. Had you not fallen, the results of the race would have been much different."

"I'm not so sure," I explain. "After the fall, I had nothing to lose. If I had not gone down, I would not have crossed the threshold that took me beyond reasonable caution. I believe we are all born to race that way, but fear of failure prevents us from doing it."

"Well said," Roman answers. He scans the street and points to a café. "Perhaps a beer or maybe a chocolate? The cafés are beginning to empty. It's the least I can offer you for giving us the medals."

I laugh. "Who owes who is of no consequence to me, but I would be pleased to share a drink with you, Roman."

We escape the crowded street in a nearby cafe and sit near the window so we might still feel the excitement flowing through the streets like an electric current. The waitress brings us two glasses of amber beer topped with thick heads of foam. We knock our glasses together.

"To these games and the spirit of brotherhood," I say.

"And to nothing more," he adds. We each enjoy a long quaff, he with the knowledge that he is now merely a spectator with his competition behind him and, me with the consolation that I do not compete tomorrow and can enjoy a beer with my new friend without affecting my performance in two days hence.

"I must formally apologize for my teammate," Roman says. "Few others on the team share his prejudice. Why him? I don't know. They are a good family. He could be a good kid, but like many of the younger athletes, he thinks his bluster and offensive attitude make him tougher in competition."

I brush it aside with a wave of my hand. "There is no need to apologize. If I read his situation correctly, he is not much more than a brash, young and spoilt boy who tries to match his sister's achievements. He's a good skier, no doubt, but he will never reach her level. Because he can't, he opens his mouth when he shouldn't. I prefer that the athlete's skill speak for him." We touch glasses again. I withhold comment concerning the boy's racist remarks.

"Aside from my teammate, how do you like my home? I am from Partenkirchen," he explains.

"Ah! So you know these mountains!"

He blushes an apology and lights a cigarette. "But I've never raced those particular courses."

"It makes no difference," I answer. "For me or anyone else to say otherwise would only be an excuse, and excuses only justify why losers aren't winners."

"Well said."

As the late afternoon sun disappears behind the peaks, and dusk conquers the waning daylight, the waitress moves through the café lighting fragrant candles at each table. They will soon cast a warm glow on the faces huddled over them.

"Your town is beautiful," I tell him, "and I think you would like mine as well. It is another mountain village that sits at the base of the Tatras in southern Poland."

"You are from Zakopane?"

I nod and take another drink.

"I have heard the snow is magnificent in the Tatras. Is it true you are building a cable car much like ours at the *Kreuzjoch* station?"

"We are. I think we are a candidate to host the international championship when it is completed. Two, maybe three years."

The cuckoo clock behind the bar announces 5:00 p.m., and with the cuckoo's final call, the bell above the door jingles to announce new arrivals, four men dressed in the black uniforms I have come to distrust.

"*Schutzstaffel*," Roman observes. "They are the *SS*, Hitler's personal bodyguard. Wherever you might find high-ranking officials, you will find the *SS*. Hitler is here, the *SS* is here." The four stroll by our table and recognize Roman as a German athlete.

"Heil Hitler," one says.

"Heil Hitler," Roman responds. They remove their overcoats and move to the bar.

"I thought only athletes can remain in the village after 5:00 p.m.," I say.

"The *SS* has its own rules and does as it pleases."

I shrug my shoulders. "I am not political by nature, and what you do in Germany is of little importance to me, but how do you feel about this new leader of yours? I don't trust him, yet Germany seems to accept him with open arms."

"Germany tries to heal the open wounds that remain from the Great War. This man may have some answers."

"Have you read his book?"

"I don't read much."

"I do," I respond, "And I read his book to improve my German. While I have no interest in politics, this man's principles concern me."

"What makes you uncomfortable?"

"His racist mentality. Hitler blames the woes of Germany and all of Europe on the Jews. I do not understand how the Jews inspire such fear in Hitler."

"Are you a Jew?"

"No. I am not, but if I were, would it matter to you? If I told you I was a Jew, would you sit at this table with me, or would you leave? If I was a Jew, your man Hitler would spit at me as soon as look at me."

"No, I would not leave, but if you are not a Jew, then why should you care what Hitler thinks of Jews?"

"Until I came to these games, I didn't think I did care and I paid little attention to him. It is true. Even in Poland, some men hate the Jews. I do not share this hatred. The Russians? They are the worst of all with their pogroms. However, as our train traveled through Germany I saw many signs, evil, wicked signs with a single purpose: to ridicule the Jews and strip them of their self-respect. Hatred in Germany is blatant. I met your teammate Rolf one week ago in a *rathskeller* where he invited me – no, he taunted me – to play a ridiculous game – a stupid board game – where the objective is to rid your country of Jews."

"Excuse my friend. He takes that game everywhere. He thinks it amusing."

"I do not, though I was very much in the minority that night. I find it offensive and beneath the dignity of any decent man to mock another man, Jew or Gentile. Makes no difference. I am not a Jew, Roman, and I am not politically motivated, but I do have a conscience, and my conscience tells me this is wrong."

One of the *SS* men turns in his seat and eyes me warily. "You must keep your voice down," Roman advises me as he smiles sheepishly and waves at the man at the bar.

"I can leave if you like," I say. Roman shakes his head and waves to the waitress for two more beers.

He leans forward and the candlelight softens his face. "I make no excuses for Hitler and how he feels about the Jews. I can only tell you that I do not share his opinions and that most people I know do not share those beliefs. I invite you to my home here in Partenkirchen. I live in a small flat. Across the hall lives a Jew, a piano teacher who instructs children. A very famous musician lives in our small town. His name is Strauss. Strauss visits my neighbor often. I've even had coffee with them in a most friendly and pleasant atmosphere. Not all Germans share Hitler's views.

"I must say, however – and most certainly not in the man's defense – there are things that Hitler has done which have been very good for the German people. Are these your first Olympic games, Bronisław?"

"No, these are my third."

"I am even more honored," he says with a broad smile. "These are my first, but I will just point to America, the great nation across the ocean. You were at the games in America?"

"I was."

"How do these games compare to those in America?"

"That depends on what you want me to compare." Before he can restrict my answer I continue, "For the spectacle alone, the grandeur of the facilities and size of the crowds, there is no comparison. The games in America were amateurish compared to what you have done in Germany."

"My point," he says but I cut him short.

"However, Olympic games should be defined by the spirit of competition and the solidarity of nations that participate. In that regard, the games in America were far superior to these. We weren't required to salute the American governor as we were supposed to salute Hitler at these games. In America, we were brothers. Here… I feel as if I am not trusted, as if I am always being watched, as if I am inferior to the hosts."

"That's not a fair assessment," Roman says. "If that was true, would you and I be sitting here sharing a drink and enjoying each other's company?"

"There are exceptions to every rule," I counter. "Maybe you and I are exceptions. You are a good man, Roman, and I want to believe all Germans are like you, but when I see public signs comparing Jews to dogs and when I hear men laughing at a board game that degrades the Jews, I'm not so sure that all Germans share your sentiments. When the thousands in the stadium raised their arms to salute Hitler, I think the Germans are more like him and are more likely to share his prejudice than your compassion."

We stare at each other in silence as the bell atop the door announces another patron.

"People fear power," Roman finally says, "And Hitler is a powerful man. He does not care what the common man desires. His objective is to insure that the common man shares his desires and his vision of what Germany should be. I don't think Germans in general share Hitler's prejudice, but I am certain that they will not voice opinions inconsistent with his. That, my friend is what is happening in Germany, and it is far more likely for a teenager like Rolf to be swept up in the tide of Socialism than it might have been for his grandfather." Roman raises his glass, and again I meet it with mine. The candle sputters briefly as a drop falls into the melted wax that pools around the flaming wick.

Black boots plant themselves next to our table. I look up to see Feldman standing with hands on hips, his peaked cap with swastika bearing eagle and *totenkopf* still on his head, black gloves in his right hand.

"And here you are again, my trouble-making friend from Poland, but this time I don't see your guardian angel," he says through pursed lips. He slaps his gloves in the palm of his left hand. "You have no special privilege here, particularly after the stunt you pulled in the stadium on opening day."

Roman leans back in his chair and boldly comments, "A man must do what his conscience compels, *Untersturmführer.*"

Feldman glares at him. "A loyal German, are you? Drinking beer with this insolent, Pole?"

"I am indeed," Roman replies with a slight bow of his head, "I am a loyal German and I am drinking beer with my Polish friend." If Roman feels intimidated, he disguises it well. "Whether you like it or not, *Untersturmführer*, this man is a guest of the Führer, and I will treat him with the respect he deserves." As Roman drains his glass he looks over the rim and sees the other *SS* men watching and listening, wondering who will make the next move.

"Hey Feldman," one of them calls, "Come join us. I think you need to relax." The others laugh and turn back to the bar.

I stare silently at Feldman while I finish my beer. Rising from his chair to meet Feldman eyeball to eyeball, Roman announces, "We've places to go and more interesting people to see. We must be on our way. Have a good evening, *Untersturmführer*." Feldman must feel Roman's breath on his face. Roman does not move until Feldman steps aside – Wörndle's fortitude is inspiring. Only after Feldman retreats a step do I stand and direct a slight nod to the men at the bar who watch us in the mirror as we walk out the door.

The temperature is colder and the crowd has thinned as the spectators give the village back to the athletes. Roman asks, "Would you like to join me for a drink in my flat? Perhaps the pianist across the hall will play us a tune."

I turn my collar up to fend off the wind. "I would like that very much, but I must return to my team." He understands. We grasp hands again, this time very firmly. "I'll say it again, Roman Wörndle: you are a good man, and I am proud to call you friend. Germany needs men like you and I pray that your moral courage and strength will be an example for your teammates, Rolf Cramer included."

My first Olympic race, the 18-kilometer cross-country in St. Moritz, seems so long ago. On that day, 49 racers skied for the medal. Eight years later in Bavaria, over 100 skiers vie for the championship and I draw the 90th position. I catch more skiers than pass me – of that I am certain – but despite my effort, I climb to the 33rd position and advance no further. Marian and Michał start well ahead of me, and Michał finishes 22nd. I am happy for him. His performance is a strong one for such a young skier. Stanisław finishes 42nd, so all of us can at least claim that we finished in the top half of the competition. There are worse things in life, and in sports.

They say this is Sonja's last competition as an amateur, that she will turn professional after these games. I don't know what to believe when it comes to Sonja, but on this eve of the final day, the crowd moves steadily like an ocean wave toward the *Kunsteis-Stadion*. Everyone wants to see her final performance. No one concedes the gold to Sonja, and other skaters – who may be no less deserving to be crowned the skating queen – push her to her physical and emotional limits. The women's figure skating competition is tightly contested, but as is her way, Sonja silences her critics with her passionate interpretation of The Dying Swan. The thousands in the stadium are stunned to silence and the only sounds are Sonja's cutting blades and the bittersweet cello as it guides her painfully but beautifully with Camille Saint-Saëns' composition. The applause that characteristically accompanies each skater's leaps, jumps and spins is absent, as if her skating on this day has achieved a moment as fragile as the finest crystal. No one can pull his eyes from her, and no one dares disrupt the performance with a sound. Emotion rises in my throat as tears well in my eyes, not for my loss of a relationship with this girl, but for the pure beauty of her skating. I am no different than anyone else privileged to be in this stadium on this day. Her performance drives me to my knees.

Seconds pass after her she lowers herself gracefully to the ice in her final spin, and the last note of the cello dissolves into the cold air. Hitler is the first to rise from his seat. Grinning broadly, he cannot suppress his applause, and he turns to the crowd to encourage each spectator to his feet, but his action is unnecessary as the 10,000 people rise as one and offer homage to this greatest of champions. If this is her final Olympic competition, it is certainly her best and one that will be remembered in legend. Sonja is weeping when she raises her bowed head, and I think they are not tears of joy, rather of anguish. She is that swan and I believe her innocence dies with it in her final death spiral.

Hitler motions her over to the reviewing stand. He remains at attention, then bows like the gentleman I do not believe he is. He leans forward and extends a single, red rose to the champion. She accepts it with a curtsy and returns to the center of the ice, to savor her triumph.

When my teammates and I arrive at the *skistadion* on this final day of the games, we are amazed at what greets us. "Look how many people have come to see me," Stashu says. Undoubtedly not to see him, but there are more people gathered together at the Gudiberg Hill than I have ever seen in one place at one time ever in my life. The stadium alone holds 60,000 people and there is not an empty seat. At least that many and probably more surround the stadium, and crowd the slopes on the sides of the jump. I am not that good with numbers, but if the stadium holds 60,000, I guess there are more than 100,000 – maybe as many as 150,000 – assembled here. That is the size of a big city, almost like Kraków, and they all converge on this slope in this small town in this customarily quiet valley to watch 50-some skiers fling themselves fearlessly into the air and all for the pleasure of sport. We are the daredevils and they love us. I am blessed to be one of the contestants.

The three of us have drawn our positions and stand at the bottom of the hill. We join hands and bow our heads as I say, "God give us the strength to soar like eagles." The cousins answer, "Amen."

"For Poland," Stashu says with conviction and void of the humor that normally accompanies every word he speaks.

"For Poland," we repeat as a team then move to our places in the line of men who slowly climb this hill, clearing their minds of all fear that might impede their efforts. The three of us are evenly spaced. Stanisław will be the 23rd jumper, I will be the 35th, and Andrzej 46th.

We use the time it takes to climb the hill to focus and concentrate on the task we face, but my musings converge on a single thought: this will be my final Olympic competition. My 28 years does not necessarily limit my ability to jump and compete, but as I watch Andrzej climb the hill before me, and as I glance back and nod at the smiling Stashu, I know they will get stronger. The very fact that these thoughts are the ones on my mind as I pull myself upward is evidence that my heart is no longer in the competition. I still love the act – I love to ski and to jump – but the battle no longer thrills me. My 11 days in Germany have given me pause to consider those things I do or fail to do that are of real and lasting value. What is truly important?

I reflect on young Yeheil, who may be somewhere in this mass of people that I look down upon. I am pleased and proud that I have brought him pleasure and inspiration, but that gratification is quickly sullied by other things with less promise. Hitler did not stage these games for the good sake of his own humanity and for the benefit of humankind. I do not believe that for a second. Hitler is intent on producing a spectacle to elicit awe for the new Germany he is building. The multitude that crams this valley tells me he has succeeded.

How I perform on this hill matters to no one and has no relevance in the grand scheme of life. What is more relevant is how people respond to what they have seen in Garmisch-Partenkirchen and in Germany, not how they respond to what they witness on the slopes and in the ice rinks. What they witness beyond the athletic competition and how they react to it ... that is what is important; that will determine the future. Will they remember my jump, or even the jump of the skier who wins this event, or will they remember what Hitler and his people have done in just a few short years? Not the grand stadiums and buildings, but the roadside signs, the parlor games and the hateful books he authors. How many will remember that we Poles, like the Americans refused to raise our arms to salute a man who openly professes his hatred of a religion different from his own? I continue up the hill knowing that my career as an Olympic athlete is finished. I am tempted to turn around and walk back down the hill with my skis still on my shoulders, but I lack the courage to pass Stashu and look him in the eye. He will not understand my gesture. No, I will jump and I will give it my best effort for Poland, but I know in the future that I will seek to do things of more lasting value.

"Czech? Are you Bronisław Czech?"

"Yes," I answer. "I am Bronisław Czech." He motions me forward to the starting position.

"Something is the matter. Are you okay?"

I look into the Captain's eyes. He is concerned.

"I'm fine," I tell him as I realize I have completed my first jump and am standing at the bottom of the hill.

"Sixty-two meters," he says. "Not a good jump for you. For Andrzej, maybe. For you, no. Even Andrzej jumped 66 meters." I nod at him. He points to the hill. "Look, Stashu is next."

The roar of 150,000 screaming voices muddles my thoughts as Stashu starts his run down the ramp. I cannot judge his speed, but he leaps from the ramp with power and confidence. He leaves the 60-meter mark in his wake, and then returns to earth after sailing a remarkable 73 meters.

"That is a jump!" I say raising both of my arms.

The Captain slaps my back and agrees. "I think that will put our young friend in contention." I lower my head and rejoin the line ascending the hill for my second jump. "Head up," the Captain calls after me.

He is right: 62 meters is not a good jump for a three-time Olympian. On my second and final jump, I extend another meter-and-a-half. It is nothing. Andrzej equals his first jump, and then Stashu performs the miraculous and approaches 76 meters. His incredible effort is good enough to raise him to fifth place. He shares the same ethereal air as the Norwegians and Swedes who exceed 70 meters and more on all of their jumps.

The three of us leave our hockey team and our other skiers in the stadium's jubilant atmosphere while we jumpers return to the hotel to change into our official uniforms. A single contest remains, a hockey match, but only about 10,000 people are allowed inside the ice stadium. The other 100,000 remain in the streets telling exaggerated stories of the previous 10 days as they wait for the closing ceremony.

Darkness swiftly descends as Stashu, Andrzej and I join our team at Gudiberg for the final moments of the hockey game. Like all but the English observers, we are surprised that the Brits have captured the gold medal in ice hockey, quite an unlikely result given the history of the Canadian and American teams. I am happy for the Englishmen.

No one notices when I lay my lips upon the flag I hold so dearly and say a silent prayer to thank God for giving me the free will to make the choices that have brought me to this wonderful point in my life. I choke back my emotion before it becomes too obvious. I note the unmistakable fragrance of the Captain's familiar pipe. He is quite relaxed, even satisfied, despite our lack of a medal.

"So how do you feel, my young champion?" He places an arm on my shoulder.

"Better than I ought to," I answer.

"How so?" he asks.

"I let Poland down and I let you down, my Captain. Three Olympic Games over a dozen years, and I fail to bring home a prize for Poland. I am humbled," I say, "but I feel no shame, some disappointment, but no shame."

The Captain stares into the lights. "You have not disappointed me, boy. You have served the team and me well. You have more jumps and races in you yet." He smiles, but the smile is bittersweet because he knows what I am thinking.

I shake my head and rub my forehead against the flag that I hold in my hands, as if it is a sacred relic worth more than the gold of Midas. "No, Captain. I will not return. Others have more promise, more years and more desire. For me, there are more important things to be won than races and medals." His expression tells me he understands. "Oh yes! I will still ski and I will still race, against myself, but the outcome of the sport is of no matter to me any longer. No, Captain, in the future, you'll have no decisions concerning the team and me. My Olympic experience is complete. Thank you for allowing me to carry this flag on my final night. Every second and every moment on my skis have blessed me. You and all the boys I've traveled with will be my friends forever." My admission is complete.

Holding his pipe in his right hand, the Captain embraces me the way my father does. "You are a champion,

Bronek, and of one thing be certain: we are teammates and brothers-in-arms not only on the mountains, but in all of life."

The orchestra inside the stadium begins to play its march. "Stand proudly with our flag, Bronek. You deserve to hold it for us." The closing ceremony begins, and all flag bearers precede the teams and enter the stadium as a single, colorful unit.

Because the other 27 flag bearers and I are inside the stadium as the teams march in, I watch closely to see how each team reacts to Hitler who stands arrogantly at the fore-front of the reviewing platform. There are no changes, too many *Hiltergruß*. I was remiss to discuss what my team-mates should do, and I smile broadly when they march by the Führer, eyes directed towards me and arms raised to the giant Olympic flag that flies majestically over the sta-dium. Their actions draw some hisses, fewer cheers, but more silence than anything. The Führer dismisses us with another wave of his hand.

Baillet-Latour awards the medals, then thanks the German people – and reluctantly, I think, Hitler – for the spectacle they produced in their beautiful Bavarian mountains. He invites the tens of thousands who still are gathered here to attend the summer games. If this was a practice session for Berlin, which I believe it was, I cannot conceive of what will happen in the capital this summer. At Baillet-Latour's command, the Olympic flag is low-ered. It descends slowly and ceremoniously until a group of German skiers collects it. Amid bright and nearly blind-ing flares, the Germans ski down the mountain holding the flag open to position it before the national flags. As precise as a drill team, they reverently fold the Olympic flag.

High on the mountain behind the jump, the Olympic flame that has burned so brightly sputters, dims and disappears. Baillet-Latour declares the 1936 Winter Olympic Games over.

Chapter Fourteen, 1939

Raphael

Time, freely given by the master of the universe. You don't deserve time, you don't earn time. You wake up every day and it is yours, just like the sunrise. A man pays no price for time. September is my favorite month. September, when the mountains blush their fever as leaves exchange their greenness for brilliant reds, yellows and oranges of autumn. The month that welcomes the first snowfalls on the high Tatra peaks and the white begins to creep slowly down the mountains towards the valley floors that wait for the serenity it brings. The air is crisp and you need but feel it once, just one time and the temperature will forever recall that palette of color in your mind's eye.

On this first day of September, much like the wind from the mountaintops, word comes rapidly that the Germans have invaded our country.

I know my countrymen. The urban population will panic while the rural population remains calm. Our legislative and military leaders are rugged men and while they may bend under the German assault, they will not break, ever. We will find a way to survive.

Shadows move like phantoms across my wooden floor. After a courtesy knock, the door swings open. The Captain and Stashu Marusarz enter with another man who I do not recognize. The stranger is a soldier dressed in a dirty, torn uniform.

"Leave the door open," I tell them. The temperatures are mild this time of year and I welcome the fresh air in my home. In a few short weeks as fall gives way to winter, we will not be able to enjoy the luxury of an open door.

"Where are your parents?" the Captain asks.

"St. Clement's."

"Then we are alone?"

"Yes."

The Captain is short on introductions and quick to the point. "Bronek, this is Stefan." Older than I am but younger than the Captain is, Stefan clicks the heels of his dusty boots and bows respectfully. "He's come from the front and detoured south to solicit our help before he returns to Warsaw."

"I've skied here before in better times and I know of you, Czech. Today, however, I have little good news to report," Stefan explains. "The Germans attack in large numbers and their equipment is new. Our men are brave but our equipment is old. We are out-numbered and we are out-gunned. We've organized a defense at Mokra that will check the German advance, but not for long. While some think the stand meaningless, it will buy us time. That is where you highlanders come in."

Mokra is a mere 125 kilometers from Zakopane, but I don't understand how our small town can concern the Nazi war machine. I am not a strategist, but I suspect they will advance toward Kraków and Warsaw, not to the mountain valleys. In Garmisch-Partenkirchen, I have seen what German technology is capable of. If the Germans can accomplish so much in peace, I fear what they will do in war, and they have proven to be a warlike people, particularly under Hitler's aggressive leadership that can only be satiated by control and conquest. His volatile oratory betrays his intention to dominate Europe. He knows but a single way to achieve his destiny, and it will involve force.

"I have served my country in peace," I tell him, "and I will do it in war." My statement confirms what the Captain has already told him.

"Good," Stefan replies. "Who would expect less from a *Górale?*" We embrace firmly, then he reaches inside his unbuttoned blouse and hands me an envelope, and another to Stashu. "As bad as things are today, they will get worse. Our general staff is convinced that the Russians will attack our eastern border. Could be tomorrow, could be next week, but it will happen. We cannot face the Germans alone, and when the Russians enter the fray…

"We are desperate for help. We need men and we need machines, and that can only come from the British and French. With luck, the Americans will join us. Our borders are sealed, and this message has to get out. The only way is over the mountains. Can you do it?"

"With pleasure," Stashu answers. "And where will you have us take this message."

Stefan taps his index finger on Stashu's chest. "You. Take yours to the *Comite International Geneve*, the Red Cross in Geneva. We have friends there who will know what to do." He turns to me. "And you. Take yours to Rome, the Vatican. The new Pope denounced Nazism years ago when he was a cardinal. He will enforce his neutrality, but I am certain he will help."

I heft the light envelope in my hand. "May I ask what it says?"

"You may," he answers, "and for that reason the envelope is open. See for yourself, and then we seal the envelopes."

I withdraw a single, folded piece of paper, open it and read the hurried script aloud, "We will stand for humanity at the tip of the spear. We are the first to fight and we will never surrender." It is signed 'Stefan Rowecki.' We nod our agreement. The message is clear and simple.

I return the folded paper to its envelope and open my shirt to stow it securely and safely where it is unlikely to be found if I encounter difficulties on my journey. I think nothing of it as my *hamsa* swings out on its thin chain.

Stefan reaches out and takes it in his fingers. "You are a Jew?"

"No," I answer. "Just a friend."

"Good," he says. "These days, Jews need all the friends they can muster. I am a Jew, a Zionist, *Betar*."

"I'm sorry," I say, "But I don't know what that means."

He studies the words on my charm and without looking up says, "It doesn't matter, Shield of Abraham, friend of Jews, but I can tell you this, it is good to die for our country and many will. If one of us does, it is not such a bad thing." He carefully places the *hamsa* on my chest and frees himself from the secret vision that held him for those brief seconds. "We must be on our separate ways. There will be little time for rest in the coming days and weeks. Question?" he concludes.

"How will we find our contacts?" Stashu asks.

Stefan replies, "You, my friend, ask for a man named Gromelski at the house in Geneva. He'll know what to do. And you, friend," he says to me, "there is a small house on the Via Sabiniano just south of the city. It is much different from the others. You will know it when you see it. There you will find an old priest they call Father Michael. If you give the envelope to him, it will most certainly reach the Holy Father. Clear?"

"Clear."

"Godspeed to all," Stefan says. He kisses our cheeks, returns his cap to his head and leaves with the Captain who pauses briefly to add, "You are men of courage. Always have been, always will be. I thank you, Poland thanks you. I am proud to be your friend."

Even though we are only two, there is strength in numbers, and Stashu and I agree to travel together for 600 kilometers or so to the Italian border with Austria. Once we cap our own Tatras, we will have to contend with the Alps – Stashu more than I will – but we'll make good time in the lowlands between them. We consider our options and determine that I will skirt the Alpine foothills and turn south to find my way through the boot of Italy to Rome and the Vatican. Stashu will continue west through the heart of the mountains to Geneva.

I leave a short, simple note for my parents: "I am with Stashu and will return in a few days." The less they know, the less to reveal and the better for them. Within an hour, we are on the mountain paths we both know so well that we could negotiate them blindfolded. We don't waste precious breath on words. As we walk silently, I ponder and prepare for the obstacles we may face so that we can avoid difficulty and make our journey a safe and swift one. Our consciences must remain clear and unencumbered in order to accomplish our task. It is likely we will rely on thievery to conceal our identities and to confiscate food and water, and faster transportation, too after we've cleared the Tatras. Stealing – no, borrowing is a given and we accept it without remorse, at least that is what I tell myself as we climb the slope.

The sun bathes us in soft, yellow light as its rays filter through the golden leaves that will soon abandon the security of their branches and carpet the forest floor, rendering the trees bare and heralding winter's approach. A stream flows on our right. The feel of the air, the temperature, the soft breeze all combine to return me to the day my father brought me here and guided me to Bolesław's grotto. My youthful revelation becomes clearer and clearer to me: as my father is, as my Captain is, I too am Bolesław. Stashu also, and Stefan Rowecki and the others who will rise against the German invasion. Our time is now.

The higher we climb, the cooler it becomes, and the forest thins. The sky is clear and there are few trees to shield us from the burning sunlight. Beads of sweat form on my forehead. I wipe them from my eyes and loosen my collar. We've no need to top Giewont, but as we pass beneath the summit, Stashu points to the cross. The sun sits perfectly at the intersection of the two beams, and the structure shimmers in the dazzling light behind it.

"It is a sign," Stashu says. We've no time to stop, but I stare at the cross and whisper a prayer to ask God to help us complete our task.

We walk slowly through the night, unfamiliar with the eastern slope that descends to the Czechoslovakian foothills a hundred kilometers to the west. The temperature drops in concert with the sun as it dips below the horizon to bring a new day to some other distant land. A full moon rises behind us and casts pale shadows that give us some comfort as they point west to our common destination. As we descend the backside in the cooler temperature, we stop at a brook to refresh ourselves.

"Why didn't we think to carry a skin of water?" Stashu comments as he stoops to his knees and drinks from the brook. "How far?" he asks.

"Not so far."

"That we've come or to go?"

Stashu's question brings a much-needed smile to my grim and taut face. "Both" I answer. Is the cup half-empty or is it half full? We are high and deep in the mountains with no sign of human habitation, but we have descended below the tree line. Though the air is still, rustling leaves to the north alert us. We hold very still and listen.

"Animal?" Stashu softly says. I put my index finger to my lips. We wait. German voices answer his question. Like mice who share a lonely house with a prowling cat, we scurry and hide in the bushes. Panic tries to take hold when it occurs to me that we have no weapons. The thought unsettles me, but I will not give in to a feeling of helplessness.

Six helmeted soldiers walk by us headed east up the path we've been navigating for hours. The Germans are not stupid and they patrol the mountains searching for messengers just like us.

"Who has a cigarette?" a young voice asks.

"I told you, no smoking," the leader responds. "And keep your voice down."

"Why so concerned," the young soldier counters. "We've not seen a soul all night. We'll find nothing in these mountains but lost goats."

"Do you know about the *górale?*" the leader asks.

"Is that some type of goat, or maybe an evil spirit?" the young man responds. The others laugh.

"You won't be laughing – or smoking or talking either – when one slits your throat," the leader says. "The *górales* are the Polish mountainmen. They roam the western slopes of these mountains. Now be quiet, keep moving and stay alert." They move on. We wait several minutes until the quiet of the tranquil, mountain air replaces the last sounds of their passing.

"Would you slit his throat?" Stashu asks me as we continue down the path.

"I don't have a knife."

We slip past one other patrol in the high mountains, and by early morning, we reach Štubnianske Teplice, a small Czechoslovakian town tucked in a quiet valley alive with the colors of the fall. We are in luck and come upon railroad tracks, which we follow like hobos northwest to the station. We are very hungry and the dawning sweetness of a nearby apple orchard draws us to it. As the day warms, bees will swarm fallen apples that deer did not dine on during the night. Our coat pockets hang heavy, bulging with fruit, when we hear a loud whistle that announces an approaching train. Its chimney spews thick, black smoke that hangs in the heavy air for hundreds of meters.

We run through the tall grass toward a stand of thick bushes 400 meters south of the station. I don't know who are more startled, Stashu and me, or the woman and the two children who hide with her. They shrink back and gape at us as we tumble into the muddy trench along the tracks. The woman stares at us through hollow eyes as her frightened children, a boy and a girl cling tightly to her coat.

I raise the palms of my hands and tell them, "Do not be afraid." She looks from me to Stashu and pulls the children to her breast. They bury their heads on her shoulders and whimper into her long, black hair. A visage of Amalia passes transparently over her pretty face, then disappears.

Her eyes fill. She struggles bravely for her children's sake, but she cannot contain her tears. "Please don't hurt us," she sobs with a wavering voice.

"We've no intention to," I say.

"How can we help you?" Stashu asks.

She hesitates, afraid to speak. "Please," I urge her, "Do not be afraid. How can we help you?"

She wipes her eyes and decides she can trust us. Does she have a choice? "German soldiers are in the town. We are Jews, but my husband is *Sokół*. He and his friends confronted these men. I watched from a distance. They exchanged angry words with the Germans." The woman begins to sob again and forces the words through her moans, "A soldier drew his pistol and fired a single shot. My husband fell to the ground." It has begun.

The train lumbers into the station and sits hissing like a huge iron snake, resting for but a few minutes before it begins to pull itself westward toward Austria and beyond.

"We've a few moments," I tell the woman as calmly as I can. "What are your intentions?"

"To flee from this place and find safety for my children."

Options are few, and Stanisław speaks up. "We will help you, madam. We cannot say where you will find safe haven," he continues, "But I am traveling to Switzerland, to the Red Cross. I do not know that it is safe even there, but if you can trust me, I will bring you and your children with me."

My duty obliges me to tell him, "They will slow you down, Stashu." I look to the frightened women and say, "I'm sorry, *Pani*, but we have important messages we must deliver, my friend's to Geneva, mine to Rome."

Before she can respond, Stashu raises his hand. "We will manage. Do not worry. I will deliver the message and this family in good time." Hope shines briefly in her troubled eyes, then fades. He places his arm around her shoulder and stares confidently at me as he repeats, "Do not be afraid. We will manage."

The engineer whistles his departure and the locomotive inches forward, straining to drag its long and heavy load. I tilt my head to the side and say, "Okay, then here is what we must do. The train will be moving slowly as it approaches us. As soon as the engine is by us, we climb to the edge of the track. We must run to keep pace until we find an open car. Stashu and I must carry your children. They will be frightened; the noise from the wheels will be very loud. You, *Pani* must stay with us. Can you hoist yourself into the car as it passes."

She is uncertain, but nods her head. "You must," I emphasize. "You have no choice." The children are afraid to come to Stashu and me until we force smiles to our tired faces. The boy may be five-years-old, the little girl, maybe seven and very petite. With little time to make friends with these terrified children, I think to show them my *hamsa*. The little girl smiles and comes to me at her mother's urging. Stashu winks at the boy and the toddler leaps into his open arms. The mother is relieved. "You '*thtink*.'" The little boy lisps as he pinches his nose with his free hand.

"Where's Papa?" the girls asks. "Isn't he coming with us?"

"These nice men are taking us to meet him," the mother responds. "Please do as they say."

The steam engine is gaining speed as it plods past us. The engineer is too busy monitoring his gauges to notice us in the bushes. We rise to our feet and scramble up the incline to get as near to the moving train as we can. I lead with the girl in my arms, and Stashu follows holding the boy in one arm and he uses his free hand to help the mother. The children cover their ears from the screeching wheels that seek steely purchase on the iron tracks. Looking over my shoulder, I glimpse an open door and begin to jog. It will make no difference what might be in that car, an angel or a devil. That open door is this broken family's only chance for survival. As the car comes alongside us, other anxious faces stare at us from the gloom, but not a one offers to help. I toss the girl inside as gently as I am able, then pull myself up. "We need help," I yell above the noise of the wheels and one of the travelers crawls forward and pulls the girl to the relative safety on the far side of the dark cabin.

Stashu releases the mother's hand so he can get the boy into the car. In a heartbeat, she falls and tumbles painfully into the ditch. Stashu hesitates for an instant, but I will not let him fail Poland or these two children. "No!" I yell at him, and grabbing the collar of his coat, somehow find the strength to haul him into the car. As his feet dangle in the wind, we watch the mother rise to her feet with hands to her face. She makes a frantic effort to crawl back up the incline to the edge of the track but fails and rolls back into the ditch. Resigned to her failure, she waves with one arm and blows a final kiss to her orphaned children with the other. She disappears from our sight as the train rounds a bend.

I drag my friend across the rough planks, deeper into the car, and hold him tightly. Neither of us has the mental strength to face the children, but it is unavoidable. Stashu's chest shudders as he fights to restrain the agony he feels at the mother's loss. The scream in my throat chokes me like a hangman's noose, but I hold it there knowing it will accomplish nothing and only heighten the children's despair. Stashu and I stare through the open door as the scenery races by. A man, 10 years my senior grunts, stands and rolls the heavy door closed, thus eliminating my fleeting desire to jump out and run away from this disaster and any responsibility we might have to these orphans. The car is old and light invades through wide cracks in the boarded side. The little boy speaks first.

"Where's Mama?" he asks. Our hearts shatter like falling icicles, but answer him, we must. His question hangs like the heavy stench of rotten vegetables that even the ventilated boards cannot clear.

I release Stashu and breathe deeply while I swallow my tears, then turn to the children and smile. "Your mother will join us with your father," I lie to them. "It will be okay. Do not be afraid." Sunlight shines directly into the girl's eyes creating a yellow mask against the shadows. Her eyes say she does not believe me. The little boy crawls to Stashu and lays his head in Stashu's lap. We speak little throughout the day, content to let the constant drumming of the wheels keep us in a suspended state of disbelief and incredulity.

I can assure you that there is a big difference between the comfort of the passenger cars I have occupied on the European and American continents and riding on the hard floor of an empty but smelly vegetable car. If there is such a thing as luck – which I am occasionally inclined to believe – then luck is with Stashu, the children and me and all who share this. Every time the train slows and stops, we wait nervously, praying that the door will not slide open to reveal our hiding place. It never happens. God cloaks us with the power of invisibility. The doors on the car in front of us and on the car behind us slowly squeal open, then close, but our door remains shut.

"It is your *hamsa* that protects us," the girl whispers to me.

"Then I shall give it to you," I reply and reach beneath my shirt, but her small hand stays mine.

"No," she says in the unselfish innocence of her youth. "It is yours and you must keep it." I smile and kiss her dirty forehead. Eternity passes while time stands still.

Many of our traveling companions leap from the car hoping to find refuge in the woods along the way, but other refugees always replace them. Somewhere not far from Innsbruck – which we glean from conversations outside our invisible car – the train turns south. We hoped it would continue west for the sake of the children, but it does not.

"It is time to part and go our separate ways," Stashu whispers so as not to wake the sleeping children. "I will take the children with me. Their chance at a new life is much better in Switzerland than in Italy." He is right, and shame overcomes me because I am indeed relieved to pass the responsibility of the children to Stashu. "I think we will be able to find another train, heaven-sent, like this one to take us to Geneva." I believe him.

Sunrise greets the train as it slowly approaches another rural station nestled in the Alps of Tyrol at the eastern edge of the range. The children stir and rub their tired eyes.

"I'm hungry," the boy says. I take an apple from my pocket and split it with my thumbs. Each child accepts the fruit gratefully, not ravenously, as one might think. They do not stuff their mouths with large bites, but rather cherish this simple meal. The girl ponders each small bite she takes and wipes the thin stream of juice from her chin and licks her fingers dry. She makes the apple last and is thankful for it.

It is best not to prolong their departure, and as the train shudders to a stop, Stashu says, "It is time for us to leave this train, children. We will find another."

The little ones are worried. Too much change, too many new people in such a short and stressful time. Lifelines are severed to what they know. Who to trust? "But why?" the little boy asks.

"It will be okay," Stashu tells them. "I will bring you to safety in the land of Heidi, cuckoo clocks and yodeling. Do you know Heidi?"

"We know Heidi, but what is 'yodeling?'" the girl asks.

"I will teach you when we are in Switzerland. For now, we must be very quiet." I peer cautiously through the space between two slats of wood and, without taking my eyes from the yard outside, wave 'okay' to my friend. There is activity several cars down the line, but it is quiet near us. Stashu slowly opens the door, just enough so he and his wards can slip through.

He drops to the ground and I pass him the boy, then the girl. She raises her large eyes to me and says, "Aren't you coming with us?"

I shake my head 'no.' She smiles and bravely wards off her tears. I place my left hand over my heart and feel the *hamsa*. I nod to Stashu. "Until we meet again," he says. Lifting the boy in his strong, left arm, he takes the girl by her hand, and they flee into the nearby forest. Stanisław Marusarz is a hero.

Quietly, I pull the door closed. I sit in the corner with my head in my hands and weep. I rue the tears that stain my life. I never even knew their names.

The train approaches a small village on the Italian coast, where the saltiness of the Adriatic Sea permeates the air. I know it is time to start out when we sit idly and unnoticed for 30 minutes. On wobbly legs, I hop from the car to the cindered ground below. With no one in sight, I stretch and steady myself, take my directional bearing from the sun and follow the road toward the village.

I approach a storefront that claims to be a market where an ancient fishmonger sits in an even older rocking chair, rhythmically moving back and forth, back and forth. He enjoys his small pipe that emits fragrant tobacco smoke, reminding me of the Captain and the simple days of my youth, but the vision passes swiftly when the old man says, "Do you hear it?" He raises the cupped palm of his hand to his ear. "Listen. Can you hear it now," he says again.

Flies greedily attack the fish that rests in the few pieces of ice in the wooden chest beside him. "I hear nothing but the hum of hungry flies," I say.

"A foreigner by your accent," he comments and adds, "You must listen more closely." He raises his eyebrows. "Ah! There it is again, the rattling of sabers!"

"Yes, old man. I hear it clearly now. I've come from Poland."

"Poland?" he says exhaling a long, thin column of white smoke. "I don't even know where Poland is."

"You will," I assure him. "The Germans crossed our borders just days ago. What news in Italy?"

He laughs. "*Il Duce* is no Caesar, though he thinks it of himself. He wants to be like that Nazi who yells and screams. I've no doubt Mussolini will take us to war. I don't care," he concludes. "Just leave me to my fish." He waves his hand in the general direction of his sweating icebox. "If you want one of my fish, please take one. It is my gift to my new friend from the land of Poland."

The man is blind. Whether or not he knows it, he has but one fish left to offer. "No, old father, but I thank you for your generosity. I must be on my way. Which way to Rome?"

"Don't you know?" he says with a grin. "All roads lead to Rome." I bid him good day and follow the dusty road inland.

I find an abandoned bicycle lying like a tired skeleton on the roadside. There's air enough in the bald tires, but I can poke my finger through spots on the rusted fenders. I will take it as far as the mountains, which rise in the west to impede my progress.

When I arrive in the foothills and the road becomes too steep, I discard the bicycle on the roadside as its former owner did. In a short time, a man invites me to board the bed of his truck. "Climb aboard," he merrily calls. The smell of the dry hay he carries is pleasant, and as we continue our journey into the mountains, I reflect on this happy farmer and the fishmonger I met earlier in the day. Why are some men so happy and so willing to share their happiness and good fortune while others are so sad and so intent on destroying what good fortune comes our way? Some men uplift our spirits, while others down trod them. Each man has the choice.

The old truck groans and its gears screech, straining to pull us over the mountains, nevertheless by noon, we have successfully crossed the uppermost ridge and our paths diverge. The driver points west to a distant valley. "It's not as far as it looks," he says. "I think you can make it before nightfall." I thank him. He's asked no questions, just given me a ride from the kindness of his heart. My legs are rested and I follow the dirt road at a good pace. At first, it winds and turns steeply, then more gradually. The width of this country is not so great and for that reason, the taste of the moist, sea air is always present, heavier now as I approach the western coast.

The late afternoon sun washes the hills in warm, golden light that will vanish in a few hours. I find another ancient bicycle, bent, beat and broken. The rusted chain breaks and disengages the axle from the pedal before I can travel 50 meters. I am not deterred. It just means I have to monitor my speed closely. I can glide down the foothills but must remember that I have no brakes other than the soles of my dirty shoes on the stones of the road. My method works quite well until the road becomes a bit more crowded as Rome rises from the plain. I have no intention of harming anyone, much less myself, so I lean the bicycle on a dry fountain on the outskirts of the eternal city and proceed through the maze of pedestrians that swarm the streets. The Colosseum confronts me as dusk gently ushers the sun to its resting place. A chill wind accompanies the long shadow the massive structure casts to the east, but despite the ill winds that blow across the continent, I find warmth in the Italians. Most are unafraid to make eye contact and when they do, they smile.

As I near the base of the stadium, a football rolls rapidly in my direction. I stop it with the sole of my foot and confront several young boys who follow it. "Which way to the Vatican?" I ask.

One wipes his sweaty brow and points west. "Walk around this stack of stones and follow the setting sun," he says with a grin. "Maybe three kilometers. Many bridges cross the river. Any one will work. You will find it."

"And the *Via Sabiniano?*"

"Even closer."

I thank them, flick the ball in the air with my foot and nod it back to the street with my forehead. *"Grazie, signore,"* the one calls out as they race after the ball and resume their game. So happy in their ignorance of what is happening in the world around them, so innocent with their thoughts focused only on the round ball they kick joyfully with their feet.

Darkness settles on the city when I reach the *Via Sabiniano*. I walk from one end of the tree-lined street to the other in less than a minute. Five large villas command the south side of the street. I consider it quite unlikely that the Father Michael I seek lives in a villa. My eyes adjust to the darkness reaching out from the north side where large trees and heavy thickets create a park of sorts. A dim light catches my eye, and stopping on the quiet street, I stare into the trees. Once again, the light briefly flickers through the bushes. Following it, I find a path that leads me to a small, unadorned wooden shack. The shimmering light of a candle emanates from the lone window, long void of glass to fend off the wind, the rain and the cold. "You will know it when you see it," Stefan told me. I am certain this is where I will find the priest.

The night is calm, but as I slowly approach the shack, an old man's soft voice disturbs the air just enough to cause the candle's flame to move. He prays his evening prayers and pleads his intercessions, but he does more than recite the ancient words that he memorized long ago from his book of prayers. He says each word as if this is the first time he has ever uttered them. His whispers bear the reverence and sincerity that are sure to carry his words to ear of God. I do not interrupt him and listen for several minutes.

When he is done, I gently rap on the door. A dog barks from the other side. "Be still, Raphael," the man says, I think to the dog although there may be someone else with him. "We have a visitor who is kind enough to announce himself with a courteous knock." The hinges creak as the door opens to reveal a small, bent man and his large, white dog.

"Father Michael?" I ask.

"It is I," he responds. "Please come in. I've not much to offer but what is mine is yours." The large, shorthaired dog sniffs my feet and I cautiously extend a closed hand to him in case he has intentions to snap at my fingers. He does not. He is a friendly brute with floppy ears and sagging jowls, and I open my hand and pet his soft head. "His name is Raphael. We have been friends for many years."

Four pieces of furniture crowd the small room: a bed, a table and chair, and a bookcase. They sit on a dirt floor. Wooden crates are stacked neatly around the room and act as pedestals, preventing his many volumes from becoming soiled. The candle shimmers on the table, its light illuminating a wooden plate, a loaf of bread and a wooden cup.

"Raphael and I are unused to visitors. You are weary, please take the chair." Father Michael is very old but he knows I will not sit as long as he stands, so he seats himself on the bed. "I have but one plate and one cup. Please share what I have. The bowl," he says pointing to the corner next to the bookcase, "is for Raphael, but we seldom use it. What's mine is his, and we take it from the same plate."

I sit while Michael breaks his bread into three, equal pieces, one for each of us. He blesses the meager meal then slides the cup toward me, "This wine is good. Go ahead, please drink it." His life lacks luxury and entitlement, yet the smile never leaves his chiseled face. I sip the sweet wine and pass the cup to him, then pull a small piece of bread and offer it to Raphael who accepts it thankfully, not greedily. He sits by me and smiles his dog smile with every morsel I offer him.

"Your unshaven face cannot hide your identity," Father Michael says. "I've seen you before."

"I'm sorry, sir, but I do not recall that we have ever met."

He hobbles to his bookcase. "These are my special books," he says as he runs his crooked finger over the spines. He pulls a volume that he places before me on the table, *IV Olympische Winterspiele, 1936.* It is the official report on the games in Garmisch-Partenkirchen. He pages through it, finds his place and points to a picture of me. The priest's eyes move from the page to my face and back. "It is you, isn't it?" he says as more of a statement than a question. The good Father leans forward, places his head close to the open page, and reads in the dim light, "Bronisław Czech. I love all sports," he tells me, "And my books are the sinful indulgence I allow myself."

"I think God will forgive your excess."

"Perhaps," he says, "And my collection will always be here for anyone who cares to see it."

The volumes on a man's bookcase reveal his soul. This man is quite learned and his many tomes suggest he permits himself to read for pleasure as well as for knowledge. I see a Victor Hugo, a Herman Hesse, even a Zane Grey, and a Mark Twain rests between a dictionary and a Darwin. What is this? *Mein Kampf* dares to show itself in this holy man's personal library.

He moves his fingers to conceal his smile and stifle his laugh when he tells me, "I cheered for the American Jesse Owens in Berlin. Please do not tell the *Führer* or *Il Duce*. They would not approve."

In some strange way, this man brings me comfort, as if we have known one another forever. He may be even older than his creased face suggests, but as the candle flickers, a youthfulness glides over his countenance, just briefly, then his aged wisdom returns again. I wonder about the dog, too. The animal is strong and healthy. At one glance, he appears not more than a pup, at another, an old friend. The odd visions of the priest and his dog distract me from the stark and simple conditions in which they live. If I asked, I know he would tell me they are blessed by poverty.

He offers the remaining crumbs to Raphael who licks the plate clean. Father Michael returns it, unwashed, to the top of the bookcase, and why not. This dog is his companion, as dear to him as a child is to his father. That they share the same plate does not strike him as odd. Father Michael purposefully slides the cup toward me and I sip again, noting that it remains full. An odd thought flashes, and then escapes me before I take time to ponder it.

"I have something for you," I reach into my shirt. The envelope is stained with sweat and I pray that the message is still legible. I stare at it briefly, then hand it to him. "It comes from Stefan, a soldier."

"I know," Michael replies. "Brave Stefan."

"You know him?"

He smiles. "Nothing deters Stefan. A man of conviction. I only wish his spiritual faith were as strong as his politics. God does not care, though because Stefan always does the right thing. Bolesław," he concludes, and as he says the name, he sees the wrinkles that emerge on my forehead. "You and he and so many others like you. I know you all. Your name is Bolesław," he says again. "Time for the king and his knights to awake from their slumber."

"Is it too late?" I ask.

"It's never too late in God's time," he says and takes more of the wine. "But I tell you this, my strong shield of Abraham…" My hand involuntarily touches the *hamsa*, which hides beneath my shirt. How does he know? "I tell you this," he repeats, "You and your compatriots will face great pain, and you will see things no man should see, things that will drag you to the limit of your spiritual, mental and physical endurance. You will gaze into the heart of darkness, and you will not like what you see." I do not understand him, but his rhetoric hypnotizes me. "They can take everything you own, Bronisław, everything you hold dear, but they cannot take your dignity unless you let them. There is a light in the heart of darkness."

He waves the soiled envelope. "I will deliver this message to the Pope, and I am certain he will act on behalf of all men of good will, but it will not happen quickly, and we are obligated to endure whatever trials we encounter no matter how dire. This is no more a test from God than it is a blight he sends to a world turned upside down. His greatest gift is our free will. The peril that we face does not come from God, it comes from the bad choices men make when they exercise their free will for personal gain with no regard to the consequences their actions can have on others."

Father Michael raises the cup to his lips and leans back. After a long drink, he dries his mouth with the sleeve of his habit. His eyes twinkle in the candlelight.

"You have journeyed long and hard," he says. "I will deliver the message this very night. Rest here on my bed for I will not return."

"I can go with you," I suggest.

"Not possible." He puts the envelope in his pocket and takes the walking stick that leans on the bookcase. "May God protect you and give you strength."

He ruffles Raphael's ears. One is white like his body, the other brown like a deer, and a brown patch covers his left eye giving the appearance that he is wearing a mask. "You, my friend," he tells the dog, "Care for this man and lead him from the city on the 'morrow." With only a confident smile and no more words, Michael leaves me in the candlelit room with his friend and the still, full cup of wine.

I yield to exhaustion and the sun is high when I wake to find myself curled atop Michael's bed. The dog sits patiently within arm's length and begins to wag his tail when he sees my eyes open. I reach over, pat his head and say, "Good boy." He moves closer and I hug his big head. His breath is warm on my neck. I sit up and rub the weariness from my eyes. A chunk of cheese, a handful of olives and the cup, filled now with water wait for me at the table. There is no sign of Michael. Feeling rested, I take my meal and share the cheese with the dog. He surprises me when he takes the olives I offer to him. His bowl is filled with fresh water that he laps loudly.

The humble meal makes me smile and think of all the grand places I have been, the banquets I have feasted on and the stately clothes I've worn to theatre and other notable places. These thoughts do not sadden me even though I cannot hide the dust from my shoes or banish the odor of sweat I am unable to remove from my wrinkled clothes. Sitting alone in this room, I consider my options. Choices, that's what Michael said, choices. In this moment of free, eternal time, I could choose to follow the smell of salt to the sea that lies not far to the west. I'm certain I could find a port and gain passage as a worker on a ship bound for America. I am strong and would be of value to any crew. I'm confident I could get to America, and I could be a cowboy, without a care for anyone or anything but me. I love America. I could return to Lake Placid and board with Mrs. Jordan and be friends with Johnny. As the thoughts and images swirl in my head, my will weakens. I can choose to leave this madness. I ponder the previous 24 hours. I've enjoyed no company more than Father Michael's, nor consider any meal grander than this cheese and these olives. I say a prayer of thanks, but the choice remains. Freedom and peace, or bondage and conflict?

I abandon my free will. I will leave it up to the dog. "Lead him from the city," is what Father Michael told this wonderful creature. I am amused: in not making a choice, I have made a choice, the choice not to make a choice.

I leave it up to the dog. I follow him out the door, lean over and pat his head. "Lead me from the city," I tell him. He barks, wags his tale and trots off with a powerful gait. When I don't immediately follow, he stops and barks again. "Okay," I call to my new friend, "My life is in your hands." We walk east and cross the Tiber, then head north to the Alps.

The dog casts my lot – though it is my choice to accept it! We waste no time returning to Zakopane. Rail traffic has increased, but no cars are empty and more often occupied by soldiers wearing the swastika than hobos dressed in rags. In three days, Raphael and I have capped the Tatras and we stand near Giewont's summit and peer into the western valleys. We have passed several patrols and I am very cautious and alert to every sound in the forest. Dark smoke – very uncharacteristic – rises from the valley and stains the sky with thin columns. I am concerned, not afraid, for fear is that undesirable emotion that weakens a man's legs.

I stay close to Raphael who leads the way into the valley toward my home. The tree line brings safety, and the forest paths I have known since childhood comfort me. As the steep slopes give way to the gentle foothills, Raphael abruptly stops. The dog is smart enough not to bark and give our position away, but I hear the low, guttural growl that he keeps in check. He backs up in short, measured steps. He does not retreat, but only seeks a better position to protect me as he considers the potentially threatening situation. There is movement behind us, and I slowly turn as three men emerge from the trees. Raphael flashes his white canine teeth. I stoop to pet and calm the dog and assure him that we will not be harmed. Two more men reveal themselves. We are surrounded, but it is okay; they are highlanders, several former teammates, and each holds his hunting rifle in his hands.

One walks forward, then breaks into a jog. "Bronek," he calls. It is Andrzej. We embrace. "What news of Stanisław, and who is your beautiful friend?"

As I shake hands with my fellows, I explain, "I last saw him four, no five days ago. We traveled together as far as the Alps where I turned south while he continued west. I have no worries for him." I find no need to tell them about the children. I know Stashu will return. He can tell his own story if he wants to. Using my hand to shield my eyes from the sun, I stare toward the village. We stoop to our haunches and form a tight circle. "This is my friend, Raphael. He is my guide. All the way from Rome!" Raphael moves from one man to the other, sniffing his boots. A pat on his head from each górale confirms new friendships.

"I've been gone a week. I have delivered my message to the Vatican and I have no doubts Stashu has done the same in Geneva. What is the situation here?"

Andrzej picks up a handful of small pebbles and shakes them in his hand as if they were dice. "Not good," he answers for the group. "Word travels quickly through the mountains despite the German patrols that wander aimlessly thinking they can seal our mountain borders." The others laugh, but the mood quickly turns dour. "Our troops retreat to the east, but will it do any good? Who knows? I think the Russians will join the fray soon and attack our eastern border. We cannot survive a war on two fronts." We agree we can't survive a war on a single front – much less two fronts – without help from the British and Americans, but no one will say it aloud.

I continue to stare at the village. "Have they come to Zakopane?"

"They have," Stanisław Karpiel answers. "Be very careful when you go home. Nazis are everywhere. Some families have lost their houses. Confiscated to board soldiers."

I respond angrily. "They cannot do that with my house."

"They have not, yet, but your mother and father prepare for the worst. I'm sorry to tell you, my friend, but these invaders do whatever they want to."

"And the Captain? What does he say?"

My friends cast their eyes to the ground. "They have him in custody and probably would have shot him already but there is an *SS* officer here who claims to know him and swears he is the key to any resistance we highlanders might organize in the Tatras."

"Who is this man who claims he knows our Captain?"

"You will know him, too, Bronek," Andrzej answers. "You crossed paths with him twice in Garmisch-Partenkirchen. Some people you don't forget; he is one of them. I remembered him the moment he stepped from the first German truck to arrive in Zakopane. I can't recall his name, but you will know him when you see him."

"So what are you telling me, Andrzej? Are we combatants simply because we are Poles? None of us wears a uniform, though I can see you are all bearing arms."

"The moment you accepted the mission from the Polish officer to deliver his message, you became a combatant", Andrzej says. "Stashu, too. We may not wear uniforms, but we will resist this invasion and will not roll over like helpless puppies. We are all afraid, Bronek, but we will not cower before these men who have no reason to be here but to steal our homes and property."

The dog barks. "What is your friend's name, again?" Andrzej asks.

"Raphael."

"Like the archangel?"

"Like the archangel."

Andrzej takes a hard crust of bread from his pocket and extends it to the dog. Raphael sits, and then rises on his haunches to receive the offering.

Like it nor not, we are all a part of this. I'm sure I was the day I instructed my team not to salute Hitler three years ago, and I became embedded in the resistance when I accepted the mission to Rome. I accept my role with some trepidation but with resolve, a resolve that continues to harden. Hitler is a lunatic. I read it in his prose, hear it in his words and now see it in his actions. Whose resolve is stronger, I wonder, and then laugh at my own doubt. Nothing will avert me from doing whatever I can, from doing whatever is necessary to prove this man and his vision a lie.

"And where can I find our Captain?" I ask.

Andrzej pushes his cap further back from his forehead. "Half the town is abandoned," he tells me. "Many pack what few belongings they can carry and leave. They think there will be safety in the big cities, though I doubt it." My friends shake their heads in denial. "But if we are to be free, we are certain our freedom is here in these mountains."

"Maybe so, Andrzej, but I will find the Captain. He's never failed us. We need to find him and take counsel with him."

"You'll get no dispute from any highlander on that point, Bronek."

"Do you know where he is?"

"Yes," he answers. "The Nazis stay at the Villa Marilor and use it as their headquarters. That is where you will find the Captain. I think it best to stay away from your parents. Your father is a tough man, but he has his responsibilities to your mother and your family. He cannot participate in the resistance like we can."

Chapter Fifteen, 1939

Bloodshed

The Nazis have the power to conquer by mere intimidation: trucks roll in, soldiers march out and just that quick, the town is captive, a very simple and direct tactic. Easy for them, harder for us to resist when we look down gun barrels. The nearest Polish forces of any consequence are in Kraków, and their backs are against the wall like all other Polish soldiers. We cannot depend on armed intervention. Kraków must care for itself and for the thousands of refugees that flood towards it from the surrounding countryside. Residents from the small towns and villages will seek safety in numbers in the cities. Not a good idea, but they are drawn to the urban centers like moths to a flame. While the main invasion force moves against Warsaw, the Germans quickly learn a handful of troops with a nasty demeanor can control the rural countryside. The people are that frightened. Of course Hitler's overconfident conclusion that the masses will shrink in the face of his storm troopers also means that a small group of determined men can disrupt the presumptive plans of their would be conquerors. I am not so bold as to think I can count myself among that group. I am no hero, and I am not ready to place the lives of my teammates in the center of harm's way.

Still, I will find the Captain, and I will free him from his Nazi captors.

I steal time with my parents. Both are distraught, but not so much for Włady and Stasia. My older brother and sister are not cowardly, but neither are they bold. They will follow the herd whichever way it takes them. Janka is different, more like I am. She is not timid and remains in Warsaw, at the university. They receive no word from her. Mother and father fear she is in the path of the beast and will not flee from it. I tell them not to worry, that I will find her and bring her safely back to Zakopane. Raphael is with me, and his eyes reflect the dancing flames in the fireplace as he sits at my mother's feet while we talk. She smiles at him and pets his head. "Such a good dog, and very handsome, too," she says, and my father agrees. "He is a big boy, and I like it when I don't have to lean over to pet him."

"Then with your permission, I will leave him with you. I have an errand to attend to, and I am not quite certain how long I shall be. You will find him grateful for whatever scraps you can spare. Kindness and love have no price, and he is pleased to accept it as much as give it."

Raphael sits obediently and does not argue when I tell him to stay.

The Germans have yet to impose a curfew and when nightfall comes, I stealthily work my way through the trees and the narrow streets on the edge of town so that I emerge in the center of the village, as if I had been there the whole time. Even without a curfew, few residents dare walk the streets. An unnatural quiet hangs in the air like an unpleasant odor. *Pani* Murach's small house is dark and empty. I pray her guardian angel has taken *pani* under his wing to whisk her to safety if such a thing is possible. A cart filled with firewood sits beside her root cellar. *Pani* will never use the wood, and the vegetables will rot. I take the cart. She will not mind, or ever know that I am the culprit who confiscated it.

I push the cart through the streets as if I belong there, only *Pan* Gromelski's shaggy pony, tied to a street lamp takes notice of me. He shakes his head as if to say, "Are you crazy, man? Get back to your house and lock the door behind you. This night is not meant for heroes." I wish I remembered his name so that I could give him a calming and confident word as I slowly pass on my way to the Villa Marilor.

Two soldiers with rifles slung over their shoulders share a cigarette on the street corner. They eye me suspiciously and one asks, "*Wo willst du hin?*"

I keep my hands on the handle of the cart and nod forward. "I'm taking this wood to the hotel. *Kann ich eine zigarette?*"

"*Dummkopf,*" the other one says and they laugh and wave me on. I smile stupidly and bow as I trudge up the dark street. The closed and abandoned shops watch me more closely than the soldiers.

I park the cart in front of the Villa and climb the few steps to the entryway. As I am about to take the final step into the bright light of the foyer, I freeze when I glimpse the officer Andrzej tells me I will recognize when I see him. Andrzej is correct: I will not forget this man. It is Feldman, the *SS* man I encountered at the games in

Garmisch-Partenkirchen.   He stands six paces from me examining paperwork with two other officers.

"Warum bist du hier?" a man says and roughly grabs my shoulder to prevent my entry into the building. By turning me away from the light in the doorway, he unwittingly saves me.

"I have wood." I point to the loaded cart.

He snaps to attention and calls out, *"Hauptsturmfürer?"*

"What is it?"

"Wood."

"Can't you make these decisions on your own?" Feldman's voice and his short temper are unmistakable. After a brief pause he says, "Tell him to take it out back."

I have no desire to tarry. I nod to the soldier at the door and return to the cart as casually but as quickly as I can.

"Hey, you!" Feldman's voice is distinctive as he shouts, and I hope he is not calling to me. I ignore him. "You there, with the wood." I stop, remove my cap and bow my head. "Next time just bring it to the back." I bow even lower as he returns his attention to the other men.

I proceed with my cart to the rear of the building where wood is stacked not 10 paces from the back door. I am very deliberate and take my time emptying the cart, piece by piece. The door opens and a large, fat, aproned man tosses steaming water from a big pan into the yard. He wears no tunic, and his undershirt bears heavy patches of yellow sweat. His pants tell me that he is a German soldier. He stands on the wooden steps, wipes his brow and lights a cigarette. "You there," he calls, "We need more wood in the stove. *Schnell.*"

I mount the stairs with an armful of wood. For no apparent reason other than his personal amusement, he uses his heavy arm and thick hand to knock the wood from my grasp, scattering it on the ground. *"Du bist ein dummer Pole und ungeschickt."* Inwardly I want to scream in his face, "Dumb? How many languages can you speak? Clumsy? When is the last time your obese body soared intentionally through the air on a pair of skis?"

"I am sorry," I timidly say to him as I retrieve the wood and climb back up the stairs. I hold my breath as I inch past him, but can still smell the sweat that betrays his lack of hygiene. He smacks the back of my head as I pass.

I have no difficulty finding the kitchen where I deposit my armful of wood. I retrace my steps to the rear of the hotel. A door opens and two soldiers enter the hallway, with them, the Captain. He looks very fatigued but his face shows no signs of physical abuse.

"Stand aside," a soldier orders me and I place my back against the wall. As the Captain passes, he mumbles in Polish, "Leave this place."

"What did you say?" the other soldier asks in German, clearly not understanding Polish.

The Captain raises his tired head, looks the man in the eye and slowly and deliberately repeats in Polish, "Leave this place." The other soldier notices me looking intently at the Captain. A man enters the hallway from the lobby to my left. Seconds pass like fleeting heartbeats; there is vague recognition in his eyes as we stare at each other. I avert my gaze and walk down the hall toward the rear door.

"I know this man," Feldman screams then commands, "Stop him," but I only walk faster. The door and the darkness beyond it are just a few paces away. "Halt, I say. You are the skier. I remember," Feldman shouts and one of the soldiers follows me. I am a single step from safety when the door opens, and I find myself face to face with the monstrous German cook. "Stop him," the soldier yells to the cook, and the big man has no difficulty snaring my collar with his meaty hand and then grasping me in a suffocating bear hug.

The Captain and I acknowledge each other, he then turns quickly, and, bringing his knee up hard into the soldier's groin, doubles the man over and sends him to the floor in a groaning heap. The other soldier, standing next to the cook and me, reaches for his holster, and as he withdraws his weapon, I kick his hand with all my strength and the gun flies from his grip and lands on the carpet at the Captain's feet.

"Move aside," the Captain orders, and when the soldier replies, "*Nein*," the Captain raises the gun and shoots the man in the face. The stunned cook loosens his grip, and the Captain quickly eliminates options. He fires a shot squarely into the cook's forehead and the fat man falls to the floor like a slain beast. As I swing the door open and leap into the darkness, I hear loud voices and another shot, this one not from the Captain's weapon. He stumbles after me. We race into the woods with flashlights gleaming behind us, and random gunshots echoing through the night air.

"You have no chance of escape," Feldman yells. A burst from an automatic weapon follows his prediction. A barrage of bullets rips through the dry, autumn leaves.

We stumble through the darkness and I bear the Captain's weight as I drag him forward. "I've been hit," he finally admits. "In the back." He falls to the ground, pain etched in deep furrows on his weathered forehead. He breathes hard and labored, as much from the pain as from our flight. "Make good your escape, Bronek. Please leave me here. I'm prepared to deal with any fate that confronts me."

I disregard his plea. Prowling vehicles search with strong lights, and barking dogs join them in the hunt. The Captain is too weak to resist me when I lift him to my back and start across what I think is a deserted street. I must be quick about it, but I fail. As I stand in the middle of the road with my Captain slung over my back, the headlights of two trucks at opposite ends suddenly cut us like a sharp knife and physically pin us to this spot. We are as exposed as climbers on an open, windy ledge are. Discovery paralyzes me, and I can only watch as the trucks creep forward holding us in their crossfire of light. Soldiers disembark and surround us. No one moves, and then a car turns the corner and pulls up to us. Feldman and another officer get out.

"I remember very, very well now," he says spitefully. I lower the Captain gently to the ground and stand as tall as I can. I do not flinch when Feldman slaps me across the face with his black leather gloves.

"I told you once before," the Captain wheezes from his kneeling position on the ground, "Do not touch my athletes."

"Yes, you did," Feldman answers. "But here, tonight, on this street ... I don't have to dirty my hands by touching you." To my horror, Feldman pulls his weapon and places the barrel to the Captain's forehead.

"He's a pig, Bronek," the Captain says and smiles while staring beyond the barrel into the nervous eyes of the *Hauptsturmfürer*. "He and his Führer. Both swine." The headlights that focus on the scene do not soften the flash of the muzzle as blood splatters on my coat and my Captain collapses, dead.

"The same for you?" Feldman asks, gaining courage with what I suspect may have been his first murder. He raises the gun to my head. I struggle to hold my bladder, as my courage deteriorates. In a quick motion, Feldman points the gun skyward and pulls the trigger. So close to my head, the roar is deafening. A loud, muted hum blocks his voice, but I can read his lips when he says, "No, not yet, flag bearer. These mountain men will listen to you.

"Put him in the car," he orders as he holsters his gun, but before they can bind my hands, shots ring out from the darkness and the three soldiers closest to me topple to the ground.

"Run, Bronek!" Andrzej and my friends call from their hiding places. I overpower Feldman as he tries to pull his pistol, and I wrest the weapon from him. Here we stand, just he and I, headlights glaring at us, surrounded by his soldiers and mine who remain concealed in darkness. "Run, Bronek!" they scream again.

I point the revolver at Feldman, and the gutless *Hauptsturmfürer* orders his men to hold their fire and to drop their weapons. He is at my mercy. I want desperately to pull the trigger and avenge the murder of the most important person in my life. I glimpse at the ground and see the Captain's lifeblood pooling around him. I will wear his spattered blood on my jacket while I flee. Feldman is too

cowardly to say something brave or bold, knowing full well
that just a word will push me over the edge and give me all
the justification I need to pull this trigger. Unlike me, he
cannot control his bladder and urine puddles at his feet. I
step backward, my hand shakes, as I will myself to remove
my finger from the trigger. I turn quickly, throw the gun
as far as I can and flee into the forest. As the German soldiers reach for their weapons, gun muzzles flash before me,
and bullets zip past me. Three more soldiers drop to the
ground while Feldman crawls to the safety of his car.

"You will not escape," he yells another time as he hud-
dles in the back seat of his car.

"Fuck you," I scream as loud as I can so the words
sound through Zakopane, as I find refuge in the night. The
Germans retrieve their weapons and fire harmlessly into the
dark. They will not find me, at least not now.

My friends whistle me to them and we flee north, always
in the trees with the railroad tracks on our right. An hour
passes before we stop to rest. The evening air is chilly and
our pant legs are damp from the dew that gathers at the
edge of the forest. We are four – Stanisław Karpiel, Michał
Górski, Andrzej and I – and we stop to rest on a large, rot-
ted log that fell decades ago.

"What now, Bronek?" Andrzej asks. I stare at the
ground searching for an answer.

They are as angry as I am, but none more than Stanisław.
He pounds the butt of his rifle on the ground and says to
me, "Why didn't you kill the bastard? How could you
not with our Captain dead at your feet? What is the matter with you, Bronek?" Tears stream from his eyes as he
shoves me. I topple backwards over the log. I don't have

the energy to argue or to defend myself. Until the day I die, the scene of the Captain's death will play repeatedly in my head like a film that never ends. I lay mute on the ground. No words I can say will satisfy Stanisław. He does not care that if I had pulled that trigger, I would have joined the murderous ranks of Feldman and his thugs and met them again in hell. I am not a murderer, and I will not let Feldman make me one, but I don't tell my fellows this, for it will make no difference to them on this eventful night. They are certainly right in one regard: most men would have pulled that trigger and avenged the Captain's murder.

"Did he not save your life in the Villa?" Stanisław continues to press the issue. We know the answer and I need not speak it. Neither Michał nor Andrzej will choose sides.

As I rise in my shame, Andrzej ends the discussion and further dissent from Stanisław when he tells him to leave it alone. "What's done is done. It's what we do now that matters, not what we did or didn't do an hour ago."

My emotions overpower me and my tears come in pitiful sobs. Even Stanisław understands how pointless and even mean-spirited his interrogation is. He embraces me and the two of us weep and share our grief. The other two join us, and standing there in the forest, we hold each other in a fruitless bid to ease the pain that each feels at the brutal loss of our old, revered and trusted friend. I raise my face to the clear sky. A shooting star streaks from east to west and burns out after a few, precious seconds of heavenly life. God himself consoles us with a burning tear from heaven.

When distant gunfire violently reminds us of where we are and why we are here, we return to Earth like the burned out meteor. We drop our arms and wipe our eyes. What would have been days of mourning are over in minutes. We have no time to grieve, and weakness of any sort will not advance our cause.

Stanisław clears his throat and says, "Okay, here's what I think. This German officer and his men know who you are, Bronek. You cannot return, at least not tonight. At the same time, no one knows any of us. I believe Stashu will return soon, and we can organize in the secret shadows of the Tatras that only we know. You, my friend need to get to Warsaw and find the man who sent you and Stashu on your last journey. I'm certain resistance remains intact, and I'm sure the men in Warsaw will need us highlanders to do what is necessary in the mountain borders.

"The three of us can return to Zakopane and still walk with some freedom. Of course, that will become more difficult in the winter, which will easily reveal our movements in the snow. What do you others think? Bronek goes to Warsaw and we return to Zakopane?"

"The alternatives are few," Andrzej agrees, "and your suggestion is as good as any I can think of. Bronek?"

Images of the past hour sear my mind. I have few choices: I can give up and they win; or I can avenge my Captain's death and join the resistance. My mind races and other images intrude, images of other bodies that lay rotting in ditches from here to Warsaw. I pull myself together and concentrate. "Yes," I answer, "That's what we'll do. I will find Stefan Rowecki in Warsaw and return with his instructions. You gather what weapons you can and hide them safely. You know the grotto?" Seconds pass without a word. We all know 'the grotto,' but no one ever speaks of it aloud. Until this moment, 'the grotto' is a very personal experience shared by all highlanders, each in his solitary way.

"Yes," Michał finally answers, "We know it."

"Then you know there is a large cave not far from it. Conceal your weapons there. If I do not return, someone else will and I will tell him to find a highlander."

We join hands and forge our collective strength and resolve into a single entity that lives and breathes, one powerful thing existing through many. "Let's be on our way, then." I leave my comrades and continue my trek north to Warsaw.

A year ago, I could have easily traveled the 300 kilometers from Zakopane to Warsaw in a day. Life has changed and who knows if it will ever be the same. Unstable borders, political calamity and conflict dictate our fragile lives. Rail traffic has ceased, at least as far as I can tell for I have yet to hear the familiar whistle that so often announces the arrival of a locomotive from the north. I keep to the woods at the edge of fields and from there follow the road. The western thoroughfares are eerily void of traffic, but the farther north I travel, the more vehicles crowd the roads and all of them bear the now too familiar German black iron cross with its white border. I have no idea how many German troops crossed our borders, but I count a frightening number of combatants, and worse yet, armored vehicles and tanks. Poland has weapons, but they are woefully outdated and can offer little opposition to this horde I must evade on my way to Warsaw. As day breaks on the horizon, columns of black smoke rise from the landscape. I fear that

I am quickly becoming too accustomed to the death and destruction that surround me. Human bodies and animals, many horses, rotting in the open fields, buildings turned to crumbled piles of brick and burned lumber, overturned vehicles on their roofs like stranded, metal turtles unable to right themselves ... The clean, crisp smell of autumn flees before the revolting stench left in the wake of Hitler's army. I accept nausea as a permanent condition.

The attacking force from the southwest sweeps through our mountains and our pastures like the devil's rancid breath. How I travel undiscovered, I will never know, but I thank God that I have. While I journeyed to Rome, the main force pushed through the larger mountain passes on its way to Kraków, which I can see smoldering in the distance. I decide it is safer to continue to Warsaw along the Wisła River. I wonder how Rowecki and our armies are faring in Warsaw, for I can only assume that Warsaw is where we may make a stand.

I circumvent the ruins of Kraków. Time means nothing as the sun sinks below the horizon, rises and sets again ... hours become days. I am tired but keep some strength scavenging garbage in the river. I risk disease with every rotten bite I am able to force down my throat that involuntarily fights to resist these putrid tidbits. Warsaw rises in the distance. With each step forward, I reflect on my physical accomplishment: in two weeks, I have traveled to Rome, returned to Zakopane and now approach the gates of Warsaw. I have evaded armies, seen men killed, watched bodies decay and yet I still believe I am sane. What if I am wrong?

The northwestern sky is very dirty, not cloudy, but dirty, and the closer I come to the city, the more clearly the rumblings of artillery become. If we make our defense to the west, perhaps the city will be spared a direct attack. As I follow the watercourse north, I see fewer and fewer signs of conflict, so I leave the riverbank in favor of the road. Another abandoned bicycle – my recently preferred means of transportation – beckons me from the ditch. I retrieve it and continue my trek north. No rail traffic, no barge traffic. Too still, but the canons continue to rumble.

I promised my mother that I would find Janka, so that will be my first priority. If I can find Amalia and Max, I can find Janka. In recent years, I have been to their apartment a half dozen times, and as I remember, it is very close to the university. I pray they are safe, but I need to be certain. The situation is not good; that Amalia and Max are Jews makes it worse.

I reach the center of Warsaw at midday and walk past the Polonia where we celebrated our film success a lifetime ago. When I entered the grand hotel that night, I entered as royalty, donned in a tuxedo with my beautiful young sister on my arm. Today, they would think me a dirty panhandler dressed in filthy rags. I resist the urge to go to the hotel; I continue north and follow *Marszalkowska* to the university. The streets are empty and quiet save for the mangy dogs that roam free and unleashed, foraging like me for what food they can find. An occasional bark echoes through the narrow avenues. Oddly, a young boy kicks a can up the street. He pulls a hand from his pocket and waves. I wave back, but he doesn't stop as he looks to the can and continues his game of solitaire. Fear rises unnaturally from the deserted streets, like steam on a hot summer day. Vehicles stand guard from their parking spots at the curbs.

Amalia's apartment building has been recently painted, quite the contrast to everything I've seen between here and Zakopane. The knob turns freely on the unlocked door and I walk inside and instinctively clean the dust of the road from my shoes on the new rug. I feel guilty. The stairs creak as I climb to the third floor. At each landing, doors open, just a sliver, and frightened eyes peer briefly from them, relieved that I am a bum and not a German soldier or some other wraith. The building's interior is freshly painted, too, and I welcome the slightly pungent aroma of paint after trudging through days of stench. The smell makes me a bit light-headed, but relieves me of the nausea that has plagued me for days.

Before knocking on the door, I straighten my jacket – why, I don't know – and within seconds, Max cautiously asks from the other side, "Who is it?"

"It's me, Bronisław." The lock releases with its metallic click, and Max cracks the door open just enough to make sure it's me, then removes the security chain and waves me in. He's quick to re-secure the door while he tells me, "Looters are already about sensing that the end is near." Amalia stands at his side and they heartedly embrace me. "Welcome, Bronek, we've prayed for your safety."

"As I have done for yours," I reply. "Where is my sister?"

"You look exhausted," Max says and leads me to the sofa.

"I will make tea," Amalia adds, "And we have honey cakes."

I sink into the thick cushions, and they invite me to forget about everything and tumble carefree into a deep, deep sleep, a sleep from which I would have no desire to wake. Through closed eyes, I ask again, "Where is my sister? Where is Janka?"

Max stares out the window toward the darkening, western horizon. "We do not know," he finally admits. "We last saw Janka before the Germans invaded. Can you believe we had no idea this was coming?" My eyes are still closed, and when Max strikes a match to light his pipe, I remember my Captain and I fight back the bloody vision of his demise.

I want to scream at the madness, instead, I swallow the bitter urge. I pretend, if I keep my eyes shut, everything bad will disappear. It won't. "And when you saw Janka a week ago, how was she?"

Amalia stands behind the sofa and strokes my greasy hair. "In love," she says. "When we saw her last, she was in love."

With eyes still closed, I smile. "It is good to be in love," I say. Max puts his arm around his wife's waist. I open my eyes to share this too brief moment of serenity. The teapot whistles.

"And who might she be in love with?" I ask.

"A soldier," Amalia responds, and places a tray with three steaming cups of tea on the table before me. Husband and wife sit with me on the sofa, one on each side.

"A soldier," I repeat. "I have great respect for soldiers, but a rather risky profession given the circumstances."

"No doubt." Max tells me Janka's friend is a cavalryman. We sip the hot tea and I take a honey cake and taste its sweetness. Few pastries have tasted so good to me. I eat it deliberately and lick my fingers of the smallest crumbs.

"He is a handsome cavalryman," Amalia adds. "Janka and three girlfriends have moved into a small apartment on *Karmelicka*. We met them in the park for a concert on a particularly hot August night. Each was escorted by a dashing soldier, all cavalrymen." She brushes the curls from her face and smiles as she fondly recalls the special night.

"And you've not seen her since that evening?" Their silence answers the question. "Then I must find her." I lean forward to rise, but Amalia places a restraining hand on my leg.

"Wait until morning, Bronek. It will be dark soon and we don't know exactly where on *Karmelicka* she and her friends live. Danger is everywhere on the night streets, and it comes not just from German invaders." She glances at Max who cannot hide his concern. "You need to rest." She stands and places her hands on her hips. "Get out of these dirty clothes and I will wash them for you tonight; they will be clean and ready for you in the morning. We will draw you a bath and Max will give you clothes for the evening."

She is right. I am filthy and I have become so used to the unpleasant odor following me like an annoying bug, that I am unaware of how I offend other people. I am very tired and I would prefer to meet my sister, alert and capable of displaying a positive disposition. I lean back into the sofa.

Within two hours, the room is dark and quiet. I smell of soap; it is a good smell, and the pajamas feel fresh on my clean skin. I pretend that the artillery fire is thunder. I surrender myself to the sound and beg it to lull me to sleep.

I rise refreshed, indulge in a quick cup of tea and take to the city early to find *Karmelicka* Street. The sounds of war have crept closer to the city and there is movement on the streets, mostly uniformed men, not quite so handsome in their soiled clothes and muddied faces. "How goes it, friend?" I say to one soldier who leans against a building smoking a cigarette.

He shakes his head. "Not well. We gained a small victory a week ago near the Bzura River, but the enemy is too strong and they are too many. We've not enough resources and have been ordered to withdraw. Most won't make it." Aircraft approach at low altitude, and drown our voices as they pass overhead displaying their black crosses beneath the wings. I thank God that they release no bombs, for I would be most certainly dead. "For now, we'll hide as best we can," he says when the planes are gone. "Our commanders think the Germans have no reason to destroy the city. I'm not so sure, but we will need all able-bodied men to resist. Can you help, friend?" He asks.

"I can."

"Then come with me," he says.

"Can you wait? I have to find my sister."

He is quick to counter, "We all have to find our sisters." He takes a final draw on his cigarette and tosses the short butt into the street. "Find your sister, then, but I must be on my way."

He limps as he walks down the street. I am trapped again. Choices. So if I find Janka, what then? What can I do? Here at this moment, what must I do? I pray for her safety, then choose to follow the soldier. Am I stupid?

"You are hurt," I say when I catch up to him.

"It's my ankle and nothing more. Running through the forest at night is hazardous."

"Like a bullet aimed at your back?"

"Like a bullet aimed at your back. I am Janusz," he says without so much as a glance and without offering his hand.

"Bronisław," I answer.

"And the dog?"

I follow his eyes and there, two paces behind me sits my dog. How long has he been with me, and why haven't I noticed until this moment?

"Raphael. His name is Raphael." I kneel and the dog runs to me. I hug him while he licks my face.

"Like the Archangel?"

"Yes. Like the angel. He is supposed to be with my parents."

"The fact that he isn't tells me your parents are okay. I know dogs, and this one would not leave his wards unless they were fine. You have nothing to worry about. That he is here is a good sign for you."

Even with the bad ankle, Janusz moves quickly. He knows exactly where he is going. As we navigate the city on streets and avenues I am not familiar with, I rationalize my decision to delay my search for Janka. Janka is strong and independent. She never shies from responsibility and faces any challenge confronting her with confidence. Włady and Stasia live safe lives and never veer from traditional paths. Janka and I are opposites of our older brother and sister. There is nothing wrong with the way Włady and Stasia lead their lives if it brings them contentment, but today, Poland needs risk-takers, and my sister and I can be counted among them. For that reason, I have no worries and know that Janka will be fine. I am in full support her decision to live independently with her friends. People of like minds seek each other out, and her friends from the university must be as strong and willful as Janka is. She will survive. I laugh aloud thinking that maybe it is I who need her, more than she needs me.

"You find reason to laugh? Tell me about it, I need to laugh, too."

"It's my sister," I tell him. "I think I need her more than she needs me."

"Big strong man like you? That is funny, but you are probably right. Where are you from?"

"Zakopane."

"Ah, a *górale*. If your sister is from mountain stock, she will be fine, for the city does not erase the lessons of the mountains. Don't worry about your sister. She will be fine." Raphael barks as he trots between us. "See. Even your dog agrees with me."

Not far from the river, we reach our destination, the *Koniecpolski* Palace. Only once have I seen the Presidential Palace. That time was when we visited Warsaw as a family. My parents and *Babcia* brought us here over 20 years ago. It was quiet then. Today, men run through the cobblestone courtyard at a hectic pace. Janusz and I rest at the bottom of the stairs.

"We wait here," Janusz tells me. "We'll know what to do when we know." I am not sure what he means, but I have confidence in him if for no other reason than he wears a uniform and I do not. The insignias he and his comrades display on their uniforms mean nothing to me, but I suspect Janusz is not an officer. No one offers him a salute, but as other soldiers pass, he is forever up and down to give them as sharp a salute as he can. I much prefer his respectful gesture than the adoration the athletes were required to offer Hitler in '36.

The flag hangs limply in the still air. In the confines of the courtyard, outlined by the Palace and other nearby buildings forming a quadrangle, the fumes from the constant flow of vehicles are sickening. As I wave my hand in front of my face, Janusz comments, "Perhaps the smoke of a cigarette will make you feel better. The vehicle exhaust is quite unpleasant." Before he can light one, he snaps to attention with another salute.

"Czech, is that you?" Stefan Rowecki and three other men approach us at the steps to the Palace. "It is you," he says warmly but without minimizing the seriousness of the situation. "And you made it to Rome?"

"I did, sir," I answer. The other men are older than Stefan, maybe 45 or 50-years old. I find their age and their clean uniforms intimidating, and starkly in contrast to the mud-streaked blouse, that Stefan wears.

He raises his hand and the older men stop. "A minute please," he says to them then takes me by the arm and we walk several paces away leaving Janusz and the others behind. "Our lines are broken," he explains. "Further, overt, military resistance at this point is futile and will only result in more, unnecessary deaths, and we cannot afford to lose more men. While we wait for the Americans and the British to help us, we have to organize an underground resistance to give the people hope. We are not giving up.

We are just taking our fight to a more practical level. Do you understand me?"

"I think so."

"You can't 'think so,' Bronek. You either understand or you don't."

His directness falls like a physical blow, but this dire situation demands affirmative action, not empty words of uncertainty. "Yes, I understand you."

"These men – all generals – and I are meeting with other military staff members within the hour. The government is in shambles. Mościcki is in Kuty, and has already abdicated his power to Raczkiewicz. I think that is a good thing although I would not have said it a week ago. Raczkiewicz is in Paris and will govern from the embassy there if that is possible, though how long the French can stand up against the Nazis, I will not speculate."

"And what of our armies?"

He shakes his head ruefully. "We've lost tens of thousands. We need lose no more. At our meeting, I will propose to order what remains of our navy to Britain. As far as our decimated armies, we need to get the survivors out of the country, to safe haven if it exists. Over the mountains, into Romania and Hungary. We will issue orders for their retreat with the hope that they can ally themselves with other belligerents sympathetic to our cause. We have to think that the Brits will join us, and the French, too.

"The Russians are massing on the eastern border, but we do not know whether they will join Hitler or stand with us to stop him. Me? I think Hitler will push through Poland and will order his troops into Russia. He is so bold as to think himself another Alexander." He glances at the generals. One raises his arm and points to his watch. "One more minute," he calls to them and turns back to me.

"You must return to Zakopane and tell your Captain to organize his highlanders." I clench my teeth and steel my jaw. "You will return, won't you?"

"Of course I will, Stefan, but you should know: the Captain is dead, murdered at the hands of an *SS* officer one week ago. I was with him but escaped with the help of my friends."

As Rowecki looks to the sky, his eyes glaze. "Goddammit," he exclaims and rubs the stubble on his chin. "And I can't even mourn him." There is nothing for me to say. I have shed all the tears for the Captain that I have to shed. There are no more in me. This man, however, does not even have the luxury to cry. In this hour, he has to show unyielding strength to everyone around him. "It's on your shoulders, then. Do you understand?"

"I do."

"You say you were with him? Are you marked?"

"Probably."

"That's too bad, but you are the man for the job. You are here. You understand the situation better than any of your mates. Get back there, organize and get ready. Starting tonight, there will be a steady flow of soldiers headed in your direction. Get them over the mountains. Get them to safety so they can rejoin the fight with the allies who must enter the fray. They have no other choice. The future of Poland," he begins to say then corrects himself, "The future of the world depends upon us and how we react.

"Men like you, Czech will win the day. Your lot was not as a soldier, but I can see you are a true brother-in-arms. In three weeks, return here for further instructions. You will be our point man in the Tatras. Come to *Smocza* 20 when you return. I'll not write that on paper. You write it in your mind: *Smocza* 20. Protect that information with your life. I must be on my way." He pulls me close and whispers the same words written on the message I delivered a lifetime ago. "We are the first to fight," and he adds, "And now the first to die. We will never surrender. Off with you, now."

I nod to my new friend, Janusz, and he waves me on with the cigarette in his hand. Urgency beckons, but I cannot leave the city without a final word with Amalia and Max.

Raphael and I race back through the city. He is fast and quick for such a big dog, and although I am careful not to lead him into a dangerous situation, he barely escapes the tires of a truck laden with troops. When I see Amalia's apartment building, I increase my pace. The front door is wide open and bounding through, I take the steps two at a time, to the third floor, but as I reach the landing, I stop cold. Painted in large, black strokes on the wall beside the open door to their apartment is the Star of David. I see another Star two doors down. I enter without knocking and call their names, but no one answers. The room is a shambles of shredded books, ripped clothing and broken dishes. Do I blame the Nazis for this? How can I when the letters below the star are Polish, "*Żyd*, Jew." Do we try to gain favor with these vile attackers by assimilating their disgusting hatred of man?

A guttural growl escapes Raphael and alerts me to an intruder, but it is only an old man, bent over and leaning on an ornately carved cane. "They are okay," he mumbles in a deep, gravelly voice. "They heard, as did we all the commotion up the hall, and I ushered them into my home. Come." I follow him across the hall to his apartment. Max hugs Amalia who still holds a handkerchief to her swollen, red eyes. She bravely forces a smile.

"Street ruffians," Max says. "We've had trouble before. There's a common thread here, this hatred of Jews. There are those who believe if they share their loathing with the Germans, the Nazis will spare them and welcome them into Hitler's world. I think they are wrong."

The old man asks if I would like a cup of tea and I respectfully decline. "Then perhaps a special treat for your friend," he says and dares to pat Raphael on the head. Food will become scarce, but he offers the dog a small bone, cleaned of its meat in the soup pot. Raphael accepts it with his dog-smile and retires to the corner to chew it in privacy.

"Did you find her?" Amalia asks.

"No. I gave up the search before I even started, but she is a survivor and she will be okay." I take my *hamsa*, and, bless myself with it, and return it to its place beneath my shirt. Amalia smiles again, this time sincerely, as she shows me the cross that hangs from her neck, the cross I crafted as a youth and gave to her a decade ago. It still hangs from its strap around her neck. Like she did then, she raises it to her lips, kisses it, then kisses her fingertips and places them on my mouth. Max takes no offense.

"I return to Zakopane," I tell them. "I've been with a friend at the *Koniecpolski* Palace. Our military staff meets there this very hour. The government is in exile. Our lines have broken and the general staff will order the survivors to flee west to the mountains. With the Russians poised on our eastern border, it is our only alternative. My friends and I will help our soldiers cross the mountains safely." My mind searches for something reassuring to tell my friends, but words of encouragement simply do not exist. "I must leave now, but you can come with me. I know places where you can hide."

Forlornly, Max says with resignation, "I am not skilled in the outdoors as you are, my friend. I cannot survive in your mountains. I have friends in Warsaw who can take us in. We will find them and take our refuge here in the city. We will be fine with our friends."

"And until they find them," the old man says, "I insist they stay here with me."

I am helpless. My Captain is dead, my sister lost, and now I am powerless to protect my friends from danger. Max understands my perplexity and says, "Fear not, Bronek. You have an obligation to more people than the few in this room. Leave now before it is too late. Like Janka, we are survivors. We will be fine."

I hesitate, lest I regret the decision I must make. "May I leave Raphael with you?"

"But of course," the grandfather replies. "He will be our archangel, Raphael the healer." The animal's wagging tail gives voice to his understanding.

I kneel again and hold my strong friend tightly for just a moment. "Stay here. I will be back." He barks, not loudly. Then to Max and Amalia, "If you find Janka, keep her with you. You protect her, and I will protect her soldier. I will return in three weeks and I will find you." A smile is better than tears. I create one to leave with them knowing we may never see each other again.

Oblivious to time and space, I put one foot before the other and move forward, ever westward as quickly and directly as I can, knowing that I must organize my friends in Zakopane before this wave of refugee soldiers reaches our borders. The rapid success of its army in the field gives the Germans confidence that they can control the rural villages and countryside with a relatively small force. With Rowecki's orders to retreat, traditional fighting is over and the Germans have taken the city. Only a miracle could have altered the inevitable outcome, and today is not a day for miracles. God will make it happen in his time, not mine. Our ability to defend our soil and retake our land rests on three pillars of strength: Stefan and his underground in Warsaw; our fleeing army's successful escape to the other side of the mountains; and the commitment of the Brits and the Yanks to support our cause with men, money and material. War is not an easy endeavor and it is more complicated in its initial stages for the defender than for the attacker. Through the first four weeks of conflict, we have reacted to the invaders. We must reverse roles and make the Germans react to us. No small task, but I have my part to play in it, and I will do it with conviction, so help me God.

The new moon spills ink on the sleeping town as I approach Zakopane in the middle of the night. Few earthbound lights complement the Milky Way that reigns above me unmindful of war and turmoil, and the only sound comes from a fearless dog who howls like a werewolf, then offers a random bark. I wish Raphael were with me so I could gain courage and confidence just from the simple act of petting his head. I've wandered these paths and mountains since childhood and I need no map to tell me where I am going or how I am going to get to my destination.

The air is so still and quiet that the slow drip of water in the grotto counts each step I take. Darkness hides the cave, but the grotto's steady beat tells me I am very close to it. The summer was dry and the fall proffers no relief, but the grotto continues to offer its water. I pray that the winter brings more dry weather and that the snow comes late to hide our movements in the mountains, at least until we can usher our men to the other side. A highlander's skill in the mountains is unmatched and these Germans know nothing of the Tatras. My friends will find me before I find them. I check my progress and freeze when the toes of my right foot begin to sink into the unseen pit I could have easily fallen into.

Certain that friendly eyes and ears monitor my progress, I dare to whisper, "It's me, Bronek." No response. I whisper again, a bit louder, "It's Bronek."

"Stay where you are," a voice issues from the thicket. I have no intention of disobeying. I raise my arms as I hear furtive movement from every direction. I am surrounded. I wait and listen, and am startled when, from behind, two arms embrace me in a bear hug.

"Bronek, you goat! I prayed for your safety."

I am so glad to hear Stashu Marusarz's voice! "And I for yours, my friend." I turn and hold my brother. "The children?"

"Safe in Geneva," he says. "I found them passage to America. They are safe and they will be fine. Come. You must be hungry and we will stuff your mouth with cheese and bread, amazing that we can still come by it, and the water is still sweet."

Starlight sparkles in his eyes and staring at them, I see our Captain. I still grieve mercilessly. I bow my head, place it on Stashu's chest, and begin to weep. He holds me tightly as I say, "He was more than our Captain."

"I know," Stashu whispers. "I know."

I raise my head and wipe the tears from my eyes. "What I do from here forward, I do as much for his memory as I do for Poland. God forgive me," I tell my comrades, "but I will have my vengeance."

"Vengeance, like hate makes a man ugly," Stashu says. "Let it empower you, but do not let it blind you."

We know the forest so well that we move through the night woods as if they were soaked in daylight. We pass the grotto on our way to the cave where my friends chance no fires to reveal our position. Until the winds of winter fly down the mountains in a month or so, we have no need for one anyway. In all, a dozen highlanders, many former members of our Olympic team – all born in Zakopane, most skiers and hockey players save one, Jerzy, a very strong man who has built and toned his muscles rowing in the rivers and then at the summer games – are gathered here. Stashu has wisely advised men with families to stay in their homes. Otherwise, they could raise suspicion and make their families targets of Nazi interrogation, of which physical brutality is routine. Four men stand guard 50 meters from the cave. The rest of us enter its dark mouth and walk 25 meters into its darkness. Andrzej lights a candle that casts enough light to allow us to feel the camaraderie that is natural among brothers-in-arms, particularly when their backs are against the wall.

Zdzisław Motyka moves to the darkest corner and returns with a goatskin of cool water and a large lump of *bundz* cheese on a thick slice of bread. I have ignored the grumbling of my stomach in recent days, and I have lost weight, so the heavy cheese and thick, sweet bread are welcome entrees to my numbed palate.

"So you have been to Warsaw. What news do you bring, Bronek?" The candlelight flickers and animates the dark shadows in the large, cool room. My comrades sit on rocks and boulders of various shapes and sizes, yet show no discomfort.

"It's not good," I tell them, "but anything can be worse. They tell me our government is in exile, at the embassy in France. Our soldiers fight bravely, but we are no match for the German war machine. The Russians mass in the east, whether as allies to the Germans or in defense of their own borders is not yet clear. We need help from the British and the Americans. Without them, our chance of survival as a nation is not good. That is the current situation, at least when I departed Warsaw. Things can change quickly."

"So what do we do?" Zbigniew asks. The others anxiously await my answer.

"Our generals have dismissed our troops," I continue.

"And that is a good thing?" Aleksander asks incredulously. "What sense does that make?"

"We have already lost many good men, thousands of good men, and thousands more are wounded or have been captured," I explain. "Continued resistance on the open battlefield will only result in more Polish casualties. That is not acceptable."

"Stashu and I received our orders to carry messages to Geneva and Rome from General Rowecki. I met him again in Warsaw this week. He orders the surviving troops to escape to Czechoslovakia, Hungary and Romania, and regroup there with the hope that they can survive and evade the Germans until the Americans and the British enter this war."

"I think you mean *IF* they enter this war," Aleksander replies.

I gaze around the dimly lit room and repeat myself, "No, Aleksander. The Brits and the Americans *have* to enter this war. We still do not know Russia's intentions. Without the Brits and the Yanks we have no chance to secure the future of Poland." Zdz brings me another slice of bread with cheese.

"So what is the plan?" When Stashu asks the question, we avert our eyes, unwilling to display our doubts and weakness to one another. The light flickers, and I draw meaningless lines with a stick on the dirt floor. We share the same, unspoken thought: the Captain is gone. He would have known what to do and would have devised a plan.

I am not a leader and have no desire to be one, but I can bear the silence no longer. "I moved swiftly through the night. I have much practice in the art of evasion in recent weeks. Our fleeing troops will band together, and many will seek escape in this direction. They will travel in small groups. We have to get them through the mountains."

My comrades agree and understand what we need to do. "These men are trained soldiers," I continue, "and have knowledge of survival. Jerzy, you take three men. Two of you mark a path through the *Hala Kondratowa*; the other two mark a trail through the *Dolina Goryczkowa*. We must work quickly, for men will arrive very soon. The rest of us will patrol the woods to the east. We'll escort men around the village, so you must set up markers south of Kuźnice."

"What can we use as a marker?" Jerzy asks.

Andrzej suggests we make simple crosses from sticks and plant them in the ground with a base of stones to secure them in place. "I think if the Germans see one, they will think it is a grave marker and will not disturb it."

"That is a good idea," I reply. "That is what we will tell our soldiers: we have marked a path over the mountains with crosses spaced some 200 meters apart. The beam of the cross will point the way."

As we emerge from the cave, the rising sun's first glow paints the eastern horizon. The air is cool, and the bread and cheese invigorate me. I need sleep, but there is no time, and things more important beckon, demanding our attention. The lives of thousands of good men depend upon us.

We descend the foothills in five-minute intervals to minimize the noise. We take no chances as we establish the secret escape route for our fleeing army. Jerzy and his pathfinders precede us, and the other nine of us follow. We have decided to fan out and space ourselves to establish a 25-kilometer arc south of the village with Zakopane at its center. I take a central position in the arc and conceal myself with pine boughs. I have always enjoyed the smell of pinesap and as I wait and watch, I recall peaceful days when my friends and I played in these mountains. Innocence, like youth, is never ours to keep and always lost, sometimes sooner than later.

I squint as the first rays of the new day pierce me from distant hills and I shield my eyes with my hand. Light, another free and priceless gift from God. A far off train whistles and awakens sleeping dogs that begin to bark. Old man Piatek's farm is not too far away, and his rooster calls, announcing the early hour. For one brief moment, I escape this madness and paint a picture with my mind's brush of happier times when my only concern was how fast I could ski down the mountains behind me and how far I could jump, how long I could free myself from earthly bonds.

My reverie is short-lived as gunshots disrupt the still morning air. A burst of automatic weapons fire – a sound new to these ancient mountains – follows the pair of single reports. The sun is higher now and no longer blinds me. As I search the panorama before me, it occurs to me that I have no weapon other than my brain. Suddenly three men in Polish uniforms emerge from a stand of trees and cross the clearing between us. When they are halfway across the open space, they veer away from me. I shake the pine boughs from my shoulders, stand and wave wildly at them. They still do not see me, and in my frustration, I whistle loudly. They run towards me just as their pursuers reach the clearing. More gunshots from the Germans at the edge of the trees. One Pole falls and disappears into the high grass, but then rises as his fellows turn back to help him. One of the Polish soldiers kneels and fires his rifle at the Germans, but his aim is not true. The Poles are 100 meters from me, and I run out to help them. The shots from their hunters raise small puffs of dirt as they strike the ground around us.

"Come quickly," I tell them. They are not about to argue. We return to the trees and scramble into the thick forest. "Halt," a German soldier yells from the distance and more bullets zip through the dry leaves. The man who is shot is a big man, heavy, and blood flows freely from his wound. Within minutes, his spirit has flown and his lifeless body is no more than an empty weight. He was a young officer, much younger than the bearded soldiers that were partner to his flight.

"Where is your weapon?" the older one asks me.

With open palms, I show him I am unarmed. He removes the belt and holster from the dead officer and checks the revolver. "Take this. He has no more use for it." I buckle the belt snuggly around my waist and with the weapon on my hip, power surges through my body knowing that I can fight fire with fire.

I raise my finger to my lips and we lay as still as the dead man whose eyes I close with my fingertips. The Germans stop at the edge of the woods and one says, "Forget about it. There were only three, and I am certain one is wounded, maybe even dead. There will be others." Another looses a final burst of aimless machine gun fire into the trees. Unconcerned and satisfied they have done their best to fulfill their duty, they return to the village.

"Warsaw?" I whisper.

The old one responds, "Fallen and occupied. We stood no chance."

"I've been told to lead you to safety," I tell him. He nods and I point toward the mountains. "You must continue in that direction. You will find two paths marked with crosses. Either path will lead you to the other side of the Tatras. The crossbeam points the way. There are

Germans in Czechoslovakia too, but not many compared to what we see here. I have traveled to Warsaw and know."

"Food, do you have any food?"

"I'm sorry, but I do not. You will find plenty of fresh water, but I have no food."

He nods and then drains the final drops from the canteen he carries. "That's okay," he says, "I never should have asked. You have done enough. We will be on our way." With his thumb, he traces a cross on the forehead of his fallen comrade, then stands and breathes deeply. "There are many others who will follow. I wish you luck so that none are left behind."

I shake hands with him and his friend. They turn west and continue their flight up the mountain.

I hold my post for three, long days, and assist a hundred Polish soldiers. Only one other time, do we contact the enemy, but we are a group of six, and bring more firepower against the pursuing Germans. All five Poles escape unharmed. I am so tired that if I did sleep during my watch, I do not remember. I am hungry but can only finger the fine crumbs in my empty pockets. On the fourth day, an unusually cold wind invades the mountain valleys and the temperature drops. Dark clouds approach from the west like an army of hellish banshees, dark clouds that portend snow. I scan the open space that I have watched diligently for three days, and when I see no movement, I curl into a fetal position and offer no resistance to the sleep that takes me captive in its merciful arms.

I wake in one of those panicked moments of disassociation and have no knowledge of where I am, who I am, where I am or what day it is. Frightening seconds pass as I return to consciousness and time reclaims its relevance.

Snow dusts me, and the clouds have thinned enough that I can tell by the sun's position, I have rested nearly 10 hours. The absence of gunfire during that quiet time suggests that our soldiers have cleared the area, hopefully to safety on the windward side of the peaks.

My comrades risk a small fire in the cave. The gray sky is apt to mask the smoke as it rises through the tiny cracks in the cave's ceiling that lead to the surface. I smell no smoke as I approach, rather the faint aroma of roasting goat, and the scent makes my mouth water in anticipation of a greasy mouthful of succulent meat.

They are tired, my mates are, but all appear satisfied. Each man's ability to smile, a contagious gesture that I willingly engage in, heightens his visible conviction in a job well done.

"How many?" Stashu asks.

"I can't remember." I answer. I tried to keep count, but that number became a part of the blur. "Maybe 50, maybe 100."

"Maybe 200?"

"Perhaps. Do any of you remember?" No one comments.

"I think over one thousand," Stashu concludes. "If 10 groups like ours operated for these days along the border, I believe we've made good the escape of thousands of soldiers." He blesses himself and we concur.

"Breakfast, lunch and dinner is served," Andrzej announces. He has gathered a collection of flat rocks that he invites us to use as plates. Upon them, he places sticks he has fashioned into forks. We pass before him with our rocks, and with his hunting knife, he slices large chunks of moist meat and places them on our makeshift plates. No king has ever dined on a grander meal, no pauper ever more grateful.

"Did no one's mother ever tell him to eat with his mouth closed?" Zdz asks.

"Did your mother not tell you never to speak with food in your mouth?" Jerzy replies and juices run freely down our chins as we laugh. It is good that we still find something that will produce laughter in such dire times.

No man leaves this table hungry; we have picked the carcass clean and only the white bones remain. The goat has served us well, and no one will criticize Andrzej's culinary skills.

"What now?" Aleksander stands and rubs his distended belly with both hands. I see that, like me, he has a revolver stuffed securely into his waistband.

They look to me for the answers. I am no wiser than they in the art of war, but I voice my thoughts. "I promised General Rowecki I would return to Warsaw, and I will. I suggest that you men remain here and await direction. We have to stay organized, and we have to have one leader. I believe Rowecki is the man. I will let you know."

"I will go with you," Stashu says. "That way one or the other of us will be sure to return with news and orders."

I agree with Stashu. "Until you receive further directions from one of us, or God willing both of us, I suggest you avoid contact with the Germans. If you stay away from them, they will have no reason to patrol these mountains. Let the sleeping dog lie, and we will slay him before he knows we are even here."

We rest peacefully through the night. Stashu and I leave well before the sun rises the next morning.

Chapter Sixteen, 1940

Into the Heart of Darkness

Six months pass. The Germans have no intention to leave, and any thoughts that the Soviets will come to our aid disappears. They sign a nonaggression pact with Hitler and cross our eastern borders simply to secure a larger piece of the changing European landscape. Although the Germans occupy our land, we are not a conquered people and we continue to resist despite the fading hope that the Americans will join the British and come to our assistance. Without the Americans, even the fabled British Army is ineffective against the German war machine.

Early in the conflict, we called ourselves the *Służba Zwycięstwu Polski*, the SZP, the Polish Victory Service. Today, we are the *Związek Walki Zbrojnej*, the ZWZ, the Union for Armed Struggle. We wear no uniforms, but I have abandoned the comfort of my highlander attire for the typical urban dress of an occupied country: cap, shirt, jacket and trousers. It is enough. Our mission is simple: to liberate Poland. Our tasks are few but complex: propaganda, reconnaissance and sabotage.

Because I have no military training or background, no one within the organization discusses strategic and tactical options with me. I do not participate in sabotage activities, but the organization respects me for my physical prowess and for what I have accomplished in the years I represented our country at the Olympic Games and other skiing championships. Though my film debut was little more than an eye blink, several soldiers recognize me as one of the skiers in *Biały Slad*. "That is my favorite film," one officer told me, "And that blonde girl is beautiful. Do you know her?"

"I do," I tell him.

"Then perhaps you will introduce me to her when this war is over," he says with a wide grin of anticipation.

"I will do that, friend," and I wonder when this war will end and what will be left of Poland when the shooting stops.

I am 32-years-old. I have performed in film, competed before thousands of cheering fans, kissed beautiful women, held Sonja Henie in my arms, I have been to America and shared casual conversation with Roosevelt ... I have done so many wonderful things that I am so thankful for, but now I am no one's hero, and never wanted to be. Today, I am a messenger boy for the *ZWZ*. I distribute and post flyers for the resistance. I promote the propaganda pieces our organization prepares for our captive population.

Stefan Rowecki organizes and leads our struggle in Warsaw. I do not see him often, but when I do, he always acknowledges my efforts on behalf of the country I serve. The General overlooks nothing. As we retreated to Warsaw in those early days knowing that the battlefield was lost, Stefan created – and others and I helped him distribute – strict guidelines for all patriotic Poles so that none of us would be accomplice to the Nazi act of aggression. "Our language is Polish," his bulletin reads, "Do not make the aggressor's life easier by speaking his language. Respond to any of his questions in Polish by saying '*Nie rozumiem,*' I do not understand." Like the Ten Commandments God gave to Moses, there are 10 directives, and all Poles are obligated to comply with them. We frequently redistribute the rules so they are always fresh in our minds. These simple and direct words exude hatred from the enemy.

On occasion, my duties include reconnaissance. I know this city now like every line of my face, I can get anywhere, through any obstacle the Germans might raise, and I can do it with my eyes blindfolded. I have carried messages to Rome, to Vienna, to Danzig and Smolensk. I take no shame in my job, rather pride that I can contribute in some way to the destruction of the Nazis and to the rebirth of my country whenever God wills that it happen.

My underground friends assure me that my sister Janka and her brave soldier, Krystian are safe. I find her and encourage her to return home to mother and father. She agrees knowing that Krystian has escaped to the other side of the mountains, somewhere in Czechoslovakia. Who knows, I may have abetted his flight. Amalia and Max are not so fortunate. The ominous words that Hitler espoused in his *Mein Kampf* are no longer just letters on paper. His maniacal oratory takes physical form in frightening ways. All Jews are required to wear their Stars of David, large yellow ones pinned to their clothing. A Jew can no longer walk the streets freely, with anonymity. I don't like it, nor do I agree with the practice, but there are those sons of David who wear their stars proudly and even dare flaunt it. Most are as proud to be Polish Jews as I am to be a Polish Catholic. The Germans ordered my friends to leave their apartment and take up residence in a small room with three other families. I visit when I can, but I must be cautious for the Germans are alert for Jewish sympathizers, and I must protect my position in the resistance. It pains me that some Poles conspire to gain favor with the occupation force. I will call no man my master, but I am not stupid and I will survive within the context of Rowecki's rules, and in time, I will put my heel on the head of the snake.

The fate of the Jews is a topic of conjecture, but it is too obvious that Hitler has special plans for them. Shortly after the invasion, all Warsaw Jews, some 400,000, are ordered into an area that is no larger than eight square kilometers. Soon, truckload after truckload of bricks arrives in the northern sector of the city. The trucks sit idle for days, as if they are breathing creatures watching the ghetto. Curiosity grows when the Germans scour the streets and assemble work crews. The *ZWZ* arranges my recruitment so that I can learn the purpose of these mysterious loads of bricks.

My work crew marches to Świętokrzyska Street not far from the Marszołkowska Street corner. Within an hour, we are building a wall of bricks. My crew and I build to the west. One hundred meters further down the street, another crew initiates its section, and I glimpse north where another group builds its wall south to connect with mine. How big is this structure, and for what reason are we building it?

On this first day, we reach the section to the west, and the northern crew joins our foundation. The wall is a full meter tall. Each of us receives a bowl of thin soup and a piece of stale, hard bread for our labor and we are told to return at sunrise. I am tired and my muscles ache from hauling bricks all day, but I walk into the shadows across the street and begin my task of mentally mapping the wall's perimeter.

I follow the brick trail two kilometers to the west, then north another two to three toward Powazkowska, but not before the wall deviates sharply to the west so that it will include the Jewish cemetery, then east two kilometers and finally south to my origin on Świętokrzyska Street. I spend two hours navigating the perimeter. During those two hours, I become a shape shifter, a shadow and nothing more. I successfully evade multiple patrols on my journey. Within the boundaries of this brick wall, Amalia, Max and their friends huddle in fear.

Before I return to our safe house, I float through the ghetto's dark streets to Amalia's residence. A street lamp sputters at the foot of the stairs. I take the steps two at a time, but slowly and quietly. No doors are locked and Amalia's door creaks as I open it. Soft, padded steps rapidly approach me. Raphael. He sniffs my boots then whimpers his request for my attention. I take a knee and put my arms around his muscular neck. He licks my face.

"Are you a friend?" a frightened voice whispers.

"Yes," I answer. "Is that you, Amalia?"

The occupation forbids lights at this late hour, but the dim starlight illumes the moonless night sky behind her, and I see her silhouette in the window.

"Bronek?" Max asks the darkness.

"Yes, Max. It is Bronek."

Other bodies stir under their blankets, but no one dares to speak. I give Raphael a final, firm hug.

"What news do you bring?"

I back to the wall and slide to the floor with my cap in my hands. My dirty fingers grope at my disheveled hair. Amalia and Max sit on either side of me, and Raphael sits before me. "The bricks," I say. "I know why they bring the bricks. The Germans are building a wall, and this house will fall within the perimeter. I am certain the wall will involve the Jews." I rub my tired eyes as Amalia puts her arm around my sagging shoulders. "That is what I believe because the wall includes the cemetery, but not the entire cemetery, only the Jewish graves."

"And Janka?" Max asks. "How is your sister? We've not seen her in weeks."

"My friends found her for me, and I have convinced her to return to Zakopane. I would advise you to do the same. You have to escape the confines of this wall. There is more danger here than on the other side. I don't like it."

"It will not be possible," Amalia says, and before I can respond, Max grabs his sleeve and thrusts the handful of cloth into my face. Even in the darkness, I make out the points of the large yellow star."

"Damn that star. Don't let that piece of cloth determine the rest of your life. You can rip it from your sleeve," I plead. "You need to get outside the confines of these walls. The wall will be complete in two day's time. You have two days – just two – to get to the other side. Do you understand me?" All so easy for me to say.

Amalia lays her forehead on my shoulder and sobs. "We understand, Bronek," Max answers.

"I will find a place for you to stay, and I will return tomorrow night to take you there." I rise to my feet and put my cap on. "Get some sleep. I will return tomorrow night." I kiss each on the forehead and leave with Raphael; I need him much more than he needs me.

As I work through the day, the dog rests in a storefront and is the beneficiary of more than one random scrap tossed in his direction. As hungry as the world is, it makes allowance for animals, and that is a good thing. At the end of the second day, the top of the wall is even with my eyes, already high enough, that it will be difficult for a woman to scale it. I shift to my shadow shape and go north to find an open area that will soon enough be a gate. This is where I will bring Max and Amalia.

What few city lights remain lit reflect from the low hanging clouds and battle the darkness. This night, the door to Amalia's apartment is locked. I tap softly. Raphael harmlessly scratches it. A minute passes, then an old, raspy voice asks, "Who is it?"

"It is Bronek."

A pause. "I know no Bronek."

"I am here to see Max and Amalia."

Another pause, a hushed whisper from a frightened woman, then from the old man, "I know no one named Max or Amalia."

I rap again at the door and say, "I was here with them last night."

More whispers. "They are not here now. I know no one named Max or Amalia. Please go away."

I place my palms and my forehead on the door. I am tempted to kick it down but think better of it. "I am only trying to help," I say and my lips touch the cold wood of the door. "Can you tell me anything?"

"Go away." I do.

We complete the wall under the early afternoon sun of the third day. Green leaves shimmer in the trees above it as they reach from one side of the structure to the other side. It is almost pretty, but a ruse to disguise the true intentions of the Germans. Do they even control the sun and the breeze? In return for my three days of labor, the Germans give me soup and several whacks on my shoulders with sticks when I wasn't working fast enough to please the supervisor in charge. Dismissed from the crew, I pace the perimeter a final time to conclude my report for my superiors. I count nine gates, and each is open, pedestrians – Jews and others – are free to come and go as they dare. I suspect that will change and it does. As a final bit of construction – but labor crews do not perform this – German soldiers crown the wall with strands of sharp barbed wire, a crown of thorns.

The following day, the Nazis send a frightening order through the city: all Jews must move into the area confined by the brick wall. There has been no rest in Warsaw since the first gunshots, but this day is as tense as any. Long columns of tired people, men and women, old and young, sick and healthy are herded like cattle through the streets, and all converge on the ghetto I am ashamed to admit I helped construct. Curious people line the streets. Some taunt this helpless parade thinking that their mockery will gain them favor with their German masters. Most however remain silent. Some pray and many rosary beads wrap the gnarled hands of old women and men, too.

In all, some 400,000 people cram into an area less than eight square kilometers. I try to put it in perspective and think that Zakopane is about the same size as this ghetto, but fewer than 2,000 people populate it. This makes no sense – mathematical, physical or biological.

I keep my distance from the procession, but constantly search for Amalia and her husband. If they are there and I fail to see them, Raphael will let me know, but there are other gates through which they can pass, unnoticed by us. Then again, is there anything I can do if I find them? I want to scream but know that my shrieking voice will achieve no purpose. I kneel and take what comfort I can from the dog.

And so, the Jews trudge through the city from sunrise to sunset and beyond. When there appears to be no more room within the confines of the wall, gunshots ring out, and the crowd at the gates surges forward again, and more bodies are packed in. Gunfire is too frequent. An old Jew – he must be at least 100-years-old – walks by me. In one hand, he carries a small but ancient case that contains his few belongings. In his other hand, he uses a cane to balance himself as he shuffles forward. Suddenly he stops and looks all around him, then places his case on the ground and takes a seat upon it. He decides he will walk no more. A soldier approaches and orders him to move. He shoves the old man, the case topples and the grandfather falls roughly to the cobblestone street. An SS officer arrives. He and the soldier exchange curt words, then the officer pulls his revolver and shoots the old man dead on the spot. People ignore the scene thinking that if they give it no notice it will disappear as if it had never happened. They are wrong, and the old one lies in a pool of blood while women shield the eyes of their children as they file past toward the gates.

I stand vigil for several more hours – into the darkest hours of the night – until the last Jew passes through and the gates are closed and locked. My heart is in there with them, but I have new orders from *ZWZ*.

The streets of Zakopane are dark and a light breeze from the mountains carries the soothing noise of chirping insects. If I concentrate on their familiar sounds, the unwelcome voices of happy German soldiers, who have become far too comfortable drinking *Żubrówka* in our taverns, are less likely to distract me. I return to post new orders from the *ZWZ*.

I commiserate with the innkeepers. At gunpoint, the enemy forces them to keep the taverns open and to serve the Germans what they want, when they want it and for just a few *Reichspfennig*. One or two smiling innkeepers eagerly comply as their coffers fill with German money, but these men and their willing subservience to our oppressors is noted, and the patriots shun their establishments.

A soft light shines in the window of my parents' home. I pray that Janka is with them, and for the safety of my brother and Stasia and their families. The light draws me to them, but I stay clear so as not to endanger my family with my physical presence. I find refuge in a barn not far from the Villa Marilor that the Germans continue to use as their headquarters, and I wait there until a distant clock chimes midnight. The parting sounds of laughter fly the empty streets as conquerors and conquered rest and wait for another day of occupation. Silence rules the night.

I choose to post my first bulletins on the very doors of the villa, a calculated action meant to rub our brazen resistance directly in the faces of our unwelcome 'guests.' I know it will piss them off. "Boycott the Invader," my bulletins read in large, bold letters, and beneath those bold words, a man can read the 10 rules that every Polish partisan should practice. I have posted these flyers before, and I am sure to do it again.

With my bag of hundreds of bulletins slung over my shoulder, I creep up the street amid the concealment of the shrubbery that lines the sidewalk. I pause and listen. No movement, so I step out when I reach the villa and climb the steps to the closed door. How stupid and careless, I think later, that I would be foolish enough to believe no guards would stand watch through the night, but with no one in sight, I softly tap a brad with a small hammer to hold the bulletin securely in place, one tack at the top, then another on the bottom. Satisfied with my work, I turn and freeze before a pair of helmeted soldiers with raised rifles.

I know what the one is telling me when he says, "*Arme über dem kopf. Hände hoch,*" but I follow the very commandments I have just tacked to the door: "*Your language is Polish... answer all his questions, 'I do not understand.'*"

"*Nie rozumiem,*" I say with a dumb smile on my face.

"*Hände hoch, dummer mensch.*" I believe the worst thing you can call a man besides a liar, is stupid. Now, I am the one who is pissed off. Holding his gun, he raises his hands above his head to demonstrate. I surprise him and reward his stupidity with a powerful, swift kick to his groin. Now, he has justification to call me stupid! The other soldier can drop me like a fly with a single bullet, but he mercifully elects to hit me hard in the sternum with the butt of his weapon. Breathless, I fall to the ground.

Gasping for air, I raise my head and see Raphael racing up the street toward me. I plant myself on all fours, and the dog licks my face and whines. No mercy for him though, and the soldier brutally kicks him. Raphael howls and drops to his haunches, but scrambles to his feet, growling, and charges the German. The soldier meets his assault with a vicious stroke of his rifle butt to Raphael's chops that renders my brave friend unconscious.

I rise and say, "Bastard," a word common to both our languages and in no need of translation. He swipes my face with the back of his hand and a small trickle of blood issues from the corner of my mouth. I am captive and escape is unlikely. It is due to my own stupidity and my inability to control my emotions. A man can control his hate for only so long, and mine has run its course. The breeze gains strength with a strong gust and I empty my bag of paper bulletins onto the street. As I watch them scatter and fly up the deserted road, I take some satisfaction that, although I did not physically nail each paper to a post, door or tree, I have indeed 'distributed' them throughout Zakopane, some undoubtedly beyond. The second German rewards me with a cuff to the back of my head. I expected worse, am thankful for less, but distraught at the sight of the dog – friend to me and an old priest in Rome – sprawled motionless at the bottom of the steps. His large chest rises and falls to a slow rhythm, and I think he will recover, perhaps not soon enough to help me, but he will recover.

With my hands atop my head, I stumble up the steps and into the large foyer. Few lights illuminate the room at this late hour but I glimpse my reflection in the full-length mirror that graces the entryway. For a fraction of a second, I see myself as the young athlete that entered this lobby in a tuxedo on his way to a moving picture debut in Warsaw. Was it a lifetime ago, or two? I have plenty of time to ponder that question. My captors push me to my knees, then order me to a sitting position on the floor between the two chairs they have taken on either side of me. One lights a cigarette, draws on it and offers it to his companion who declines it. He waves it in front of my face and the smoke burns my eyes. "Cigarette?" he asks. I do not respond. He shrugs his shoulders. As my eyes adjust to the dim light, I note five other soldiers in the room. One snores loudly, another reads a newspaper. There is no chance for escape and I resolve to play this waiting game through the night.

After sleeping on the wooden floor for several hours, a knock to my head rouses me. I open my eyes to the first rays of the morning sun, which filter through the trees that surround the villa. I am more rested than I have been in recent weeks. Though hungry, I will ask for no food or comfort from my captors. If they offer it to me, I will accept, but I refuse to ask for anything. Rule number seven: *"Do not complain to the enemy."*

I stare at the floor as several men confront me, one in shiny black riding boots. "On your feet." A hand hauls me up by my collar. For the third time in my life, I stand face to face with *Hauptsturmführer* Feldman, promoted twice since our original encounter at the games in Garmisch. I am taller than he is, and standing as straight as I can, I look over the top of his head. The smell of sausage on his breath makes me want to gag, but I force my stomach to remain calm.

My height forces him to look up into my dirty face. "Do you never learn?" he barks. Then he slaps me hard. "If it were up to me," he stresses each word, "I would kill you here and now. I can do it that fast, you know." He snaps his fingers before my face. "But I have other plans for you, my friend, plans that will make you beg for the quick death I could give you in this instant." He draws his revolver and places the cold, steel barrel against my temple. I will not budge. In my peripheral vision, a photographer stands ready to take a picture. With the gun at my head, I smile, thinking it will make quite the clever picture for the Nazi propaganda machine. Feldman hungers to pull that trigger, he aches so badly to wipe the smile from my face. He draws the hammer back with his thumb and it clicks loudly into place. The barrel shakes nervously on my head, then he moves it beneath my chin and points it at the ceiling while returning the hammer to its closed position. He holsters his weapon. "Take him to Tarnów," he orders his men. My gaze is steady and fearless as he turns and walks away.

Without preamble, the guards shackle my wrists and ankles, and I march from the villa with other men — some of them friends — to waiting trucks. We climb into the open beds and depart the villa without formality. The convoy follows the road that I would normally travel to walk from town to my home in the foothills. From my position on a bench, I stare beyond the armed guard and through the cab. A solitary figure, a woman walks on the side of the road. It is Janka. Her hair flies freely and wildly in the wind, and she carries a package.

She hears the approaching trucks and turns to watch them pass. My first inclination is to leap from the vehicle, but I know my captors would shoot me on the spot, and my sweet sister does not deserve to see me murdered on the road like a criminal, discarded like worthless trash. As we pass her, I lower my head so she will not recognize me, but tilt it enough to look at her through the cloud of dust that rises behind us. Janka bends slightly and reaches out her arm. Standing beside her is Raphael.

I cannot remember the last time I bathed. If the odor that follows me like my shadow is repulsive, I do not know it. After 30 days in the Tarnów prison, I am accustomed to the aroma of unwashed bodies. My fellow prisoners and I have no chance of escape, the walls are too high, the guards and their dogs, too many.

Each day is the same: we wake, attend roll call, receive a cup of cold soup and walk the prison yard. From dawn to dusk, we walk the yard and do little else. This routine will not last forever, but we dare not speculate when it will change – though most hope each day is that day – or what that change will be. We know change will not bring freedom. The ability to smile is a lost art. I, however have not forgotten, and the guards must think me a dunce as I pace the compound back and forth, round and round all day, every day with an idiot's smile on my face.

Today becomes 'that day' as precedent breaks. The soldier in charge reads from a list and calls out hundreds of names, mine among them. The few prisoners not chosen are dismissed and ordered to their quarters. The rest of us proceed out the gate in a single file. This is my first experience beyond the prison walls since I walked in a month ago. Our long line bends around corner after corner and extends through the town. Word reaches us that we march to a bathhouse. It takes hours to get there, but as I near the entry to the bath, I see a commotion at the door. German soldiers with heavy sticks are beating two men. I know little of Jewish custom, but another prisoner tells us that the bathhouse is a special one to the Jews in Tarnów, who use it for ritual cleansing, but like everything else, the Germans have confiscated it for their own purpose. The few Jews among us apparently refuse to enter the bathhouse, and their refusal to follow orders results in violence. They finally give up their fight and walk into the building.

By late afternoon, it is my turn. I do what everyone who has preceded me has done: I remove my dirty clothes. Like Adam during those first days in Eden, I am not ashamed of my nakedness. There is no reason to be, but others are quite conscious of their condition. I am careful to take my *hamsa* and cup it securely in my hand. No one notices.

Why we are afforded this cleaning, I'm uncertain, but the cold water, steadily flowing over my dirty body on this warm June day is most certainly welcome. I wish I could stand here forever, but the guards prod me forward and I enter the next room. It contains large baths, empty now, the bricks that contain them as dry as the road outside. Moisture drips and evaporates from my body as I walk through this room, shivering in the shadows as goose bumps rise on my flesh. I pass through an area where two men dust me with a white powder, a disinfectant I think. I cover my mouth and cough but continue moving forward, dry now but I look like an albino. In the final room, an expressionless man gives me a new change of clothing. Today the clothes are clean, but I doubt they will remain that way for long. I leave the bathhouse and join my prison mates in the bright sunlight. We wear identical uniforms: a thin, jacket-like shirt and trousers, both striped in gray and blue, a cap and wooden shoes. I am lucky because my shoes fit. Others are not as fortunate, and they hobble in their ill-fitting footwear hoping that sooner than later their feet will shrink or the shoes will grow. Neither will happen. The painful condition will be permanent.

Scattered among us are a handful of Jews. They are the older men in the group, men in their fifties. Even dressed in their new 'pajamas,' none can escape the professional and refined air that hovers above each. They appear to be scholarly men, and not men who toil with their hands. They cannot disguise their attraction to book learning. I suspect they may be doctors and lawyers, maybe a professor or two. Fear and uncertainty are etched on each face. Most of us are men in our prime. I have learned during my 30 days in Tarnów that, excepting the few Jews in our midst, the rest of us are here because of our association and activity with the ZWZ. We are told we are criminals and, true or not, I find pride in that moniker if standing against the Third Reich qualifies me to be a criminal.

Our number grows as more men garbed in the striped uniforms leave the building and congregate with us. I look for an opportunity to escape. Prison walls no longer confine us, but then I consider how obvious I would be dressed the way I am, I realize evasion would be very difficult.

Daylight drips from the trees as evening descends. On this warm night, the air is still and no birds coo; not even the crickets in the nearby fields dare play their fiddled legs, and no dogs bark. It is so quiet that I know exactly when the last man showers, when the water is turned off. It is so quiet I fear I am deaf. The Germans allow us to sit, but they do not feed us. I am hungry. We wait. Someone whispers to me the Germans will kill us tonight. I tell him that might be the best thing for us. The perfect half moon rises above the buildings, and sheds its silver light on the 700 prisoners who continue to wait, patiently, no, but there is no other choice. Sleep takes all of us at one time or another. I judge how long my eyes are closed by the position of the moon as it crosses the night sky. I watch the stars like an astronomer seeking a new discovery.

A train whistle is the first notable sound all night and announces that daybreak will be here soon. An entourage of officers approaches. The one in charge shouts briskly, "Jeder aufzustehen. Auf eure füße." I think that many of the prisoners know that he has told us to get up, but only a few respond. I want to believe it is because we are committed to our resistance and refuse to follow the orders spoken in German. The officer waves his hands, and someone yells in Polish, "W górę!" One by one, we rise. I stretch my arms, and then rub the tiredness from my eyes. The train's whistle blows again, much closer now and the approaching engine slows somewhere nearby.

The officer raises his pistol and fires a shot into the air. We move quickly in an awkward trot. Rising dust causes several men to cough. I cover my mouth. Prior to this war, I traveled Europe and then America in comfortable passenger cars. I will not be so fortunate on this ride to our unknown destination. Even at this early hour, I would expect activity in the streets as vendors prepare their shops for the day's activity, but on this morning, the streets are eerily deserted, as we shuffle through them, now four abreast. Curious faces peek around window curtains pulled aside just enough to offer a look, then the faces disappear and the curtains fall. Our guards shout constantly at us, and anybody who slows the group is withdrawn from the serpentine line for a quick beating, and then thrust back into the parade.

An invisible hand mercifully reaches out to us as a small bouquet of red roses floats over a narrow wooden wall between two buildings. The bouquet hangs supernaturally, as if it is immune to the laws of gravity. Then, the flowers fall to the ground and the nearest soldier tramples them under his heavy boot and scatters the red petals to mix with the dust on the cobblestoned street.

The locomotive rests and heavily breathes a vestige of white steam that quickly disappears. The sun rises early in June and bursts over the western horizon. This is no passenger train; it is a freight train with at least 30 boxcars, doors drawn open and gaping like a hungry animal. I'm reminded of my experience with Stashu as we mounted the moving train with the children.

If the Germans show any mercy, it is that they allocate only 25 men to each car. I suspect they could have crammed 25 more into each hold if they had a mind to. I board a car midway up the tracks. As soon as the 25th man boards, soldiers slide the heavy door shut, bolt and lock it, with a disturbing sense of finality. Because we've recently showered, the odor of cleanliness lingers, but as the minutes approach an hour, it gives way to the pungent smell of perspiration and passed gas that we are helpless to contain. My hunger grows, but I will not whine or yield to the cramps it causes me because I share my predicament with others who choose to remain silent. Not a one complains. Some might think it is fear that keeps our mouths shut. It is not; it is courage.

When we are all aboard, the whistle announces the train's departure and the cars jerk one after the other as the engine brings its retinue into motion. I lean against one wall of this old boxcar where large spaces allow the sunlight to shine in. The sun's position tells me we move west toward Kraków. I think that is our destination, but as we approach the outskirts of the city, the train continues to power forward with speed and no sign of slowing down. I am not the only passenger surprised we do not stop in Kraków, and for the first time since we boarded, men begin to mumble.

We speed through the city and hold our course west. Though not far from my home in Zakopane, I am unfamiliar with the small bit of countryside I am able to discern through the rough wooden planks. Thirty minutes beyond Kraków, the train slows as we move toward a small town, then creep through it. "Oświęcim," the man next to me whispers aloud.

The train stops and the doors open to a wall of loud, maddening noise. Shouts and orders assault us like physical implements intended to inflict harm. Most of us fall several meters directly onto the ground for only the first several cars have the luxury of a loading platform. I am lucky and land on my feet. Others are not so fortunate, and more than one twists his ankle and starts his life here in pain, as if he needs any more. Most of us are freedom fighters of sorts who have worked with the *ZWZ* for many months, but it takes mere minutes, no, seconds for our captors to break our resistance. They beat us into submission with the butts of their guns, some even wield whips and I feel the lash through my thin clothing that somehow refuses to tear. No German needs an excuse to use his weapons. They kick us, slap and punch us. I lock eyes with a soldier about my age hoping I will see a glimmer of compassion. There is none, rather the opposite. He is enjoying his task — I cannot call it his work. He grins and then doubles me over as he drives his closed fist into my stomach. I fall to a knee then rise. I do not want to lie on the ground and let him, or one of his compatriots use me as if I were a football. I want him to know that I am a better man than he is, and I will not stay on the ground in a subservient position beneath him. I say nothing, raise my eyes, and stare into his. I steal his smile and the hateful grin leaves his face. He knows what I am thinking and when he can stand my silence no longer, he turns to find another victim to intimidate.

The fracas continues for several more minutes, and then a harsh whistle sounds, and the yelling immediately stops while cries of pain linger. We march in single file to a building, and enter one by one. It is not a hotel, of that I am certain. The day drags on and I am weary when I finally walk in. The building houses an office complex with many desks, tables and chairs.

The spectacled soldier who sits behind the desk never looks up as he waves me to take a seat. This is the first

time I have been off my feet since we boarded the train
in Tarnów. Smoke rises from the cigarette he holds. He
rests his elbow on the desk, chin in his hand, and he leans
over the paper in front of him. "What is your name?" he
asks.

"Bronisław Czech."

Still not looking up, he turns his head curiously. "Place
of birth?"

"Zakopane."

"Occupation?"

"Ski instructor."

He sits up straight, removes his spectacles and looks
closely at me. A hint of a smile crosses his lips. "You *are*
Bronisław Czech," he whispers so as not to draw attention.
I don't know what he means; of course I am who I say I am,
though it might have been better had I offered an alias.
His eyes flit left, then right to ascertain how closely we are
being monitored. "One moment," he says, then looks at
the nearest guard and nods as if to tell him to keep watch
closely on me. He walks to the cooler for a cup of water
and returns to his desk. He nods again to the soldier who
directs his attention elsewhere. He takes a sip from the
cup, then places it in front of me. After glancing cautiously
in all directions, he looks at me and points to the cup with
his pencil. "Please," he whispers again, then says loudly,
"Year of birth."

I hunch forward and dare to raise the cup to my
mouth. The wetness flows over my parched lips. The
water is cool, though stale and not sweet. I take a single,
long draft – quickly – then return the cup to the desk.
"Nineteen-oh-eight."

"Oh-eight," he repeats, then looks up again and whispers through glimmering but sad eyes, "You don't remember me, but I remember you. St. Moritz," he says, "Twenty-eight. We jumped together."

I think back a dozen years as I stare into his face, and then recall the second jump in St. Moritz, when the officials moved our starting position so much higher up the hill, that the crowd below us looked like ants. This man preceded me and I remember his apprehension that day. I sought to dispel his fear, so I placed my hand on his shoulder, a simple gesture. We exchanged no words. As we look into one another's eyes at this moment, I remember it as if it was yesterday. Perhaps he detects the fear in my eyes that I saw in his, though I try to be stoic, if not brave as I sit surrounded by the enemy. It is the uncertainty that unsettles me, not the enemy.

Someone behind him yells, "*Schnell,*" an unspecific command to everyone in the room, and the German jumper whose name I cannot remember looks back to his desk and concludes his short interview. He waves me to my feet, gives me the sheet of paper and shouts over his shoulder, "Three-hundred-forty-nine." He glances nervously around him a final time, then touches the back of my hand and whispers loud enough for me to hear, "May God be with you." I return his blessing with a smile and move on.

Two men roughly escort me into a hallway that extends to the far end of the building. Sudden and unexpected screams escape from the interior doors that are open. The screams are unnerving, but neither guard prevents me from looking into the rooms where grimacing men, some doubled over plead with their eyes for mercy. My escorts shove me into a room where two other men in white coats tinged with drying blood and black marks, wait impatiently for me. The soldiers back me up and firmly pin my outstretched arms against the wall while the taller of the other two opens my shirt and pulls it aside to expose my chest.

"What is this?" he asks when he sees the *hamsa*.

One of the soldiers bends close and says, "It's a Jew thing with Hebrew letters." He appears afraid to touch it.

"Fucking Jew," the white-coated attendant replies. I expect him to rip it from my neck. Instead, he ignores it and swings it to my back as if it isn't there.

His partner looks at my paperwork and says aloud, "Three-hundred-forty nine." He picks up a strange implement from the table and makes some adjustments. The tool is rectangular, maybe 10 centimeters and looks like a postman's stamp with its rounded handle. Many small needles extend from the opposite side. With one quick, unexpected movement, he slams it into my chest, buries the needles and then extracts it in a smooth motion. Now I know the source of the screams. I want to cry out, but I hold my pain inside. My head falls forward as I restrain the shriek I've trapped in my throat, and I see the dripping, red numerals "349" punched into my chest. The white-coated man wipes away the blood then stays it momentarily by applying pressure with a dirty rag. With his other hand, he dips a different rag into a can of what I can smell is black ink, he then presses the ink into the needles marks on my chest and holds the rag there for a full 30 seconds. The soldiers release my flexed arms and order me to button my shirt. As I do, I glance down at the black mark on my chest, a tattoo that reads "349." The pain was sharp and instantaneous but did not last long. They take me to the steps at end of the building and deposit me into the street to join my comrades who form up in files of five men abreast. Each bears the dirty, damp spot on his shirt from this unholy initiation.

Though painful, the registration process goes much faster than the bathing procedure at the prison. Those in charge at Oświęcim are better trained and are more organized than those at Tarnów are. The expediency of our overseers may give us a clue as to why we are here, but we are given no time to consider it. By noon, we have received our numbers and the soldiers move us forward into a containment area. Watchtowers stand at regular intervals along a high, barbed wire fence, surrounding a large group of buildings. This place appears more a compound than a prison. We pass through an iron gate and above it is an iron sign with large, iron letters that read, *"Arbeit macht frei,"* work makes you free. While I enjoy the fruits of labor, I am not so sure that freedom comes from work alone, particularly when I am about to be caged behind barbed wire.

We march through the camp in groups of 50 men – 10 rows, 5 deep – and each group stops in front of a two-storied, brick building. There are more barracks here than what our contingent from Tarnów can fill. More men will come to this place. Forty-nine others and I leave the thinning parade to stand and wait silently in front of the building, which will be my new home. Soldiers stand guard, but no single person seems to be in charge of my group. We count minutes, not willing to risk doing the wrong thing that could bring some undeserved punishment upon us.

When the final group stands before its barracks, a large, fat man ambles to take his place in front of my company. Although his clothes are the same as ours, I do not recognize him as one of the prisoners who rode the train from Tarnów with us. The only difference in our attire – other than the fact that his shirt is so big that it looks like a tent – is the badge he wears. Like my confederates who accompanied me from the prison, I wear a small, red triangle with a 'P' on my left breast. This big, bald man lumbers forward with a green triangle sewn on his jacket. He stands with his hands on his bulbous hips and stares, no, glowers at us. In his right hand, he carries a stick. We only have time to wait.

He faces us, then raises his right arm perpendicular from his side indicating that we should do the same and space ourselves at arm's length. He points his arm and his sausage-like fingers forward, and we follow suit so when the exercise is complete, we stand at arm's length from one another, side to side and front to back. He begins to pace. His path takes him from left to right, and with each turn at the end of our rank, he inches closer to the front row. He removes his hands from his hips and begins to slap his left hand with the stick, hard enough to make a sharp, stinging sound.

I am in the back row and sense movement behind me, but I dare not turn and look. The fat man with the green patch is now within arm's length of the front file. He slows his pace and stares into each man's eyes as he struts down the row. Does he know how stupid he looks with his obesity straining the buttons of his jacket and his belly sagging over his pant waist as if he were pregnant? Every prisoner block before every building is subject to the same exercise, and when all blocks are identically formed up with all men in their proper places, a loud voice booms a single word over the loudspeaker system, "Begin!" Shouting commences immediately, interspersed with pleas for mercy and then screams. The volume and intensity increase.

A man in our front row coughs and raises his hands to wipe his mouth. The fat man walks toward him and asks, "Are you sick?" Before the man can answer, Fatman delivers a fierce blow to the prisoner's face, and knocks him to the ground. The fallen man tries to rise, but Fatman kicks him twice, very hard in the mid-section. The prisoner collapses and curls into a ball in a useless effort to protect himself.

Why I think I have the power to intercede, I do not know, but even as I take a step forward, I receive a blow to the back of my head that sends my cap to the ground. As I bend to retrieve it, a foot strikes my backside and I stumble and fall. I roll to a sitting position to confront the soldier who struck me. "Don't cause trouble," he says and jerks his head. "Get back in line." Pity wipes the anger from his face for a split second to reveal the innocence that the Reich steals from this young man, and the words run from his lips like a plea rather than an order. I follow his instructions. We are the same height, he puts his face directly in mine, and we are so close I can feel the rim of his helmet on my forehead. "Your will may be strong," he breathes at me, "but you have no power here. Stay where you are and follow orders." I clench my teeth and look past him with the briefest of nods. "Please," he adds.

This place changes everyone who walks through its portal. Prisoners, guards, staff ... this compound in Oświęcim makes exceptions for no one. Every man is part human and part beast, a Minotaur in this labyrinth of life. In this place, the beast rules and only a special man will contain him and disrupt his mission to destroy our humanity in favor of Hitler's bestiality. The men with power are cruel men and rule without compassion. The men trapped here are little better, perhaps worse than caged animals, who must rely on their masters for the basic essentials to sustain their miserable lives. What fate has delivered me to this evil place? The yelling and screaming become a single, unintelligible sound that rings painfully in my ears. Beaten men fall before me. Those who attempt to resist are murdered on the spot. I wonder if death may not be the better alternative to life, as I see it in a place that Death is pleased to call home. I receive my share of blows and no one escapes unscathed. A single, loud whistle quiets the melee and brings order to the camp.

The soldiers move back to their positions behind us, and Fatman returns to the front of our ranks. "I am Frederick," he introduces himself with a threatening smirk on his ugly, swollen face. "Each of you should be my friend." He pulls one man forward and turns him around to face us, then uses his stick and slaps the red triangle stitched to the prisoner's jacket. "You see this?" he says and does not wait for an answer. "This means this man is a political prisoner. All of you wear this red triangle. You have all offended the Reich, and the Führer is not pleased. He has brought you here to work off your debt to him, the debt you incurred for your insolence and your worthless efforts to affront him and his army." He shoves the man back into line then uses his stick to point to the green triangle on his jacket. "You see this?" he asks again. "This means I am a criminal. I have killed many men in my time, not in war, but just because I wanted to do it. I have no particular reason, I need no particular reason." He laughs. "I just like to kill men, not animals, only men." The smirk returns to his face. "You will want to be my friend."

We learn that Frederick is a *kapo*. He is a prisoner, but privileged and therefore given some minor authority over prisoners like us. He is not important, but he has the power to make life miserable for us, not for any reason – as he explained to us – but only because he can.

I have always regarded a prison as a building with cells, barred cells to keep criminals separate from 'civilized' society. By that definition, this is not a prison. We are guarded and we have no freedom to come and go and we do not interact with any society other than what exists within these barbed wire fences, but we sleep in brick barracks like soldiers in training. Unlike soldiers, we have no beds or cots. Frederick introduces us to our building. The smell of fresh mortar hints at recent repairs. The exterior has received a sloppy whitewash, but the interior walls, though clean, emanate a moist and musty odor. Each of us receives a thin, straw mattress and a thinner wool blanket. The blanket is unnecessary during the summer months, and I hope we receive another before the winter comes because this flimsy thing will not protect anyone from the cold winds that will assault us from the open fields to our west.

"Sleep where you like in this big room," Frederick tells us, "but in the morning, stack your mattresses and blankets against the wall to keep the floor open and orderly."

The thin mattress offers no comfort and the building creaks its annoying sounds at night as the wood expands and contracts with the iron nails that pieced it together not so long ago. That music plays regularly for several months until the wood ages and becomes accustomed to our regular comings and goings.

We have no simple tasks, and we are expected to perform miracles to keep ourselves alive and maintain some sense of hygiene. Bricks without straw. The liquid diet forced upon us can cause serious problems, so I minimize my liquid intake to reduce the swelling I see prevalent in the population. Bread becomes my primary staple but I allow myself some soup as a source of liquids. My chosen diet helps me control my bowels, a basic function beyond the capability of many other inmates. I tolerate the smell of my smitten comrades, whose greedy intake of liquid either dehydrates them as it rushes uncontrollably through their bodies, or bloats them and swells their extremities because it won't. Death in its naked most gruesome costume is everywhere.

The conditions drive us together. No Olympic team is as close as we are and will become.

Other than the German jumper who I have not seen since the day I arrived, no one recognizes me; my fame as an Olympic athlete means nothing, it is unnoticed and of no consequence to anyone, particularly to me. Ten years ago, if asked, 'Who are you?' I would have answered, "Bronisław Czech. I am an Olympic skier from Poland." Today, I would

answer, "I am Bronisław Czech. I am a man. I once skied."
Man first, athlete second. My dignity is all I have, commendations be damned. I left any pretense of self-importance
behind me when I walked through the gate. I cannot help
but ponder those three words that greet each man who walks
beneath them, *"Arbeit macht frei."* No, I do not believe that
work makes a man free. I believe that a fair day's work is
worth a fair wage, but we do not work here for wage or for
freedom. I begin to doubt we will ever know physical freedom again. Here, we work for one thing only: to survive, and
it may not be worth the fight. A man who cannot work in
this camp writes his own death warrant. In the real world, a
man who cannot or will not work is a bum. In Oświęcim, he
is dead. The Germans care little for those men who worked
in the real world with their minds and not their hands. A
man who arrives here fit has difficulty enough surviving the
atrocities he confronts; a man who walks through this gate
not fit, will see his life pass in weeks, sometimes days. No
war is kind to humanity. If it is possible, this war, even less,
and I've no reason to believe the end will come soon.

We rise before the sun each morning. With mattresses
stacked in the corner of the room, we carry our tired bodies into the cool, morning air, sometimes lucky enough to
watch the last star fade. Today, I am a demolition man, and
my barracks mates and I march through the gate to complete the destruction of the small houses that once graced
these quiet streets just beyond these barbed wire walls.
I wonder where the former inhabitants are. I pray they
moved on peacefully, or perhaps they just disappeared, but
more likely they are dead for I think the Germans would
not like to have witnesses to what they do here.

As I move the broken lumber from these fallen houses to trucks that wait nearby, I am thankful that this is my task and not something more heinous. Tadeusz and Józef, both from Zakopane have told me their work is not so innocent. No graveyards in Oświęcim serve the compound. No one who dies here finds his peace in a cemetery. No, not here. When a prisoner dies, his body is burned, cremated, ashes to literal ashes, dust to unholy dust. Tadeusz and Józef tell our barracks mates that they are building another crematorium, and they believe yet another is under construction nearby. We conclude that many more men will arrive on these hell-bound trains, some to work, more to die.

Adam Dziadulski, another friend from Zakopane says there is a factory not far from here where the lucky ones get to work. He marches two kilometers to the east each morning where they build a massive factory that will soon belch rotten smoke that will mix with the ashes that rise from the crematoriums. When the wind blows in our direction, we fall silent.

November brings the first taste of winter. "You must love the cold," my *Babcia* would tell me when I was a young boy. "You must let it be your friend." I followed her advice as a skier, and her guidance never failed me, but it is different here. As children, we could always escape the cold. In Oświęcim, there is no warmth nor is there reprieve from the inescapable claws of the wind when the temperature drops intolerably below freezing. When I was a boy, Father Stolarczyk would gather the children and tell us holy stories of the saints. I remember the tale of the French maiden Joan, Joan of Arc. She was a saint and she died a martyr's death, burned at the stake! How gruesome, I thought, to be burned alive at a fiery stake! The story haunted me and it forced itself into my dreams for a long time. I would wake in the middle of the night to dispel the vision of flames engulfing me on earth and in hell too, if I was not good and did not say my prayers. As an adult, however, when I recollect the story of Joan, I think she may have suffocated quite quickly, and although the pain would have been excruciatingly intense, her exposure to it was over in minutes, if not seconds. I have seen worse things here than the fate that took Joan. We are not martyrs in Oświęcim. Martyrs willingly give up their lives for what they believe in. We will die, but not willingly, and there are those prisoners who would gladly renounce their beliefs if it meant their freedom. It would not.

On this night, we receive our first taste of the frigid cold that can bring Poland to its knees. It is very early in the winter for such conditions, but it has arrived nonetheless. Frederick enters our barracks accompanied by several soldiers, one an officer. Frederick points to three prisoners and grunts, "You, you and you." The three march quickly out the door with Frederick and his cohorts. Several of us gather at the window.

"What now?" Tadeusz asks. No one ventures an answer. The Germans have built a large fire and their bonfire roars to life casting orange light to reveal 12 prisoners under guard, including the three from our building. They stand erect and visibly shiver. At first, I think the soldiers will burn them alive, but we learn their end will be crueler still. The guards assign the prisoners to three groups of four, and then arrange them in semi-circles facing the fire.

The closest group is about five meters from the flames, close enough to be teased by the warmth the fire offers, but far enough away to be gripped by the cold air. The other two groups are spaced at five meters beyond the first, then a final five beyond the second group.

Within minutes, the Germans' deadly game becomes obvious. They have no intention to burn these men. They mean to freeze them to death and have spaced them in such a way as to create several hours of unspeakable agony, which those soldiers and *kapos* gathered around the fire refer to as entertainment.

Perhaps it would be wise to follow the lead of a handful of older prisoners in my barracks who leave the glass and return to their mattresses, wrap their blankets about them and roll toward the walls. A handful of friends and I stand vigil in our feeble effort to honor these hapless victims. Our captors' muffled laughter penetrates the frosted windowpanes, but not a man who faces his death in the frigid wind utters a sound. One by one, they fall to the frozen ground, no longer feeling the sharp cuts the ice makes in their last moments. We are too far away and the light too dim for us to see each man's final shudder as his spirit welcomes its release from his broken and abused body. I pray that the final release of their souls brings an ecstasy that overpowers their time of agony. As each body collapses, the soldiers cheer and throw more wood into the fire. The flames reach for heaven, and the soldiers toss the dead bodies onto the pyre. The final man dies in his place, and those of us who stood at the window for two hours return to our mattresses. I envy the fallen their deaths, but I acknowledge my obligation to live.

Chapter Seventeen, 1942

Pater Noster

Two years pass like twenty, and our camp in Oświęcim is much larger than the town ever was. Thousands have died but more prisoners arrive every day to replace them. I came here in 1940 with less than 1,000 men. Today we are 30,000 – probably more – and we have constructed another compound, much like ours but larger, a kilometer across the railroad tracks to the northwest. The completed factory stands two kilometers to the east, on the other side of the town, which now houses only German soldiers and the *SS* men. The *SS* have the final responsibility for our camp. I hate them though I try hard not to. Yet another reason why God is God and I am not.

Why I am still alive is a question I no longer deliberate. It is God's will, but even as I believe that, I cannot escape the devastation and hatred, which surrounds me. Is this God's will, too? I think God's will is a reflection of a single gift that he bestowed on Adam in the beginning, the gift of free will. God will never revoke that precious gift. Because each of us has free will, our life evolves from the will of God based on the decisions we make, choices that face us every day. Some days we make good choices, other days, our choices are bad. I smell the stagnant, rotting air around me and say, "Someone made bad choices to create this hell on earth." God did not will this place. God did not build this place. Man exercised his free will and made this horrible choice to do it.

There was an old man in Zakopane who was quite fond of my *Babcia*. One day he told me, "You have to re-invent yourself, Bronek. Re-invent yourself all through your life." I was no older than 10 when he told me that and it meant nothing to me at the time. He was just an old man, rocking in a chair on our front porch, vying for *Babcia's* favor. Intentionally or not, I have attended to his counsel. I have experienced many things in my life, more things than most people do, including this unpardonable imprisonment in my own country. However, even here, I re-invent myself, and I believe that is the one reason I am still alive.

As we assemble for morning roll call in the raven dark, Tadeusz says, "How are you today, Bronek?"

I cannot hide the thick sound of phlegm in my throat when I cough into my hand, but I say, "I feel wonderful today, Tad. I feel much better than I deserve to feel." He does not believe me, but he smiles anyway. Again, choices confront us every minute of our lives. I can answer as I do and maybe make the day a bit brighter for my wretched friends, or I can frown and complain, knowing my personal depression cannot help but make them feel worse. No matter how I feel, I *will* feel fine for my friends and fellow prisoners, who endure this dismal life with me.

"Even so, I think your day will improve." He winks at me. I have no idea what he means, but it is better to believe him than to question him.

Frederick recites every man's name and number. Most inmates answer with a whisper, a few, like Tadeusz and me and some of our friends, with as much gladness as we can inject into our voices. When the call is complete, Frederick walks down the lines and assigns us to our work details. He gets to Tadeusz and me, hesitates then looks twice at his papers. "Hmmmm? What's this?" he says rubbing his unshaven, triple-folded chin. "To the carpentry shop, both of you."

Tadeusz and I walk through the camp toward the front gate. Gallows rise up before the kitchen, a sure way to rob any man of his appetite. They are never empty and by not averting my gaze from them, I honor those souls whose bodies swing. We pass other large groups assigned to other tasks, and find the contingent fortunate to be assigned to the carpentry shop. Tadeusz exchanges a glance with a man called Peter who I grew up with in Zakopane. Peter is a highlander, too, but never skied with the passion to find his way to our team. Like many highlanders, he is good with wood and I recall seeing his work in and about Zakopane. Peter looks at me and offers a slight nod that I acknowledge with a shadow of a grin.

We march out the gate with our guards and follow the snow-covered road lined with sturdier buildings than those we reside in on our side of the barbwire. The white smoke rising from the chimneys comforts me because it is a product generated from wood for the purpose of warmth, not smoke spawned from an unthinkable fuel and for a less than noble purpose. As I walk through the cold, I imagine the warmth I might experience if I am fortunate enough to enter a building. I am not disappointed as we climb the steps to the building designated for our woodwork. The cast iron stove on the far wall of the room radiates warmth as strongly, it seems to me, as the sun on a hot August afternoon. In addition, the heat from the stove drives away the dampness that forever plagues us in our barracks. I am grateful, and my hand moves instinctively to my chest and I touch the *hamsa*.

As the new workers in the shop and unfamiliar with the environment, Tadeusz and I watch the veterans move mechanically to their respective positions, most behind work tables covered with wood shavings. Fine sawdust rises from the floor and the workbenches as we sidle between tables looking for some direction. I sneeze.

"Bless you," a man calls from the other side of the room. He smiles and with outstretched fingers pointing skyward, carves an invisible cross in the air before him.

"Shut up," another man says as he picks up a hammer. "That one is a priest," he says. "He blesses everyone. Doesn't do much good, does it?" He holds the hammer by its head and points the wooden handle toward Tad and me. "Peter is my friend," he says matter-of-factly, "And he tells me we need two more carpenters from Zakopane. That is why you are here. Have you any skill?"

Before I can shrug my shoulders and display ignorance, Peter steps up and says, "This one is Tadeusz and the other is Bronisław. They have been here a long time and they are still strong. Just feel their arms. They'll be good with the saw and the hammer."

"I am Czesiek. This is my shop, but I keep that to myself. The SS think it is theirs." He winks. "Let me see your arms." He takes my wrist, and rolls up my sleeve.

He is not looking to test my strength; he is looking for the number and expects to see the tattoo on my forearm like most prisoners. "No number? What is this?"

"We've been here since the beginning," Tadeusz tells him as he unbuttons his jacket. "In the beginning, the number was stamped on the chest." He opens his blouse to reveal the dark and blurred '346' that will remain inked in his skin until the day he dies.

I do not offer to show my number, but Czesiek sets his hammer on the bench and opens my shirt. "Three, four, nine. And the two of you are still alive?"

"And strong," Peter says again.

"And this?" Czesiek holds the *hamsa* in the palm of his hands and inspects it closely. He does not know what it is, but he recognizes the characters etched in it as Hebrew. "A Jew? You are a Jew?" He drops the *hamsa* and steps back as if the charm has caused him physical pain, as if I am a leper and have defiled him. Czesiek looks to the guard who stands outside the door with a cigarette hanging from his lips. Before Czesiek can summon him, the priest says, *"Pater noster, qui es in caelis."* He halts and pleads to me with his eyes to continue the prayer.

I do. *"Sanctificetur nomen tuum."*

Confused, Czesiek spins towards the priest and says, "What sort of magic is this, you crazy holy man? Are you casting a spell?"

"It's a prayer," Peter interrupts. "Don't you know your prayers, Czesiek? 'Our Father, who are in heaven.' They say it in Latin. He is no Jew, though why he wears the charm, I do not know. I think he is more Catholic than I am if he knows his prayers in Latin."

"What do you think, Max?" Czesiek asks the priest. "Catholic?" Father Max holds his broken spectacles to the bridge of his nose as he nods, yes.

Czesiek raises an eyebrow and asks, "Is he right? You are not a Jew?" I shake my head. "Then be careful with that thing. If I were you, I'd throw it away." He is not me and I will keep it.

"We have much work to do here, more each day. You, Tadeusz is it? Can you carve with a knife?" Tadeusz says he can. "Then you will make spoons. What about you?"

"I can carve since I was a boy," I respond.

"Good. We always need more spoons. You will start with spoons and maybe in time you can make shoes." He moves on after a final word of caution. "Those knives on the table are for the wood." His eyes sweep the room by habit. "For the wood. Not for the SS, and not for your own wrists. *Rozumiesz?*"

I weigh the knife in the palm of my hand. The blade is sharp and reflects the light to make the beams dance in the room. "*Rozumiem.* I understand."

Czesiek directs us to a table with other workers who stand hunched over small blocks of wood. Shavings fall rapidly from their knives and soon each produces a spoon that we place into a box that will find its way to the kitchen. Peter is on the opposite side of the table. "This is good work, here in this shop," he whispers. "We are not allowed to talk, but Czesiek isn't all that bad. He puts on that gruff, mean face for the benefit of the SS, but he leaves us to our task. He is not a cruel man like so many *kapos*. Other workers are not as lucky as we are."

As I take a block of wood and begin my work, I glance at Peter and say, "Thank you."

The days pass quickly in the warmth of our shop, the nights so slowly in our cold, brick building. I carry guilt with me each evening as we march back to our barracks and pass under that sign, "Arbeit macht frei." Less than one hundred of us are blessed to work in the comfort of the carpentry shop while thousands trudge sockless in our wooden shoes down the frozen streets to toil in open areas constructing more buildings. Why I am favored remains a mystery. Peter is correct: Czesiek is a decent sort and his gruff manner is balanced by his affability, a trait that is natural for him when the SS is not present, which more often than not is the case. The SS understands its power, and knows it is in absolute control, that we fear it as we fear hell. There is no middle line in Oświęcim. The *kapos* know that the more brutal they are, the more favor they gain with the SS. Still, the *kapos* weigh on the extreme sides of the scale: there are those like Frederick – a convicted murderer – who finds pleasure in brutality; and fewer like Czesiek who – as improbable and difficult as it might be – cling to a merciful bone as their final link to humanity.

I never remember what day it is, but common to each is hunger. I am always hungry, even though we receive a bit more bread in the shop than what we received in the construction groups, an odd gesture given that one would think the laborer in the field requires more strength than the artist does, wrapped in the warmth of his shop. I torture myself by withholding a mouthful of the bread I receive at lunchtime so I have it in the evening as I lay on my straw mattress. My mouth waters as I stare at the morsel, while my guilt beats me as ruthlessly as any *SS* man. In the end, I always offer my extra bread to one of my barrack mates who I consider less fortunate than I am.

Christmas is a special time, particularly for children. I thank God that there are no children here, nor women, at least not that I am aware of. I know the Christmas season approaches because tonight the Germans erect many Christmas trees around the camp, one directly in front of our barracks. They do not use electric lights but carry on the old custom of miniature candles. Yes, it is Christmas, but this Christmas brings few blessings and more curses.

A drunken *SS* man, and an equally inebriated Frederick, staggers toward our barracks and I fail to return to my mattress quick enough. Frederick sees me move as he stumbles through the door.

"That one," he slurs to his companion. "That is the one we want." He kicks me hard and grabs my collar. "Come with us." They force me out the door without my shoes and the hard ice quickly numbs my feet.

The smell of beer hangs over the soldiers gathered round the Christmas tree in front of our barracks. The alcohol smothers the otherwise pleasant scent of pinesap from the freshly cut tree.

"He's one of the first ones," Frederick explains as buttons fly and scatter when he rips open my jacket exposing my chest to the cold and to the soldier's scrutiny. "See there?" He points to my chest with his stick. "Three, four, nine."

One soldier squints and looks closer. "Hmmm? And this, number 3-4-9?" He flicks the *hamsa* with his finger. "These are Hebrew letters. You are a Jew?"

"He's no Jew," Frederick answers for me. "I've already checked his prick. Just like you or me. Me, anyway. I can't speak for you."

"Be careful, Fatman," the soldier is quick to respond, "I'm no friend of yours either, so you better be careful with that big mouth you always flap."

"Sorry, sir," Frederick says with a bow. "I mean you no disrespect. This one, though?" He cracks the side of my head. "Thinks he's a Jew, probably wants to be a Jew. Why else would he wear this heathen magic charm?"

"Climb the stool, boy," the soldier orders me, and I almost laugh to think that I am over 30 years old and someone calls me 'boy.' He is drunk or stupid. Probably both. Laughter however is reserved for our captors, and I will enjoy none this night.

"Do you know what day it is, number three-forty-nine?" the soldier asks as he stares up at me. I take what pleasure I can from my elevated position over this drunken sot, and I clench my teeth to maintain my silence. "Another dumb one," he says and they all laugh. "Of course you don't. A Jew wouldn't know what day this is. Look at these fine trees we've put up." He opens his arms towards the dark sky and twirls unsteadily on his feet like a broken ballerina. "It's Christmas."

I dare to touch my forehead, heart, left, then right shoulder to draw the invisible sign of Christ's cross as I stand freezing on the stool.

"No, no, no, no," he says. "That won't work for you, number three, four, nine. No, no. God has no mercy for Christ killers." As he stares up at me, he extends his arm toward Frederick. "Give me that stick, you fat Pole." They are drunk with laughter. "It's Christmas, three, four, nine. Christmas has 12 days." He slams Frederick's stick down on my freezing toes. I catch the cry in my throat, and I bend but hold my balance.

"That's one!" the soldiers gathered around us shout in unison. He strikes me again, this time on the back of my legs and my knees buckle but I do not fall. "Two!" they shout, "Two for turtle doves!"

"What a stupid song," someone slobbers.

"He's right," another says as the stick falls once more on my legs. "It is a stupid song. It's Christmas and Christmas falls on the 25th day of December." They all cheer. "That's it, twenty-five. Not twelve days, but twenty-five days."

"Then I shall give him twenty-five lashes with this stick, that way the Jew will never forget when to celebrate Christmas."

The pain intensifies with each blow and I want to scream out, "Stop! Please, stop!" Don't, I command myself. Even if you die here on this night, do not cry out. I wobble after six lashes, and the seventh knocks me to the ground. I struggle to rise to my knees but fail. I am numb and cannot feel the final strokes. They throw cold beer on me, and feeling returns as icy fingers form in my wet clothing and reach for my bruised and bleeding wounds. A final thought passes through my mind as my vision fades to darkness: God forgive us, me and them.

The warmth of a dog's breath breathes life back to my lifeless body. A distant gunshot opens my deaf ears. Raphael's hopeful eyes peer down at me. I think it is a dream until he licks my face with his soft, wet tongue. I taste blood in my mouth, smell burnt ashes and feel every aching bone and muscle in my body. Once more, God robs me of death. I will accept his gift of life, again.

The guards have had their fun and left me for dead, to be hauled off like garbage as I have seen so many bodies dragged through the compound. I must return to my barracks before Frederick sobers up and assembles a detail to dispose of me. I try to move but the pain is too great. Raphael whispers to me, and I will to smile but the impulse does not reach my lips. Suddenly, an arm folds behind my back, and another moves under my bent knees. More pain as my limbs extend, but there is mercy in the touch, mercy in a merciless place. Through my clouded eyes, I see the *kapo* Czesiek. He says nothing, only lifts me in his arms.

"Here, this way," a voice whispers urgently. It is Tad and he scurries across the ice to lead Czesiek to our barracks. The *kapo* carries me inside, gently places my beaten body on my mattress and leaves without a word. Tad, Jożef and three others cover me with blankets then huddle close to give me as much of their own warmth as they can. Raphael whimpers and works his way into the pile.

My teeth are intact. The hardest blows fell upon my legs, and when I force myself to extend them to their limits, I conclude that no bones are broken. I curl fetus-like, and extend and retract my legs several times. The muscles are bruised, but my bones are unbroken.

"And this dog," Tad asks, "How could he enter the camp? Surely, the guard dogs would tear him to shreds."

"This is my dog," I whisper through swollen lips. "His name is Raphael."

"And where did he come from?"

"Heaven."

I struggle to raise my fingers to the dog's lips. He appreciates the gesture.

"*Wesolych Swiat Bozego Narodzenia*. Merry Christmas" I tell my friends. "I am blessed with life. It is my gift."

In the distance – barely audible – a soft and soothing sound rises from the real world on the other side of the fence. I have heard this carol many times before. "Silent night," a baritone sings softly and then others join him. "Holy night," they continue. My chest hurts, still I manage to hum along but the sound only comes intermittently. Maybe my music and the singing I hear are only in my mind. With my dog in my arms, darkness cloaks me. I close my eyes and sleep.

The deep bruises in my legs restrict my movement and force me to shuffle like an old woman, but with my friends' assistance, I stand erect at roll call. Frederick's eyes are puffy and red, and his self-induced ailment disgusts me in this environment where a man does not have to search far to find sickness. When I respond after he calls my name, Frederick stops and stares stupidly at his paper. He is confused. Perhaps he was so drunk last night that he has no memory of it. He steps closer and peers through the ranks. "Czech?" he says again with one eye closed and his eyebrow arced sharply above the other. Raphael sits at my feet and barks, but the Fatman takes no notice.

"Present," I repeat and then dare to add in a loud, clear voice, "Merry Christmas." Time explodes like a bomb and the men in my formation gasp in unison.

The Fatman scowls, waves his stick at me and says, "No it's not." He resumes his roll call. When he is finished, he tells us to stay where we are and we wait several minutes. The loudspeakers click and crackle with their static. We hear muffled voices in the background, and then Rudolf Höss, the SS *Obersturmbannführer*, the commandant of this camp tells us that his men deserve to rest this Christmas Day. He tells us to return to our barracks. With pleasure, I think, and I thank God for another Christmas blessing.

My body is sore, and the day of rest gives me some relief. Throughout the day, I exercise my legs as best I can. I extend them forward and then pull them back tightly to my chest, forward and back, forward and back. By nightfall, I am able to move about without assistance, slowly, but without help. No one has difficulty falling asleep, and many snore through the day and do not regain consciousness until morning.

Refreshed is too generous a word for how we feel when Tadeusz and I take our places in the carpentry shop the next day. Czesiek makes no mention of the incident. I thank him with a wisp of a smile to which he does not react.

Mid-morning rings with sharp orders outside the building. They are non-specific and mean nothing, and are only intended to be loud and bothersome so that we never forget that the Germans are the masters and we are the slaves. Boots climb the stairs and the door creaks open behind me. Czesiek calls the room to attention, which means we all stand upright at our workstations with our hands at our sides and our heads bowed in submission.

"Czesiek?" the man behind me asks. Czesiek steps forward so that the man can recognize him by the *winkel* stitched to his clothing. "Which one, *Kapo*? Which one is he?"

Czesiek looks at me then back to the man. "That one, *Obersturmbannführer*." He nods in my direction. "That is Czech."

"Turn around then, Czech," the man commands, and I turn to face Rudolf Höss, the commandant of this way station on the road to hell. His pursed lips suggest a strict formality as he stands with hands clasped behind his back. He looks at my feet then raises his head slowly, almost as if he were smelling me, studying me with his nose to determine if I am fit to eat. He takes my chin in his hand and turns my head to the left and right. He sees the marks from the beating but does not comment.

"Do you like flowers?" His question puzzles me and I hesitate to respond. "Flowers," he repeats, "Do you like flowers?" When I fail to answer again, he brushes me aside, reaches into his pocket and lays a postcard on my workbench. It is the last card I sent from this place, and on it, I had drawn a flower. He points at it and looks at me impatiently.

"Yes. I like flowers."

"And you can draw?"

"I scribble and sometimes my scribbling looks like a drawing."

"I like this," he says and taps the card with his fingertips. "Follow me." Before we leave the building, he says to Czesiek, "Get these men back to work."

Höss and his entourage lead me down the road on the east side of the compound. I have not been to this area before. Trees prevent me from seeing the nearby river, but I can smell it in the cold. We are very close. I consider bolting toward the water and regret that I did not steal my knife from the carpentry shop, but when I look at the guns slung over my escorts' shoulders, I know I would have no chance to reach the tree line, particularly with my bruised muscles and bones. They would shoot me like a fleeing rabbit.

We walk past a small house. A white fence encloses the front yard, covered now in snow, and a snowman stands guard with crooked arms made of sticks and a toothy smile of stone. A woman and several children wave from a window. Höss smiles, waves back, and comments to his entourage, "My wife does not like the cold and tries to keep the children inside." He snatches a handful of snow, packs it loosely into a ball and tosses it towards the window. He throws like a girl.

We enter the spacious hallway of the third house beyond the Höss home. The smell of clay and paint floats comfortably in the air, and I deduce that this is a studio for artists of all sorts, painters, sculptors, potters. A large bed of red ambers glows in the fireplace and welcomes us.

Höss points to a room through the doorway on our right. "In there. That is where you will work." A table and an empty chair greet me. Two men occupy their own desks, but rise immediately, and bow to the commandant when he enters. "As you were," he says. "This is Koscielniak." He waves his glove at a gaunt man whose stern look etched into his young face makes him look much older than I think he is. "Koscielniak will monitor your work, Czech. Your skill has saved you from a worse fate, at least for now. Postcards. Make me postcards with your decorative flowers. Simple enough. Understand?"

I am trained to answer 'yes' to every question I'm asked, and his tone of voice suggests Höss does not like to repeat himself.

"See that he gets started right away," Höss tells the artist, then leaves us to our work.

As soon as the Germans leave, Koscielniak takes a handful of my postcards from his desk and spreads them on my table. Without looking up he says, "Please call me Mieszko. My friends call me Mieszko, and I will call you …" He rotates the card to read my name, "Bronisław." Now he looks up and asks, "Or do you prefer 'Bronek' or maybe something else?"

"'Bronek' is fine."

"No skiing here, aye Bronek?"

"That was another lifetime."

"And so it was for all of us," Mieszko sighs with resignation.

"It seems my cards were never delivered."

"Good for you, and good for the person to whom you addressed the card. Most are delivered, and by the SS so they can further investigate our friends and families. But your cards caught the attention of the postmaster who seeks favor by bringing your pictures to the commandant's attention. Seems like he succeeded, and that is good for you. Höss believes he has an eye for art. Perhaps he does. Your luck continues. The carpentry shop is good. This studio is better. You can gain favor, too."

"I have no desire for favor, only freedom," I respond.

Mieszko smiles. "You can be a hero without being arrogant. In this place, we fight to live. It is our duty.

"These Germans are as stupid as they are brutal. Look around you. No guards. I say what I please to myself – aloud – and to you. They think because we are artists that we are powerless and have no desire to fight because artists are weaklings. They respect our work, but to them, we are no more dangerous than children are. They are wrong. Because we work in this studio, we are important to the underground that operates within the camp, we are an important element to the flow of information to the world outside the barbed wire. We continue to filter and process information through this shop. Sooner or later, someone on the other side will believe."

"Are you a soldier?"

"What is a soldier?" he counters. "Must a man bear arms to be a soldier? Must he wear a uniform? I know soldiers of God and they are peacemakers. I think that weapons of war will do us no good in Oświęcim. We must seek other ways to find victory here." He raises a thin paintbrush and waves it in the air like a sword. "Rowecki tells us you are a man we can depend upon." He raises his eyebrows waiting for my confirmation.

One day since the worst beating of my life, I am back in the underground and soon learn that we are one of many cells that function within the Oświęcim complex. Polish leadership tasks us to disseminate as much information as we can, and it flows from our pens not just in words, but also in pictures.

New prisoners report that the war goes well for the Germans. The Nazi truce with the Russians, though

tentative holds fast. Hitler assaults the west and resistance falls before him like wheat to the farmer's sickle. The
Channel remains uncrossed by either the British or the
Germans, but the Nazi invasion of England appears a certainty. America is strong but so very far away. I remember
the games in 1932, and I recall the man Roosevelt whom I
met in Lake Placid. He is now the President of their entire
country. Our leaders say the Americans are our only hope.
I believe them. It has been nearly two years since Stashu
Marusarz and I delivered our messages to Rome and to
Geneva, messages written from our government pleading
for American help. Nothing has happened. America stands
by and waits, an ocean away. Why? And the Vatican? The
Pope maintains neutrality and keeps his distance. I cannot
say the Catholic Church condones Hitler's fanaticism, but
the Pope is cautious not to condemn anything Hitler does,
at least as far as I know. The Italian leader Mussolini is as
crazy as the Führer and they have pledged their forces to
each other. What is *Il Duce*'s relationship to the Vatican?
Why no help from America?

"Listen to me, Bronek," Mieszko says, "We are not as
helpless in our prison as some may think, and we must help
bring this war to an end. Look at this." He opens the bottom drawer of his desk and moves some papers aside to find
the envelope he is looking for. He shows me several pictures sketched in pencil, depicting life in our camp. "I send
these out to a friend who takes them to General Rowecki
and his newly organized *Armia Krajowa*. By the way, they
call Rowecki *Grot* now, Spearhead. The *AK* disperses them
to places beyond the boundaries of German control, even to
America, I'm told.

"The SS has no suspicions of me, and the commandant has an eye for your work. Soon, I think no one will search envelopes with your mark on them. That is how we will get more and more of these pictures outside this camp. Someone, somewhere will believe and understand what is happening here.

"As bad as our predicament is, it will continue to get worse. As long as Hitler has success on the battlefield, he will tolerate us. If he suffers defeat, we will be his scapegoat. Of that, I am sure. The beatings we suffer are humane compared the things that happen in the bigger camp to the west they call *Birkenau*."

Guilt haunts me. Surrounded by so much death, I do not deserve this easy life in the studio – if that is what I can call it. Frederick no longer singles me out for punishment or for his own, cruel jokes. Those of us in the studio are the favored ones because the SS purports to appreciate our work. I hate everything about it.

Locomotive traffic increases. Because the studio is in the village, I am able to watch the trains as they pull their hundred cars slowly around the town. If each car contains a full cargo of prisoners, the population of Oświęcim is swelling. The numbers in our camp remain steady; if one man dies, another replaces him. We learn that more and more arrivals are Jews, and we can see the activity at the crematoriums increases in proportion to the train arrivals. That tells me two things: *Birkenau* grows, and that many of the new arrivals go directly to the crematorium.

Four new faces join my block. The other prisoners ignore them. Why learn the name of a man who could die tomorrow? Prevailing wisdom suggests that we refer to each other as numbers, not names. I will not diminish the dignity of any man, so I approach these four and learn their names: Jakob, Abraham, Schmelke and Miksa, all Jews.

"I am Bronek."

"No number?" Jakob asks. I open my shirt and point to the blurry, black digits on my chest. He stares at the *hamsa*, and I know what he is thinking.

"I am not a Jew, grandfather." Jakob is old, but he is fit.

He shrugs his shoulders and lets the matter drop. "I suppose I am happy to have a number," he says. "Those that don't ..."

"You and your friends are able to work and the *SS* needs healthy bodies. Who is better off: you with your numbers; or the others? Who's to say? Not I."

Chapter Eighteen, 1943

Vengeance is Mine

I work through my guilt only because Mieszko and some of his friends tell me the *AK* is making progress, whatever that means. Oświęcim has been my home for three years. The only progress I see is our captors' ability to murder more people, more quickly. If anyone on the outside cared, our misery would end in a shower of bombs. Either they don't know, or they don't care. My struggle to keep meaning in my life is the most daunting challenge I face.

I no longer pray for myself, and conclude that prayer can take one of three forms: I can pray to thank God, to praise God, or to ask his blessings on other people. I pray for my family and wonder if they are safe. Are my parents still alive? Janka, Włady and Stasia? I sent one letter to my home, though I doubt it ever arrived. I wrote to say I am fine, better than I deserve to be, and that I would see them soon. 'Soon,' just another word that is no longer relevant. I wait for eternity.

I think of escape and discuss it with Tad who is still with me. We even made plans, but after the *SS* demonstrated it would execute 10 men for every escapee, we determined it is best to abandon our plans. People still make independent escapes, but 10 innocent men die in the wake of the escape effort. Tad and I stay where we are; we want no more blood on our hands. Freedom is a foreign word, unknown to me in any language.

Raphael only comes to me at night, and less often than I would like. My eyes are failing. His image is less clear. Perhaps he returns to Zakopane to check on my family. I hope he does.

The colors on my desk are brilliant, but the palette of my existence is bland. I stare dumbly at the picture I work on, blooming crocuses on a snow-covered field at the foot of the mountains. I focus on the paper and do manage a smile. I still remember how to do that, smile, and I will not allow them to steal that gift from me.

Visitors climb the steps, and when the door opens in the front room, Höss says, "Koscielniak, we have some guests." Bent over my work with my back to the door, I listen intently. "We are honored with the presence of *Reichsführer* Heinrich Himmler. Hedwig and the children have just entertained the *Reichsführer* and his staff in our home. He happened to see one of these postcards, and is most taken by it. We've come to commission a set from your man. He is still here, isn't he?"

"Yes, commandant, he is still here," Mieszko answers. When the visitors enter my room, Mieszko calls us to attention. I rise and turn to face the commandant and the *Reichsführer*. If the blood had drained from my face, my visage could not be paler, for every prisoner has the wan look of death lurking about him. Such is not the case with one member of Himmler's entourage. Standing behind Himmler is Feldman, and he's instantly lost the ruddiness of the others when he sees it is me who Himmler has come to meet. Feldman is dumbstruck. I am dizzy and light-headed – not because I stand before Himmler, but because I am once again within an arm's length of my Captain's murderer. I breathe deeply to maintain my composure.

"I remember now that I see him," Höss remarks. "You must enjoy your work here ... What's his name, again?"

"Czech," Mieszko says.

"You must enjoy your work here, Czech. It continues to improve." Höss steps aside and defers to Himmler, who comes forward to examine the current project on my desk. The man wears spectacles and his moustache is exactly as I remember Hitler's, too narrow and mousey, quite unlike a highlander's bushy handlebar that reaches well beyond the corners of his mouth.

Himmler leans close. "Ah, yes. Quite good, Czech. I have my own Hedwig, and she would be pleased with a collection of these. Twelve. I want twelve, one for each month. Do you understand?" I bow. "How long? When will you have them done?"

"At your request, *Reichsführer*."

"What do you others think?" he turns to the four aides who accompany him.

Each vigorously approves, and only Feldman offers criticism. "I'm not so sure I like his choice of colors, *Reichsführer*."

Himmler places his hands on his hips. "And you can do better, *Hauptsturmführer*?" Himmler laughs at his joke and Höss and the others join him while Feldman lowers his eyes and retreats. "I leave this afternoon," Himmler tells me, "And I do not want you to rush. My Hedwig deserves

your best work. I expect it." He turns to his aides and
his finger floats above them, and finally rests on Feldman.
"You, Feldman. You wait until he is done, then deliver
these to me personally." Himmler looks at me, "You can
have 12 done in 12 days?"

"I can, *Reichsführer*."

"It is settled then." No emotional combination can
have a more visible affect on a man than hate and humili-
ation. That combination can make the handsomest man,
ugly. Both are plastered on Feldman's countenance, but
he dares not question or interrupt the plans of his superior.
He is the whipping boy, not I. The pleasure I get from seeing the look on his face exceeds the pain I received from my
Christmas beating. My physical wounds healed. Feldman's
embarrassment will haunt him forever.

As the party leaves, Höss tells Mieszko, "Give your man
whatever he needs to get this done. Understand? Good."

I have 12 days to complete a project I would normally
take much longer to do, but as with all my work for the *SS*,
I am not concerned with quality, only quantity. If Höss
and Himmler like these scribblings of mine, they would
be amazed at what I could produce in another time and
place. I tell Mieszko I need to stay in the shop around the
clock. "Please tell my friends in the block that I am taking a vacation from Hell. No cause for celebration. I will
return." He agrees and arranges the details with the commandant. When the shop closes late each afternoon, two
guards arrive and spend the night in the anteroom playing
cards and drinking coffee. I work until midnight, then rest
for a few hours on the cot they've erected in the corner of
my workroom.

As if he actually knows anything about drawing and painting, Feldman arrives promptly at noon each day to inspect my work. "Twelve cards in 12 days. Maybe easy enough for you to do, Czech, but know that your days are numbered. Your life belongs to me, and I will tire of it very shortly: in exactly 12 days." His is not an idle threat, but he fails to understand what his presence in Oświęcim means to me. I've lost count of time, but my soul remembers that moment years ago when I left the Captain dead on the street and ran through the dark forest with his blood, splattered on my jacket. That night I swore vengeance, though I refused to allow Feldman to make me a killer, too. I am ashamed that I have forgotten, but I no longer care if I become a murderer at the expense of this man. He deserves death, and death by my hand. As Pharaoh's own words called the final plague upon Egypt, so does Feldman's threat seal his own sentence. I swear it.

I learned to love Greek mythology as a child, and when I consider Feldman's threat, I remember Penelope's trick to buy time from her suitors so that her husband, Odysseus could return to Ithaca. She spent her days weaving her husband's burial shroud but would unravel her work at night. I can do the same with my paintings. Himmler wants my best work. Surely he will understand if I need more time, but to delay Feldman's action is only to defer mine, and I will avenge my Captain, sooner than later.

"I see a crudeness in these drawings that does not appear in your other work," Mieszko comments after four days.

"Would you prefer that I begin again?" I ask him.

He smiles. "Not really. I don't care if Himmler likes them or not. These postcards will not determine our fate, even though this *SS* man Feldman suggests that they will. He is an angry, arrogant man, isn't he?"

"I've come to believe anger, hate and arrogance are pre-requisites for *Schutzstaffel* positions."

Five, six, seven … my drawings capture winter, spring and into the summer. Less than one week. Feldman no longer speaks when he comes to our studio. He grunts at Mieszko but says nothing to me. He smiles cynically and pats the luger, holstered on his belt. He can intimidate other men, but not me. I've held his own gun to his head and watched urine drip down his pant leg. I do not fear this man.

The first 11 postcards depict flowers, trees and leaves in soft pastels. The final piece, the 12th card, the card for December is different. I work quickly and sketch the cross on Giewont atop the barren, windswept peak. No color, only black, white and pale gray. Even the sky is ashen. On this final day, Feldman does not appear.

"I wonder where he is today." Mieszko asks.

By 4:00 p.m., I am finished. I arrange the 12 post-cards on my table for Mieszko and my fellow artists to review. "They are beautiful," Mieszko says. "The twelfth, an odd complement to the other eleven, but beautiful in its simple and stark way." My co-workers congratulate me.

The guard detail arrives just prior to the routine con-clusion of our workday at 4:30 p.m. Two remain with me and four return the other workers to the compound.

"I guess this means you enjoy a final night in purgatory so that you can present the cards to Feldman tomorrow. Then you'll return to the fiery pit with the rest of us," my friend Bogdan remarks. "I hope you enjoy your final night on the cot. Is it like heaven?"

"Yes, Bogdan. It's like heaven in here at night when you all leave," I speak in Polish. "Just me and these two donkeys." I bray. My fellows laugh and depart for the night.

Other nights, I would draw at my table until midnight. One of the guards looks in and finds me sitting quietly on the cot so early in the evening. "Why aren't you working?" he asks me. Few of our captors speak to us without vehemence. This one does, he simply asks the question with no preconceived answer, nor is his hand cocked to strike me.

"My work is finished."

"May we look?" he asks politely.

"You may." Both are so young, maybe still teenagers. He turns on the overhead lamp and calls his friend. They closely study each line and each color on each individual card, then step back to view them as a collection.

"This is wonderful," one says. "I will be an artist – after the war that is – but I haven't the skill to match this." He brushes aside the hair that hangs on his forehead.

"One day, you will," I tell him. "Believe in yourself and know that you have it within you. I'm sure your work will be famous someday." He smiles. "Would you like a postcard?" I ask him.

"Oh, no," he says. "I cannot take one of these."

"I am certain of that," I answer and walk behind the desk. "I'll make one for you. What is your name?"

"I am Franz, and my friend is Wilhelm."

"Nice to meet you. I am Bronek. Do you have a sweetheart, Franz?" He blushes.

Wilhelm grins and answers for him. "He has a sweetheart."

"That's good. Everyone needs a sweetheart." Bittersweet portraits of Amalia, Janina the actress and, of course Sonja materialize, then quickly vanish in my mind. Oh, how I wanted to have a sweetheart! "What is your sweetheart's name?"

"Lilah," Franz whispers, as if he utters the name of a goddess.

"Lilah," I repeat. "Like 'Delilah?'"

"Yes. Like Delilah."

"Let me think," I say as I take the postcard paper. The left half is pre-printed with a space for a message. I draw my image on the right half. I close my eyes. "Breathe deeply, Franz. Can you smell it? I can, and it smells as beautiful as it looks." I dip by brush into the green and create a grassy background, then add tiny yellow flowers, and next, a blue cloud.

As they watch over my shoulder, the two guards are careful not to block the stark light that beams from the conical lampshade above us. Minutes pass and Franz asks, "What is it? I see the tiny yellow flowers, but what is the blue splotch."

I smile. "Here. Now you will know what it is." I clean my brush and begin working with the purple paint, then white, and purple again. After several minutes, they see what I am creating. I finish in little more than an hour. I blow softly on the paper to help it dry then hand it carefully to Franz. "A lilac for your sweetheart, Lilah!"

The young man beams brighter than the naked bulb. "Thank you. I will send her my love with this card in tomorrow's post. She lives with her parents in Munich and I have not seen her since I became a soldier one year ago. I know she still loves me."

"And if she doesn't," Wilhelm adds, "this postcard and whatever words of romance you can write on it will rekindle her feelings toward you. You are a master, Bronek."

"No, Wilhelm. I am no master in Oświęcim. You are the master, I am the slave." My response hangs like the man who swings from the gallows, the man that no one wants to look at but no one can avoid. As soon as I speak those words, I regret saying them to these two decent, young men who were probably pulled from their university studies and forced into these uniforms, unwilling accomplices to Hitler's madness.

Before we can gather ourselves, Feldman throws open the front door and enters the empty, dark lobby. The glint from the gun barrels draws his attention to the two weapons leaning in the corner and then to the helmets on the desk. Wilhelm calls, "Achtung!" and he and Franz snap to attention as the *Hauptsturmführer* strides into my studio.

Feldman stares angrily from my doorway. "Where are your weapons, *gefreiter*? Ah, not here?" He points impatiently behind him. "Oh, there. In the corner." No one moves. "Good place for them, yes?" When neither man answers, Feldman screams, "No! That is not the place for your weapons when your job is to watch this prisoner. Is that what you are doing? Watching this prisoner?"

He looks at me and demands "Are you finished?" I do not answer, but smile smugly and point to the postcards arranged on my table. He glances briefly at the cards, and notices that Franz holds another in his hand. "What is that?"

Fearfully, Franz hands the postcard to the *Hauptsturmführer*. Feldman turns it over and carefully studies both sides as if the card contains some secret message. "I see, *gefreiter*. You are taking one of the *Reichsführer's* cards?"

"No, no, *Hauptsturmführer*. I would never do that. This is my card. This man made it for me."

Feldman throws the card at Franz, and shakes his head disdainfully. "These are the reasons I am a captain and you will always be a corporal. I have no more need of you. Go sit and drink your rotten coffee." The two soldiers edge cautiously around the table and return to their posts in the lobby.

"And you," he says to me. "I see 12 cards on the table. You have completed your task?"

"For the *Reichsführer*, yes. His cards are ready."

"Then I've no more need of you, either." We stare across the table at each other. I know exactly what he is thinking, but he has no idea what is going through my mind. If he numbered my days, which I've no doubt that he did, then my number is up. His vanity demands he carry out his threat by himself. He believes my three years in the camp have dulled my reflexes and weakened my muscles. There is some truth to that, but even a weakened Olympian is the better man to such as Feldman. He thinks his uniform, his rank and his weapon will protect him. He is wrong.

"This way," he orders me. As we pass through the foyer, he tells Franz and Wilhelm to stay at the studio for the remainder of the night. "This man's work is done. I will personally take him back to his block. He no longer deserves the comforts of these accommodations."

I smile with my eyes as I exchange brief glances with the two Germans. Walking out the door, I tell them, "I am not afraid." Feldman cuffs the back of my head. My smile remains intact.

The moon is full and the dark shadows it casts will be witness to my vengeance. Feldman does not know how pleased I am when we reach the river and turn right, away from the camp. I am surprised he wants no witnesses to my execution – far worse atrocities occur here every day – but he must feel that I have value to Himmler, at least until the *Reichsführer* says otherwise. Feldman's hands cannot be stained by my death. He can stage a feigned escape on this warm and humid night and emerge the hero. No one will know or suspect differently.

The searching lights from the watchtowers and the dim lights from the village are behind us. Phantoms rise from the industrial plant's smokestacks to the east. A night bird sails across the moon and follows the Great Wagon to the North Star. Feldman proceeds with such confident immunity, that he has yet to unholster his pistol.

"Thirty-six," he says. "You remember, don't you? At the great Olympic Games in Bavaria in 1936. In '36, you merely pissed me off with your impertinence. I could live with that and frankly, I forgot about you within days of our final encounter there. But, people like you do not go away. You are always lurking about looking for trouble.

"Have you enjoyed your stay here in Oświęcim? Wonderful place, don't you agree." He laughs while an owl calls to the moon, and then I hear the deliberate 'click' when he releases the snap on his holster. "I have wasted two opportunities that would have saved you this miserable experience at our camp. Both times in Zakopane. Are you not grateful for the peace I brought to your old friend, the one who was always there to protect you?"

His words are pointed and he simply does not understand how he continues to fuel my hatred. True, he could have killed me twice, but I remember standing over my Captain and holding a gun to this fool's head. I so much wanted to pull that trigger, but I refused to let him turn me into the murdering bastard that he is. He lives because I allowed him to live. And for what? So that he can continue to taunt and humiliate less fortunate men? I made my decision over a week ago. "Your days are numbered," he told me. With his very words, he seals his own fate. If I become a murderer by taking this worm's life, so be it. I will face my judgment day with a clear conscience. No hell can be worse than this one.

We reach the bank of the river. My heightened senses capture each stimulus directed at them. I feel the sweat run down my face and taste its saltiness when I lick my lips, I smell the rot of decayed carp and see the lazy river carry their bloated bodies toward the Vistula. My pulse quickens when he tells me to stop and stand where I am. At last, I hear the sound I have been waiting for, the almost silent pull of his luger from its holster.

I reach to my innermost being and for one, final time, take from it the speed, power and quickness I once used to explode from icy hills in quest of gold medals. I spin on Feldman, and catch the pistol before it is clear of the holster. I raise my knee to his groin as I wrench the weapon from his small hand. Can any warrior ever have moved quicker than I have? The instant splits the universe with the keenest of blades. History is past and I care nothing for the future, only for this moment. He makes one feeble effort to wrestle the gun from me, but falls to the ground when I strike him hard across his face. In the moonlight, his blood flows gray from the gash.

I pull him to his feet. He does not struggle. I step back and extend my arm so that the gun barrel rests on the bridge of his Nazi nose. I will not taunt him as he has taunted so many innocent souls. He is numb and expressionless. Three words only, "For my Captain."

My being is reduced to my index finger as I apply pressure and slowly draw the trigger. Before I can fully understand what an eternity is, a large, white blur flies from my right, disturbing time and illuminating darkness, knocks me to the ground and takes the weapon, unfired, from my hand. I roll to my knees, hands raised to do battle with the demon that dares defend the cowardly Feldman. When I realize who it is and what has happened, I clasp my hands to pray, for it is no devil, rather an angel. It is Raphael.

For an instant, Feldman thinks he is saved. He wipes his bloodied face and takes a single step toward me. Thinking the dog his savior, Feldman ignores him. No matter. Raphael charges once more, leaps high and strong, and throws his 50 kilograms on my unsuspecting nemesis. The Nazi is helpless as Raphael takes the man's throat in his strong jaws. No human hands have the strength to break the dog's death grip. Feldman kicks and swings his arms blindly for only a few seconds, then falls limp. Raphael holds him in his bloody jaws and shakes the body several times before releasing it. Breathing heavily, he stands above the bleeding mess and stares coldly at me.

Though my intent was murder, I rise from the ground an innocent man. The dog saves me and bears the burden of my sin.

I consider disposing the body into the river, but Raphael has different plans. Each time I take a step toward the corpse, Raphael growls to back me away. He does not need to speak, for his message is clear. "Leave this place," he tells me. It is finished.

What course, now? I can flee, but if I do, what fate will greet my fellows in the morning? Wiseman or fool, I follow the river back to the village and walk through the empty streets to the studio. Thinking it is probably the *Hauptsturmführer*, the two guards stand at rigid attention and hold that position for several seconds after I enter.

Wilhelm speaks first. "Where is the *Hauptsturmführer*?"

"Not here." No more questions, no more answers. I collapse on the cot, and remain there undisturbed until Mieszko and the others arrive promptly at 6:00 a.m. with their escort. Frederick is with them. "You are finished?" he asks me.

Mieszko answers. "He is."

"Very well," the Fatman says. "I've been told to bring you back to the block. One day of rest for you, then you'll be back here tomorrow. Commandant's orders." He sniffs the coffee pot and refills his tin with the cold liquid that would make most men gag. "Just so you know," he tells Mieszko, "Someone else will retrieve those cards. That *Hauptsturmführer*, Himmler's aide, killed by a wolf last night near the river. Serves him right wandering around alone in the dark. I never liked the man. Throat ripped clean out. I think it was a werewolf." No one laughs with him.

Franz and Wilhelm show no reaction to Frederick's report. No questions. No answers. They walk with Frederick and me a short way up the road. When they turn toward their barracks, Franz pats his pocket and says, "Thank you." I nod.

"What was that for?" the Fatman asks.

"Don't know." No more questions. No more answers.

According to Mieszko, Höss personally delivered the postcards to Himmler, who dismissed Feldman's death as unfortunate, but was more pleased with the cards than he was distressed at his aide's gruesome demise.

Chapter Nineteen, 1944

Into Your Hands

I see more of my new friend Franz, whose last name I learn is Drescher, Franz Drescher. I suspect he is running a modest business after showing his friends the postcard I made for him. "Can you make one for my friend, Peter?" he asks. "His girlfriend's name is Lily." That is an easy one, so is 'Bertram' when I learn the name means raven. For one man's friend, Eva, I paint the tree of life from Eden. More challenging requests for names like Bertha follow. Mieszko encourages the activity because it diverts attention from our covert work and encourages our masters to lower their guards. While Franz's pockets jingle with more spare coins, he rewards me with small pastries and other delicacies. I share them with my mates in the studio and smuggle pieces back to the block to share with Tad and my other friends.

I forever struggle with feelings of guilt that I should have such an easy life in the studio, while other prisoners face brutal cruelty and death in unimaginable ways, and merely by walking on the wrong side of the street, or staring at the wrong person in the wrong way. However, on an unseasonably warm spring day, my conscience clears when the commandant visits me in the studio for the second time.

"How are you, Czech?" As soon as Höss asks, he realizes how stupid the question is and brushes it aside quickly. I save him any embarrassment in front of his staff or my own colleagues in the studio by not answering. "Yes, well ..." he stutters while adjusting his hat, "I have very good news for you." He notices that the other artisans and Mieszko are paying close attention, probably thinking the 'good news' will affect all of us. "Yes. Please gather your workers, Koscielniak. All of them should hear this."

Hope teases us as we gather in the foyer. "I have good news for this man, Czech," he announces, and the smiles fade; this good news is not to be shared. "You men are in the presence of a great, Polish athlete. You are," he raises his hands and claps, encouraging us to join him. I stand with head bowed. "Yes," he continues, "Three Olympic Games for Poland. A skier and a jumper. Did you know that?

"*Reichsführer* Himmler personally requested this man's file, and when he saw the occupation listed as 'ski instructor,' he recalled seeing Czech jump at the games in Garmisch-Partenkirchen in '36. Himmler's memory is so sharp, it is no wonder that Hitler loves him so. Isn't that interesting that he would remember?" Not a man reacts.

"As you know, the Reichsführer has commissioned Czech on several occasions. With the realization of who this man is, Himmler has called me personally. 'The camp is no place for this talented man,' he says to me. 'He has earned his freedom.' Axmann says his *Hitler-Jugend* is in need of athletic trainers and instructors." Höss smiles at me and concludes, "Himmler asks me to send you to Bavaria to train our youth in mountain skills. How about that, Czech? You are a free man." While my compatriots politely applaud, I refuse to shake the commandant's hand. He eyes me suspiciously and says – now, more formally and less friendly – "What do you say, Czech? Are you ready to leave this behind you?" With hands on hips, he stares hard at me awaiting my answer.

Freedom. He says I can be a free man. I have an opportunity to leave this factory of death, not just to leave, but also to return to the mountains, to breathe clean air, to search for the eagle, to once again feel the wind on my face. Is there such a thing as freedom in Hitler's Germany? I think not, but the temptation to flee Oświęcim is strong and powerful. I cannot resist it. I stare at the floor and will my feet to move, to take that first step toward the open door. I raise my face to see Mieszko and my fellow prisoners waiting for my answer. They wait as they would for a clear glass of cold water on a hot summer's day. From their pleading faces, their silent voices scream "Leave!"

"Well, Czech? I'll ask you a final time. Will you accept the *Reichsführer's* generous offer?"

A lifetime in the mountains, maybe with Sonja, certainly joined by my family, the image burns in my mind like a moving picture, but it is not silent. Laughter drowns the clicking projector that no one else in this room hears, while my friends frolic in the hills. There is a small boy. Is he my son? I shade my eyes and watch as Janka and her soldier build a man with snow in the blinding sunlight, and there, Amalia and Max wave merrily as the small boy runs to me and hugs my legs. He is my son. I know he is.

I raise my eyes from the floor and return the commandant's stare. The clock ticks. "I have no desire to instruct

Hitler's Youth or to assist in any way with his war effort." Apology is not appropriate.

Höss frowns, visibly affronted. How can anyone decline Himmler's generosity? "Very well, then. All of you, back to work. You will regret your decision, Czech." He spins sharply on his heels and leaves the building.

I spend the night deliberating the wisdom of my decision, but what I've done, is history. I have no regrets and harbor no ill will.

I stand before the block with my fellows for morning roll call. As I proceed toward the other artists to go to the studio, Frederick detains me. "No more pictures for you, pretty boy. Your days of leisure are behind you. Bad choice on your part. Until told differently, from now on you go with them." He shoves me in the direction of a large detail of unhappy prisoners.

We are a group of 20 and leave the compound in the familiar direction of the town, but we pass east. Some days, we march the two kilometers to the Oświęcim rail yard, while on other days we continue six more kilometers to the Dwory rail yard by the factory. Regardless, we unload raw iron, sometimes bricks, other times chemicals that burn our hands and lungs. If one man falls, another like me takes his place. I put the studio behind me and immerse myself into the exhausting, manual labor. At first, my muscles – as thin as they are – actually grow stronger.

God has blessed me with health through 36 years, even in this damnable place. My rare bouts with sickness have been no more serious than the common cold, but as colds go, nothing can slow a man down faster than a summer cold. It is warm and humid by the river where we unload trains. A fellow worker from our block contracts a summer cold, and his fever and lethargy become too obvious at the evening roll call. Albert is a good worker and Frederick is not yet ready to dispose of him, so he orders him to the camp infirmary.

Why we have such a medical facility in our compound is a mystery. Rumors abound that nothing healthy transpires in that 'hospital,' if it can be referred to as one. Too often, prisoners sent to the infirmary do not return to their blocks, so we are surprised when Albert is in his room three days later, sleeping soundly on his mattress.

"They gave me medicine and put me on a cot where I slept uninterrupted for a day," he tells us. "I am still very weak and tired, but my fever is gone."

"What is it like? The hospital?" Karol asks.

"Not a good place. It is true, the medicine they give me works, but the place is not a good place to be. A man cannot lie there and block out the screams and cries that issue steadily from dawn to dusk and throughout the night. It is bad here in our own building; it is unbearable in the infirmary. The worst thing, though," Albert shivers and dusts his clothes, "the worst thing is the lice. They are everywhere, and they give life to lifeless things."

We hang on his every word.

"I have seen a blanket crawl across the floor, dragged by an army of the abominable creatures. No sane man would desire to stay in the hospital. It invites death. Those who are forced to stay there, at least the ones with me who are mobile, spend their time hunting lice, and the bugs are not difficult to find. You kill 10 … 100 more take their place."

As Albert tells his story, several prisoners back away. How do we know for certain that Albert does not carry a single louse into our block?

Within three days, we know he has, and we battle the infestation the best we can. There are so many, and they multiply so quickly, that even Frederick and the other *kapos* are offended by the rancid bugs that threaten to wrest control of our block from the Nazis.

Frederick announces at morning roll call that no one goes to work until he has been de-loused. He explains that the blocks will be de-contaminated, and that anyone who cannot participate will be escorted to the hospital. Every man finds the strength to participate.

In the warmth of the late spring, the process is easier for us to bear. With no ceremony and less modesty, we remove our clothing. Our shirts and pants are thrown into a waiting truck, which will deliver the infested garments to a special block. There, they will be steamed in order to kill the unwanted guests. While our clothes are steamed, we march through the rarely used shower that is supposed to serve four blocks. Like our clothes, we are 'steamed;' the water is so hot, I think I am cooked. Then, we are heavily dusted with powder, probably the same thing we were treated to in Tarnów. Meanwhile, a detachment scours our rooms, mattresses, floors, anything we may have touched. Everything is treated with the same white powder.

We stand naked in the warm breeze until the trucks return with our clothing. These are the first clean clothes that have touched my body in three years.

The exercise is successful. In the evening, we sweep thousands of louse carcasses from our rooms, down the steps and into the yard. We pray they are dead and that the wind will carry them to places far from us, perhaps, if we are lucky, to the German field barracks scattered throughout Poland.

Nonetheless, I awake in the morning with an itch. I investigate the area as secretly as I can, and dislodge a single large and live louse. Damn you! Please, God. Let this be the last one I will ever see. It will be.

One year ago, we built bunks in our buildings. The room reminds me of my steerage experience on the boat to America. Big difference, however between the gaiety of hundreds of people embarking on new, exciting lives, and the hundreds who sleep here robbed of anything better to hope for than death. We are so crowded. There is barely enough room for two men to pass through the center aisle, then just enough for one to squeeze between the beds for his personal berth. Each bunk has three tiers. I am lucky. Those who survive the longest 'earn' the bottom beds nearest the door, so I am grateful for my special space. On this warm evening, we leave the door and windows open, hoping to create a soothing breeze.

Most often, sleep comes quickly when I take my place on my thin mattress, but it hides from me on this night. I am restless. The beds are so narrow there is no way to toss and turn, so I lie on my side and listen to the labored breathing of my fellows. I note a slight rasp in my own breath and try unsuccessfully to clear it. No matter. It is nothing.

Soft, padded feet – not the harsh 'clop' of a block mate's wooden shoes or the 'slap' of a soldier's leather boots – climb the stairs,. Too quick to be a barefooted prisoner. The white apparition hesitates at the door, then comes straight to me. It is Raphael. I reach out and run my fingers through the soft, short hair atop his head. I flop his ears. He likes that and thanks me with a slobbery lick to my face. I cannot remember the last time I saw him, not long after the final encounter with Feldman, I think.

When I swing my legs to the floor, Raphael moves closer and I hug him with more love than I would hold a woman, maybe even a child. He allows it. I walk outside and sit on the top step. He follows me and lies down with his large head on my lap.

The night sky is brilliant. Earth bears the light without damage and watches as Draco threatens the North Star. Softly, I hum the highlander's song as if it is a lullaby for my dog. Raphael's pulse slows.

"Bronek, what are you doing out here?" Tad walks down the steps, stands tall and stretches as he studies the Milky Way.

"Watching the stars and soothing my tired dog with a favorite tune."

"The universe is quite humbling, isn't it?" Tad sits on the bottom step with his face skyward. "Raphael. I remember. Your dog's name is Raphael. That is a good name. And where is this Raphael?" He looks at me and then scans the courtyard.

"He's just here," I answer.

Tad nods his head. "Tell him I say hello. Get some sleep, Bronek." He walks back to his bed.

Raphael dreams of good things and makes soft, happy sounds. I lean close to feel his warm breath on my cheek. I so envy the dog the peace that follows him. My time will be finished soon. I take the chain with the *hamsa* from my neck, and put it to my lips. It smells of ancient clay and perspiration. I wash it with a single tear and see that the letters are very worn and unreadable. *B'hatzlacha*. I think of little Yeheil in Bavaria. He would like Raphael. I kiss the *hamsa* and place it reverently around the dog's powerful neck. As I do, he raises his beautiful eyes to me, and they say, "Do not be afraid." I place my lips close to his ear and whisper, "I am not." His head falls to my lap and he breathes his final breath. I try to hold him, but his spirit knows it is time for him to leave me. He follows the voice and is gone. My arms grasp only air. I weep into my hands, empty save for the *hamsa*.

I return from the rail yard late this afternoon with help from my mates. Without them, I fear I would have keeled over and found what comfort I could in some putrid ditch. My head aches and I burn with fever. My muscles are so sore, I cannot believe I have completed any productive work.

"I'm sorry, Bronek," Tad says, "I will take you to the infirmary. Albert says they have medicine."

I sigh deeply and cough painfully. "They have other things, too, other things I want to stay as far away from as I can. No. I will stay here, in the block." Before Tad can say another word, I cover his mouth with my hand. "I will stay here," I repeat with as much authority as I can muster.

As he leads me slowly to my bed, I ask him, "Please promise me one thing: wake me when the stars appear, and bring me outside. I know there is a light in the heart of darkness, and I will see it." He gives me his word.

The louse has done his work. Typhus is a painful affliction, but is there really any point tending to it with medicine from the infirmary? To heal a broken arm may make sense, but to heal me of typhus so I can live more days here defies logic. No, my time has come.

I toss fitfully in my bed, but true to his word, Tad carries me to the front steps when night rules the sky. My block mates sleep, some soundly, others restlessly, but all sleep. My clothes are soaked with perspiration, and my body is racked with chills.

"Please drink," Tad whispers. Somewhere, he has acquired a cup of water. I smile and tip it to my lips. I thirst for it, but it belongs to the living, not the dead. I thank him for his kindness and struggle to sit upright on the top step with my palms on the floor and elbows locked behind me.

Tad stoops to take a seat, and I deny him with the wave of my thin hand. "No my friend. I seek no comfort from another human in my final moments. God has been with me from the beginning, and he will be with me at the end. That is enough. You've hardship enough without tending to mine. My misery is over. I am certain we will meet again soon."

Tad chokes back emotion and dares not speak as he clenches his jaw to bar the sounds of sadness so frequent and common in Oświęcim. With a final touch to my dirty head, Tad walks slowly back to his bed. The heavy snores of our mates drown his sniffles and throttled sobs.

I fight the delirium characteristic of my condition. Will Albert rue the morning when they find my lifeless body on these steps? Will he blame himself for carrying the single bug into the barracks? Probably, but he should not. We are not victims of disease or fatigue in Oświęcim. We are victims of one powerful man's misguided choices. We are victims of our own humanity. If life is not fair, it is only because we make it unfair.

I ache. The stars are too bright and hurt my eyes, but I am too weak to raise my hand to shield them. I want to believe I leave this world with dignity, the same dignity that I entered with on the night of the bright lights when the skies glowed at midnight.

It is too warm. It is too cold. Rather the cold of June than the cold of January. I am pleased with my life. I could have done worse, not much better. If I am remembered, let me be remembered as a good person, not as an Olympic athlete, or a highlander or even a Pole, just as a good person. I think Mrs. Jordan and Johnny will agree that I am. Do they remember me? Where is Johnny? He is old enough to be a soldier. The Yanks have entered the war. Hurrah! Is Johnny with them? He is a good boy, like Yeheil. I fear for Yeheil. Too many children, not enough compassion. Too much hate.

My eyes recover and they no longer burn. I look at the sky and drink of the million stars there. One shines brighter than the others do. I used to know its name; now I forget, but whether or not I remember, it brings light to this dark land. I will not see the sun tomorrow. Please God, answer creation's request 'to be' once more, and bring your sun over the horizon another day. Man will heed your word, I know he will. Keep your covenant and do not let us destroy ourselves. Bless us with wisdom to make better choices.

I hold my *hamsa* tightly as the star grows in blinding intensity, then dims as a silhouette appears within it. I am not delirious! This is real! My vision is clear. A mighty angel with outstretched wings descends towards me to take me home. I commend myself to him and to his God.

The End

Epilogue

Bronisław Czech was posthumously awarded the Cross of Valor in 1967 and the Auschwitz Cross in 1987.

Six million Poles died in World War II. Half of them were Jews. No other country lost a greater percentage of its population.

Glossary

2,000 kilograms: 4,400 pounds, 2.2 tons

18 kilometers: 11 miles

50 kilometers: 31 miles

Armia Krajowa: Polish home army formed in 1942 from the ZWZ

Babcia: Polish for 'grandmother'

Behatzlacha: 'good luck' in Hebrew.

Betar: a Revisionist Zionist youth movement founded in 1923 in Riga, Latvia.

Biały Slad: White Track

Bolesław: and his knights at Giewont.

Bonne chance: "Good luck" French

Boże Coś Polskę: God Save Poland

Bright nights: glowing skies observed across Europe in the summer of 1908 in conjunction with the Tunguska event in Russia.

Charybdis: In Greek mythology, a sea monster that created large and dangerous whirlpools, confronted by both Odysseus and Jason and his Argonauts.

Chamonix: Site of the first Winter Olympic games in France, 1924.

Domowoj: Polish house spirit

Dziadek: grandfather in Polish

Föhn: a type of dry, down slope wind, which occurs in the lee of a mountain range. Föhn winds can raise temperatures by as much as 30°C(54°F) in just a matter of hours. Central Europe enjoys a warmer climate due to the Föhn.

Giewont: highest peak in the Tatras

Górale: Polish mountaineer

Great Wagon: The Big Dipper, Ursa Major

Hala Kondratowa: pastoral valley in the Western Tatras.

Hamsa: a Jewish good luck charm often called "The Hand of God."

Herring-boning: a method of moving up a steep slope by planting the skis outward on their inner edges roughly at right angles to each other.

Jagerstutzen: Austrian-made rifle

Juden Raus: A board game produced in Germany. Players take turns rolling the dice and moving their "Jews" around the map toward "collection points" outside the city walls for deportation to Palestine.

Kapo: A Kapo was a prisoner who worked inside German Nazi concentration camps during World War II in certain lower administrative positions.

Karpaty: Carpathian Mountains

Konzertina: a free-reed musical instrument like an accordion.

Kopa Kondracka: A peak in the Carpathians in the Tatra Mountains on the border of Poland and Slovakia.

Kozice: Chamois, goat

Lettland: Latvia

Leszy: a male woodland spirit who protects wild animals and forests.

Mośckicki, Ignacy: President of Poland from 1926 – 1939.

Na początku Bóg stworzył niebo I ziemię: In the beginning, God created the heavens and the earth. Polish

"Na drowie": Cheers! To health! A toast. Polish

Naleśniki: pancake. Polish

"Nie chwal dnia przed zachodem słońca:" "Don't praise the day before sunset." Polish

Obersturmbannführer: Translated as "Senior Storm Unit Leader", *Obersturmbannführer* was junior to Standartenführer and was the equivalent to Obersleutnant (Lieutenant Colonel) in the German Army.

Old Black Dope: early commercial ski wax composed of sperm whale oil and pine pitch.

Oświęcim: Auschwitz

Pan: Polish for mister.

Pani: Polish for 'lady,' 'Mrs.'

Parzenice: decorative embroidery on highlander's woolen pants.

Pączki: traditional Polish donuts

Pęksowym Brzyszku: Peksa's brook. Land behind
St. Clement's church in Zakopane where the old grave-
yard is.

Placki: pancake

Pogrom: from the Russian word "to destroy and wreak
havoc." A form of a riot directed against a particular
group characterized by killing and the destruction of
homes, businesses and religious centers.

Powodzenia: "Good Luck" Polish

Raczkiewicz, Władysław: The first president of the Polish
government in exile from 1939 until he died in 1947.
Until 1945 he was the internationally recognized Polish
head of state, and the Polish Government in Exile was
recognized as the continuum to the Polish government
of 1939.

Sachertorte: a chocolate cake invented in Vienna by Franz
Sacher in the 19th century.

Sanacja: from 1926 until 1939, Sanacja was the dominat-
ing political force in Poland. The movement was com-
prised of former military officers who were disgusted
with the corruption in Polish politics.

Schutzstaffel: the SS. Hitler's personal bodyguard.
Responsible for many crimes against humanity.

.S. Kraay

Służba Zwycięstwu Polski: the first Polish resistance organization in World War II. The organization was tasked with the continuing armed struggle to liberate Poland. In November 1939, is was renamed Związek Walki Zbrojnej, ZWZ.

Sokół: Czech and Slavic youth movement. They were brutally suppressed by the Nazis and the majority of Czechoslovakians who died in Auschwitz were members of Sokół.

Sturmabteilung: Nazi storm troopers, often called "brown-shirts" because of the color of their uniforms.

Tarantella: Italian folk dances characterized by a fast upbeat tempo.

Totenkopf: German "skull of a dead man" military insignia similar to the Jolly Roger skull and crossbones.

Untersturmführer: junior storm leader of the SS, equivalent to a second lieutenant.

Winkel: patches used by the Nazis to classify prisoners in concentration camps

Z Dymem Pożarów: With the Smoke of Fires. Polish

Żyd: Jew, Polish

Żydówki: Jewess, Polish

Żubrówka: Bison grass vodka manufactured in Poland since the 16th century.

Związek Walki Zbrojnej: Poland's Union of Armed Struggle, abbreviated *ZWZ*. Formed in 1939 in response to the German invasion.

ACKNOWLEDGEMENT

This project began when, by chance, I found and read the report Witold Pilecki wrote following his voluntary incarceration and subsequent escape from Auschwitz. Further research led me to Bronisław Czech. That is when the story began to materialize.

While I remain convinced that too many evil minds were at work in the Third Reich, I am equally as certain that the majority of soldiers on both sides of the line were men of good will trapped in a world too ready to solve its problems with conflict. I acknowledge all those who served for the preservation and honor of their respective countries with the hope of securing a lasting peace for the entire world.

How my wife tolerates my passion to write, I do not know, but I am indebted to her for it, and to my dogs who enjoy the cool, Saltillo tile in my office.

Once again, avid reader, aviator and good friend, George Mehrtens pushed me from start to finish.

I am very thankful for the assistance I received from Alison Haas, Archivist, at the 1932 & 1980 Lake Placid Winter Olympic Museum in New York.

To Hilary Evans and The OlyMADMen who continually feed data to Sports-Reference.com, the most comprehensive collection of sports information I know of. These folks are terrific and very cooperative.

Somehow, my Boonville pal Dave McGrath always seems to touch base at the right time to get me through those days when my brain won't work without a shot of Upstate wisdom and humor.

Lastly, to my spiritual mentors Father Alexei and Father Greg who continue to open my mind to new perspectives and visions. As SP says, we have to continue to re-invent ourselves.